The Other Son

ALSO BY NICK ALEXANDER

The Bottle of Tears

You Then, Me Now

Things We Never Said

The Photographer's Wife

The Hannah Novels

The Half-Life of Hannah

Other Halves

The CC Novels

The Case of the Missing Boyfriend

The French House

The Fifty Reasons Series

50 Reasons to Say Goodbye

Sottopassaggio

Good Thing, Bad Thing

Better Than Easy

Sleight of Hand

13:55 Eastern Standard Time

The Other Son

nick alexander

LAKE UNION
PUBLISHING

This is a work of fiction. Names, characters, organizations, places, events, and incidents are either products of the author's imagination or are used fictitiously. Any resemblance to actual persons, living or dead, or actual events is purely coincidental.

Text copyright © 2015, 2019 by BIGfib Books
All rights reserved.

No part of this book may be reproduced, or stored in a retrieval system, or transmitted in any form or by any means, electronic, mechanical, photocopying, recording, or otherwise, without express written permission of the publisher.

Previously published by BIGfib Books in Great Britain in 2015. This edition contains editorial revisions.

Published by Lake Union Publishing, Seattle

www.apub.com

Amazon, the Amazon logo, and Lake Union Publishing are trademarks of Amazon.com, Inc., or its affiliates.

ISBN-13: 9781542018999
ISBN-10: 1542018994

Cover design by @blacksheep-uk.com

Cover illustration by Jelly London

Printed in the United States of America

The Other Son

PART ONE: THE MARRIAGE

1

NOVEMBER

Alice slides the shoulder of the shirt over the end of the ironing board and slowly smooths out the creases, working the iron gently back and forth. In front of her, beyond the windowpane, the November rain lashes down, hammering the roses. They'd been so pretty in summer, but now, like everything else, like her, really, they are merely hanging in there, waiting for winter to pass.

From the lounge, she can hear the sound of a football match on TV. She flips the shirt over and starts on the other sleeve. She doesn't mind ironing, in fact it's probably the only household task that she enjoys. There's something satisfying about turning that basket of jumble into piles of neatly folded order.

She smooths the cuff and thinks of the coming trip, for this is Ken's best shirt, now ready for Mike Goodman's funeral. There have been so many funerals recently and she'd love to be able to skip this one. She imagines herself standing up to say a few words. 'Mike was always good for a sexist joke,' she could say. 'Mike never failed to turn up to dinner empty-handed! Mike could always be counted on to shock everyone with a good juicy racist remark!'

She glances back out at the rain, follows, briefly, the movement of a droplet as it makes its way down the glass. She wonders how long it takes to get from Birmingham to Carlisle. Too long. She's dreading the drive. Hours and hours trapped in the car with Ken.

He scares her with his driving, always has done. He looks at you when he talks to you, that's the thing, and on the motorway, she'd really rather he didn't do that. Sometimes when he turns back to the road, he actually swerves as he corrects his trajectory, and she ends up being terse just to dissuade him from talking, just to stop him looking at her again. He gets angry in city traffic, too – turns into a monster, in fact. And God forbid that she insult his manhood by asking him to slow down! At weddings he gets drunk, so at least she can drive home. But at a funeral it's unlikely. Three or four hours each way . . . At home she can move to another room or she can nip out to the shops. In the car, there's no escape.

She drapes the shirt on a coat hanger, then fastens the top button. She unplugs the iron and crosses to the window to peer outside. She chews the inside of her mouth then turns back to face the interior, crosses to the fridge and, hoping for an alibi, looks inside. She needs to get out. This weather's making her stir-crazy.

As she pulls on her coat in the hallway, Ken glances up at her briefly, but she can tell from his glassy-eyed stare that he hasn't even assimilated the fact she's going out. His mind's on the match, and when his mind's on the match it's not available for anything else. It's not so much that women are better at multitasking, she thinks, it's that men can't do it at all.

By the time she gets back, the match has ended and the presenters are discussing what went wrong. 'You've been out in this?' Ken asks, like a hypnotist's subject suddenly back in the room now the football is over.

4

'We needed bread,' Alice explains, waving the carrier bag at him, then shrugging out of the wet coat. 'And I needed the walk.'

'It's raining up there as well,' Ken says, nodding, presumably at the out-of-sight television set. 'In Manchester.'

'Rain stopped play?'

'No. Nearly. They played badly though. They were bloody awful, to be honest. Any chance of a cuppa?'

Alice thinks that Ken could get up and make his own cup of tea, that he could even, Lord forbid, make her one. 'Of course,' she says, managing to say one phrase even as she thinks the other. 'I was just about to make one anyway.'

She's pouring the water on to the teabags when Ken appears in the doorway. He leans on the doorjamb and looks at her blankly. He smiles but actually looks a little sad – it's probably because of the match. Football is generally the only thing that elicits much of an emotional response in him these days.

'They've started selling Christmas decorations at Tesco,' she says. 'Imagine that.'

'A bit premature,' Ken agrees.

'I asked the woman on the checkout if anyone actually bought Christmas decorations at the beginning of November and she said I'd be surprised. I wondered how she could tell.'

'How she could tell what?'

'Well, how surprised I'd be!'

Ken frowns at her. He's never quite grasped Alice's sense of humour.

Alice squashes the teabag thoughtfully against the side of the cup. 'Do you think Tim will invite us this year? Or should I plan to do something here?'

Ken shrugs. 'We're barely into November, love,' he says.

'I think we're still allowed to envisage events that haven't happened yet, even in November. They haven't made that a crime yet.

5

And what about Matt? Do you think Matt will come home for Christmas?' She pours the milk.

'I doubt it,' Ken says. 'He didn't bother last year, did he?'

'Here.' She proffers the mug.

'Thanks.'

'He was in Sydney last year, so it wasn't really an option,' Alice points out as Ken turns away down the hall. 'But now he's in . . .' She lets her voice fade away and exhales slowly. Because Ken has vanished from view. 'Spain maybe?' she mutters. 'Or is it France?' She glances at the countertop and wonders where Matt's most recent postcard has got to.

She imagines Matt sleeping under a bridge somewhere, like that singer he used to go on about all the time. The one who killed himself. Nick something. She has always feared that Matt will somehow end up badly. Perhaps it's just because every pop star he ever worshipped was dead. Nick Drake, that was the one. And that chap from The Doors. There was the guy from that Australian band, too, and the one from Deaf Tiger or whatever they were called. He talked about dead pop stars so much that she knew all their names, became quite the expert. Tim liked ABBA and ELO. He liked bright bouncy music that even she could sing along to. Whereas Matt was always drawn to the dark side. Dead poets with miserable songs. The Smiths – that was another one. What was that song he used to like? Something to do with being run over by a double-decker bus. He used to sing it all the time; he sang it so much that she knew all the words as well. She became quite a trendy mum at one point, thanks to her boys.

But, yes, it's hard to wonder about Matt's future, hard to think about his whereabouts and not feel concerned. It's almost impossible to picture him contented and happy somewhere, not when he's spent his life pulling the plug on anything that looked like it was about to be remotely successful.

6

She remembers Matt aged thirteen, proudly presenting his report card to them. He had been graded 'C' for every subject. 'C' meant average, he declared, and he seemed as proud of that fact – of the universal averageness of his grades – as he had ever been of anything. It was as if being average was a new pinnacle of achievement, as if it beat, hands down, the straight 'A's that Tim had been getting. Ken had disowned him over that report card, had told him he was no longer his son. Which was harsh, admittedly, but they'd wanted him to do better, that was all. They'd been afraid for him, even then.

Alice sips her tea and remembers Matt's graduation from university. Or rather, the absence of his graduation. How she had been looking forward to that! She takes a teaspoon and taps the rounded back of it against a thumbnail. Yes, thinking about Matt makes her nervous. Sometimes it makes her short of breath. Occasionally she fears that she's slipping into an actual panic attack.

'Don't think about him then,' Ken tells her if she ever admits that she can't breathe properly. 'Think about Tim instead.' And of course, Tim has done so much better than Matt. But for some reason, thinking about Tim doesn't make her feel that much happier, and it definitely doesn't stop her worrying about the other one.

'It's over!' Ken shouts from the lounge. 'You can reclaim your sitting room. The coast is clear!'

'Oh joy!' she murmurs. She glances at the clock. It's almost time for *Coronation Street*.

It's the day of the funeral, and Ken, wearing black suit trousers and a white singlet, is at the top of the stairs looking down. 'Where's my shirt?' he asks.

'Oh, I tied it to the television aerial,' Alice replies. 'Seemed like a good idea at the time.'

7

'The television aerial? What?'

Alice sighs. 'It's in the wardrobe with all your other shirts.'

'The white one's not there.'

'It is.'

'Only it isn't.'

Alice tuts and climbs the staircase. It's nine already and they should have left by now. She crosses the bedroom to the open wardrobe, swipes the shirt from the rack and pushes it into her husband's arms as she leaves the room.

'Huh,' Ken exclaims, '. . . must've been hiding.'

'Only from you,' Alice murmurs, pausing on the landing. 'Now can we please get a move on? You know how stressed you get when we're late anywhere. All we need is a bit of traffic or some bad weather and—'

'We're sure to get plenty of both,' Ken says, now buttoning the shirt.

'I know,' Alice says. 'That's my point.'

By the time Ken has checked the locks and looked for the map, by the time he's found and jingled his keys, then lost them and then found them again, it's 10 a.m.

'Ken!' Alice protests, one hand on the latch. 'We're really going to be late.'

'We won't,' Ken says. 'It's easy to make up a bit of time on a long journey like this one.'

At the end of the street, as Ken waits to pull out into the traffic, Alice spots a length of tinsel draped across the top of the 'open' sign in the Chinese takeaway.

A minute later, as they drive past the golf course – transformed into a lake by all the rain – she asks, 'So how do I find out if Tim

8

is inviting us for Christmas without sounding like I want him to invite us?'

She glances at Ken enquiringly and he turns to face her just long enough for her to start to feel nervous. 'Please look at the road occasionally,' she says.

'Don't start that already. We've barely left the house.'

'I'm sorry. But the idea of your ploughing two tonnes of Renault Mégane into a shop full of people makes me slightly nervous. I'm funny that way.'

'Don't you want to?'

'Want to what?'

'Go to Tim's place? For Christmas?'

'I suppose so,' Alice says. 'Compared to the alternatives, I suppose it's preferable.'

'What alternatives?'

'Well, there's always the Dignitas clinic in Switzerland. But I still prefer Tim's place, I think. Just about.'

'If you want to go then, just ask him. Why does everything have to be so complic—'

'I don't want him to feel obliged, is all,' Alice interrupts. 'And Natalya was very frosty last year. Do you remember how frosty she was? Actually, frosty's not the word – she was arctic. She was antarctic.'

'Yeah,' Ken says vaguely. He's momentarily distracted by the heavy traffic on the roundabout.

Alice runs a film of last Christmas through her mind's eye. And yes, Natalya had been very prickly. She had left the sprouts Alice had prepared in the fridge – a special River Cottage recipe with chestnuts it had been, too. She had 'forgotten' to defrost the chocolate log they'd brought as well. Fridges and freezers – that's how chilly things had been.

9

'You know, she never once wore that scarf I bought her,' Alice says. In fact, it's a general rule that nothing Alice and Ken have ever given them has ever been seen again. Perhaps she has a black hole in her chest of drawers, Alice thinks. Perhaps it just sucks things up and casts them into a parallel universe where they join Ken's missing socks.

'Not that you know of,' Ken comments, checking his mirror as they merge on to the A38.

'What do you mean?'

'I'm just saying that as we're not with them twenty-four hours a day, it's hard to be certain that she's never worn the scarf.'

But Alice is certain. She's perfectly certain. And it was a nice scarf, too – a very nice turquoise cashmere scarf. If Natalya didn't want it, then she would have liked to have worn it herself. It's particularly galling when you give people nice gifts – things that you don't dare buy for yourself – only to see that they never use them.

Perhaps it's because Tim and Natalya are so well off these days. Perhaps anything Alice and Ken buy just pales into insignificance against the rest of their wealth. Perhaps they need to up their game this year, gift-wise. Then again, it's not like Natalya makes much effort. She gives Alice a bottle of perfume every year without fail, and it's never even perfume that Alice likes. She only wears Yves Saint Laurent's Parisienne, and she's told Natalya that enough times. Though never at Christmas. That would be rude. Alice has lost count of how many full bottles of perfume she's given to Dot, how many she's taken to the Oxfam shop.

'Well, I still think she was a bit off last year. Tim was funny, too. Do you remember all that fuss about the missing Champagne glasses? As if it mattered what kind of glasses we were drinking out of.'

'It was very expensive Champagne, apparently,' Ken says.

'Oh, it taste so dee-fferrent from prroper glass,' Alice says, rolling the 'r's, mocking Natalya's Russian accent.

10

'I think they were just getting on each other's nerves. It happens in a marriage. Especially at Christmas.'

And yes, it's true. It happens in a marriage. Ken has been getting on her nerves for fifty years now and no doubt vice versa. She wonders again why Ken was so determined to marry her. It hadn't been for her wit, that's for sure. He can barely tolerate that. She had been pretty enough, she supposes. But there had been prettier girls out there. It's a strange one, because she's never been able to detect much pleasure in the arrangement, not on Ken's side. Not on either side, really.

Marrying Ken had not been Alice's first choice. In fact, it hadn't really felt like a choice at all. Her grandparents (whom she'd never met – they'd died by the time she was born) were Jews who'd fled Russia in the late 1800s. They'd arrived in Norwich and then in the Midlands as penniless refugees.

Despite widespread myths about the wealthy, successful, businesslike nature of the Jewish people, they'd remained pretty much paupers their whole lives, right up until their premature deaths in their forties. Poverty and persecution do not a long and happy life make, it would seem.

Alice's own parents, her mother no longer officially Jewish (she had seen how dangerous that could be) and her father of Irish extraction, had suffered terrible deprivation during their childhoods and had barely managed to drag themselves out of the gutter by the time Alice came along. Her father was a street cleaner, so in some ways he was still very much in the gutter.

Though Alice herself had never known hunger, she had grown up with the terrifying all-pervading knowledge that poverty was never far away. Her parents had lived as if destitution were imminent, hoarding tins of food in the cellar and worrying, to the point of near-insanity, about every political upheaval, every downturn, every distant conflict . . . It didn't take much, they told their

11

children, over and over, for everything good to vanish. All it took was an injury or an illness, or another economic depression – all that was needed was another Alexander the Third, or another Hitler for that matter, and they'd all be scrabbling around in the dirt all over again.

By the time Alice hit nineteen they'd been pushing her to marry for a while. Marriage was about the only hope that people like her parents had for their daughters, and they were concerned, unnerved, by the lack of suitable suitors and by her ever-deepening friendship with Joe. Joe who came from the wrong side of the tracks in so many ways.

Alice wonders where Joe is now. She wonders if Joe is even still alive, wonders whether Joe went on to have the exceptional life that Alice always imagined.

And then Alice came home one night from the soap factory, the stink of fat and lye still on her clothes, and there was Ken, leaning on the mantelpiece, fiddling with a pocket watch, looking suave. Her parents were smiling nervously up at her, being – what's the word? – obsequious, that's the one. Ken had seemed bright-eyed and smart in his Sunday best – he always was a snappy dresser – and he had been polite and generous towards her, even enabling, insisting, that she quit that horrible factory job. Yes, he had been nice enough, at least at the outset.

People complain about the Muslims and what have you, complain that they arrange their marriages, that they hang people, that they still treat homosexuals badly, that they don't give women proper rights – but it really wasn't that long ago that all those things happened right here in Britain. People pretend to have forgotten these things because it makes them feel better, it makes them feel superior. But Alice remembers.

So yes, Ken had been polite and well dressed and, above all in her parents' eyes, generous. He was to inherit his father's business.

12

He had good prospects. He was declared to be a 'catch'. There was no reasonable opt-out clause.

Just after one, Ken pulls into the motorway services. They run through the drizzle and then stand in the midst of the food court to survey the various offerings, blasts of freezing air chilling their backs every time the sliding doors open.

'Well, what do you fancy, love?' Ken asks, as if choosing between these grubby little kiosks, between Burger King or Famous Fish or Señor Taco, might actually be considered a treat.

Alice bites her lip and turns her head from side to side as she takes in the options. 'Fish and chips might be the best option,' she says, thinking that at least the deep-frying process will be hot enough to kill any microbes. Nothing looks very clean here.

'Yes, fish and chips and mushy peas,' Ken says, sounding almost enthusiastic. But the girl in Famous Fish is already wiping down the counters with a greasy cloth, inexplicably closing up at ten past one, so they end up with Ocean Catch menus from Burger King, which Ken declares are 'almost the same thing'.

But an Ocean Catch menu is not the same as fish and chips – not by a long stretch. Alice nibbles at the bun and then samples the burnt, greasy fish-finger-type thing within. She disdainfully lifts a few of the powdery fries to her lips and ponders the mysteries of British food. Because the lad in Burger King sounded a bit Italian, and the girl in Famous Fish was definitely French. They live after all on an island of green fields, surrounded by seas, encircled by European countries with fabulous cuisines. Half the people in the restaurant industry are French or Spanish or Italian or Indian, and yet the entire country has ended up opting for these American food-like synthetics. Burgers and 'French' fries and tacos. It really is a terrible shame.

13

Alice watches Ken wolfing down his burger. He has never cared much about food, which is also a shame because once upon a time she had pretensions to being a good cook. Her pies had been to die for – everyone had said so. These days, after fifty years of indifference, of hearing Ken proudly tell people that he 'eats to live, not the opposite', she has abandoned any culinary aspirations. Nowadays they mostly eat ready meals. An occasional home-made cauliflower cheese or an actual cooked breakfast is about as adventurous as it gets in the Hodgetts household.

A child on the far side of the hall starts to scream and Alice glances over and briefly remembers Matt shrieking in a shop somewhere. She scans the food hall again, taking in the true horror of its dilapidation: the chipped, grubby Formica tables, the economy light bulbs sprouting from fittings designed to take pretty spotlights that once must have cast a warm glow on fresh, shiny tables. She feels a bit like the food hall herself – tired and worn out and a bit depressed. The food hall suddenly seems like a metaphor for her life. Something that should be, that could be, that once was sparkly and appealing, but which is now chilly, grubby and worn out, lit with flickering, yellowish, cheap-to-run lighting. The whole place is beyond repair, really. It needs to be pulled down and rebuilt from scratch.

The door opens behind her again, and she pulls her scarf more tightly around her already stiff neck. Alice isn't getting any younger, either. She's getting older and achier. She remembers her parents complaining about their aches and pains, remembers thinking that they exaggerated it all. But youngsters, learn this: your body really does get older. Joints actually do creak when you get up in the morning, really do seize up when you sit in a car for two hours. She knows what's at the end of that particular tunnel. By the time you get to seventy, by the time you've been to as many funerals as they have, you've got used to that idea – you've had time to grasp the

14

concept of your own mortality. But that doesn't make it seem fair. It doesn't mean that you necessarily feel as if you've lived everything you were supposed to live.

'You all right?' Ken asks.

'Fine,' Alice says. 'Just thinking about poor Jean, really.'

Ken nods. 'Yeah. She'll be in a right state,' he says, then, pointing, 'Are you eating those, or . . . ?'

Alice shakes her head, smiles weakly and pushes the packet of fries across the table.

Yes, it feels like a small life, looking back on things. Even smaller these days as the high points – the summer holidays, the days on beaches with the kids, and the dances of her youth – shrink and fade in the rear-view mirror. It's not that she aimed high and failed, because she never expected much. She didn't come from the kind of people who hoped for much more than enough to eat and a dry, warmish house. To her parents, even these things were incredible, unexpected achievements. So no, she had never hoped for miracles, never expected a vast Premium Bond or lottery win. But she did think that at some stage she would have a sense that there'd been some point to it all. She had thought that at some point she would be overcome by a sense of contentment, like a cat on an armchair perhaps, in the sun. She had expected to be able to stretch and yawn and look back on it all and think, 'There, I did it! Now I can relax!'

Perhaps her problem is that she never took the time to define what 'it' was. If only she had defined some goals for herself, then maybe she would feel like she had achieved them.

Ken is clapping his hands and standing, so she wrests herself from her sombre reverie and pulls her attention back to the here and now of this day, this journey. They're on their way to a funeral. Of course she's feeling a bit down. Who wouldn't?

15

'Well,' Ken is saying, 'that's put some fuel in the old furnace. Shall we make a move?'

It's still raining when they merge back on to the motorway. Alice thinks that she hates winter, that she truly, honestly hates it. She has always felt as if she isn't genetically adapted to survive an English winter. Perhaps her great-great-grandparents weren't from Russia at all, but the Middle East. Seeing as they were Jewish, it's surely not impossible, is it? She wrinkles her nose at her own shocking lack of grasp of Jewish history. Their Jewishness wasn't something her mother had ever wanted to discuss.

Ken swings out to overtake a petrol tanker and has to drive through an opaque wall of spray from the tanker's vast wheels. Alice winces until they come out the other side and vision is restored.

She wonders how Mike felt on the night of his death. She wonders if his life flashed before his eyes as it always does in films. And if it did flash before him, she wonders if Ken featured even briefly, if it contained glimpses of their shared fifty-year careers in the tyre remould business. She wonders what his happiest memories were. His kids perhaps. His daughter has always seemed nice enough.

Alice has had moments of contentment, too. Dozing off in a deckchair on a beach when the kids were younger, swimming in the sea with little Tim clamped to her back, shrieking in her ear with excitement . . . They went to Cornwall for a few years in a row when Matt was a toddler. Ken had found a bargain cottage to rent, and they'd gone back every year until the owner sold it. It had felt quite traumatic not being able to go there once the cheap deal ended.

'How many years did we go to Durgan?' she asks.

Ken looks at her and frowns. 'Four? Five?' he says.

'That's what I thought. Four.'

'Why?'

16

'No reason. I was just remembering.'

'You remember when Matt fell down those stairs?'

Alice is surprised that Ken dares mention that day. To stop Ken looking at her, she glances out of the side window. 'Yes,' she says. 'Yes, I do.'

It had been a beautiful summer's day, and Matt had been, what? Five? Six? Something like that. They had meandered through the higgledy-piggledy Cornish town, bought dribbling ice creams, had Coca-Colas on the seafront . . . And then they had wandered along the pier. Alice had wanted a photo, so she had asked Ken to pose with the kids, but they were on a sugar rush and had run off. And while she was looking through the viewfinder framing the stunning coastline in the background, there had come a shriek from behind her. Matt, it transpired, had run straight over the edge of a flight of stairs, had somehow failed to see them, had quite simply not stopped. He had cut his forehead, grazed his knees, split his lip and chipped a tooth.

Secretly, because she would never dare say such a thing, Alice held Ken responsible. He had, after all, been staring straight at Matt. 'What happened?' she had asked him. 'Did you see? How did he fall?' The sun had been in his eyes, Ken said, and she was their goddamned mother, not him.

They had held on to their anger long enough to assure themselves that no bones were broken, long enough to buy sticking plasters, and long enough to drive the howling children (Tim had joined in by that point) back to the cottage.

And then Ken had started drinking. Matt had 'ruined' the day, he kept telling him. It was a waste of time trying do anything nice for any of them.

By the time he had downed his third beer, the focus of his fury had turned on Alice.

17

Those moments of contentment, those moments of relief, were so often ephemeral, so often terminated by one of Ken's thoroughly unreasonable temper tantrums. If her life flashed before her, Alice thinks that the happy snapshots would be as rare and fleeting as the English sun that shone upon them.

Perhaps that's the real truth – that she just needed to live somewhere warmer. Because she has always been something of a sun-lizard, has never missed a single opportunity to turn her face to the sky and close her eyes. And all of her good memories were of moments lit by sunshine, moments eased by warmth. She remembers herself at eighteen, lying in Canon Hill Park with her head on Joe's stomach. Some kids had been playing with a football and it had whacked Joe on the shoulder. Joe, always energetic, always full of beans, had jumped up and kicked it back across the green with surprising expertise.

She tries to push the image from her mind. It's amazing how tenacious lost dreams can be. Incredible, really, that such a simple memory as that, a simple memory of a sensation of uncomplicated happiness, can still haunt her fifty years later.

'Look at that idiot,' Ken says as one of those new oversized cars squeezes itself into the tiny gap between themselves and the car in front.

'Everyone's driving too fast anyway,' Alice says pointedly.

'Bloody wankers in their Porsches,' Ken says.

And it's true, Alice thinks, that the people in the big expensive cars are always a bit worse than everyone else. They're always a little more pushy. They probably consider themselves invincible in their big steel boxes.

'Is that really a Porsche?' Alice asks. She's always thought Porsches were little sports cars designed for insecure middle-aged men with tiny todgers.

18

'Yep, it's basically the same car as a VW Touareg,' Ken informs her, as if that's supposed to mean something. 'They're made in the same factory.'

'Right,' Alice says. 'Well, it's very big – it's like a lorry almost.'

'Awful in an accident,' Ken says. 'It would flatten that little Panda in a pile-up.' From the corner of his eye, he sees Alice gripping the roof handle. 'Just relax, will you?' he says. 'You're making me nervous.'

'You're just a bit close, that's all.'

'It's not my fault if that idiot's inserted himself bang in the middle of my braking distance.'

'No, but you can still slow down. That is allowed, I believe, even when it's not your fault.'

Just as Alice says this, the Porsche lurches back out into the fast lane and accelerates away.

'There,' Ken says. 'Better?'

'Yes,' Alice says, forcing herself to breathe. She looks at the little boxy car in front. It's the same model she and Dot rented in Spain six years ago. It was such fun driving that little car around those winding Spanish roads. She had been nervous at first, of course – driving on the wrong side of the road and everything. And she had kept searching for the gearstick and the handbrake in the door pocket – that had been embarrassing. But once she had got used to it, it had been lovely. The car had a leaky exhaust pipe, too, she remembers now. It had made it sound like a sports car.

They'd had too much fun on that holiday, really. Dot had had a fling with . . . Alice can't remember his name now . . . Anyway, he was the father of the young man who ran the hotel bar. Now there's a story never to be told! Imagine if Dot's husband ever found out about that! And while Dot had been otherwise occupied with Jorge – that was his name, pronounced *Hor-hey* – Alice had been wined and dined by Jorge's best friend Esteban. Esteban had not

19

been Alice's type at all, thank God. He had been way too hairy, way too . . . What's that word? Ugh! It's so annoying the way when you get older that words start to hide from you. Sometimes when she tries to explain one word, she can't think of the other similar word either. It happens more and more with people and places, too. 'She looks like that actress,' Alice will tell Ken. 'You know . . . the one who's in that film. The film made by . . . oh, gosh . . . by that actor who's also a film director. The one who made . . .' And of course, she can't then remember the film he made either. Sometimes she has to dig down three or four levels before she can start digging her way back out again.

Anyway, Esteban had been just too hirsute, that's the term. No one says hirsute any more. It's strange the way words go out of fashion. Alice has always preferred clean-shaven men, and the mere thought of a hairy back has always been enough to make her shudder. Beards and moustaches look a bit sinister, don't they? But the attention – Esteban's attention – had been lovely. So she had let him believe. She had led him on a little. She had allowed poor Esteban to take her to dinner. And then she had pretended once she got home that the holiday had been uneventful, boring even. In fact, she had so overcompensated the misery side of things that it became impossible for her to justify going with Dot again the following year.

Dot's going again next summer, but to southern Spain this time, to Alicante. It's even hotter down there, she reckons, and Alice would love to go with her. She thinks a proper holiday in the sun would do her the world of good, reckons it would ease her aches and pains, too. But how to approach it? It's a bit like Christmas at Tim's. She can't work out how to organise it, how to mention it even, without sounding like she's asking Ken for his approval. Because what if Ken says 'no'? And he's pretty likely to say that. He's bound to say that they can't afford it, or that she didn't

20

even enjoy it last time or something like that. Even worse would be if he decided he wanted to come along! But that's unlikely. Ken's not keen on foreigners.

'Where's Matt at the moment?' Alice asks, trying to forge a bridge she can use to move the conversation towards where she's hoping to go. 'Is he in France or Spain?'

'France,' Ken says, 'as far as I know.'

'He was in Spain though, wasn't he?'

'Yeah,' Ken says, 'he was in Madrid. But now he's in France, down south somewhere. He's been in France for a while.'

'Dot's off to Spain next summer.'

'Dot's off to Spain every summer.'

'Maybe I'll go with her and meet up with Matt somewhere.'

'Matt's in France,' Ken says again, starting to sound exasperated.

'They do share a border, you know, France and Spain.'

'What, you're hoping to wave to Matt from over the border?'

'No . . . it's got nothing to do with Matt really, I just . . .'

'I'm not the one who brought Matt up.'

'No, I was just thinking it would be nice to go to Spain again.'

Ken shoots Alice one of his looks – a mixture of confusion and disdain.

'So what do you think?' Alice asks. 'About Spain?'

'You know what I think about Spain,' Ken says. 'Sweaty spics and girls with moustaches and greasy food and tap water that gives you the squits. That's what I think of Spain.'

'That's verging on racist,' Alice says.

'It's the truth,' Ken says. 'And the last time I looked, Spain wasn't a race. It's a nationality.'

'It's a country, actually. Spain is a country, and Spanish is the nationality of those who live there.'

Ken blows out through pursed lips and shakes his head. 'I can't win with you, can I? I don't know why I still try.'

Alice doesn't risk replying. She laughs lightly to defuse the tension.

She thinks about Matt in France. She wonders what he's doing. She wonders if he's OK. She wonders if he'll ever come home again.

He'll be working some dead-end job, cleaning or packaging sausages or waiting in a restaurant – he's done all of these things. It's such a waste, that's the thing. Because, like herself, he could have done so much more.

'Dot says Matt's just trying to find himself,' Alice says, unsure even as she says it why she's chosen this particular phrase to say out loud. 'But I think it's the opposite. I think he's trying to lose himself.'

'Dot should mind her own onions,' Ken replies, misunderstanding entirely the context of Dot's remark. And that's Alice's fault far more than it is Ken's. She hadn't, after all, provided any context.

But Ken doesn't like Dot much, that's for sure. Dot is a busybody. She's pernickety and sarcastic. She has an overactive thyroid which she claims explains much of her nervous disposition. But whatever the cause, she rubs Ken up the wrong way. Not that he has ever really approved of any of Alice's friends. Even Lisa, her best friend all those years ago, he hated with a passion. Though that was probably Lisa's fault, too. Lisa certainly hated Ken first. But what with Lisa moving to New Zealand, and Jenny Mayer dying; what with Jenny Parson now a full-blown alcoholic, that only leaves Dot. So no matter what Ken thinks, Alice isn't going to give Dot up.

Lisa has been gone over twenty years now and still Alice misses her. She was the friend Alice felt closest to, the only one who ever really laughed at her jokes. It was a shock when Lisa and Jim moved away, a shock to have to realise that your biggest, most important friendship just didn't weigh that much in the grand scheme of things, not when balanced against a better lifestyle, a bigger house with a pool and a major promotion for Jim. It's normal to lose friends over the course of a lifetime: you fall out with some, you grow apart from others. A few die, too. But to have someone just move to the other side of the world, well, that's tough. And one thing's for sure – it's less and less easy to make new friends as you get older; there are so few opportunities for it.

Still, she has Dot, thank God. Dot gets on with her own husband Martin about as well as Alice gets on with Ken, so it's a relationship based largely on bitching. But bitching, it turns out, is a surprisingly solid basis for a friendship. At the thought of the things they say, at the conversations they have about their respective husbands, Alice snorts almost undetectably. Ken, usually so slow to pick up any kind of subtlety, catches this one immediately.

'What?' he asks.

'Oh, nothing,' Alice says. 'I was just thinking about those Christmas decorations in Tesco.' When you have a tetchy husband, you develop coping mechanisms, such as always having an alibi at the ready.

One time, a couple of years back, Alice had been telling Dot what a relief it was that Ken no longer wanted to have sex. Dot had been laughing, lapping it up, goading Alice to go further, to be funnier and ruder. Alice had said something about Ken's wrinkly wiener – a phrase she had heard on an American sitcom – and Dot had spat her wine all over the dining table. But then they had heard a tiny voice coming seemingly from nowhere. 'Hello, hello?' it said. Alice finally traced the little voice to her new mobile phone in her handbag. It had somehow dialled home, had mysteriously and, under the circumstances, dangerously, called Ken.

Terrified that he had overheard part of their conversation, and wracked with guilt, Alice had literally been trembling by the time she opened the front door that evening. But she had found Ken sober, calmly watching television. He had complained about the

23

phone bill, of course. He had reminded her 'for the thousandth time' to lock the keyboard – whatever that meant. But that was it. She had got away with it. She was always very careful with her mobile after that.

'Chinese tyres,' Ken says, prompting Alice to look out of the side window at the lorry they're overtaking. It says 'Imperial Tyres' on the side.

'"Imperial" doesn't sound very Chinese,' Alice comments.

'Well, it's not meant to, is it? That's the point. That's why they do it,' Ken says. 'So you think they're English.'

'I suppose they did have an empire once.'

'The Chinese?'

'I think so.'

'Well, empire or not, their tyres are rubbish. Dangerous rubbish, at that.'

'You just don't like the fact that they're cheaper than remoulds,' Alice says. She's heard Ken say this enough times to know that it's true.

'You're right. I don't,' Ken says, 'but they're still rubbish. That *Which* magazine tested them all and the braking distances on the Chinky ones were terrible.'

Alice watches as the truck indicates, then veers away from them, apparently taking its slippery Chinese tyres to rainy Blackburn. It's funny, because she thinks she can smell the load it's carrying from here, but it's probably just her memory, it's probably just because of the conversation and the fact that the odour of tyre rubber has permeated their entire lives.

Even when Ken had a whole chain of Re-Tyre stores, even when he was spending all day in the offices towards the end, he still came home smelling of rubber, still sat down of an evening emanating that bitter, metallic smell of recycled tyre rubber. No, her first choice would not have been to marry a tyre remoulder, even if they

24

are still here, fifty years later. Who would ever have guessed that they'd turn out to be quite so tenacious?

It's not that she hates Ken, per se. She's so used to him that it's hard to define quite where Ken ends and Alice begins these days. He just . . . irritates her, really. He irritates her the way certain aspects of herself irritate her. He annoys her the way her own brain annoys her when she can't remember a word, the way her own hand annoys her when she discovers that it's put the teabags in the freezer or her glasses in the fridge for no reason that she can identify.

If she hates anything, she hates her marriage to Ken rather than Ken himself. She hates the opportunities, the life that marrying Ken precluded. She should have had a career, that's the thing – that's the real disappointment, her real mistake. She was clever; she knows she was. She was good with numbers and good with words. Her parents used to get her to do all the adding up in her head. She was the one who had to help Robert with his schoolwork. Yes, like Matt, she could have done so much more. That's why his lack of ambition upsets her so much.

Alice remembers their father drilling them at the kitchen table. 'Alice!' he would shout, 'What's seven plus nine plus twenty-three? Robert! What's eleven plus nine take thirteen?' And even as Alice was adding up her own numbers, she would be bracing herself for the slap, either across Robert's hands should he dare to start counting on his fingers, or across the back of his head if (as usual) he gave the wrong answer. 'Tuppence short of a shilling,' that's what people used to say about Robert. 'A sandwich short of a picnic.'

If they'd known how long he was going to be around, how transient his passage on the planet would be, then they might, just might, have been nicer to him. But they didn't know, and the truth was that their parents' generation had no idea whatsoever how to bring up a child with what these days they'd call special needs. Other than drilling him to be better and beating him when he

25

failed, they were at a loss when faced with Robert's unique brand of stupidity. Sometimes Alice managed to add up her own numbers and Robert's numbers at the same time. On such occasions, she would announce her own answer while simultaneously indicating Robert's answer discreetly on her fingers. But though she had explained the system often enough to him, he was rarely sharp enough, when placed under duress, to notice the unnatural splay of her hands.

Poor Robert; he had never known when to shut up, never known how to avoid their father's wrath. One time, he had been supposed to make a toolbox in woodwork lessons. He had gone with their father to the ironmongers for wood, and Dad had been so proud, so hopeful that for once here was something his son could actually succeed at, that he had purchased not the cheap pine specified by the school, but expensive sheets of sheer, beautiful mahogany. And that was always going to be a bad move.

Poor Robert, perhaps overly stressed by the cost of the wood, or more likely, simply no better at woodwork than he was at anything else, had repeatedly failed to dovetail the corners correctly, and as he repeatedly cut them off and started again, his box had got smaller and smaller. By the time he was finished, it was not a toolbox he had made but a so-called jewellery box – a tiny, ugly trinket box with inch-thick walls and wonky corners that the daylight shone through.

Dad had raged about the cost and the waste, and Mum had tried to make the most of the situation. She had even fetched a pair of earrings to put in that shoddy little box – her attempt at calming everyone down.

In a chilling silence, they'd begun to eat dinner, Alice nervously tapping one foot against the chair leg, silently pleading with her eyes, secretly begging Robert, opposite, to remain silent. Because that was the thing about Robert, that was the one thing he could

26

always be counted upon to achieve without fail: once the eye of the storm had passed, when everything was done and dusted, when everyone was finally starting to relax again, Robert could and would produce the one phrase, seemingly precision-engineered, to make everything kick off again. Alice hated him for it. And she hated herself for hating him.

That night, the night of the jewellery box, once everything was calm again, once dinner had been eaten and the box had been moved to the kitchen counter behind her, no longer the centre of attention; once their father had, for once without blows being administered, moved on to a different subject and their mother was serving up bowls of banana and custard (Alice's favourite), Robert had piped up.

'We're going to make picture frames next week,' he had said brightly. 'We have to take in a picture to frame and some lengths of special wood called beading.'

Their father had cleared his throat. The effort he was expending in order to ignore his idiot son was palpable.

'Do they sell beading at Johnson's, Dad?' Robert had asked. 'Can we get some?'

'I'll give you beading,' their father had said, standing sharply enough to knock his chair over. 'I'll give you bloody woodwork, you cheeky little shit.'

'Don't, please!' Mum had shrieked, moving between Robert and their father.

And Alice, hating Robert in that instant as much as she had ever hated him, had started to gulp down her bananas and custard, trying to get as much of it inside her as possible, trying to eat her favourite dessert before it was too late, before it ended up on the floor.

'Can you remember Lizzie's kids' names?' Ken now asks her out of the blue.

27

Alice frowns. She had actually been having trouble even remembering Mike's daughter's name, let alone her children's names. 'Lizzie?' she says. 'Oh, do you mean Linda?'

'Oh yes, you're right – Linda. And the kids' names?'

'Terry, Tim? Something with a T?' Alice offers. 'Tom?'

'Yes, Tom and . . . Lucy maybe?'

'That's it. But I doubt they'll be there, Ken. They're only four or five or something.'

'They're at least ten.'

Alice frowns. 'Really?'

It's another cliché about getting older that's always guaranteed to get the youngsters groaning, but, yes, time really does go by faster as you get older. Alice remembers when she was a child, how the long hot summers seemed endless. Nowadays, it's winter, summer, winter, summer, like Monday, Tuesday, Wednesday. And yes, it honestly does seem only yesterday morning that the kids were still living at home, Tim working conscientiously in the dining room on his homework, Matt clomping around in his Dr Martens boots singing The Smiths songs. She had felt terrified when Matt left home for college. Alice had always felt that the children's presence somehow protected her, like a good luck charm. If Ken was capable of being angry and occasionally violent in front of the children (and he was), then what on earth would he be like once they were gone, once there were no longer any witnesses to his rage? But Ken, in fact, became calmer once Matt left home, as if, perhaps like Robert, it was the kids' presence that had been winding him up all along.

That's not to say that Alice is happier now the boys have gone. For most of her marriage, the children felt like the only reason she was staying. If she's honest with herself, she has no real idea why she's still here. At first it was because of her parents – they'd wanted this so much. Once they had died she had convinced herself that she was staying for Tim's and Matt's benefit. After they had left

28

home, the idea of grandchildren kept her going for a while – she had been so excited about their arrival. But now they're seven and nine and she hardly even sees them – Christmas is not the only time that Natalya is frosty.

She glances over at Ken and allows herself to ask the question: *Why are you here, Alice?*

Could it really just be a bad habit, like biting fingernails? Is it really possible that she's still here merely because she doesn't have enough imagination to picture an alternative, because she doesn't have enough courage to pursue anything different?

Ken clicks on an indicator and starts to pull over into the exit lane.

'Are we there?' Alice asks, trying to catch a glimpse of the road sign they're just passing.

'Nearly,' Ken says. 'We just need to get across town now. I hope there's not too much traffic.' He shoots her a smile and Alice responds in kind before turning back to face the windscreen.

She has, she realises, been lost in her thoughts. The rain has stopped and she has no idea when that happened. There are even glimpses of blue sky to the east.

The main reason she never left Ken, she decides, is that no one else ever seemed to believe in the possibility. Because yes, she had been serious about it a few times. She remembers telling Tim, maybe ten years ago, maybe much more – time does fly – that she was leaving his father. Tim laughed. 'You'll never leave Dad,' he predicted, and he was right.

Lisa, too, said almost the same thing. 'We all feel like that sometimes,' she said, managing not to see the black eye behind the sunglasses even as Alice pretended that she herself had walked into a door. 'Sometimes you just have to hang on in there until it gets better,' she said.

29

If one single person had ever responded with, 'You're right, you should get out,' or even better, 'I'll help you,' then Alice would have left – she knows that to be true. Only they didn't. They'd found it as impossible to imagine Alice leaving Ken as she did herself. And here she still is. With hindsight, it looks as though they were right. It looks as though they were all right, all along.

One part of Alice's brain questions why the other part is pondering all this, today of all days. Because the truth is that things haven't been that bad recently – their marriage has certainly known more challenging periods. In truth, they've progressively settled into a routine of old age that one could almost call comfortable. There are few surprises, good or bad, but the days are not unpleasant. Ken reads the paper and watches the football and Alice loses herself in her endless stream of novels. With the Kindle that Tim bought her (she had been struggling increasingly with the small print in paperbacks) she doesn't even need to go shopping between books any more. She just clicks and downloads the next recommendation and off she goes.

'She's always got her nose in a book, Alice has,' Ken jokes, never pausing to wonder why, never stopping to think about the fact that even the grimmest of fictional realities feels like escape to her.

Alice thinks about the novel she's reading right now – one of Dot's suggestions. It hasn't really been doing the trick, hasn't quite been hitting the spot. The story – of a woman in a miserable marriage dreaming of escape – is a bit close to home, that's the thing. But Alice will finish it when she gets back. She always finishes every book she starts if it's humanly possible to do so, because until you get to the end, there's still hope. Until you reach that final page, there's still the possibility of sudden, unexpected, thrilling escape.

30

Alice supposes that the same principles apply to life. Until you get to the end, there's still hope. It's why we don't give up on life until the very end, until life gives up on us.

'Oops . . . running on empty now,' Ken says, tapping the flashing petrol sign on the dashboard.

'Why didn't you fill up at the services?'

'Too expensive,' Ken says. 'I'm not paying silly motorway prices. I'll fill up at Asda round the corner from Mike's.'

'If we make it that far.'

'We will. We'll be fine.'

Running on empty. Alice runs the phrase through her mind, because it kind of sums things up. She and Ken have been running on empty for years, and it's amazing how far you can get just coasting along on a wing and a prayer, just rolling along on hope.

Her lot has been infinitely better than anything her parents had to live through. And what her grandparents (on her mother's side) had to survive must have been horrific. So perhaps she's done OK after all, considering . . . Her parents even had to pawn their wedding rings to pay for Granny Miriam's funeral – imagine that! They never managed to save enough to redeem them, either. It became a standing – if rather sour – family joke. 'Where are you off to then?' her dad would say. 'Me?' Alice's mum would reply. 'Why, I thought I'd treat myself. I'm off to Herbert Brown's to get me wedding ring back.' 'Ooh, pick mine up while you're there, would you?'

Alice dreamt for years of recovering her parents' rings for them. Long after they would have been melted down and turned into something else, she was still scheming to save enough money to get them back.

Alice looks down at her hands and sees that her right hand is fiddling with her own wedding ring, twisting it around and around on her finger. Considering what could have been, she's probably

31

being ungrateful. She should probably make more effort to see the positives.

She tries to list some of those now.

They have two reliable cars, her little Nissan Micra and this one, the Mégane. They have a comfortable home and a fair stash of money in the bank, even if Ken won't ever let them spend any of it.

They have two healthy sons, though one of them is married to a crotchety Russian who won't let her near, and the other is too busy losing himself on the Continent to come home for Christmas or even pick up the phone.

If she keeps tagging negatives on the ends of her positives then this isn't going to work, Alice reminds herself. She downloaded a book about positive thinking a few months back – it had been free on the Kindle – and not tagging negatives on the end of your positives is one of the few things she remembers. She tries again.

They have two healthy, clever sons, and two gorgeous grand-children. They're in good health for their age, and they have a nice home and enough money to get by. She has never had to pawn her wedding ring, or anything else for that matter, and she has never once gone to bed hungry. She has a good friend in Dot. And . . . She chews the inside of her mouth as she tries to think of some-thing else, anything else, and at that moment the sun finally breaks through the cloud cover. There, she thinks, she has all of this, and the sun's come out.

'Almost there,' Ken says. 'Good job, too. I'm bursting for a pee.'

Alice glances at her watch. It's a quarter to two. They might still arrive in time.

The house, which they have visited before, is a slightly pretentious, vaguely oversized new build. It looks a little like the ones they have

32

in American sitcoms. They park the car and walk to the shiny blue Downing-Street-style door. It's opened by a woman wearing an apron. She's holding a butter knife and a tub of I Can't Believe It's Not Butter not-quite-butter.

'Hello,' she says, 'I'm Karen, the caterer. Are you here for the funeral?'

Ken nods. 'We are. Sorry, love, but can I use the loo?'

'It looks like we're a bit late,' Alice says, glancing around at the empty rooms.

'They've just left,' Karen tells her, 'but you'll be fine. It's not even half a mile away.'

'Can I give you a hand with the sandwiches or something?' Alice asks. 'There's no reason why I have to—'

'No, really, I'm fine,' Karen replies. 'Jean will be happier if you go. She was worried about numbers . . . There aren't . . . you know . . . as many as she had hoped.'

Once Karen has given Ken directions to the crematorium they walk briskly back to the car. Though the pavement is still wet from the recent rain, it's turning into a bright, crisp day. The clouds are rapidly dissipating to reveal a light, hazy blue sky. It's somehow the perfect kind of weather for a funeral.

Once they are reseated in the car, Ken hesitates, his hand on the ignition key. 'This isn't going to look great, is it?' he asks.

'What?'

'Turning up in the middle of the bleedin' funeral.'

'It'll be fine,' Alice says, restraining the urge to remind Ken whose fault it is that they're late. 'She said it's just five minutes away.'

'Yep. And it's already five to,' Ken says.

'Just go, will you?' Alice prompts, nodding at the road ahead. 'Or it will be too late.'

33

'You reckon? It's not better to, you know . . .'

'No, Ken. It's not. Go!'

Alice begins to feel emotional even as they're arriving in the crematorium car park. Outside the building, they pass between people gathering for the next funeral, or perhaps, judging by the blurred mascara and the shiny cheeks, stragglers from the previous one. It seems to be something of a production line.

A very young man in a badly fitting suit greets them and leads them to the chapel where the service is already in progress.

Ken attempts to walk towards the front rows where the other mourners are clustered, but Alice grabs his wrist and tugs him forcefully to the nearest pews at the rear of the room. She knows the protocol for late arrivals at funerals and weddings and, despite what Ken may imagine, barging your way to the front isn't part of it.

Jean, already at the lectern talking tearfully about her husband, catches Alice's eye, pauses, nods, and then continues. 'It's left such a big 'ole,' she says, sounding with her dropped h's a bit like Pat from *EastEnders*. 'That's the fing. It's so 'ard to know 'ow to carry on.'

Alice observes Jean struggling to speak, watches the tears running down her cheeks, notes the shuddering shoulders of those in the front row, and then begins to cry freely herself.

In the car on the way here, Alice had found herself thinking a shameful thought. She had wondered if she would cry if Ken died, and had found herself coldly imagining the sheer embarrassment of a funeral where she might fail to summon a single tear for her dead husband. She had pushed that thought from her mind and labelled herself a terrible person for even thinking it, but realises now that she needn't worry – of course she would cry. Even Alice isn't hard enough to go to a funeral and not cry.

34

She looks at the plinth supporting the coffin and wonders if it'll smoothly vanish the way it did at Betty Johnson's funeral.

That unexpected movement, that silent slither from view, had seemed creepy and somehow too smooth, too technologically perfected to be suited to the occasion, as if the process of death needed perhaps to be violent and shocking rather than sleek, sanitised and aesthetically pleasing.

She wonders, as she wondered at Betty's funeral, if they burn the coffin – which would seem a waste – or if they remove the body and reuse it – which would be a little gruesome. She wonders what the ovens look like, if they're in the same building, wonders if they're the same kind of thing the Germans used during the war. She's read somewhere that Siemens had made those. They have a Siemens oven at home. It's very fast to heat up, very efficient. Alice shudders.

Friends are taking it in turns to speak now, and they all agree on one thing: what a marvellous guy Mike was. Despite the fact that Ken worked with Mike pretty much his whole life, Ken has declined to speak today, thank God. Ken has never had much sense of decorum and Alice can just imagine the sort of toned-down wedding speech – all anecdotes and inappropriate jokes – that Ken might have delivered.

'He was always there,' a middle-aged man is saying now, his voice gravelly with emotion. 'That's the thing. You could always rely on Mike.'

Alice reflects on the fact that every person you pass on the street, every person you have dealings with at the post office, every person your husband ever worked with, has been important to someone. Everyone has, at some point, deeply touched the lives of those around them. Even racist, bolshie, flashy Mike.

The man sits down and is replaced by Mike's daughter Linda. 'This is really hard,' she says, her voice wobbling like a toy that

35

needs new batteries. 'So I'm not gonna say much, except that he was the best dad anyone could have. He was my whole world really . . .' Linda collapses into tears and is led away by a very good-looking young man, presumably her new husband. Alice pulls a tissue from her sleeve and dabs at her eyes, prompting Ken to reach for her hand, and she lets him take it and squeeze it.

Alice wonders if Tim and Matt would say the same thing, if they would say, 'She was the best mum, he was the best dad . . .' She doubts it, because they weren't the best mum and dad really, were they? Even if they did do their best.

She had been too soft on them, and Ken, no doubt about it, had been too hard. She should probably have stood up to Ken more about that, but he was never an easy man to stand up to. So no, they hadn't been perfect parents by any stretch of the imagination, but she truly had given it her best shot.

Nobody taught you how to raise children back then, that was the thing. These days there's the television and the self-help books, there are pamphlets to read and the school psychologist to fall back on. In Alice's day, you just had to wing it, you just had to get on with it as best you could.

They hadn't been exactly bad at it, either. There had been worse parents around, parents whose kids ended up killing themselves, parents whose kids died of overdoses or ended up in prison. Her own parents had been very cold, very distant – they hadn't seemed to consider it their role to adapt themselves to their children in any way; it had been the child's role to be quiet, to shut up, to fit in. 'Children should be seen and not heard,' they used to say. 'Children should not speak unless spoken to.'

At least Tim and Matt will never have doubted that they were cared for. At least they have known that they were loved, even if Ken's parenting did become increasingly authoritarian as they got

36

older. At least they must never have feared that their parents were indifferent to their fates.

Mike's son is reading a poem now – it's the one from *Four Weddings and a Funeral*, that poem by Auden that everyone and his dog seems to have chosen for every funeral ever to have happened since that film came out. Alice groans internally.

It's a lovely poem, but honestly, you would think there were no other poems out there. Alice must remember to tell someone that she doesn't want Auden read at her own funeral. She can't think of anything worse. She wants something quirky, something unusual from her big poetry book. Something by Sylvia Plath, perhaps.

Alice wonders who will die first, she or Ken. Generally, it's the men who go first, but you can never be sure. Betty Johnson was five years younger than Will, so no one expected her to go first. It's the men who go suddenly, as far as she can see. Like Mike: one minute laughing, and the next just gone. The wives tend to favour years of battle with repeated surgery and toxic chemotherapy drips, before finally expiring in the cold light of a hospital ward, dosed to the eyeballs on morphine. Better to die like a man, Alice thinks. Better to suddenly, unexpectedly check out. Better to go laughing, like Mike.

She tries to imagine how she would feel if Ken suddenly keeled over, but her mind comes up with a blank. Perhaps it's just too massive to be imagined. Or perhaps it's too insignificant. Perhaps its significance would turn out to be precisely its insignificance. She thinks of a character in a novel she read a few months back. The girl in the novel kept waiting for her break-up to hit her, kept waiting to collapse over the unceremonious way her boyfriend had dumped her (by text message) only to realise eventually that she was happier without him. Could Alice's biggest life trauma turn out to be losing her husband, only to discover that her single fifty-year relationship hadn't been that important after all?

37

It crosses Alice's mind that if Ken died, she could go to Spain with Dot. She could go to Spain every year. She could go and live in bloody Spain. Disgusted at her own thought processes, Alice glances guiltily across at Ken. He looks up at her. His eyes are shiny with tears.

You really are a terrible person, Alice tells herself again.

Back at Jean's house, Alice nibbles a sandwich and makes conversation with first Jean herself ('It will get easier, I know it doesn't feel like that now, but it will') and then with surprisingly together daughter Linda and her husband, James. They're both rather lovely.

Beside her, Alice can hear Ken having one of his pointless blokey conversations about cars and routes and traffic. Something about the A58.

'And what about your lads?' Linda asks. 'They've got two sons the same age as me and Doug,' she tells her husband as an aside. 'We used to play together when we were kids.'

'They're well,' Alice tells her. 'Tim's married with kids. He works in finance, which he seems very good at. He was the only child I ever knew who had more money at the end of the week than when you gave him his pocket money! He actually used to lend money to Matt with interest, can you believe that?'

'I think I remember that,' Linda says. 'And he's still with . . . ?'

'Natalya,' Alice says. 'Yes. And the boys are lovely – Boris and Alexander.'

'And Matt? What's he up to?'

Alice clears her throat. 'He's good. He's in France at the moment.'

'France! What's he doing in France?'

Alice licks her lips; for how can she tell Linda that she doesn't have much of an idea what Matt's doing in France? How can she say that without sounding like an uncaring mother?

38

'He's working in a hotel,' she says finally, 'and working on his French.' And it's only half a lie. Working in a hotel is the last thing she can remember Matt doing. And seeing as he's in France, he's bound to be working on his French.

'And he's still single?' Linda asks. 'I was a bit in love with Matt,' Linda tells her husband in a confidential tone of voice.

'I'm not sure how I feel about that,' James says.

'Oh, it was when she was about ten!' Alice explains. 'And yes, he's still single.'

But the truth, again, is that Alice has no idea if Matt is single or not. He's been gone so long – almost three years now – and even before he left he was always such a private person, such a secretive child. Neither she, nor she suspects, Ken, ever had much of a sense of who Matt really was or what kind of person Matt would end up with.

From his lack of competitive spirit to his dark, grungy clothes (what was it he called them? Goth?), from his strange friends to his penchant for dead pop stars, he was always somehow 'other' to them. He was always just out of reach.

Tim had been the only person who seemed to understand Matt, and even then it was only up to a point. They'd always seemed close, or at least until Matt went travelling. But even that closeness looked more to Alice like a kind of blanket acceptance on Tim's part than any profound understanding of what made Matt tick. 'It's just how he is, Mum,' Tim would say whenever Alice asked him about Matt. 'Why is all his music so dark?' she would ask. 'Why do all of his clothes have to be black, Tim?' 'Why is he wearing black eyeliner?' 'Why would anyone get their nipple pierced?'

'That's just Matt,' Tim would reply. 'Don't worry.'

The one reassuring thing was that Matt did tend to land on his feet. Despite failing all of his science subjects, he had managed to get into university to study art. And he'd been good at it,

39

apparently. When he dropped out, Matt had been, Tim said, in line for a first-class degree. It had been just months before his finals.

Alice had so been looking forward to that ceremony. She had chosen a dress for herself and had been eyeing up new suits for both Ken and Matt. She had never even seen Matt in a suit before and had spent happy hours imagining the pride she would feel when they handed him his degree.

With both sons long gone from the family home, she had been well into the lonely phase of her marriage by then, and had learnt to cling to such scheduled moments of happiness like a monkey to a tree in a hurricane. But then Matt had phoned home – he had wanted to borrow some money – and Alice had asked him to confirm the dates of his final exams, and he had admitted that he wasn't even in Manchester any more. He was in London, he said. He was living in a squat.

The phone call over, Alice had sat and wept at the telephone table, not for Matt, but selfishly for herself, for the dress she would no longer get to wear, for the hotel in Manchester that Ken wouldn't book, for the restaurant where they would no longer celebrate, for the pride she wouldn't get to feel. And when she was done with feeling sorry for Alice, she had sat and chewed her nails and worried, yet again, about Matt. But Matt bounced back. Matt always bounced back, and often this actively annoyed Alice. She frequently wished that life would teach Matt a lesson once and for all. Was that mean of her, to want her own son to stop getting away with blue-bloody-murder? Partly it was, she supposes. But partly it was borne of a genuine fear that if Matt didn't learn soon that life wasn't all-forgiving, then he would end up falling out of the tree.

But life, it appeared, wasn't out to teach Matt harsh lessons. Not this time. Not, seemingly, any time. Within a month of moving into the squat he had found a job – a good, well-paid job working as a graphic designer in an advertising agency. Not that

40

he would deign to stay there for long. He must have had ten jobs in the ten years he was in London. He would just walk out of a job any time someone annoyed him. And that was often. Yes, he would walk out and never go back, as if jobs were unlimited. And for Matt, it seemed, they were.

And now he's travelling. Travelling! As if travelling were a 'thing'. As if travelling, like life, wasn't meant to be about actually trying to get somewhere.

'We were going to move down to Manchester,' Linda is saying when Alice tunes back in. 'We even had a house lined up, but we're thinking we might stay here a little longer now, you know, for Mum.'

'Yes,' Alice says. 'Yes, I'm sure she'll appreciate that.'

She attempts to take a deep breath, but fails – it feels as if someone is sitting on her chest. She turns to Ken, still citing the numbers of various roads to the man beside him. 'I need to get a breath of fresh air,' she tells him. 'I'll be out in the garden.'

Alice steps out of the kitchen into the chilly twilight of the garden. It's a long strip of land leading down a gently curved hill to a PVC-and-glass summerhouse at the bottom, lit by the almost blood-red sun setting behind it.

Drawn by the pretty summerhouse, Alice starts to cross the garden, her shoes crunching on the frost of the immaculate lawn. It's literally freezing out here, and the air makes her lungs smart as she struggles for those still-elusive deep breaths. She thinks about this breathlessness, now so well known to her, so familiarly linked to thinking about, to worrying about Matt.

But it's not just Matt today, she realises. It's a kind of all-encompassing anxiety about . . . what, exactly? As she walks she tries to break down, to categorise, to analyse the component parts of this strange mix of emotions.

41

She's feeling a little ashamed, she realises. That's part of it. She's ashamed of her lack of relationship with her second child, of her inability to even speak confidently of his whereabouts. She's also, if she thinks about it, ashamed of her relationship with Ken.

She's feeling jealous, too. Jealous of Jean's relationship with Mike, which, even if Alice didn't much like him and even if it has now ended, was apparently powerful enough to leave Jean struggling to imagine how she can even carry on without him. And she's jealous of Jean's relationship with her daughter. Jealousy – it's not a pleasant feeling to have to face up to, one of the seven deadly sins. But this feeling that she is having has a name, and that name – there's no getting around it – is 'jealousy'.

Linda is so pretty and together; she makes a perfect couple with elegantly suited, affable James. Other people's families always look smoother, look more together from the outside, and that's only because outsiders never get to see all of the hidden resentments, all of the grimy compromise, all of the unspoken tensions that lurk behind the scenes. Alice, of all people, knows this. And as Ken would point out, she can feel just as proud of Tim, who with slim, pretty Natalya provides a similar tableau of success to that displayed by Linda and James. Yes, plenty of people would look at Tim and Nat with their matching Rado watches and their kids running around in those outrageously pricey Dolce & Gabbana outfits and feel jealous of her and her own wonderful, successful, well-balanced descendants.

As for the other one, well, Alice loves him too, of course she does. Is her problem with Matt just that she would so have loved her second child to be a girl? The thought has occasionally crossed her mind. Alice has always believed that a daughter would have been an ally for her in that house of men, whereas not only was Matt not her ally, but seemingly he did everything he could to make himself incomprehensible to both of them. Sometimes, just

42

occasionally, Alice has even wondered if he really is her child, wondered if someone didn't accidentally swap the name tags around in the hospital.

There's no doubt about that any more though. Matt has grown up to have Ken's humpy nose and Alice's strong chin, her good teeth, and occasionally, when she looks at the back of his head, she's unable to tell if it's Matt or Tim she's looking at. But psychologically, it was, for much of his childhood, like having a foreigner in the house, like having a guest from a different culture, someone from a faraway place with incomprehensible customs. Ken blundered through pretending that his relationship with Matt was 'fine', but Alice could tell he felt the same way that she did. She saw the difference in the way he treated the two boys.

Alice reaches the summerhouse and peers inside to look at the interior. With the exception of one of those Japanese paraffin heaters and a three-piece suite of basket-weave furniture, it's entirely empty. Too cold to use in winter, probably even with the heater on, but it must be a lovely place to sit and read in summer. It's a shame she and Ken don't have a bigger garden. Alice would love to have a summerhouse. She shivers and turns back towards the wake, still thinking about Matt.

One time, Ken's father had given the boys some money to spend and Ken had driven them all to a big toyshop – a rare treat. Tim, who must have been eleven or twelve, had chosen a Hot Wheels racing set. It had clip-together plastic tracks and a loop-the-loop and a chicane and four little metal cars to race down the slope. Cars with genuine rubber tyres being something that Ken could relate to, he had seemed almost as excited about those Hot Wheels as Tim was.

Meanwhile Matt, holding Alice's hand, had led her on a random meander around the shop, choosing a box of watercolours, and a lampshade that projected stars on the ceiling, and a fluffy

43

pink monkey with battery-operated cymbals, and an Action Man with Eagle Eyes who came equipped with three different military uniforms you could dress him in.

At the cash register Ken had frowned in disbelief. 'This is what you want?' he had asked the boy, brandishing the monkey, which looked, with its stupid expression, almost as surprised at Matt's decision as Ken was. 'This rubbish?!'

'It's fine, Ken,' Alice had said. 'He can have what he wants. That's the whole idea.'

'A monkey and a doll and paints?' Ken had asked, struggling to hold back something akin to anger. 'A bloody lampshade?'

Matt had said nothing; he had merely nodded solemnly and stared at his feet. He had looked as if he might cry at any moment.

'It's fine, Ken,' Alice had said again. 'Let him have what he wants. He's a child!'

'Fine!' Ken had declared, pulling the ten-pound notes from his pocket. And Alice had bitten her lip and sighed in relief that Matt had not mentioned the purple plastic horse with brushable mane and tail that he had also chosen, the one toy that even Alice had baulked at, the one thing she had removed from the shopping basket.

With the image of that My Little Pony still in her mind's eye, Alice reaches the back door. She steps back into the kitchen.

'Oh, there you are,' Jean says. She's redone her make-up and looks almost normal. 'Ken's looking for you. He says he wants to head off before it gets dark.'

'It virtually is dark,' Alice replies. 'The sun's setting now.'

'I know,' Jean says with a shrug. 'But you know what Ken's like.'

'Yes,' Alice says. 'Yes, I know what Ken's like.'

44

2

APRIL

Alice stands in front of the bathroom mirror brushing her hair. She needs to go to the hairdresser's, she thinks – her roots are showing through. But she doesn't look so bad this morning; at least she doesn't look as old as she has been looking. Winter has never been kind to her skin generally, but the flu she suffered in March seemed to age her by about one hundred years, dried up her complexion and left her looking as wrinkled as a tumble-dried sheet. Luckily this morning it looks like she might be returning from the dead, though it could just be an impression caused by the softer glow of the sunlight filtering through the frosted window of the bathroom. Or perhaps it's just that her mood is also lifting now that the flu is behind her, now that the days are getting longer and the first flowers are blooming in the back yard.

From downstairs she hears the sound of the front door and notices as her body relaxes. Today is Sunday so Ken will be off to the newsagent's for his *Sunday Times*. It's one of the few of his many, many rituals that Alice actually likes, because if she's honest, she would probably rather get up to an empty house every day. She's not much of a morning person, never has been really, and these silent Sunday mornings where she can just stare into the middle distance instead of talking to Ken, where she can listen to the house creaking instead of struggling to ignore the bad news spewing from the television, have always felt like little gifts from God.

She puts down the hairbrush and quietly opens the bathroom door. She holds her breath and listens. She hears the central heating boiler fire up. Other than that, the house is silent. She really is alone. She exhales slowly and heads downstairs.

In the kitchen, she fills and switches on the kettle, then looks out at their small back garden. Yes, the light this morning is lovely, and it makes her want to be somewhere else, on a beach perhaps, or in the woods. On a mountain in Scotland or on a ferry going somewhere new. She suddenly wants to be anywhere but here – a familiar spring feeling that has haunted her regularly throughout her life. Perhaps she can convince Ken to go for a drive in the country when he gets back.

Automatically, unconsciously, she pulls a mug from a hook, drops a teabag in and pours on the boiling water. She sits at the kitchen table and warms her hands on the cup, notices the steam rising, sees dust motes floating in the sunlight.

She reaches for her Nokia and checks the screen. She has missed two calls from Dot and has a voice message. She smiles at this unexpected good news. Dot has been strangely absent for the last two weeks – it happens occasionally, generally when things are bad with Martin. She's glad Dot's back. Perhaps, if there's football for Ken to watch, she can go for a walk with Dot instead.

Alice raises the phone to her ear and simultaneously raises the mug to her lips. But at the sound of Dot's brittle voice, she frowns and puts the cup back down, somehow the better to concentrate on the voice message. Because Dot doesn't sound much like Dot today.

46

'Hi, Alice, it's me,' the message runs. 'I've finally done it. I've left him. I, um . . . I need to talk to you. I'm staying in a little place in Edgbaston. It's near Edith's place but don't tell Martin; he doesn't know where I am. Oh, and don't tell Ken either, please. You know those two are thick as chalk and cheese. Anyway, um . . . call me back, will you? Bye.'

Alice lowers the phone and frowns at it. As thick as chalk and cheese? Dot means as thick as thieves, surely. She swallows with difficulty. She wants to listen to the message again, but can't remember which button to press and can't risk deleting it, so she hangs up and dials her voicemail again. But even on the second and third listening, the message makes no sense to her. She understands what the words mean, she can hear what Dot is saying, but their meaning seems so out of context as to be almost an impossibility. Because when Alice last saw Dot she had not been about to leave Martin, not at all. In fact, no woman in her seventies that Alice has ever known has been about to leave her husband. It's simply not something that happens in Alice's universe. She hangs up, then redials and listens to the message for a fourth time, and then she puts down the handset and stares at it – suddenly strange, suddenly alien to her, the bearer of surreal news. Eventually, after fifteen minutes, her brain starts to adjust. The idea that her best friend might truly be leaving her husband begins almost to make sense.

She reaches for her phone again and is dialling Dot's number when she sees Ken's shadow fall upon the patterned glass of the front door, hears his key in the lock. 'Hiya,' he says, stepping into the hallway.

'Morning,' Alice replies, putting down the phone.

Ken approaches, the soles of his brogues tapping the hall tiles as he walks. He enters the kitchen and drops the considerable weight that is the *Sunday Times* on to the kitchen table. 'It's all Greece again,' he says.

47

'Grease?' Alice asks.

'Greece. The country. The euro and all that palaver.'

'Oh,' Alice says, nodding, still stroking her mobile phone.

'Are you all right?' Ken asks.

Alice nods. 'Yep,' she says. 'You?'

'Of course,' Ken tells her, pulling off his coat and hanging it in the hall before returning to the kitchen. He looks at Alice questioningly. 'Are you sure you're OK?' he asks with unusual perspicacity.

Alice forces a smile. 'Yes,' she insists. 'I'm fine! I, um . . . I was thinking that I might nip out to the shops.'

'Really?' Ken asks. 'We went yesterday. We got a whole carload of stuff, nearly a hundred and fifty quid's worth.' Trust Ken to bring everything back to money.

'I know. But I fancy some fish. You know how it is when you just fancy something, and today I fancy fish.'

'There's fish in the freezer,' Ken says.

'I fancy some fresh fish. It's almost a craving.'

'Maybe you're pregnant,' Ken laughs.

'Maybe.'

'Anyway, it's Sunday, love,' Ken says. 'You'd have to go to—'

'Tesco,' Alice says. 'Yes, I know.' Tesco is perfect, Alice thinks. Tesco is in Edgbaston.

Knowing that Ken will find out about Dot soon enough and wondering why she is bothering to lie to him, Alice pulls on her coat, grabs her car keys from the hook and glances back at Ken.

'You're sure you're all right?' he asks one more time, frowning deeply.

'Yes,' Alice says crisply. 'I just want some fish, that's all.' She'll have to come clean later, but for now, she simply doesn't want to deal with Ken's reactions until she has at least some handle on her own.

Outside in the sunshine, in something of a daze, she slides into the car, fastens her seat belt and pulls sharply away. She accelerates

48

quickly to the end of the road, drives faster than usual through King's Heath, and then unexpectedly, even to herself, pulls abruptly off the main road on to a lane leading to the cemetery. She feels younger this morning – younger and, like life, unpredictable. It's strange.

She parks on the gravelly hard shoulder, turns off the engine and then pulls her phone from her handbag.

Dot answers immediately. 'Alice?'

'Yes, it's me. Is it true?' she asks, aware that she's sounding abrupt.

'I've been trying to phone you,' Dot says.

'I know. I heard your message. Is it true then?'

'That I've left him?'

'Yes.'

'Of course it's true. It was the Spain trip that, you know . . . broke the camel's back. D'you know what that bastard did? He only went into Thomson's and cancelled my whole—'

'Dot,' Alice interrupts. 'I'm in the car. I'm on my way to Tesco's.'

'Tesco here? The Edgbaston one?'

'Yes.'

'Then come. I'm just around the corner. And I need to see you.'

'That's what I thought.'

'I'm in the same building as Edith from gym class. On Skipton Road. Do you remember?'

'Yes, just about.'

'Then come. I'll make a pot of coffee.'

'I'll be there in ten minutes.'

'Park in bay thirty-four.'

'I'm sorry?'

'That's my space. They get funny about that stuff here.'

49

'Oh, OK. Bay thirty-four,' Alice repeats. She clicks on a button to end the call then returns the phone to her handbag. She shakes her head vigorously as if to dislodge something, then exhales slowly, starts the engine and swings the Micra around, spitting gravel as she does so.

She's feeling most peculiar, she really is. This Dot thing has left her feeling quite shaken up. She feels jittery and nervous. Her heart is beating faster than usual. She has a bead of sweat on her top lip. And then she works it out – she's feeling excited. She hasn't felt excited about anything for so long that the feeling is barely familiar to her, but, yes, that's definitely it. She's excited. But why?

When she gets to Avery House, she finds Dot standing in the car park. She's wearing a rather Vicky Pollard purple velour track-suit, which is so out of character that Alice has to blink twice before she manages to convince herself that this is indeed Dot.

The second she climbs from the driving seat, Dot hugs her.

'What on earth are you wearing?' Alice asks.

Dot looks down at herself and then laughs in surprise. 'Don't worry, these are just my pyjamas,' she says. 'Lazing around in your jim-jams until ten in the morning is just one of the pleasures of being single. One of many pleasures. Come inside. Come see my new place.'

'Are you really single?' Alice asks as she locks the car. 'Or is this just some—'

'It's real,' Dot tells her. 'Come and see.'

She leads Alice across the car park and into the shabby lobby of the small tower block. It's not an elegant or refined building in any way, but it is clean, and when she opens the front door to her apartment the sun is shining on to the sofa, a pot of coffee is steam-ing on the table and a novel lies open next to it.

'Home sweet home,' Dot says, gesturing at the space.

50

'You need to tell me what's going on here,' Alice says, 'because this is all a bit too much for my brain to take in.'

'I know,' Dot replies, sitting on the sofa and patting the space beside her. 'Take your coat off, come and sit down, and I'll tell you everything. I've been dying to tell you, Alice, but I couldn't. I hope you'll understand. I hope you'll forgive me.'

Over coffee, Dot tells Alice her story. She tells her about the secret bank account she opened three years ago. She tells her how she squirrelled money away. She tells her about her surreptitious hunt for an apartment and how Edith from gym class mentioned this one to her a month ago. 'It's only one hundred and twenty a week,' she says. 'That's cheap for round here.'

Alice listens and struggles to get her brain around the fact of Dot living alone. She also tries to forgive her for keeping the secret for so long. Because in Dot's own words, she's been planning this for years. She's been saving and house-hunting, consulting divorce lawyers and seeing pension specialists, and all of it without a word to anyone. And Alice can't help but feel a little hurt by her best friend's lack of trust.

But then they start to talk not of the past but of the future, specifically of Dot's future as a single woman. Alice asks her how she feels, if she's scared, if she feels lonely. And Dot replies that no, she's not scared, and no, she doesn't feel lonely. She feels, for the first time in years, relaxed, she says. She feels, for the first time since her thirties, optimistic and excited. The tears in her eyes reveal her words to be true and they are so convincing and somehow so familiar to Alice (who only this morning was savouring Ken's hour-long absence) that her happiness for her friend drowns out her resentment. She feels proud of Dot's bravery and surprisingly jealous, too. And there, again, is that strange feeling of youthful excitement. Her heart is racing again. What's that all about?

51

It's only when Alice gets home that she realises she has completely forgotten to buy fish – her supposed alibi for the trip out. But as she enters the lounge – hesitating between the truth and a 'surprise run on fish products at Tesco' – Ken glances up at her looking outraged, and says, 'You'll never guess who phoned while you were out.'

'Martin?' Alice offers.

'You know about this?'

Alice nods. 'Dot phoned me while I was out. I was, um, so surprised I forgot all about the fish.'

'It's un-ber-loody-lievable,' Ken says. 'What did she say? Martin doesn't even know where she is.'

'I don't know either. She didn't say. I think she's in Brum some-where, staying with a friend.'

'Which friend?'

'I really don't know.'

'She's gone crazy, that's what Martin says. She needs help, you know – proper professional help.'

'She sounded OK. I think she just had enough of him,' Alice says, fiddling with her headscarf, reluctant to remove her coat, not with Ken looking this angry.

'Enough of him?!' Ken says. 'They've been together thirty years. More than thirty years.'

'Well, quite. I think that's why . . .'

'She's a selfish cow,' Ken says. 'That's what I think. That's what I've always thought.'

'Selfish?'

'Martin reckons she's made off with a load of money, too.'

'Money?'

'That's what he said. That she stole a load of money from the joint account.'

Alice frowns. 'The joint account, you say? Now, let me see—'

'A thief!' Ken interrupts. 'That's the kind of person your best friend is. A thief who steals from her husband. Lovely.'

'It's their money, Ken. They're married. It's a joint account.'

Ken laughs meanly. 'You're pulling my plonker, right? Dot's never worked a day in her whole life. You know that.'

'She's brought up three children, two of whom weren't even hers,' Alice says, struggling to contain her own anger. It's hard to remember that they're talking about Dot here. It's hard to feel that they're not also talking about Alice. 'That's quite a lot of work, actually.'

Ken's jaw drops. He shakes his head in disbelief. 'And how are they going to feel? The poor kids?'

'They're in their forties, Ken. They're hardly kids.'

'They're still not going to think much of their mother abandoning their dad, are they?'

'Abandoning? You make him sound like a do—' Alice starts to say. But then she restrains herself. Ken's going red, and that's not a good sign. 'Anyway, I'm sure it's like everything. I'm sure there's two sides to the story.'

'Well, you're not to see her any more,' Ken says.

Alice pulls a face. 'I'm sorry?'

'You heard me. I don't want you seeing her. I forbid it.'

Alice laughs. Even though she regrets the laughter – it's like a red rag to a bull as far as Ken's concerned – she can't help herself. 'You forbid it?'

'Yes,' Ken says, now removing the *Sunday Times* magazine from his knees and standing.

'Last time I looked, we weren't living in Saudi Arabia,' Alice says. And then before Ken even has time to implode, she turns and walks from the room.

'Alice!' Ken calls behind her. 'ALICE!'

53

After a second's hesitation, Alice walks to the front door and, ignoring Ken's calls, lets herself out. She walks towards the car, then changes her mind – she's too shaky to drive – and spins on one heel to head the other way, towards The Dell.

Once or twice she glances over her shoulder to check that Ken isn't following her, but she knows that he won't be, not yet. It takes Ken half an hour to find his keys, and another half an hour to find his shoes. And after that he has to check all the locks on the doors and the windows.

As the distance between herself and the house increases, Alice starts to feel calmer. Yes, Ken's being an idiot, but it's still a beautiful day. The sun is shining. She did the right thing by leaving. The argument about Dot was precisely the kind of situation where Ken's anger gets out of hand. Because, though there's nothing to be won by arguing, Alice knows that she was right, knows that she is not going to back down, is not going to accede to some crazy demand that she stop seeing her best friend. The problem is that Ken will never climb down, not even when he is patently wrong. 'I'm sorry, I was wrong,' are words that Ken simply cannot say. So the only way for this argument to end is for Ken to overreact to such a degree, for him to spin into a maelstrom of anger and violence that is so out of proportion to whatever is going on that even he can see that he has behaved badly. Only then does a path to contrition appear. Only then can he apologise, not for the original argument but merely for his overreaction. So Alice's best bet is to stay out of his way long enough for him to calm down.

She reaches the entrance to the nature reserve and weaves her way around the waiting cars in the car park. It's a Sunday, so it's bound to be busy.

As she starts to walk along the little track into the woodlands, she crosses paths with a family – three generations out together, laughing and joking, the grandchildren tearing around the

54

grandfather's feet. She nods 'hello' to them, and tries to remember the last time she got to go out somewhere with Alex and Boris. Between crotchety Natalya and Ken, who complains like crazy any time he has to walk anywhere, such outings are getting rarer and rarer.

On days like this she hates Ken, she really does hate him. Perhaps she should . . .

She freezes. She takes in the sensations in her body. Because it's there again. That feeling of youthful, crazy excitement. And this time she knows why. Suddenly she understands why Dot's rupture with Martin, unimaginable only twenty-four hours ago, has left her feeling so edgy. It's because Dot has opened a door. Dot has made the unthinkable appear to be not only thinkable, but really quite appealing. Should she, Alice . . . ? Could she . . . ? Is she really going to let herself even think that thought?

She glances at the path behind her. If she goes back now, the storm will become a tornado. She could choose that though, couldn't she? She could spin on one heel and walk right back into the firestorm. That's all it would take to get the justification she needs.

She winces at the thought and raises one hand to her cheek. Yes, she could simply go home, defend Dot and refuse to back down. Ken, she knows, would explode. Still caressing her cheek, she imagines herself turning up at Tim's place in tears. 'Look what he's done to me,' she would say, and then she would tremblingly lower her hand to reveal the bruise.

But then she'd feel guilty, wouldn't she? She would know that she had brought it upon herself. She imagines Tim saying, 'Don't be silly, Mum, you're not going to leave him. You know you're not.' He has said it before, after all.

She shakes her head and starts to walk deeper into the woods.

It's late afternoon by the time Alice returns home. She lets herself in quietly and stands in the hallway as she tries to get a feel for the atmosphere within the house. The smell of anger carries from room to room – you can pick it up from a distance if you've developed the knack. Surprisingly, everything seems calm, and when she peers into the lounge, she understands why. Ken is asleep on the couch, snoring lightly.

She tiptoes through to the kitchen – she's in no hurry to wake him – and gently closes the kitchen door, wincing as the catch of the door clicks into place. She crosses to the sink and looks out at the garden, at the beautiful green of the lawn and the elegant shapes cast by the shadows of the trees. Then she turns back to face the kitchen. Her sight falls upon the oven. She'll bake a cake, she thinks. That'll smooth things over.

By the time Ken pokes his head through the door an hour later, the rich smell of Victoria sponge has filled the kitchen. Ken's face looks puffy from sleep and, without a doubt, all the beer he will have consumed earlier in the day. 'I slept too long,' he says. Then, 'Something smells good.'

Alice lets herself breathe again. He's not drunk and he's not angry. They might get through this day without an actual fight. 'I'm making a sponge cake,' she says.

Ken nods. 'Nice,' he says. 'Make me a cuppa too, would you?'

Alice reaches out to switch on the kettle. 'Sure,' she says. 'Go sit down. I'll bring it through.'

When she returns to the lounge with the tea, Ken asks, 'So, Dot . . . ?'

Alice braces herself.

'Did you see her?' Ken asks.

'No,' Alice says, begging him silently not to ask if she intends seeing her, and wondering what she'll say, what path she'll choose if he does, if he forbids it again.

56

But the silent begging seems to have worked. 'Good,' Ken says, taking the mug of tea from Alice's outstretched hand. 'Now, when's that cake ready?'

◆ ◆ ◆

The next morning, Alice finds a note on the kitchen table. 'At the accountant's,' it says simply. She wishes that she had remembered Ken's appointment. She wouldn't have lingered so long in bed had she known that he was out.

She makes a mug of coffee and then phones Dot. 'I was just going to call you,' Dot tells her. 'Can you take me to Ikea? I need plates and pans and things.'

'Ooh, yes!' Alice says. She finds the idea of a trip to Ikea quite exciting. 'I could do with some new pans, too.'

Not only is finding the entrance to the Ikea car park difficult, but the store itself would appear to have been designed to be as hellish as it can be, from the labyrinthine car park to their careering caddie to the one-way racecourse for aggressive caddie pushers they find themselves on. The entire store has been laid out so that it's impossible to visit any one department without visiting every other part, so, like sheep, they follow the stream of other shoppers around the loop.

But despite Ikea's apparent worst intentions, shopping with Dot for furnishings feels youthful and fun. They argue good-naturedly about whether orange faux-fur cushions look modern or simply 'tacky'. They bitch like an old couple about whether it's best to buy the cheapest saucepans, or, as Alice believes, the ones 'designed to last'. They slump in a big red sofa together and both agree that it's too 'squidgy' and that it would be terrible for their

57

ageing backs. And by the time they've negotiated the checkout queues, found the car and unloaded the shopping from Alice's jam-packed Micra, it's almost one o'clock.

'I'll put the rest away later,' Dot says, chucking two cushions from the top of a blue Ikea bag on to her sofa.

The sun is streaming into her apartment and the new cushions contribute to making the place look bright and optimistic.

'I was wrong about the cushions,' Alice admits. 'They look nice. Not tacky at all.'

'You see.'

Despite Alice's protestations that she needs to get home, Dot makes them sandwiches to eat. They slump on to the sofa, sigh simultaneously, and then laugh because of it.

'I feel like I've done one of those army assault courses,' Dot says.

'Yes,' Alice agrees. 'Me too.'

'I did buy a lot of rubbish I don't need,' Dot admits, glancing at the pile of bags by the door. 'That's the trouble with Ikea.'

Alice laughs. It's exactly what she kept telling Dot every time she added some new impulse purchase to the caddie. She closes her eyes and feels the warmth of the sun on her skin. It's a funny little thing, but she always dreamed of having a sofa in the sun where she could sit and read her books. You wouldn't think that it was a complicated ambition, but it was an important one, and it's something they never quite managed. The windows and sofas, the east-west lie of the houses they lived in, they all conspired to make her sunny sofa a permanent impossibility.

'Still, what the hell,' Dot says. 'You only live once, huh?'

'Are you going to be all right for money?' Alice asks. She can't quite get her brain around Dot's new-found independence.

'I squirrelled away about five grand,' Dot says. 'So I'll be all right for a bit. Plus the pension should be sorted out soon. I'm see-ing some pension chap tomorrow to get them all separated out and

58

everything. Then Martin's will go to him, and mine to me. That's the theory, anyway.'

'Squirrelled away how?' Alice asks.

'I'm sorry?'

'How did you manage to siphon off five grand without him noticing? You were always saying how mean he was.'

'Oh!' Dot laughs. 'That . . .'

'Yes, that.'

'Cashback, love.'

'Cash back?'

'Every time I did the weekly shop, I added twenty or thirty quid cashback. It shows up on the statements as a single purchase so he never spotted it. Been doing it for years. I put all the cash in my Nationwide account.'

'And he never noticed?'

'Let's just say I complained a lot. About the cost of living, like.' Dot snorts. 'Actually, Martin complained a lot, too.'

When Alice gets home, she finds Ken at the kitchen table, eating. 'You took your time,' he says. 'I had to make myself a sandwich.'

'Poor you,' Alice says, shrugging her way out of the coat. 'That must have been exhausting.'

'No,' Ken replies, sounding confused by her sarcasm. 'But I was worried about you.'

Alice raises an eyebrow at this and pulls the two new frying pans from the Ikea bag and places them on the kitchen table. 'We needed new pans. I left you a note.'

'Yes . . .' Ken says doubtfully. 'I didn't think it was going to take all morning though. I suppose you were with that friend of yours.'

Alice returns to the hall to hang up her coat. 'Dot?' she asks lightly. 'No, why would you think that?'

'I know you were,' Ken says when she returns.

'Well, I can assure you that I wasn't,' Alice lies, looking Ken straight in the eye and smiling blandly. 'Actually I don't think I even want to see her at the moment. I'm finding all this separation business a bit disturbing.'

'Oh. Well, good,' Ken says. 'So how much were these new toys?'

'They're not toys. They're tools for making your dinner. And the big one was twenty, and—'

'Twenty quid? For a saucepan?'

'There's no point buying rubbish,' Alice says. 'That cheap one you got hasn't even lasted three months. And the small one was fifteen.'

'So you've spent thirty-five quid on saucepans?' Ken asks. 'You'll be the ruin of me, woman.'

Alice laughs. 'We can afford a couple of decent frying pans, and you know it.'

'You're not safe to shop alone,' Ken says. 'You always just buy the most expensive of everything. That's how you choose. You just look at the prices and choose the most expensive one.'

'You can come next time,' Alice says. 'You'll love that.'

'OK,' Ken says. 'I will.'

Alice laughs again. 'You like shopping like a ferret likes fennel.'

'Why wouldn't a ferret like fennel?' Ken asks. 'Jim Perry had ferrets and they ate just about anything you threw at them. I never actually saw them eat fen . . . Oh . . . You're just being daft again. You and your ferrets!'

Alice shrugs and turns her attention to removing the labels from the new frying pans. Fifty years together, and Ken still hasn't got the hang of her funny similes. How can anyone be so resistant to humour? Alice wonders. Fifty years she's been saying that things are as slow as a sausage, as quick as a quibble or as finicky as a

60

finicky ferret, and still Ken doesn't get the joke. It had been Joe who'd started that one, by describing an obnoxious bus conductor as being as fat as a ferret.

'But ferrets aren't fat,' Alice had protested.

'OK,' Joe had retorted. 'As fat as a fat ferret then!'

Alice gently washes the remains of the labels from the pans. Yes, they're just frying pans, but they're really rather lovely. Heavy, and stainless steel, and smooth shiny Teflon. If you whacked someone around the head with one of these, they'd be a goner. And yes, they were expensive, but like Dot says, what the hell?

'So are you going to make me an omelette in that new pan of yours?' Ken asks.

'I've just seen you finish a sandwich.'

'It was just a sandwich, love,' Ken whines. 'A man can't survive on a couple of slices of bread.'

Alice nods slowly. 'Maybe,' she says, 'if we have eggs. And if you're nice to me.'

'But I'm always nice to you!' Ken says. He might be joking. And then again, he might not. He might just believe it.

That night, Alice is awoken just after two. At first she's not sure what woke her, but then the noise comes again: two cats fighting in the back garden.

She closes her eyes and waits, but sleep does not return. Her knees and ankles ache for some reason. She wriggles in the bed, struggling to get comfortable. She rolls to the right and looks at the strip of moonlight shining through a gap in the curtains. It must be a full moon. That's why she can't sleep. That will be why the cats are fighting as well. A doctor once told her that the psychiatric wards all fill up on full-moon nights, that the hospitals even lay on extra staff. It's an actual fact, one of those commonly accepted facts of life that everybody knows to be true, but that no one can explain, that science will perhaps never explain.

She rolls to the other side and looks at Ken's shiny head. She sighs and then snorts gently in surprise at the fact that it's there again – that thought, that forbidden idea. She's thinking about leaving him again, actually playing the scene on the cinema screen in her head: Alice packing a suitcase; Alice walking away; Alice buying pans for her own little flat somewhere, perhaps in the same building as Dot; Ken sitting alone at the kitchen table, eating a sandwich, reading and re-reading her goodbye note. She wonders if he'd cry. She reckons he wouldn't.

It's all madness though. The full moon has turned her into a lunatic. And isn't the French word for 'moon' where the *lune* in 'lunatic' comes from, after all?

Where would she live? What would she live on? She doesn't even have her own bank account. And if it's taken Dot three years to sort it all out . . . well . . . she's almost seventy already.

She's not going to sleep now, she can tell. Those familiar insomnia sensations are with her – she's thirsty and hungry. She's achey and fidgety. She moves towards the edge of the bed, then gently eases herself into a sitting position. She doesn't want to wake Ken up and have to share the early hours with him complaining about his lack of sleep. She really doesn't want that. She listens to the ticking of the clock for a moment, then pulls her dressing gown on and sneaks from the room. To avoid the creaking floorboard on the landing, she edges along the wall like a cowboy in a shoot-out.

Downstairs, she makes herself a cup of tea and a slice of toast. She sits and stares out at the garden. It looks alien and unfamiliar in the moonlight, like some photograph by a modern artist, like perhaps a dream scene. It's almost like daytime out there, except that the colours are all wrong.

She's still thinking about packing a suitcase. It's more of a feeling than a thought, really – a compulsion almost. Ideas that come at night-time are always more forceful, more obsessive, more seemingly clear-cut than the complicated real-life world of daylight. She knows this from experience.

She needs some task to distract her until daybreak. She needs something to keep her busy until the gravity of reality yanks her back to earth. She scans the room. Perhaps she'll clean the oven. Ken will call her mad if he catches her. He'll call her a lunatic, in fact. But she's been meaning to do it for ages and that cake had a distinct smell of roast chicken about it. She crosses the room and pulls the oven cleaner and the rubber gloves from beneath the sink.

Yes, she'll clean the oven, and then maybe she'll defrost the fridge. And then perhaps, just perhaps, she'll pack a suitcase. She laughs at the absurdity of the idea. As she pulls on her rubber gloves she imagines Dot sleeping in her own bed in her own little flat and feels a fresh pang of jealousy.

◆ ◆ ◆

'I said I wasn't going to come here any more,' Dot says, looking up at the Starbucks sign.

Alice, who already has one hand on the door, says, 'Oh, don't be silly. It's just for a quick coffee.' She pushes into the cafe and Dot reluctantly follows.

Once they have joined the queue, Alice asks, 'Why, anyway? What's wrong with here?'

'I saw a thing on the telly,' Dot says. 'They don't pay their taxes, apparently.'

'I don't think any of them pay their taxes,' Alice says.

'No one rich seems to, that's for sure,' Dot agrees, eyeing up the cakes behind the counter. 'Though they said the other one – Costa, I think – they do.'

63

'Well, we'll go to Costa next time,' Alice says, 'but today I'm in a hurry. Tim's coming round, so I need to get home with the shopping and cook lunch.'

'Is he bringing the little ones?'

'No, just Tim today. He's got a meeting nearby. A work thing.'

'Still, that'll be nice.'

'Yes.'

'Can I help you, ladies?' the barista asks.

Once they have their drinks and are seated, Alice says, 'He forbade me to see you any more. Did I tell you that?'

'Tim?' Dot asks. 'Oh, Ken, you mean.'

'Yes, Ken.'

'He forbade you?'

'I know!' Alice laughs. She sips her cappuccino, then wipes the froth from her top lip. 'Men, huh?'

'What did you say?'

'Oh, you know what it's like with Ken. I stood up to him at first, and then decided it was easier just to lie. You can never win an argument with Ken. I agreed I wouldn't, but here I am.'

'I don't know how you put up with him,' Dot says.

'You put up with Martin for long enough. That should give you some idea.'

'Yes, I suppose I did.'

'It's just habit, I think.'

'Go on, have half of this,' Dot says, prodding her slice of brownie with the knife. 'It's delicious.' For someone who's in the middle of a boycott, she's unexpectedly enthusiastic about Starbuck's brownies.

'No, not half. Just . . . a little . . . Yes, like that,' Alice says.

'Did you never even nearly do it?' Dot asks, slicing the cake. 'Leave Ken, I mean.'

'Oh, of course I did. Lots of times.'

64

'When he used to hit you?'

'Oh, he never really hit me,' Alice says. 'We just, you know, used to scuffle.'

'Scuffle . . .' Dot repeats doubtfully, through a mouthful of cake.

'Yes.'

'If you say so.'

'If I'd ever had, you know, a proper plan . . . an escape plan, like you did . . . I might have done it, I suppose. There were certainly times . . . But we can't all be as organised as you.'

'Maybe you need to make an escape plan.'

'Oh, I'm not going to leave Ken now,' Alice laughs. 'I'm too old to go wandering off into the sunset.'

But as she says it, she realises that it's true, but also untrue. She realises that whatever part of her brain is speaking is having to choose from a swirl of different, conflicting Alices. One of these knows that she'll never leave Ken. And the other Alice could walk out tomorrow, could almost be persuaded to simply not go home today. 'So you've got no regrets then?' she asks, trying to move the focus away from her own marriage and on to Dot's.

Dot laughs. 'You've got to be joking. Martin was worse than Ken.'

'Well, Ken's not that bad,' Alice says. And again, the Alice that says it believes it to be true. It's just that there's another Alice who knows she's talking complete nonsense, knows, in fact, that she's lying.

'I don't even have a bank account,' Alice says. She frowns as she says it, because she realises that she has briefly channelled the other Alice, has let a slither of that other version of the truth slip out.

Dot has picked up on it. She puts down her fork and reaches across the table for Alice's hand. 'If you need help organising things, you know I'm here for you,' she says earnestly.

Alice pulls a face. 'Organising what?'

65

'We can go and see my young man at the Nationwide. He was ever so nice with me. Tom, his name is. Ever so helpful. He looks a bit like that guy from the telly – Alan Carr. Talks a bit like him too.'

'No,' Alice says firmly. 'No, I don't think so.'

'Why not?'

'You just think everyone should be like you, that everyone should do whatever you've just done,' Alice says. 'You always did.'

'But even if you're not going to leave Ken,' Dot says, ignoring the barb, 'you should still have your own bank account. I bet you still have that five hundred pounds stuffed away under a mattress somewhere, don't you?'

Alice looks surprised. She doesn't remember telling Dot about the five hundred pounds.

'Think how much interest you would have earned if it had been in a building society all these years. It would have been worth thousands by now.'

'We've managed just fine as we are,' Alice says. 'And I have my own debit card and everything. I don't need a separate account.' Dot pulls a face, so Alice insists, 'I really don't.'

'Sometimes just feeling that you can do something takes the pressure out of needing to actually do it,' Dot says. 'Sometimes—'

'Look, I know what you're saying,' Alice interrupts. 'But I think you're projecting your life on to mine. You left Martin and that's great. But I'm not going to leave Ken. We all know that.'

'OK,' Dot says, raising her hands in surrender at Alice's suddenly strident tone of voice. 'OK. You know best.'

Alice glances at her watch. 'I really do need to get a move on though,' she says. 'I've only got two hours before Tim arrives. I wanted to make a quiche. He loves my quiche.'

'Yes,' Dot says. 'Plus you don't want your husband realising you've been visiting forbidden friends, do you?'

'It's not that,' Alice says. 'You know it's not that.'

66

3

MAY

Alice hands over the wad of cash. The notes are secured by two faded elastic bands. They once, Alice remembers, held two bunches of asparagus together. She had used the tips to make risotto and the stalks had gone into soup. And how can she possibly remember that now?

As Tom starts to count the banknotes, Alice feels a little sad at the loss. Though Dot's logic is unarguably correct (at least this way her cash will keep up with inflation), she's already missing the concrete reassurance of their existence. Though she hadn't known this until now, she has liked knowing that the cash was there, waiting, should she need it.

But Dot is right. It's safer this way. And Tom, who is indeed a great deal like Alan Carr, has been very pleasant about it all.

'And the cash card definitely won't be sent to her house?' Dot is asking.

'No, as I said,' Tom replies, 'we'll call your mobile once it's ready and you can come here and collect it.'

Outside in the street, Dot claps her hands together. 'There!' she says triumphantly. 'Done!' It has taken her the best part of a month to convince Alice to open her own account. 'And don't look so forlorn. The money's still there. It's just in a safer place.'

'I know,' Alice says. 'It just feels funny, sneaking around like this.'

'It's no more sneaky than keeping it hidden in a tin for twenty years.'

'Forty,' Alice says. 'More than forty years.'

'Coffee?' Dot asks. 'There's a Costa up there, and it's my turn.'

'No, thanks. I really need to get home. I'll drop you off on the way.'

'Oh, go on. I'll treat you.'

'No, really. I have to get home. Plus it looks like it's going to tip it down at any moment.'

In truth, there isn't any particular reason why Alice can't stay out a little longer. But despite what Dot says, the opening of the bank account does feel sneaky, and a little monumental, too. Alice wants to go home to the quiet of the house so she can sit and think about it all.

The rain starts almost as soon as they reach the car, first spitting on the windscreen as Alice pulls away, then lashing at the streets until all the cars have to slow down. It's only a short-lived spring shower, but they would have been drenched had they been caught in it.

'You see?' Alice says, vindicated. 'Rain!'

'Yes,' Dot agrees. 'You should work for the BBC. Do the weather, like.'

Back at the house, Alice makes lunch for Ken – she's not hungry herself.

Once Ken has headed off for his afternoon kip and the kitchen is clean – when the only sound in the house is the rhythmic chug

68

of the dishwasher – she pulls the old flour tin from the cupboard. She sits and stares at it on the kitchen table, then prises open the lid and peers inside as if to prove to herself that she really has done this, that it wasn't a dream.

It's pure stupidity to have kept the money in cash for so long.

The money had been a Premium Bond win, and the true significance of the event was that it was the first time she had ever kept anything from Ken.

Her 'aunt' Beryl (who was no aunt, but her mother's best friend, in fact) had bought her the tickets. She had given five to Alice and five to Robert. And when Robert died, she had somehow transferred Robert's numbers to Alice's name as well.

Alice has never been sure whose actual tickets won the prize. She purposely never checked the numbers. Knowing that the prize had been destined for her deceased brother would have been too hard to bear, and it would have taken all of the pleasure out of the win.

She had taken Tim, still less than a year old, to visit her mother. She was still, after two years, grieving her husband's death, and the only thing that seemed to cheer her up back then was to see little Timothy.

Her mother had handed her the letter and once she had ripped it open, they had struggled to believe their eyes. They had gone to the post office to claim the cash together. 'Safety in numbers,' her mother had said.

Five hundred pounds – well, five hundred and sixty, to be precise. She had given fifty to her mother (she wouldn't take a penny more) and had stopped on the way home to buy a bonnet for Tim. It had been January and a cold January at that, and Tim's bonnet had been insufficient to the task at hand.

She had been so excited at the prospect of telling Ken the news; had suffered no qualms at the idea of handing over the money.

They had just bought their first house, and though they have never really struggled – Ken always earned a good living – money had been tighter than usual. Four thousand six hundred pounds the house had cost, she remembers. She wonders now if that's really possible. Perhaps she's got that wrong. But five hundred pounds was a lot of money, of that she's sure. It had been more than most people earned in a couple of months.

When she got home, she had found Ken drunk and angry. It happened a lot in those days. He had been too angry for her to want to tell him about the money, and too drunk to take any pleasure from it anyway, so she had tucked the money in the food cupboard. She would tell him, she thought, in the morning.

But when Ken had got up the next day, he had been no longer drunk and angry but hungover and angry instead. And that was almost as bad. He had shouted at her about wasting money on the bonnet, too. Did she have any idea how much this house had cost? he had asked. Did she really think they were rich enough to waste money on silly, pretty baby clothes?

So she had moved the money to the flour tin. She would wait for a more propitious moment to break her good news. And with each day that passed, it got harder to tell him. And with each day that passed, her desire to tell him faded.

The tin had eventually rusted, so she had bought a new one to replace it. And she'd had to change the banknotes twice, once in the seventies – that must have been when decimalisation happened – and once because the banknotes simply changed for no apparent reason, in the nineties perhaps?

And yes, Dot was right. If the money had been invested, it would have doubled, tripled, even quadrupled by now. But in the sixties, it would have been no easy matter to open a bank account without your husband knowing. And by the eighties, when such things were conceivable, she had all but forgotten about the money

70

in the tin. The galloping inflation of the seventies had made it worth much, much less. And the truth was that they weren't hard up, not by any means. They didn't need her cash anyway.

Ken may have spent his life smelling of rubber, but his business had done well. He has almost one hundred and fifty thousand pounds in his savings account these days. She knows, because she has caught glimpses of bank statements from time to time over the years. She remembers checking the meaning of commas and points in large numbers the first time she had seen them. She had been unable to believe that they had tens of thousands of pounds, so frugal was their lifestyle.

Though she has never alluded to her knowledge of the extent of Ken's savings, she has dared, once or twice, to ask him why they have to be so thrifty. Ken's answer has always been 'for our retirement', but now they've retired, he still won't spend a penny. And even retired, he still seems to save more than he spends – those numbers on the bank statements are still creeping up.

Still, having grown up in fear of poverty, it's reassuring for Alice to know that the money's there. Something could happen, or one of the kids might suddenly need helping. And it certainly puts her sneaky five hundred pounds into perspective.

It's like the tins her mother kept in the cellar really. Once you've experienced real hunger, once you've truly been down on your uppers, having a safety net, no matter how insignificant, takes on unreasonable importance.

But they're getting old now. Alice wishes they could use some of the money to make life a little easier for themselves, to even, dare she say it, have a little fun. A cruise, for example, would be nice. She laughs at herself. A cruise! Ken would go crazy if she even suggested it.

71

She fingers the blue flour tin and remembers the yellow of the previous tin, and then thinks again of the reserves her mother kept in the cellar.

She had treated them like a talisman, rotating them religiously, so the oldest ones got consumed and replaced, so they were never out of date. She remembers her mother telling her something about people dying from rusty tins of tuna – the rotational thing was important.

Robert, God rest his soul, opened one of their mother's tins once, and they had shared the contents – tinned peaches, slippery and sugary and forbidden. He had done it not because they were hungry, nor even because he particularly liked tinned peaches (though Alice did). No, he had simply done it because he could, because it was exciting, because, with the feisty mother they had, it was risky, a brave thing for a boy to do.

They had filled the tin with stones afterwards and replaced it in the middle of the stack. And their mother had never noticed.

But they had lived in terror of her rotational system reaching that tin, or even worse, of something happening and her suddenly ploughing into the reserves. She was always complaining about how tight things were, and every time she mentioned money, Alice and Robert glanced at each other. They were both always thinking about the stone-filled tin.

Eventually Robert shoplifted a tin of the same Del Monte tinned peaches, but the label was shiny and new compared with the other tins – the colours overly vibrant. So they had steamed off the old label and taped it on to the new can. Robert had even rolled it around in the coal dust in a vain attempt at dulling the telltale shine of the tin.

Within hours, not even days, but hours, their mother had spotted it. 'Do you know anything about this?' she had asked, brandishing the tin, running a fingernail along the ridge of tape. Alice had

72

shaken her head. Let Robert carry the can for it, she had thought. It had been his idea, after all.

But that was the day that Robert ran out into the road. He had been buzzing around like a wasp in a box all morning because he'd been invited to a children's birthday party. He wasn't the most popular child around, so such invitations when they came sent him into a frenzy of excitement, and in his excitement he had failed to look both ways. To everyone's surprise, that was all it took to end a life.

Her parents were devastated. The house was silent and as dark as the cellar for months. It's an overused cliché perhaps, but it truly was as if the sun had gone out. The faked tin was never mentioned again.

To listen to her parents, it was as if Robert was no longer the 'stupid one' they had spent their time whacking around the head, but the best son any parent had ever had. He was her 'angel', her mother kept saying, over and over. Her 'poor little angel'.

Alice had cried, too. She had cried for days. And Robert's disappearance left a hole in her childhood, a hole in her life, in fact, that never got filled.

But she had felt something else, too, an emotion so shameful that she never mentioned it to anyone. She had felt relieved as well.

Because the truth was that Robert drove her father insane, and once he was gone, things were sadder, they were far less exciting. But they were also so much calmer.

She forces herself to return to the here and now of the kitchen. She looks at the flour tin again, no longer a hiding place or a secret or a symbol. Just a flour tin for the first time in years. She reminds herself that even though it doesn't feel like it, she still has the five hundred pounds.

As emergency funds go, it's not much these days. She supposes that she could, like Dot, siphon off a little extra if she wanted to.

She could even use Dot's cashback system. Ken rarely helps with the shopping. He almost certainly wouldn't notice. But she would feel as if she were stealing – she's never earned a penny, after all. Not since she married Ken, anyway.

'Consider it pay for all that childcare and housekeeping,' Dot said, ever the devil on her shoulder. 'Count the hours you used to put in and multiply it by the minimum wage. And if you do decide to leave him one day, just write yourself a big cheque on the joint account before you tell him. You earned it. Do the maths.'

Alice fingers the tin one last time and then stands and returns it to the food cupboard.

It would be stealing though, wouldn't it? And she's not really going to leave him anyway. She's still not sure why she keeps thinking about it. It's not like Ken's even being particularly difficult these days. It's because of Dot, no doubt. It's because of Dot and her flat and her sofa in the sunshine.

'Alice?' Ken's voice, coming from the lounge. 'ALICE?'

'Yes?' she calls back. 'I'm here.'

'Alice!' Ken shouts again.

She rolls her eyes. She knows he can hear her. She heads down the hallway towards him.

PART TWO: THE SON

4

OCTOBER

Natalya glances up at the clock on the mantelpiece then returns her attention to filing her nails. It's gone seven and Tim is not home, which means that despite their argument this morning he has decided to visit his parents after all.

From upstairs she can hear one of the children wailing. It sounds like Boris but from this distance it's hard to tell – it could equally be Alex.

She splays her fingers, tilts her hand from side to side as she appraises her work, and then swaps the nail file to the other hand. Let Vladlena deal with the children. It is, after all, what she's paid for.

She focuses briefly on the muted television screen. An image of Putin has caught her eye. They will be talking about the gas supplies to Ukraine again – it's one crisis after another these days.

She hears the front door open and, stuffing the nail file down the side of the sofa, rises and crosses the room. She finds Tim in the hallway hanging his coat on the coatrack. He's wearing his checked

Paul Smith suit and the gold tie she gave him for his birthday. She thinks he looks particularly handsome in a suit.

'Hello,' she says, crossing the tiled floor and pecking him on the lips. 'You're early.'

'They weren't in,' Tim says. 'Right bloody waste of time . . .'

'Oh, that's a shame.'

Tim cocks his ear towards the staircase and frowns. 'So what the hell's going on up there?'

'I know,' Natalya says. 'I was just go seeing.'

Tim restrains a smirk at her. *Just go seeing.* He loves Natalya's English language mistakes; he finds them endlessly cute.

Natalya strokes his arm. 'You relax,' she adds, starting to climb the stairs. Letting Vladlena deal with the screaming children is one thing. Letting Tim see that this is what she does when he's not here would be quite another.

Upstairs in the rumpus room she discovers Vladlena trying to tug a reluctant, red-faced Boris through the door of the bright red playhouse.

'*On ne budet spat*,' Vladlena says. He won't go to bed.

'Boris, come out!' Natalya orders, leaning through the window to tug ineffectually at Boris's other arm. 'Is bedtime!'

'No!' he says, then again in a scream that sounds like she's about to perform dentistry without an anaesthetic, 'NOOOO!!!'

Natalya lets go. 'You want I get Tim perhaps?' she asks Vladlena, matter-of-factly.

'No, I'll be fine,' Vladlena tells her, speaking in Russian.

Natalya nods, stands, then walks from the room, closing the door firmly behind her to seal off the noise.

'Is nothing,' she tells Tim when she reaches the lounge. He is pouring himself a whisky. 'So your parents weren't home?'

'No,' Tim says. 'Really annoying. I swear they're getting worse. It might even be the start of Alzheimer's.'

78

'And you phone them?' Natalya asks, pulling a glass from the bar and pouring herself a shot of Stoli.

'Yes, at lunchtime. Oh, you mean now? Of course. But you know what Mum's like with her mobile. She picks up about one time in ten.'

Natalya nods and shrugs her shoulders. 'Well, they are not so young now,' she says. She has to tread carefully where Tim's parents are concerned, has to walk a fine line between not contradicting Tim's assessment of them while not joining in his criticism either.

Personally, she's relieved that they weren't in. She doesn't like how his visits to his parents affect him. She doesn't like how irritable he is afterwards, nor how much he drinks when he gets home.

'Anyway, you were right not to come,' Tim says, putting his drink on the coffee table and collapsing into the comfort of the leather chesterfield. 'It's bad enough that I had to traipse all the way over there.'

And this is the other reason that Natalya is glad they weren't in: because it lets her off the hook. They had argued, this morning, about whether Natalya and the boys should visit the grandparents as well. Natalya simply hadn't felt up to it, hadn't been able to summon the necessary reserves of courage to cope with taking the two boys all the way to Birmingham just to listen to Alice's thinly veiled criticism of their parenting techniques, of the boys, of Natalya herself.

You would think that Alice and Ken would be happy that one of their offspring has finally given them grandchildren, but their dissatisfaction is endemic, is made of the same stuff, as far as Natalya can see, as their dissatisfaction with their own children, with each other. Nothing Tim and Natalya do is ever enough for Alice and Ken and it riles her. It perhaps riles her even more than it should do because she feels the same way. She too would like her children to be extraordinary. She too would love Tim and her to

79

be perfect doting parents of a united happy family. She would love to be the rich, beautiful, placid daughter-in-law she pictures in her mind's eye, rather than a desperate, grasping Russian, swamped by dark thoughts and random moods, by inabilities and insecurities. She would love Alex and Boris to be beyond fault, to be perfect models of politesse and creativity, demonstrations of their wonderful upbringing.

But despite her best efforts, her humble origins trap her, her lack of education belies her. She uses the wrong words and everyone laughs at her. Tim insists that they're laughing with her, but they're not. They're really not. And only too often the kids speak like her too, they make the same mistakes. Half of that comes from Vladlena, not from her, but Natalya still gets the blame. 'Is OK,' Boris will say, and Alice points it out every time. 'Is OK?! That's from you, Natalya,' she'll say.

And then Boris will steal from Alice's biscuit jar and smear chocolate all over her white sofa, and Alex will open her purse and start taking her money out, and when everyone asks her, 'Why, Natalya? Why does Boris steal food?', she's unable to give them the only answer that might make any sense: that Boris's mother grew up in an orphanage, that she had to steal potatoes and hide them under her mattress just so she could get through the night, just so the rumbling of her stomach and the pain of hunger wouldn't wake her.

Memories of the orphanage fill her mind now, the weak light drifting through the grubby windows, the echoey voices in hallways from stern people making decisions about their futures, the stench of the cheap disinfectant they used everywhere – it's as much as she can do not to wrinkle her nose.

And could that really be why Boris steals food? Could that really be why Alex, at seven, collects coins he finds around the house and puts them in a jar, why he once even buried the jar in the garden? Is it really possible that Natalya's own terror of poverty

80

has transmitted, via her genes, to her children? People say that kids pick up on things, but this surely goes beyond that?

She looks at Tim lighting a cigar and remembers the taste of cold potato, remembers the sound of other children snoring (or crying) around her as she ate it, remembers the fear of being caught.

'So how was your day?' Tim is asking, blowing smoke rings as he speaks, already turning up the sound on the television, already looking for American families that are brighter, funnier or more dangerous than his own.

'Fine,' Natalya says, her mind partly still in those horrible Mazanovsky corridors. 'Busy.'

'Good,' Tim says, tugging at his tie, loosening his collar.

'And yours?' Natalya asks.

'Other than traipsing all the way over to Mum's for nothing? Yeah, fine. Normal,' he says.

Upstairs, the screaming has stopped. 'I go kiss the children goodnight,' Natalya says, 'then I get dinner. Is Veal Orloff.'

'Sure, great,' Tim says, his attention shifting to *The Simpsons*. 'Tell 'em I'll be up in a bit as well.'

Twenty minutes later, once Vladlena has left and Natalya has read the children a story (it's good for improving her English) she returns to the lounge. Tim has fallen asleep in front of the television, the half-glass of whisky miraculously still held in one hand.

She looks at him sleeping for a moment and reminds herself that she has little idea what his days in banking involve. She only knows that they're stressful and tiring, and that they pay for all of this for all of them. She gently prises the glass from his fingers, momentarily waking him.

'Um? Uh!' Tim grunts.

'It's OK,' Natalya says. 'Sleep a little. I wake you when dinner is.'

81

She is just pulling the tray of Orloff from the oven when Tim appears in the doorway. 'Perfect timing,' he says.

'Yes.'

'Smells good too.'

'Thank you,' Natalya replies. Vladlena actually made the dish this time, but there's no point telling Tim that.

'Did they go off OK?' Tim asks, crossing to the huge refrigerator and pulling a half-consumed bottle of wine from the door.

Natalya looks confused, so he rephrases. 'The kids. Did they go to sleep all right?'

'Oh yes,' Natalya replies. 'I read them a story from new book. The Russian one. Is funny reading these stories in English, you know?'

'Baba Yaga again?' Tim asks.

'No, this time they choose Ivan the Fool.'

'You wanted to call Boris Ivan,' Tim reminds her.

'Yes, you are right. Not such a good name after all.'

Tim hangs his jacket over the back of the chair. Natalya always overheats the house, but the oven has left the kitchen feeling quite tropical. He pulls the cork from the bottle of wine with his teeth and sloshes servings into both his and Natalya's glasses.

'So where do you think they go?' Natalya asks. 'Alice and Ken.'

Tim shrugs. 'I'll call them after dinner. I thought we could invite them over on Sunday. They haven't been for ages. What do you think?'

Natalya licks her lips, then forks a large chunk of still-too-hot Veal Orloff into her mouth as an alibi for not replying.

'They're my parents, Nat,' Tim says. 'I have to see them sometimes. And the boys need to spend time with their grandparents. Family's important.'

Natalya pulls a face, all innocence, and shrugs and points at her full mouth. She thinks about these feelings she has about Tim's

82

parents. She disguises her wince as being caused by the hot food in her mouth rather than by the pain of her jealousy.

Because, yes, she's jealous. She wishes she had parents she could visit, grandparents she had known. She wishes she even knew what that meant – to have a family you want to see, even though they drive you mad. Because they do drive Tim – quite literally – mad.

After a proper visit from Tim's parents (the real thing, not a half-hour pop-in), Tim is irritable and he drinks too much, but beyond this, something more profound happens to him. Something goes wrong with his brain; something happens to his logic circuits. All his decisions for twenty-four hours afterwards – sometimes for days – are skewed, and only Natalya can see that he's not making any sense. So he'll decide to drive all the way into Birmingham for a new watch battery even though he works next to a watch shop every day of the week. Or he'll attempt to fix something they both know he can't fix, and only make it worse. He'll decide to cook the one thing they don't have the ingredients for, or he'll throw away something they need to make space for something they don't, or he'll lose his keys, or his phone, or his wallet. And without fail, he'll complain to her about Alice and Ken afterwards. Interminably.

He'll moan about their negativity, about their lack of recognition for his achievements, for Natalya's cooking, for the children's progress. But she's not allowed to join in; she can't even hint that she agrees, otherwise he jumps to their defence with the vigour of a lioness defending her cubs. He'll turn on her in an instant, and suddenly the problem's not his parents but Natalya herself.

So she's supposed to listen to these endless complaints – many of which are justified – yet somehow remain neutral about seeing them the next time, and the time after that.

In fact, she's not even supposed to remain neutral; she's meant, somehow, to remain positively enthusiastic about entertaining them. She has to be keen, because, yes, they're his family. Whatever that means.

'I say nothing,' she protests, once she has finally managed to swallow. 'Yes, of course we can have them. I can make rassolnik again. Alice liked my rassolnik.'

'Great,' Tim says. 'I'll call them after dinner.'

Natalya sips at her glass of wine and imagines them all sitting around the table eating. She wishes they had a separate dining room, but it's been knocked through by the previous owners to make for a bigger lounge. If they had a separate dining room, she could cook and serve up without Alice questioning everything she does, without her saying doubtfully, 'Oh, so that's how you do that, is it, Natalya? Okaaay . . .' She could escape just long enough to breathe.

She thinks about the big house in Broseley. She shouldn't mention it now; it's not the right time. She should wait until the weekend. She should wait until Tim is relaxed and amenable, but she's never been that good at self-control.

'So what was all the fuss about?' Tim asks, saving her from herself. 'It sounded like Vlad was torturing them up there.'

Natalya nods with fake sadness. 'Yes, she try the waterboard thing.'

'What waterboard thing?'

'You know, like in Guantanamo. She say if it's good enough for the Yankees . . .' Natalya smiles wryly.

'Oh, waterboarding, yeah,' Tim laughs. 'We could get them little orange jumpsuits too. And leg irons.'

'Yes,' Natalya says flatly. 'I already order them from the Internet.'

After dinner, Natalya stacks the dishwasher before returning to the lounge.

84

Tim has changed into jogging trousers and a sweatshirt. He's thumbing through a copy of *What Hi-Fi?*.

Natalya joins him on the sofa and snuggles against him. She glances over his shoulder at the magazine. The centre photo shows a man standing next to a loudspeaker the size of their refrigerator. His scarf looks like it's being blown sideways by the sound from the speaker.

'It's so big,' Natalya says.

'Yeah.'

'This is for concerts, yes? Or rave party?'

Tim laughs. 'No, these are home speakers. About the best you can get.'

Natalya glances over at their existing hi-fi. 'I think ours are big enough, yes?'

'Maybe,' Tim says vaguely.

'You don't think to buy these?'

Tim shrugs. 'I'd love to hear how they sound.'

Natalya leans in more closely and studies the picture, then attempts to imagine these monstrosities in their lounge. 'This is crazy,' she says. 'They look just silly.'

'Yes, but it's not about how they look, is it?' Tim says. 'It's how they sound.'

Natalya snorts quietly. But she restrains herself from pointing out that Tim rarely even listens to their existing hi-fi these days. He's always at work or asleep in front of the television. And when he's not, he's fiddling with his phone or surfing on the iPad.

But no, Natalya does not say any of this. Instead, she does a deal with herself, mentally exchanging not saying this for saying the other thing, the thing she promised herself she would not say. Because she has just realised that she can link the one to the other.

'Well, those are too big for this room anyway,' she says. And this is a fact that even Tim would struggle to argue with. 'We

85

cannot even move if we have these speakers. Oh! Talk of big house. You know which house they are going to sell now? The big white one on the hill in Broseley. I saw the . . . how you call that?' She makes a shape with her fingers.

'For Sale sign?'

'Yes, that one.'

'The architect's house?' Tim asks, glancing sideways at her, his interest awakening. 'The one with the big windows?'

'Yes,' Natalya says. 'Now this is house for big speakers.'

Tim raises an eyebrow and she sees that he has picked up on her strategy, has spotted the bridge she has been trying to build. She shouldn't have mentioned it twice.

Tim flicks through a couple more pages of the magazine before saying, 'I wonder how much they want for that. A fortune, I bet.'

'Yes,' Natalya says. 'I expect so. Too much for people like us, anyway.'

'It's too big as well,' Tim says. 'We'd get lost in it. We'd never find the kids.'

'Hmm,' says Natalya, 'maybe not a bad idea.'

Tim puts down his magazine, so Natalya reaches for the remote control and turns the TV sound low. She begins to flick through the channels, but it's just a distraction, just something to do while she waits for the idea of the house to percolate through Tim's mind. Because after nine years together, she knows the way his mind works. It's the same as this hi-fi obsession, which she knows, despite what Tim may say, has nothing whatsoever to do with sound. Houses and speakers are just things to aspire to, they're just things to grasp for. Grasping and aspiring are the fuel that Tim runs on, they're why he gets up in the morning. Natalya understands this, because she too works the same way. She too has an infinite list of things they need next.

Tim sits and stares blankly at the television.

86

'This guy is funny, yes?' Natalya says, nodding in the direction of Harry Hill onscreen.

'Yeah,' Tim says, then, 'Did you notice which estate agent it was?'

'Um?' Natalya asks, feigning being distracted by Harry Hill's bloopers.

'The house in Broseley. Which estate agent was on the placard?'

'Oh, I'm not sure,' Natalya says, furrowing her brow, even though she knows exactly the name of the estate agent, even though she has a photo of the placard in her iPhone. 'Right-something maybe?'

'Rightchoice?' Tim asks, reaching down the side of the sofa for the iPad.

'Yes,' Natalya says. 'Yes, I think so. Maybe.'

Still half asleep, Natalya rolls to the right, expecting to find the warmth of Tim's body beside her. But the space is empty, the mattress barely warm. She can hear him moving around downstairs.

She peers at the blurry numerals of the alarm clock. It's barely six-thirty. She rolls on to her back and drifts back to sleep.

When she next wakes up, she can hear him in the bathroom. She realises she's been dreaming of a rainstorm falling into a swimming pool – no doubt caused by the sound of the shower next door.

After another ten minutes, Tim appears, naked. She watches him from behind, checks out the cuteness of his arse, his muscular thighs. Considering all the business dinners he goes to, he remains surprisingly trim. He crosses to the chest of drawers and quietly retrieves underwear, socks and a T-shirt.

'You're early,' she says.

'Oh, I woke you.'

87

'No,' Natalya says. 'I just wake myself.'

'I'm in London today,' Tim explains, glancing back at her as he sits on the bed and pulls on his socks.

He crosses to the wardrobe and takes out his suit trousers, then a shirt – pale blue with white cuffs and collar.

'You're late tonight?' Natalya asks.

'Yeah. I'll probably end up eating with the HSBC boys,' Tim says. 'I'll text you during the day, OK?'

Natalya watches him button his shirt, then fix his tie. He crosses to her side and holds out one wrist and proffers cufflinks with the other. Once she has attached the ends of his flapping cuffs with them, he attempts to kiss her, but she turns her head sideways. Her mouth is gunky with sleep, and she's worried about having bad breath. She doesn't want his wife's bad breath to be the one memory he takes with him.

Tim pecks her on the cheek instead, then saying briskly, 'OK, gotta go, have a good one,' he leaves the bedroom.

Natalya lies, listening to the sound of his shoes on the stairs, then the click of the front door and finally the crunching gravel as his car pulls away. A metallic bang from the kitchen tells her that Vladlena has arrived. She can relax – there's no hurry for her to get up.

She tries to remember the dream, but it has drifted beyond reach. Only the sensation of warm, wet concrete beneath her feet remains. Perhaps she was dreaming of a pool. Perhaps she was dreaming of the long, thin lap pool beside the house in Broseley. Maybe the dream was a premonition.

She allows herself the pleasure of luxuriating in that thought. She imagines herself on a sunlounger with Vladlena bringing her drinks. Only Vladlena would never bring her a drink. She would tell her to go and make it herself. Such are the disadvantages of hiring Russian help. All those years of Soviet propaganda about

88

equality have left their mark. So maybe if they do move to the house, they should hire someone new.

Natalya has always been in two minds about having Vladlena around. On the one hand, their private language – Russian – makes her specifically Natalya's maid rather than Tim's. And she enjoys the not inconsiderable sense of power and status that this brings. Everything else in their lives is so very clearly Tim's, after all.

On the other hand, the fact that Vladlena can tell – must be able to tell – that Natalya is from the same humble origins as herself always feels like a risk. Any time Natalya criticises her about the state of the windows or the laundry lingering in the washing machine, she imagines Vladlena sneaking off to tell Tim the truth. 'Your wife is a tramp,' she might say.

Then again, the fact of their shared origin also makes Natalya feel better. It's as if Vladlena is a fixed point in space and time from which Natalya can measure her own progress. They may have started in the same place . . . Vladlena may even be fifteen years her senior . . . But it's Natalya handing over the cash now. It's Natalya giving the orders.

She thinks again of the pool. Maybe if Tim's business goes well enough, they can keep Vladlena and get someone new in, too. A butler maybe.

She smiles at the thought, imagining Boris's friends telling their parents that the Hodgetts have a butler, that the Hodgetts have a pool. Then she would feel like she had arrived. Then she would feel like she had truly escaped and the nightmares would end and she would have dreams of plenty instead – dreams of tables laden with exotic foods instead of that recurring horror of trading favours for chocolate. She can remember the taste of that cheap chocolate even now. She can remember the other taste, too.

She sighs and forces the memory from her mind. Instead, she imagines the butler, dressed in a dinner jacket, bringing her a vodka and tonic on a tray. She closes her eyes and makes him dark, muscular and bearded. She slides one hand between her legs, then opens one eye and checks the door. Yes, he would have white gloves as well. She closes both eyes and imagines him sliding a smooth, gloved hand up the inside of her thigh.

It's the following evening before the house gets mentioned again. Natalya loads then switches on the dishwasher. She dumps the big frying pan in the sink – Vladlena can deal with that tomorrow. Because today has been Vladlena's day off, Natalya is exhausted.

As she crosses the hallway, she hears the boys still talking upstairs. It's almost ten, but they've been running riot all day and she's too tired to care – she leaves them to it. They're just talking, after all.

In the lounge, Tim is surfing the Internet. She slides in beside him and he moves his knees so that he can rest the iPad on them and continue to look at the screen while sliding his free arm around her shoulders.

'Ah,' she says, glancing at the screen. 'You find it.'

'Yes,' Tim says. 'Two point eight mill. Bloody nice though.'

'Show,' Natalya says, and Tim starts to swipe his way through the photos.

'Big pool,' Natalya comments.

'Yes, and look at the . . . Hang on . . . There! Look at that window,' Tim says.

'Wow.'

'Yes, wow,' Tim agrees. 'Very James Bond.'

Onscreen in the photo, beyond a vast three-by-five-metre picture window, an empty sunbed has been placed next to the turquoise pool. Beside it, on a small table, is a bottle of wine and a bowl of fruit.

90

Natalya imagines herself on the sunbed reaching for the glass of wine. She pictures Tim inside, looking out at her.

Unbeknown to Natalya, Tim is imagining exactly the same scene: himself, inside the house, looking out at Natalya on the sunlounger. The only difference in his version is that music is blaring from his new speakers and Natalya is not drinking, but eating grapes.

The photo reminds him of a Renault advert from a few years back. What had the tag line been? Something about space. 'What if space was the real luxury?' perhaps. And suddenly, in his mind's eye, he's the guy in the advert, he's the impeccably dressed man – not suited, just an Egyptian cotton shirt and jeans – reclining on that absurdly long sofa, looking out at his beautiful wife lounging by the pool.

He glances down at Natalya now, and seeing the tops of her breasts peeping through her low-cut T-shirt, he changes the image in his mind's eye so that she's topless on that sunlounger. Topless and rubbing in suntan lotion.

Natalya is tiny and skinny – has even managed, after many hours at the gym, to lose her baby fat since the kids' births. She still looks, even at thirty-five, like a top model, albeit a miniature one. She'd look even more like a top model next to that pool.

He'd be inside, looking out, music playing, something modern, something angular, Apparat perhaps, or if he was feeling good, if things were going well, maybe something bouncy, something fun, something like Metronomy.

Alice would say it's crazy to have so much space. She'd say the speakers are too loud, too big as well. He can hear her exact words in his head now, like a guaranteed prediction of the future. But she'll be proud all the same, he knows she will. She'll tell her neighbours, her friends, his brother, what an amazing house Tim and Natalya have. She'll tell them all how well he's done. She just won't let Tim ever have the pleasure of hearing her praise, but he'll know how proud she is all the same, because how could she not be proud? It's a fucking palace.

Natalya, without realising it, sighs.

'What's up?' Tim asks.

'It's maybe not so good to look at houses we can't afford,' she says. 'This one we have is good house. This is very good house.'

She alternates hourly between trying to manipulate Tim into wanting the new house as much as she does, and wanting instead for him to be happy, to stop striving, to be contented with what they have. And right now in this instant, she realises that the vast, crazy, three-million-pound house is out of reach, and just for a moment she's able to access a bigger truth – the truth that it really doesn't matter. They have already come so far; they have already come far enough. And what really matters is this – being alive, being (still) in love, being in good health, being happy, having the two boys upstairs and a refrigerator full of food and a reassuring arm around your shoulders.

'Anyway,' Tim says, 'who says we can't afford it?'

Natalya frowns and looks up at him. 'Really, Timski?' she asks, genuinely surprised.

Tim shrugs. 'If the Greek deal all goes to plan, then maybe,' he says. 'I'm not guaranteeing anything, but, yeah . . . we might just manage it.'

5

NOVEMBER

It's Guy Fawkes Night, and a gentle drizzle is falling as they park the car in the stadium car park.

Despite Tim's best efforts to keep everyone happy, precisely nobody is happy this evening – it happens that way sometimes. Tim is praying that the rain stopping (as predicted by the icons on his phone) combined with a spectacular firework display will have the power to turn things around, leaving him a family hero after all.

Boris, who has spent half the day in a temper tantrum (Natalya tried to warn him that the fireworks might be cancelled due to rain – a psychological miscalculation of massive proportions), seems no happier now they're actually here. He's hungry, he says. He's cold.

Alex, holding Natalya's hand, is watching him closely. Alex looks to Boris for guidance; he watches his older brother constantly in order to know how to react to events. If Boris doesn't cheer up soon then Alex will start to cry, and if that happens then Tim might just cry himself.

As for Natalya, she has the hump with Tim on multiple counts. Firstly, she's furious that he agreed to visit his parents after the fireworks. It's too late, she says, for the boys. Of course, it's only too late because it's Tim's parents they're visiting. She never has any objections to their staying up for anything else. But beyond her fury at having to spend an hour with his parents (and how could he come here – less than two miles from their house – without visiting them?) she has a more deeply held grudge that has been undermining their relationship for days. In short, she thinks that the offer he has put on the house in Broseley is too low. She's convinced that they're going to lose it, just as Tim is convinced that they won't.

She's been bitching about it for three days now, mainly in a low-level way, but with spikes of actual Russian feistiness. And all of this from a woman who only a week ago was insisting that they didn't need to move at all, that their current house was perfectly fine.

Tim gave up trying to understand his wife's logic circuits many years ago, and knows with certainty that there's absolutely no point in trying to decode her moods at this particular time of the month. You have to grin and bear it. You have to just wait for the weather to improve.

'Look at queue,' Natalya is saying. 'We will be soak before we get in.' To Alex, who is dragging on her arm, she mutters, 'Walk properly.'

'That's the queue for tickets, Nat,' Tim says. 'We've already got ours. We go in the other door.' He nods at the shorter queue for the turnstile. 'But first, we're going to the funfair round the other side, aren't we, boys?'

'Hmm,' Natalya says. 'Funfair in rain. So nice!'

'I'm cold,' Boris says. 'I want to go home.'

'This is not cold,' Natalya tells him. 'This is like five degrees or something. Cold is minus twenty, like where I grow up.'

'I don't care,' Boris says. 'I'm cold.'

94

'It doesn't mean anything to him,' Tim points out, trying to defuse Natalya's anger before it gets started. 'He's never experienced minus twenty.'

'If he doesn't stop to complain, maybe I send him to Russia,' Natalya says. 'Maybe he needs to find out what cold means.'

Tim wipes a drip from his nose, pulls his hood further down and tugs Boris to the right. The funfair should come into sight soon. Perhaps then everyone will stop complaining. 'We'll get you a nice warm drink in a bit,' Tim tells the boy. 'Hot chocolate maybe. How does that sound?'

'I don't want hot chocolate,' Boris says. 'I don't like hot chocolate.'

'This is such lies!' Natalya says. 'I remember this the next time you ask me to make you chocolate!'

'And you really don't want to go home, Boris,' Tim says. 'You love fireworks. Do you remember last year, how excited you got?'

Boris doesn't answer, he simply trips along miserably, doing his best to scuff his new shoes.

Family life! Tim thinks. *Maybe I could send them all to bloody Russia.*

'Timmy?' Natalya whines. It's her special miserable voice, both nasal and plaintive. 'What time do these firework start anyway?'

'Eight.'

'But is only seven.'

'I know, darling,' Tim says, barely keeping his voice under control. 'That's why we're going to the bloody funfair first.'

When they reach the house, it's Alice who opens the front door. 'Hello boys! Come in! You must be freezing!' she says, ruffling their hair as they squeeze past her legs. 'Hello, Natalya . . . Tim.'

95

The boys run straight to the lounge. They have an unexpected and, as far as Tim's concerned, inexplicable preference for Grandpa.

'Gosh, we thought you weren't coming,' Alice says. 'It's so late!'

'I know,' Tim says. 'Getting out of the car park was a nightmare.'

'Yes, very late,' Natalya confirms, 'so we won't be stay too long. It's past bedtime for the boys.'

'Huh! Hardly here and she's leaving already!' mocks Alice. It's her way of powering through Natalya's quasi-constant state of reluctance. She turns and heads through to the kitchen. 'I'll put the kettle on,' she shouts back. 'I made sandwiches too.'

'We've eaten, Mum,' Tim says, hanging his parka on the coat-rack, then taking Natalya's and hanging that up too. She catches his eye, prompting him to ask, 'What?'

'Nothing!' she says.

'We had fish and chips, and the kids had hot dogs,' Tim says as he starts to follow Alice to the kitchen.

'Hot dogs?' Alice says. 'You don't know what rubbish they put in those. You can't bring children up on hot dogs.'

'We don't bring them up on hot dogs,' Tim says, changing his mind and lingering at the doorway to the lounge. 'It was just one night.'

'Well,' Alice says. 'I've made some nice cheese sandwiches with Branston. They like Branston.'

'They won't eat them, Mum,' Tim calls back as he enters the lounge. 'They're stuffed full of hot dogs and candy floss and chocolate.'

In the lounge, he finds the boys sitting together on Ken's lap. It's an image of family unity, which strikes him as a little out of place, slightly absurd. The boys are eating fun-size Milky Ways from Ken's secret chocolate tin. The secret chocolate tin is probably, on reflection, the reason they like him so much.

'So how was it?' Ken asks. 'The boys seem to have had a good time.'

'Dad kept making silly noises,' Alex says.

'Yes, he went "oooh" and "ahh" every time a firework went bang,' Boris explains.

'That's something he got from me,' Ken says. 'I always got them to make silly noises when they were little. Timmy always loved shouting out the "oohs" and the "ahhs", didn't you?'

Tim clears his throat and licks his lips, then, muttering, 'I'll, um, help Mum with the drinks,' he heads back through to the kitchen. Ken's fathering stories always make him feel uniquely uncomfortable. It's as if he'd rather just pretend that none of it ever happened. He doesn't know quite why he's so allergic to these memories, particularly the positive ones – perhaps it's because it always feels like Ken's using them to erase all the rest.

'Did you enjoy it, Nat?' Ken asks Natalya as he leaves the room.

In the kitchen, Alice is putting mugs of tea and plastic beakers of hot chocolate on a tray. 'Can you take that plate of sandwiches through, love?' she asks.

'I told you, Mum, we ate already. None of us is going to eat anything.'

'If they've only had hot dogs, then I'm sure they'll eat something,' Alice says.

'They won't. And if those drinks are for the boys, they don't like hot chocolate any more either.'

'Since when?'

'It's brand new. Just came out tonight.'

'What rubbish!' Alice says. 'It's freezing out there. This'll warm them up.'

'It was cold,' Tim admits, 'but at least the rain stopped.'

'You wouldn't get me standing out in the rain to watch a load of money go up in smoke.'

97

'Why not? You used to take us to the fireworks every year. And often enough it rained.'

'Yes, well . . .' Alice says, adding the sugar bowl and three teaspoons to the tray. 'I suppose it's just one of those things you have to do when you have kids.'

'Exactly! Oh, Mum, Nat will want coffee. Can you do her a coffee instead? Or d'you want me to do it?'

Alice shakes her head and puts the tray back down. 'Now he tells me!' she says.

'So how have you been, Mum?' Tim asks as she pours the tea down the sink, rinses the cup, and reaches for the instant coffee.

'Oh, you know . . .'

'Not really. That's why I'm asking.'

'Your father's been very difficult.'

'Yeah, well . . .' Tim says. His father's difficult nature is not really a conversation he's prepared to have any more. His mother has been married to him for long enough, in his opinion, for that difficult nature to have become a given. His mother's shock, her supposed outrage at each new distasteful episode of his father's (mis)behaviour smacks somehow of dishonesty as far as Tim is concerned. It's like moving to Finland and then complaining about the cold.

'He's been complaining about the gas bill all week,' Alice says. 'He says I use the oven too much.'

'But the central heating is gas,' Tim says. 'That'll be what's putting the bills up, not the bloody oven.'

'Well, quite!' Alice says. 'But you just try telling him that. And it's your father who keeps nudging the thermostat up all the time.'

'Cook slowly, gas mark three, forty years,' Tim murmurs.

'I'm sorry?'

'Nothing. I was just being silly.'

'He says he's got Alzheimer's now,' Alice says. 'That's the latest thing.'

'Really? That's worrying.'

'Oh, it's only any time I ask him to do or buy anything,' Alice says. 'He never forgets his own stuff.'

'Who has Alzheimer?' Natalya asks. She has appeared in the doorway. Both she and Tim do absurd amounts of back-and-forthing when they visit Alice and Ken. Neither can ever quite decide which room, which parent, makes them the least uncomfortable.

'Dad says he has it,' Tim says. 'But Mum says it's selective.'

'Very selective,' Alice says, handing Natalya her drink. 'Here, I made you coffee.'

'Selective?' Natalya asks.

'He only forgets things he wants to forget,' Alice explains.

'Hmm, well,' Tim murmurs. 'At least he'll never run out of those.'

'Don't be like that, Timothy,' Alice says.

'Sandwiches?' Natalya questions, frowning. 'For who? Not for us, I hope.'

'I told her,' Tim says. 'But you know Mum.'

'If you don't want them you can take them home,' Alice says. 'You can have them for lunch tomorrow. I don't know what all the fuss is about.'

'And these are for the boys?' Natalya asks, pointing at the plastic mugs of hot chocolate.

'Yes.'

'Ha!' she laughs. 'So now we see how Boris don't like chocolate!'

'Doesn't,' Alice corrects. 'Doesn't like chocolate.'

'Sorry.' Natalya's expression darkens. She hates it when Alice corrects her.

'But your English is getting much better, dear,' Alice adds, trying to lessen the blow. 'You just need to take more care with your does and doesn't. And all that trouble you have with your prepositions.' She lifts the tray and heads down the hallway towards the lounge.

'I don't even know what is prepositions,' Natalya says quietly, once Alice has gone.

'Nor me,' Tim says, lifting the plate of sandwiches. 'I wouldn't worry about it.'

As if to prove their parents wrong, Boris and Alex dive into Alice's sandwiches. They look like they haven't been fed for days.

'You see!' Alice says triumphantly. 'The poor things are starving!'

'Boris ate almost two whole hot dogs,' Tim says, 'plus a load of other junk.'

'It's all the excitement,' Ken says, jiggling him up and down on one knee. 'Isn't it, Boris?'

'Hot dogs are lovely,' Boris tells him. 'With ketchup but not that horrible yellow stuff.'

'He tried mustard,' Tim says, '. . . wasn't keen.'

'Hot dogs are full of rubbish,' Alice says again. 'It's all the rubbish they sweep up off the floors of the abattoirs. All the bits they don't know what to do with. I saw it on television. They zap it all with some chemical to kill all the bugs. Jamie Oliver was going on about it.'

'Mum . . .' Tim protests.

Alice purses her lips, sighs, gently flaring her nostrils as she does so, then adds, in a controlled tone of voice, 'But kids do like that stuff. You two were the same.'

Tim observes her struggle between light and dark, her fight between Jekyll and Hyde. He watches the effort it takes for her to be positive and mentally thanks her for it. At least she makes some effort these days. At least around her grandchildren, she tries.

'So how much are they charging for tickets these days?' Ken asks, his obsession with the cost of everything ever-present.

100

'Fifteen quid a head,' Tim replies. 'Nine for the kids. Nine quid each, that is.'

'Fifteen pounds?' Ken says. 'That's madness. It used to be ten bob in my day.'

'Yeah, but the minimum wage wasn't six-seventy an hour then, was it?'

'No!' Ken says, as if this somehow proves his point. 'It wasn't! It was more like eight quid a week. It wouldn't even get you a couple of hot dogs now.'

'It's not that now though, is it?' Alice says. 'Surely it's not really six-seventy, is it?'

'Yes, Mum. The minimum wage is exactly six-seventy. And anyway, it was worth it, wasn't it, boys?'

Boris frowns at him.

'You enjoyed the fireworks and the funfair?'

Boris nods.

'So it was worth it. Sometimes you have to pay the price to make everyone happy, Dad,' Tim says, a disguised barb at his father's increasingly problematic relationship with money. *And why do old people get so tight?* Tim wonders. He actually opens his mouth to ask his father the question, but thinks better of it just in time.

Natalya, who has spotted an opportunity, speaks instead. 'Is like the house,' she says, avoiding looking at Tim, afraid of his glare.

Tim had specifically asked her during the drive not to mention the new house. He knows how his parents latch on to things and worry about them. There really wasn't any point provoking nights of insomnia for his mother until the deal was confirmed, he had said. And Natalya had agreed. But it's too late now. 'What house?' Alice is asking.

'It's not even a sure thing, so just . . .' Tim shakes his head.

'You're not thinking of moving again, surely?' Alice says. 'Poor Natalya has barely finished unpacking from the last time.'

101

'Oh, I don't mind!' Natalya tells her. 'Is beautiful house.'

'It's beautiful,' Alice says. '"It" plus "is" makes "it's", so "It's beautiful", not "is".'

'Sorry, yes, "it's",' Natalya says.

'So when is this happening?' Alice asks, leaning forward in her chair and already, Tim notices, starting to wring her hands.

'It might not be happening at all,' Tim says, still glaring at Natalya.

'Tim make a very low offer. He hopes they will cave.'

'I'd hardly call two . . . I'd hardly call that much money a low offer,' Tim says.

'This is what the estate agent say,' Natalya says. 'Not me. So . . .'

'Where is it?' Ken asks.

'Really!' Tim exhales, laughter in his voice. 'Can we all just wait and see if the bloody thing happens before we get our knickers in a twist?'

'I can't see why we're not allowed to discuss it, Tim,' Alice says. 'You're the only one getting his knickers in a twist. Unless it's a long way away . . . Is it a long way?'

'No, not far,' Natalya says, still keen to get the in-laws onside, even as she begins to doubt the wisdom of having mentioned it, even as she senses the capacity for the conversation to spin completely out of control. 'Just Broseley.'

'Broseley?' Alice says. 'But that's in Shropshire!'

'It's fifteen minutes more, Mum,' Tim says. 'Not even that. And, as I keep saying, not that anyone's listening, it's not even—'

'Yes, not even a sure thing. We heard, Timothy. We all heard you.'

'The thing, these days,' Ken says, 'is that you have to pay the asking price. I saw it on that programme. The one with the bald chap and the lassie – the bloke with the posh suits and the lisp.'

'It's not a lisp,' Alice says. 'He just can't pronounce his r's.'

'*Location, Location*,' Tim says.

'Yes, that's the one. It's because of the housing crisis, apparently. Whenever they put in a lower offer, the houses get snaffled by someone else these days. He's always telling them – what's his name?'

'Phil Spencer,' Alice says.

'That's the one. Well, he's always telling them to go in at the asking price, and they never listen.'

'Thanks to you, Ken,' Natalya says, bowing theatrically. 'My point exact.'

'Why are you moving anyway?' Alice asks. 'What's wrong with the current place?'

'Nothing's wrong with the current place.'

'Well, then, why change? Are you sure it's going to be worth all the angst?'

'What angst, Mother?' Tim asks, starting to feel exasperated. 'There is no angst.'

'Well, the cost, and the move, uprooting everyone . . . The boys will have to change schools.'

'That's not what you're worried about though, is it?' Tim says. 'You're worried about the extra five minutes' drive.'

'It was fifteen about a minute ago,' Alice says. 'I'm glad it's getting closer. By the time you've bought it, it'll be in the back garden.'

'It's about another ten minutes. That's all. Ten minutes.'

'We hardly see you as it is.'

'And now you know why,' Tim says, opening his arms to embrace the scene of family bliss.

'I don't know what that's supposed to mean,' Alice says. 'I'm sure I don't.'

'Is very beautiful,' Natalya says, trying to nudge a smidgen of positivity back into the conversation, though she suspects that it's a lost cause. 'It have five bedroom and a pool and—'

'Five bedrooms?' Alice interrupts. 'What on earth would you want five bedrooms for?'

'Unless they're thinking of—' Ken starts.

'We're not thinking of anything,' Tim tells him. To Natalya, he adds, 'And Nat . . . please . . . just button it. Christ!'

Natalya shrugs. 'I discuss our life with my in-law,' she says. 'If this is not allowed, maybe you should deliver me a new copy of *Little Red Book*.'

'What red book's that then?' Ken asks.

'She means that we're not in Soviet Russia,' Alice explains. 'She means that we're still allowed to discuss things.'

'Thanks to you, Alice,' Natalya says graciously, even though the *Little Red Book* was Chinese, not Russian.

'Five beds in Broseley, huh?' Ken says. 'That's gotta cost a pretty penny. That's got to be over a million, hasn't it?'

'I'm not discussing this any more,' Tim says. 'You won't get one more word out of me. We'll let you know if anything actually comes of it.' He glances at his watch. 'And now we need to get going. It's almost eleven and the boys have had a long day.'

'But you've only just arrived,' Alice protests.

'It'll be a quarter to twelve by the time we get home.'

'It would be gone midnight if you lived in Broseley,' Alice says pointedly. 'In fact, I bet you wouldn't have even come this far for the fireworks if you were living all the way out there.'

Tim closes his eyes and pinches the bridge of his nose, then opens them and gets to his feet. 'Right, that's enough. I'm suddenly very, very tired.' He shoots Natalya his harshest glare, and she, in return, curves her shoulders, bulges her eyes, and opens her hands at him in a 'What did I do?' gesture.

'Just get the kids together, will you?' he says, shaking his head and heading for the door.

◆ ◆ ◆

'So what was that all about, Nat?' Tim finally asks, as he pours himself a whisky.

Tim has driven them home in silence and carried the boys, already sleeping, to their beds.

Natalya, looking unusually sour, is already on her third shot of vodka by the time he reaches the lounge. 'What is what?' she says, looking back at him from the sofa.

'We agreed. We decided, together, not to worry them.'

'Huh!' Natalya says. 'You want me to be friend with them, then you want me to not tell them anything! This is your problem, not mine. Perhaps you should decide how you want me to be one time for all.'

'That's not the point. The point is that we discussed it, in the car,' Tim says, attempting to keep the discussion within the narrow confines of their agreement and Natalya's failure to respect that agreement.

'So how you want me to be with your parents, Tim? How?' Natalya asks. And this is the problem with trying to discuss anything with Natalya. This, Tim reckons, is the problem with trying to discuss things with women in general. Whereas men tend to keep each subject in a separate folder in a labelled filing cabinet so they can extract one subject and discuss it before carefully putting it back, women prefer to hurl everything into one big pot. It's all just spaghetti with every subject knotted up with every other, so that it's almost impossible to discuss any one thing without discussing everything.

'The point isn't how I want you to be with my parents,' Tim says. 'The point is why, after we decided not to mention it, did you go ahead and bloody mention it?'

105

'You agreed to not tell them, Tim,' Natalya says, rising and crossing to the bar for yet another refill. She's feeling trembly and unsure of herself, yet angry and accused at the same time. It's a complex and uncomfortable mix of emotions and the vodka seems to be helping. 'It's what you do,' she says. 'You decide things and then you tell me, and then you decide that I agreed.'

'You make me sound like some kind of dictator,' Tim says, 'when that's not what happened at all. What happened is that I explained how my parents work, and we agreed it was best not to tell them, and you told them anyway because you had some half-baked idea that they would tell me to up my offer. Which is to really misunderstand my parents' relationship with money. And now Dad will talk of nothing else for a month, and Mum won't sleep for worrying about it, and all for nothing because we don't even know if we're going to get the damned place.'

'Because of low offer,' Natalya says. 'Yes.'

'Two point five million is not a bloody low offer!' Tim says.

'Even Ken understands that this is not how market works,' Natalya says. 'Even the bald man on the television knows this.'

'So now you're going to give me lessons in property prices?' Tim says. 'You're going to give me tips on negotiating techniques? Really?'

'Perhaps you need!'

'So you really want to go there, do you?' Tim says. 'You really want to demonstrate that you have absolutely no idea what your husband does for a living, what he does all fucking day while you're sitting around drinking vodka?'

'Oh, Tim!' Natalya says in horror. 'How dare!'

'Look, I . . .'

'You are like dictator,' Natalya says, her voice rising. 'It's like Timski Putin. No one can discuss. No one can share. It all have to

106

be secrets and silence. Because Putin can't do when people disagree. Oh no! Everyone must bow to the great Timski Putin.'

'You're shouting,' Tim says. 'You're losing the plot.'

'Oh . . .' Suddenly the only words Natalya can think of are Russian ones. It happens when she gets really angry. '*K Chortu!*' she says, waving one hand dismissively at him. Tim knows what it means – go to hell.

She grabs the bottle of Stoli from the bar and struts from the room.

In the kitchen, she slumps at the kitchen table and pours herself another drink. She stares at the darkness beyond the kitchen window and tries to calm down.

She's being unreasonable. She can sense that much, even as she fails to control it. And it's true that she had agreed not to tell Tim's parents, even as she had agreed with herself that she might tell them all the same if she suddenly felt like it. It was just that Tim hadn't known that. But it was a kind of treason, she can see that now, and the fact of her treason makes her feel both guilty and angry at the same time.

But there's a larger picture here as well. There's the fact that Tim is always convinced that he's right, that he knows best about every bloody thing. There's the fact that no discussion has been possible about how much they might offer on the house, the subtext being that it's Tim's money, after all. Which is all the more annoying because it's so patently true.

She feels scared, too, she realises. It's not reasonable, this sensation of fear. The fact of not getting the new house doesn't mean that they'll lose this one, it doesn't mean that they'll end up on the street, even if that's how it feels to her. But she's scared. Now she has imagined herself in this new house, she's scared, irrationally scared, that it won't happen.

107

It's a dream house, that's the thing. It's literally a house of dreams, a vast, overblown symbol of wealth, of security, of safety, of finally being beyond reach.

Every time she watches an American sitcom she looks at the ridiculously big houses they all live in . . . (And how is that even possible? How can Susan the writer, who dabbles at her laptop about once every season, earn enough to pay for that house? Because Natalya knew a couple of writers when she worked in London, and they couldn't even pay their rent. Does Mike the plumber pay for it all? Is it possible that American plumbers earn a lot of money?)

Anyway, yes, every time she sees their mansions, their entrance halls bigger than her lounge, their shiny, happy, perfect lives (with the exception of the occasional murder) she thinks of the house. She thinks, soon this will be us. Even Susan and Mike don't have a lap pool.

She would feel safe in such a house. She's sure she would feel settled and centred, and finally safe. No one is going to drag a woman lounging by a pool back to her old life, but even as she thinks this, she is visualising a man, a big-built mafia type in a badly fitting suit, dragging her by the hair from the sunlounger. Her heart starts to race.

'Natalya!' It's Tim's voice. He's standing in the doorway behind her. 'Come to bed.'

'Go away!' she says. 'I hate you.' She's a little surprised at the sound of those words. They weren't the ones she had been intending to say.

'You're a fucking lunatic sometimes, you know,' Tim says, but his voice is soft, loving even.

Natalya chooses to focus on the words themselves rather than the tone. The vodka has made her reactive. 'Oh, I am lunatic?' she says, now standing and turning to confront him, her eyes fiery. 'And you? You are so very macho! So very clever. So very bloody

108

everything. You decide this, you decide that. And now you think you'll decide what I can say?'

'Nat . . .' Tim whines.

'What?'

'I don't know. Stop shouting.'

'Me? Shouting!' Natalya says, though she realises that she is shouting. 'Oh yes, Mister Putin. And perhaps you would like . . .'

'You're impossible when you're like this,' Tim says, interrupting her. 'Call me when your period's happened. I'm going to bed.'

'My period?!' Natalya says, now pursuing him down the hallway. 'My period! Well, that's one problem Mister Putin doesn't have, isn't it! Because he has such a big dick between his legs! He has his money and he decide everything. He doesn't bleed either! Oh, Timski Putin is so fucking clever!'

Tim stops walking away now and turns back to face his wife. She's out of control, momentarily possessed by some demon from her past. He knows that she has these demons. He has heard her nightmares and knows that she'll never tell him what she dreams of. And it's probably best that way, too. Because he's pretty sure that a beautiful, tiny, fragile Russian girl from the middle of nowhere doesn't get to be working in the luxury hotel in London where he met her without breaking a few psychological bones along the way. He loves her, whatever she had to do to get there. He loves her, in fact, partly because of what she had to do to get there. But it's best not to know. That's something they both agree on.

Right now, she's shrieking at him and he can't stand it. He literally can't stand it.

He asks her to stop. He begs her to stop. He needs her to understand his need for her to stop.

But it's like being King Canute facing the tide. Because Natalya's anger is like a breaker, rising from the calm flat of the ocean into a huge terrifying swell and then racing towards the

109

shore. And the only way to deal with it, like a swimmer before a tsunami, is to attempt to bob over the top, to hope it will crash on a beach behind you.

But the kids are upstairs. That's what Tim can't stand. The kids are upstairs, and they'll be listening to all of this. And he can't let that happen.

Without thinking, acting out of animal instinct, he physically pushes her, still raging, back into the kitchen. He closes the door behind him. He sees her fear at the gesture, sees that she has misinterpreted it as something far more sinister than him simply wanting to spare the boys her absurd screaming.

And now he's lost in his memories, lost in a different set of screams in a different house, even as Natalya's flailing arms start to slap at him ineffectually, even as she exhausts her vocabulary of English swear words and switches again to angry, incomprehensible Russian.

He is remembering being at the top of the stairs, looking down. He is remembering watching Ken slapping Alice, remembering trying to come up with some strategy whereby a small boy like him – for how old had he been, eight perhaps? – might intervene should that become necessary. He remembers grasping for any little idea that might stop the raging bull that was Ken on a roll.

He's remembering the terror as Ken glanced up and caught sight of him there, peeping through the banisters, remembering running, his heart racing, back upstairs to his room, plugging his ears against the screams with his fingers, wondering if his mother, his beautiful, gentle mother, would still be alive by morning. They haunt you forever, those childhood memories. You run them and rerun them until you're not even sure they happened any more. Except that they did happen. They really did.

Natalya asks him about his nightmares, but he can't tell her because they contain nothing concrete. They're just the sensation

110

of fear, just the feeling of wondering if Ken's drunken anger will result in his mother being hit – or worse, being killed – or whether instead the terrifying wave of madness will come crashing up the stairs into their bedrooms, into their safe space. Whether, no longer safe, he or Matt will get ripped from the bed. Because they – Matt, Alice, himself – were the beach Ken's anger always crashed upon. They were the only way it ever dissipated.

And so he dreams of that feeling, that apprehension, that fear . . . He dreams of the guilt, too, the guilt of hoping, of actually praying that this time it might be Matt's turn, that this time it might just be Alice. As long as he doesn't kill her. Please don't let her die. Because what would they do then?

So he doesn't want his kids to grow up with that, he really doesn't.

Right now, Natalya is leaning over him. She's stroking his hair and speaking softly, saying his name, and he, Timski, a child again, is wincing at her touch. He's crying, he realises. He's crouched down against the kitchen door, and he's weeping. And Natalya, thank God, has stopped.

Natalya ends up tearful too, so they hug each other and cry together on the kitchen floor. Neither asks the other exactly what their tears are about. They would both have trouble explaining anyway.

When the crying is over and Natalya is feeling silly about her shouting and Tim is feeling embarrassed about his crying – once Tim has blown his nose and declared that he isn't going to buy the bloody house anyway, and Natalya has summoned every modicum of self-control she possesses to tell him that it doesn't matter, that she doesn't care, that this, each other, is all they need – they end up hugging on the sofa. The hugging leads to nuzzling and the

111

nuzzling leads to kissing, and soon enough Tim's getting hard and Natalya is wriggling out of her jeans.

And then he's half-naked on his back, his own jeans around his knees, and Natalya is sliding over him, pulling him inside her. She's bouncing like a kid on a space hopper and pinching his nipples, and none of it matters, because this, this sliding and slipping, this tingling in his spine, this ecstatic animal thrusting, really is all they need.

Natalya pulls off her top and throws it over the back of the sofa and Tim reaches behind her and unclips her bra releasing her breasts and, yes, Natalya is amazing, because on top of everything else, on top of being a great mother, and a good cook and a great friend (most of the time), she really does fuck like a porn star (and where did she learn to do that?).

Tim pushes the thought from his mind because who cares where she learnt it – it's brilliant, it's amazing! She's the best lay he's ever had, and fucking Natalya (yes, 'fucking', because though they do sometimes 'make love', that's really not what's happening right now) makes him feel like a porn star too, and it's all rising within him, the electrical charge increasing, the fragility, the fears, his childhood, poor Alice, that bastard Ken . . . all receding, and his mojo is returning and he's himself again, he's broken free from it all and he's the wildly successful banker he decided to be, he's the man who does multi-billion-dollar deals, he's the father who takes his family to firework displays, he's the husband who pays for everything. And on top of all of this, he's just momentarily a porn star. He's a master of the fucking universe and his wife is sim- ply . . . God, her beauty, her body, the joy of being inside her . . . it's beyond words.

And he's getting there now, it's rising within him and Natalya is almost there too, and he wishes he could hold it longer, because

112

it's so good, this making it last, and yet it's so good to just let it happen too, such a relief to allow this different wave to envelop them, to feel it wash over them and crash on a different, sunnier beach, and all that anger, all that fear will be magically transformed into sweaty, glorious deliverance.

But Natalya has stopped dead. He tries for an instant to continue to writhe beneath her but she locks him in with her knees so he can't move a muscle. She grabs her sweater and uses it to hide her breasts.

'Go to bed!' she shrieks, causing Tim to look up behind him to where little Boris is peering through the banisters at them.

'Fuck!' he mutters.

'Go to bed!' Natalya shouts again, now rolling away and grabbing cushions with which to make a wall she can hide behind. Boris peeping through the banisters is reminding her, shockingly, of the punters in the peep shows. 'GO TO BED!'

But Boris isn't moving. He's still there, his little pale fingers gripping the banisters, his tiny face poking between them. His expression looks glassy, neutral. He could even be asleep.

Tim stands, pushes his semi-erect dick back into his jeans and buttons them up. 'It's all right, buddy,' he says as he crosses the room, but it's not really all right at all because Boris has ruined his porn-star moment and Natalya is lapsing back into semi-madness.

'Don't stare at me, Boris!' she's shouting. 'Go to bed! Tim, make him stop stare. Is creepy!'

'Mum and Dad were just playing,' Tim says reassuringly as he climbs the stairs. To Natalya, now muttering unnervingly in Russian, he casts a, 'Button it, Nat, for Christ's sake!'

When he reaches the landing, Boris looks up at him and blinks confusedly, and Tim still can't tell if he's sleepwalking or in shock at what he's just seen. He waves a hand in front of Boris's eyes. It's

113

what they do in films to find out if people are conscious or not, but right now it reveals nothing.

'Did you have a nightmare?' he asks as he lifts the boy into his arms. As he carries him back to his bed, he feels the full weight of guilt for this dishonesty. It's exactly what his mother used to say to him when he was Boris's age, and often enough he had chosen to believe her. The idea of a bad dream had seemed at the time to be so much easier to live with than the truth.

6

APRIL

'Shall I put these in boxes or bags?' the guy asks. He's standing in the doorway to the bedroom holding a pile of sheets from the airing cupboard. He's irritatingly good-looking and slightly more muscular than the average superhero.

Tim's generally fairly proud of his body – he has worked hard to avoid a paunch – but being around this guy, specifically having this guy peering in at him when he's in the process of getting dressed, makes him feel insecure. He has already decided as soon as this move is over to up his hours at the gym.

Natalya has spotted Steve's muscles too. (Yes, Tim remembers now: the guy's name is Steve.) She's all flirtatious and girly whenever she's around him, which makes Tim's comparative lack of musculature even harder to bear.

Tim pulls a shirt from the wardrobe and starts to button it. 'I don't know,' he replies, irritated more by the guy's Californian-surfer head of hair and his pecs than by his question. 'Ask my wife.'

Steve nods thoughtfully. His regard seems to hover just a fraction too long over Tim's chest as he rushes to hide it beneath the blue cotton shirt.

So he's gay, Tim thinks. Figures. The gay guys are always more built than everyone else. But then the hours that Tim spends taking Boris and Alex to funfairs, the gay guys get to spend at the gym. No wonder they're ripped.

'She's not . . . um . . . that clear, this morning,' Steve says, vaguely smiling, seemingly unaware of any danger in what he's saying. But even if Tim knows exactly what Steve is hinting at, Steve has misjudged the situation. This is not that moment when Tim and Steve bond over the state of Tim's dippy, hungover wife.

'I don't know what the fuck that's supposed to mean,' Tim says, watching with a certain pleasure as the smile slips from Steve's lips.

'Sorry,' Steve says. 'I just . . . I didn't mean anything really.'

And suddenly, the guy whose muscles are so big that he doesn't seem able to walk naturally looks like he might cry, and a vision of Steve as a small, spotty, bullied child flashes into Tim's mind. He doesn't know where the vision comes from – some shared pool of consciousness perhaps – but he understands now how young Steve is, how recent those terrified walks home from school were, and he understands and forgives Steve's musculature for what it is: a defence shield, and not a very good one at that.

'Look,' Tim says, his voice softening. 'You're the packing expert, OK? And my wife's the boss in all of this. And they're sheets – they're just sheets. So pack them any way you want, OK, dude?'

Steve nods. 'Bags are best, I reckon,' he says.

'Bags it is then,' Tim agrees. He grabs his shoes and squeezes through the small gap Steve provides by stepping only partially aside. He's happy to escape the strange intensity of the guy. He'll break with routine and put them on downstairs.

In the living room, another, older man with another instantly forgettable shortened name, Burt or Mike or Joe, is busy loading Tim's CD collection into boxes.

'Careful with those,' Tim says, for no reason except that he can. 'Some of those are collectibles.'

'Oh, we're careful with everything, sir,' Burt/Mike/Joe says. 'We go on special training sessions. It's written in our company motto and everything.'

Tim suspects that he's meant to enquire what the company motto is, but a) he isn't in the mood to chat to the guy, and b) he isn't interested anyway, and c) he suspects that he's already seen it on the side of their lorry and like Burt/Mike/Joe's name, has already allowed himself to forget it.

In the kitchen, he finds Natalya having what she calls her Russian Breakfast – alternating between sips of Bloody Mary, strong gritty coffee, and drags on a cigarette.

'You OK?' Tim asks, lifting the vodka bottle from the table and placing it out of view in a half-packed carton on the counter. 'It's a bit early for vodka, dontcha think?'

'But is so stressful, Timski,' Natalya says. 'I read it in a magazine.'

'You read what?'

'That the move is as stressful as losing partner in car accident. Someone measure it.'

Tim nods blankly. He tries not to feel insulted by the comparison. 'Well, thanks!' he says. But Natalya doesn't spot his irony.

Yet Tim knows what she means. It is stressful. Tim too has had a tightness across the chest for days, an occasional inability to breathe smoothly. Even Boris and Alex are unusually wired at the moment, are waking up with nightmares at night.

And despite the moving company's motto – it comes to him now: 'Every Item As Safe As Houses' – things do get broken. Not

117

the big expensive replaceable things, but the little worthless family heirlooms.

It wasn't Steve's fault though. There was no way he could know (unless Natalya had told him – which she hadn't) that if you took everything off one end of that glass shelf, it would tip up. Only Natalya could have foreseen that, but she had been upstairs, sleeping off yesterday's Russian Breakfast.

'I'm so tired, Tim,' she says now. 'I'm so glad when this is all done.'

Tim has been working eleven-hour days trying to close the deals that will pay for the bridging loan, the deals that will pay for the Safe As Houses moving company, the Dash of Flash interior designer, and the Spic and Span industrial cleaners who are due to swoop in behind them once they've left. And he has dedicated his weekends to driving around with Natalya to look at furniture, to taking the kids to the park while she sleeps, to feeding them while she drinks . . . And yet despite all of this, despite the fact that she has a virtual army of people at her beck and call to clean, move, decorate and furnish, he has to listen, on top of everything else, to her complaining about how fucking tired she is.

Perhaps he's just tired, too. Yes, he's tired and it's making him irritable, which isn't helping things. And it really shouldn't come as a surprise that the process of moving house is exhausting. As Natalya says, it's well known to be as stressful as having your husband drop dead.

But he is surprised. His vision, the vision he had of this house did not include the moving process, did not include the thousands of little tiring, irritating, personal-space-invading details. It did not include being cruised by tearful Steve, or the glass shelf that would inevitably crash down on Natalya's grandmother's Babushka doll. Just as picnics in films never feature those bastard red ants biting everyone's ankles, and just as sexy pool scenes are never interrupted

118

by those horrifically carnivorous horseflies, his vision of moving house had been carefully edited to exclude specifically anything to do with actually moving house. But here they are. And it's more nightmare than dream sequence.

Tim returns to the lounge, relieves the packing guy of the iPad (which it seems he was about to bubble-wrap) and instructs him not to unplug the broadband box until the very end. 'I need Wi-Fi till the last possible moment,' he says.

He returns briefly to the kitchen. Natalya is standing over the espresso machine making coffee. At least she's not hunting for the vodka bottle.

'Nat?' he says. 'You said the broadband's sorted in the new place, right?'

'The Internet?'

'Yeah.'

'Yes,' she says. 'I tell you. The Virgin will come this afternoon. The only thing you care is Internet.'

'It's work, hon,' Tim says, now returning to the lounge.

She's right though. Tim's biggest fear is being deprived of access to the Internet during the move, and of suddenly, on reconnecting, discovering that the world has changed and that he has missed some vastly important boat. Things move fast these days, and as mobile reception in the new house seems patchy, he's worried. They could stay in a hotel for a few days and he wouldn't care one bit. They could eat every meal out of a Pizza Hut box for a week, and he would barely even notice. But to find himself without an Internet connection – that would be a disaster. As far as Tim's concerned (and it's probably the case, he reckons, for about half of his genera-tion) Wi-Fi has replaced food or water or sex, or very probably all three, at the base of Maslow's triangle of human needs.

119

In the lounge, on a garden chair (the sofa has been dragged away, either to the new place or to the tip – he's not sure what they decided any more) he logs into his share account and misses a heartbeat as he looks at the column of red figures. This move has stretched him to breaking point, and he really doesn't have any spare capacity for a failed deal. But Greece, bloody Greece, is dragging the Euro even lower, and his Gazprom shares are down too. That's because of Putin sizing up to Europe for a fight. (Actually, Natalya, who occasionally blindsides him with her lucidity about international affairs, says it's NATO pushing Putin into a corner, not the other way around, and she may well be right.) Still, whoever's fault it is, it's not good for Tim. He needs one of three things to happen: either Greece to pull through, to be saved by the EU, or Putin to back off and let things calm down in Ukraine, or for Greece to do a deal with Russia to get all that Gazprom gas flowing into Europe by the back door. Actually, they could even just look like they're going to do a deal for long enough for him to sell his damned shares. Ten minutes would do, hence the importance of the Internet connection.

And right now, in the midst of Tim's international stress, here's Natalya who promised to organise ALL of this asking him about every bloody item they own. 'Should we take this or get new one, Timski?' she's asking, over and over as she points to the bookcase, or the coffee table, or the CD rack. And Tim really, honestly doesn't give a shit.

'Take it all, or replace everything, or do both,' he tells her, dragging his eyes from an article about the Greek finance minister (who may or may not have stepped down). 'There's enough bloody room, isn't there?'

'But is expensive, no? To change everything,' Natalya says, revealing her preference.

'It honestly makes no odds, Nat,' Tim says.

120

Natalya blinks at him confusedly. She wonders if her husband is telling her they're so rich that money's no object.

The truth is slightly more complex. If Greece gets saved and Tim can flog his Gazprom shares, then Natalya's interpretation will be spot on – they'll be so loaded it won't matter. If neither of these happens, they'll be down millions. Either way, the cost of a new sofa is neither here nor there.

7

MAY

Tim pads down the polished concrete staircase to the lounge, and thinks, yet again, that he needs to buy slippers. His feet are freezing.

They've been living here two weeks to the day, and he has had the same thought thirteen mornings in a row.

It's just before five, so the sun isn't up yet. Natalya and the kids are still sleeping, and the house feels boundless and empty and as cold as a train station at 3 a.m. Tim glances around, almost expecting to discover a tramp sleeping in a corner.

He crosses the lounge and enters the galley kitchen, another over-designed, oversized space, shaped, in this case, like a canal boat. The six-metre countertops running along either side look absurd and empty. They need, Tim thinks, more stuff on them. But Natalya's against. Natalya likes her surfaces.

At the far end, he switches on the little espresso machine, waits for it to warm up, and then makes himself a cup of coffee before returning to the lounge where he sits on the sofa and stares at the blackness of the window. He watches as the sky beyond begins to lighten. He's never, as a general rule, awake before dawn, but has managed it three times this week. It's all the stress of the move, his worries about the markets and the novelty of the new house. It will pass.

He checks his trading accounts on the iPad. There's been no surprise reprieve overnight and everything's as grim as it was when he went to bed. He mentally calculates how long he can continue paying the loan on this place as well as the bridging loan on the old one before the well runs dry. He reckons they'll be OK till July, maybe August. And surely something will give by then, won't it?

The sky is edging towards pink now, the sun peeking over the horizon, and, seemingly automatically, like a mathematical result, the imminent arrival of daylight makes him feel a little better. There are things you can still count on, the planet seems to be telling him. The sun will still rise.

Tim shivers and looks around for a jumper or a blanket he can throw over himself, but Vladlena has tidied everything away and he can't be bothered to return upstairs. He notes again the strange space surrounding him and feels vaguely surprised. He keeps finding himself doing this. It's as if he forgets that they've moved houses and has to remind himself of the fact every time he wakes up, every time he looks up from the iPad or switches off the TV. It's not a comforting feeling. It's the opposite of comforting, in fact. He tries now to remember why they did all of this, tries to remember the vision he had of this house and momentarily it's there again: Tim, relaxed, trim, well dressed, smiling; Natalya, beyond the window, rubbing in suntan lotion beside the pool; Tim's music blaring from the hi-fi; the kids running around upstairs . . .

The rising sun is highlighting a series of ugly smears on the big picture window – Vladlena, apparently, can't reach any higher than five feet from the ground. The sofa beneath him is their old

124

one and, lost in the vastness of the lounge, it looks like a small tatty armchair that doesn't fit the space at all.

Tim hasn't bothered to set up the hi-fi yet because he's holding out for new speakers and it's too cold outside to use the pool, which in any case has turned in the two weeks since they've been here from translucent turquoise to a deep shade of algae green. Tim shivers again. The much-dreamt-of picture window creates a permanent downdraught of chilled air. It's all a long way from his original vision. Thank God summer will be here soon.

He turns the thermostat up to twenty-three, grabs an overcoat from the entrance to use as a blanket and soon he's asleep on the sofa with the iPad on his chest rising and falling as he snores.

He's woken at seven by Boris climbing on to his legs, and opens his eyes to see Natalya in her dressing gown, looking down at him concernedly.

'You can't sleep again?' she asks softly.

'Uh huh,' Tim says.

She strokes his hair. 'Poor Timski.'

'Have you seen the state of the pool?' Tim asks.

Natalya nods.

'When's the pool guy supposed to be coming? It looks like bloody pea soup out there.'

'Pea soup!' Boris repeats. He seems for some reason to find this funny.

Natalya frowns. She reckons Tim knows perfectly well that the pool guy was supposed to come yesterday. She's pretty sure his question is nothing more than disguised reproach. 'Today maybe,' she lies, removing her hand from his head.

'And have you seen the state of the windows?' Tim asks. 'It looks like Vladlena's been cleaning them with a dead cat.'

'Maybe she did. Is Russian tradition, you know?'

125

'Seriously though, can you buy the woman a stepladder or something? Or maybe even get someone new who knows how to actually clean windows?'

Natalya pulls a face, shakes her head, and blows out through pursed lips in an apparent indication of despair.

'What?' Tim asks, as she turns back to the staircase. 'Seriously? What did I say?'

'And good morning to you, darling,' she says sarcastically.

Once she has gone back to bed, Tim turns his attention to Boris, wide awake and attempting to bounce on his stomach. 'Whoops. Looks like Daddy's upset Mummy,' he says.

'Whoops,' Boris repeats, smiling mischievously.

'We'll buy her some flowers later,' Tim says, realising that he has been mean to Natalya recently. It's the shock of the new house. It's waking up at 4 a.m. and not knowing where he is and never being able to find anything. It's all been getting to him, and he's been taking at least part of it out on his wife. He vows to make up for it today. 'She likes flowers, yeah?'

'And chocolate?' Boris asks.

'Yes, chocolate too.'

'For me?'

'Sure, OK,' Tim laughs.

'Not for Alex though.'

'Why not?' Tim asks.

'Alex is baaad,' Boris says, starting to bounce up and down again.

By the time Natalya resurfaces, Tim has left for work. Vladlena is playing with the boys on the big grey rug.

'*Dobroye utro*,' Vladlena says, looking up and smiling – good morning.

126

'Good morning,' Natalya replies in English. 'Tim is gone, yes?'

Vladlena nods and raises an eyebrow. '*Da*,' she says. 'He told me off about the windows, but I told him, I'm only little – I can't reach that high.'

'I know,' Natalya says. 'It's fine.' She kneels between Boris and Alex. 'What are you two making?' she asks.

Alex shrugs. He's holding a block of randomly stuck together Lego pieces.

'Mine's a space motorbike,' Boris says.

Vladlena glances at her watch. 'We need to be off soon,' she says. 'You want a coffee before I go?'

Natalya nods. 'Yes,' she says. 'That would be nice.'

She lies down on the rug and allows herself a brief moment of comfort as the boys' physical presence swarms around and over her. What with the move and everything, she's been ignoring their needs almost as much as she's been forgetting her own need for them. As Alex drives his unnamed object through her hair and Boris runs his space motorbike along her leg, she glances up at the ceiling, so high above them. She notices the way the sunlight cuts across the room. *Wow*, she thinks. *We did it.*

Once Vladlena has returned with her coffee and has whisked the boys off to school (the school is on her way home, after all), Natalya's emotions shift slowly but surely from awe of the new house, through pride, to a strange sensation of loneliness.

It's peculiar, the effect that space, that the shape of space, can have upon your psyche. She never once felt lonely in the old house, but it's the sheer volume of the rooms here. They make her feel smaller than usual, as if she's dominated by the building, as if the house perhaps is winning some unnamed battle.

She shrugs off the feeling and takes a hot shower. The downstairs water pressure here is amazing, more jet wash than shower.

Afterwards, she dries herself, gets dressed and begins to hunt for her make-up bag. It's not where it should be.

She checks the upstairs bathroom three times, checks the bedroom twice, then returns downstairs to look there. This search, this wandering from one unfamiliar semi-furnished room to another does nothing to lessen her sensation, this morning, of being lost. There are so many damned rooms here. There are so many unpacked cartons still to get through – boxes and boxes containing thousands of individual tiny items that each had their own place in the old house, items she can't even think where to put now they're here. Perhaps she can just leave them all in boxes in one of the rooms. Perhaps she can just close the door and forget them forever. But her make-up bag – she had that just yesterday. So how can it be lost today?

She starts checking unlikely places. The kitchen. The refrigerator. The children's rooms. She returns upstairs and checks the bathroom, which is silly because she's already looked three times. But sometimes things do vanish and reappear. She has no explanation, but she knows it to be true. Poltergeists maybe. She should look for her glasses first, she decides, and so she starts to hunt for those instead.

Eventually, almost distraught, she hurls herself on to the sofa, and there beside her, poking from beneath a cushion, is the goddamned make-up bag. And inside it are her glasses. She feels almost tearful at the discovery, or perhaps at the wasted hour. She's not sure quite which.

This move, it's true, has worn her out. Tim thinks she's exaggerating when she says that, but it really has. She's on the edge of tears all the time. She's feeling stressed and exhausted and lonely. She's waking up every morning feeling disoriented, wondering where she is. Yet she can't be seen to complain because it's her own fault: she pushed for this move. It was she who wanted it, after all.

128

And this getting people to do things . . . Getting the pool guy to actually drop by when she's here, getting the delivery guys to unbox things in the right rooms, getting Vladlena to clean the windows properly; it all turns out to be as hard, if not harder, than doing it all yourself. Who knew?

She looks up at the smears of Windolene. It's true that in the sunlight they really do look horrible.

She walks to the kitchen where she snatches a roll of kitchen towel from the counter, takes the proper window cleaner from the cupboard (not that horrible white cream Vladlena uses), and returns to the lounge. She drags the new coffee table to the window and puts a chair on top of it. She climbs up uncertainly and begins angrily to rub away Vladlena's smears. It really does look like she used a dead cat.

Her anger, Natalya realises as she works, is not against Vladlena, and it's not against Tim. She's angry, it transpires, with life. She's angry with life for making everything so difficult, with making everything so goddamned disappointing.

Vladlena, she thinks, as she climbs down and drags the table and chair to the right, is going to leave them. She's not sure where the thought came from, but she's certain, now she's thought it, that it's true.

Vladlena has been complaining about the distance she has to travel to get here. She's been complaining about dropping the boys at school, too. And she's upset about not being able to manage the windows. They do, it has to be said, have acres of the damned things, and whoever the architect was, he doesn't seem to have ever planned for quite how they might be cleaned. To do them properly you'd need to be that comic hero who climbs buildings . . . Spider-Man – that's the one. And even Spider-Man would leave little sucker traces. Natalya needs to have a word with Tim about

129

that. He needs to lay off criticising Vladlena until he's tried to do them himself.

Yes, unless they sweeten the deal, perhaps reduce her hours or up her pay, Vladlena will leave them. And that would be more than a shame.

Natalya remembers the search that led them (eventually) to Vladlena. Jenny, the previous girl – a live-in au-pair – had slapped Boris across the face. She had threatened him with another slap if he told his parents about it, too. If it hadn't been for his bright red cheek and Natalya's intuition, her tenacity in interrogating the boy, they might never have found out. Natalya had slapped Jenny back and then fallen out with Tim, who insisted that slapping employees was not acceptable behaviour even if they had abused your children.

Natalya remembers how happy she had been once Jenny had gone. The house had been a mess, and their dinners had all been takeaways, but she had loved being with Alex all day. She had loved picking Boris up from school.

The chair on which Natalya is standing wobbles and slips a little, and she realises that she's taking risks by leaning too far out, so she climbs down and drags the table and chair a little farther.

And poor Tim, what is the move doing to her lovely Timski? He's working more than ever in an attempt to pay for everything. He's trying to sell the old place and worrying about Greece, and when he isn't at work he's staring into the middle distance through these same smeary windows, looking almost as lost as Natalya feels.

She peers back at the window to her left – it's definitely an improvement – then returns, encouraged, to the task at hand.

Yes, Tim looks lost and his brow seems permanently furrowed these days. And they haven't had sex once since they moved here; not since Boris interrupted them in the old place, in fact. And that's not like Tim at all.

He's waking at three in the morning and complaining of chest pains as well. And it's all Natalya's fault because she knew. She had read the damned article about how moving house was as stressful as bereavement and yet pushed for this all the same. If she had never mentioned seeing the house on the market, then Tim wouldn't be having chest pains and they'd still be having sex, and Vladlena wouldn't be thinking of leaving them, and Natalya wouldn't be standing on a wobbly chair on a table trying to clean Vladlena's smears of Windolene from these stupid bloody windows.

There had been a moment when she realised, when she had grasped briefly the meaning of the word 'enough'. There had been a short window of opportunity through which she had been able to identify the comfortable advantages of stasis, of being happy and contented with what they already had. And then something had happened and she lost it again.

The doorbell rings, making her jump. The sound is still unfamiliar.

She climbs down and chucks the wad of paper towels on to the sofa and places the cleaning spray on the coffee table beneath the chair, wondering if this will be the new sofa, or the kitchen table, or the pool guy.

She trots excitedly through to the hallway and opens the front door where she signs disappointedly for a recorded delivery envelope. The delivery, it turns out, was nothing more than paperwork for Tim from HSBC. It's probably something to do with the loan.

Back in the lounge, she looks up at the window. Yes, it's better, but the smears, though fainter, have not vanished entirely. From this angle, in this light, they still look pretty bad. Tim won't, as she had imagined, be congratulating her after all.

She sighs, murmurs, 'Oh well,' and lifts the chair from the coffee table.

The chair legs, she sees now, have left deep, ugly dents in the surface of the brand-new table. She has been thoughtless, idiotic, to use a table and a chair as a stepladder.

She sinks to her knees to study the scarred surface of the table, runs her fingers around the edges of the dents. In anger at herself, she groans and bumps her forehead gently against it.

All she has ever wanted was to make things better, to make them nicer for Tim, for herself, for the boys. But even when she tries to make things better, she only makes them worse. Her eyes, she realises, are misting.

Once the aged pool guy with the missing front tooth has finally tipped his buckets of foul-smelling chemicals into their swamp, and once the new five-metre sofa has been delivered and the old one whisked away, Natalya glances at her phone and decides that she just about has time for her plan.

She phones Vladlena and gives her the evening and morning shifts off. She's decided that she really doesn't want Vladlena to leave them right now, and she also wants to spend more time with the boys herself. Giving Vladlena a break kills two hares with one shot. Or as Tim would say, two birds with one stone.

The traffic this afternoon is terrible and there are roadworks and temporary traffic lights to get through, so the drive back to Dudley takes almost an hour. They have, in theory at least, been sharing the school runs three ways. In reality though, Natalya has only done it twice since they moved. She realises now just how tiring the journey must be for Vladlena, who has to do it five days a week. She realises that even with them paying her travelling time and costs and letting her stay over whenever she wants, the system is unsustainable. It's amazing, in fact, that she hasn't been complaining more.

132

It's almost five by the time they get home and Natalya's too tired to deal with the raucous boys and too tired even to cook them a proper meal. So she lets them load up the Xbox and slings a frozen pizza in the oven before setting about ripping the bubble-wrap from the new sofa. She wonders what Alice would say about her parenting techniques. Nothing nice, she reckons.

At eight, she puts the kids to bed and, worried by Tim's absence, texts him and then just three minutes later phones him instead. In those three minutes she's already started obsessing about his chest pains. He could be in hospital. He could be dead. By the time he answers, her own heart is racing.

'Hi, babe,' he says. 'Sorry I'm late but I stopped off to get those speakers. I'm just about to leave. We'll be there in forty minutes.'

'Speakers?' Natalya asks, then, 'We?'

'Me and the guy from the hi-fi shop. He's gonna come and set everything up.'

'But it's eight fifteen, Tim,' Natalya says. 'The shop is still open?'

Tim laughs. 'For fifty grand, he'd stay open to midnight, sweetheart,' he says.

Once she has hung up, Natalya lounges back on the new sofa – it's incredibly comfortable. It's just a shame the leather is so cold to the touch. She looks around the room and tries to remember the speakers Tim showed her in the magazine, tries to imagine how they will look in this room, how they will impact upon the decor that she and Graham from Dash of Flash so carefully conceived.

She's a little angry at Tim for not discussing it with her, and a little concerned about what Graham will say, too. But she's also glad that Tim has found the time to treat himself to something that makes him happy. She's a little bit proud, too, that they've gone from being the kind of people who hide potatoes under the mattress to the kind of people luxury stores stay open for.

133

◆ ◆ ◆

Edwin from Midland Hi-Fi leans his back against the second box and pushes it inside the open rear of Tim's BMW X5. The first one is already filling the rear of his own white Peugeot van.

'My wife's getting tetchy,' Tim says, sliding the phone back into his shirt pocket. 'This won't take long, will it?'

'Once we get to yours, half an hour tops,' Edwin replies.

'I hope they sound good,' Tim says. 'It's a big investment.'

'It'll be like having a band in your lounge,' Edwin says. 'TAD are the best you can get in this price range. And for the moment, these are the top of their range.'

Tim nods vaguely and frowns, but before he can pursue that thought to its conclusion, Edwin has climbed into his van and started the engine. 'So I'll follow you, right?' he calls out.

As they turn on to the ring road, Tim runs the conversation through his mind and chews the inside of his mouth. Something's worrying him, something about those two qualifying statements. He wants to stop the car right now. He wants to pull on to the hard shoulder and sort it out before it's too late. But he doesn't. He carries on driving – just a little faster than usual. Edwin follows on.

When they get to Broseley, Edwin parks too close behind Tim in the driveway, so Tim has to instruct him to reverse up so he can open the hatchback.

'So just before we do this,' Tim says, once Edwin has joined him behind the X5. 'What did you mean when you said they're the best "in this price range"? And what about them being top of the range "for the moment"?'

'Ha!' Edwin says, laughing unconvincingly. 'Worried you, did I? Sorry.'

134

'Not worried,' Tim says, though this pain across his chest is surely something not far off worry. 'I just want to understand what you meant.'

'Oh, it's nothing,' Edwin says. 'It's just that the new range comes out in September. They fly us out to Düsseldorf to see it, which is cool. Well . . . to hear it, I suppose.'

'So these are what? An old model?' Tim asks, slapping the box with the flat of his hand.

'No!' Edwin says, looking scared at the thought that his sale might be evaporating. 'No, these are the best they do at the moment. None of us know what's happening in September.'

Tim nods. 'And what about in this price range? You said they're the best thing in this price range.'

'Stay cool,' Edwin tells him. 'These are amazing. These are great. You'll love them. They'll be fine.'

'Fine?' Tim repeats. 'I didn't think I was getting fine. I thought I was buying the best speakers that money can buy.'

Edwin laughs at this – he actually laughs. 'Oh, I doubt I ever said that,' he says. 'If you really want the best that money can buy, then you'll be needing about six hundred grand for a pair of Omega Ones. And I bet if you look hard enough, there's something out there even better than those.'

Tim swallows with difficulty. Edwin has pricked his bubble and, like a leaky airbed, all of the pleasure, all of the optimism he had associated with buying these speakers is leaking out. Because evidently there's always something better somewhere, and yes, there's already something better than these TADs, worth a 'mere' fifty grand. He feels sick.

'They'll sound amazing,' Edwin says again. 'And if they don't, I can take them back.'

'Right,' Tim says.

135

'So are we doing this or not?' Edwin asks, now lifting the end of the box and starting to slide it out of Tim's car.

'I suppose so,' Tim replies, but without any of his former enthusiasm.

When Natalya opens the front door, her expression shifts from initial pleasure through annoyance to shock. 'Oh my God!' she says. 'Is so big!'

'Hi, Madam,' Edwin says. 'Don't worry, there's a lot of packing around them. The speakers are smaller than the boxes.'

'New sofa,' Tim says, as they edge their way into the lounge with the first package.

'Yes, is good, huh?'

'Beautiful,' Tim says, now lowering his end of the carton to the ground. 'My music sofa,' he tells Edwin proudly.

'Nice!' Edwin agrees.

Beneath Natalya's critical gaze, they unbox the first speaker, then return outside for the second one. And even though the speakers are taller than Natalya herself, even though Vladlena will need a stepladder just to dust them, they don't look unreasonable given the scale of the room.

'Nice space,' Edwin says as they pull the packing away from the second speaker.

'Thanks.'

Edwin returns again to his van, then begins to unroll ten metres of thick, outrageously expensive speaker cable.

'We must have wires?' Natalya asks. She's still seated on the sofa, her hands beneath her thighs as she watches events unfold.

'Of course,' Tim says. 'How do you think they work otherwise?'

Natalya shrugs. 'Wi-Fi maybe?' she says.

'Wi-Fi's not hi-fi,' the man from the shop tells her. 'In fact, it's distinctly lo-fi.'

Once wires have been uncoiled and ends have been stripped, once Tim's amplifier has been connected and the valves have started to glow, the moment of truth arrives.

He selects a CD – John Grant – but then changes his mind and chooses St. Vincent instead. He slips it into the player and then glances back at Natalya. 'Ready?' he asks.

She nods. 'Not too loud,' she says, her eyes flicking towards the stairwell. 'The children . . .'

Tim laughs. 'I'm afraid that tonight, for once, if it wakes them, it wakes them!' he says, glancing at Edwin conspiratorially.

Boys, Natalya thinks. 'OK,' she says, rolling her eyes. 'But just for trying. Just short time.'

Tim checks the track list on the back of the CD case and then, deciding on track one, he simply hits the play button. 'Rattlesnake' starts to whisper from the speakers. He reaches for the volume dial. And as the sound increases, the music sounds . . . terrible.

'Um, that's a difficult track,' Edwin says, his forehead furrowing as he heads towards Tim in a damage control operation. 'Perhaps start with something more . . .'

'Wait,' Tim says, raising one hand to hold him back. He switches to track two. Then track three. He fiddles with the base and treble controls. He ups and lowers the volume, pivots the speakers left and right. But whatever he does, St. Vincent sounds truly horrible.

'Hmm . . . let me check the phase,' Edwin says, scampering behind each speaker to check the connections. 'No, they're fine . . .'

After having played a few seconds from each track on the album, Tim ejects the CD and puts in Metronomy's *Love Letters* instead. It's his favourite album of the moment, mellow and sweet, but it too sounds horrible, worse even than in the car.

'I think is the room,' Natalya says, looking around. She can hear the sound bouncing off all that polished concrete. It seems to be assailing her from all directions. It's making her feel like her head will explode.

'Yeah,' Edwin says, 'I think you have too much space. I think you need more furnishings. More textiles.'

'Too much space,' Tim repeats. *Tell that to the guy in the advert*, he thinks.

It's almost eleven by the time Edwin pulls away down the drive. Tim closes the front door and returns to the lounge. He turns off the hi-fi, then lies down on the sofa and puts his head on Natalya's knees. He reaches, automatically, for the TV remote control.

'Don't, Tim,' Natalya says.

'Huh?' Tim asks, straining to look up at her, his finger hovering over the on/off button.

'Don't turn TV on,' she says.

'Why? You wanna listen to those fuckers?'

'No, I want to talk with you,' Natalya says. 'We don't talk so much now.'

'Oh . . .' Tim says, laying the remote across his chest, and then, deciding that the implied temporary nature of the gesture is rude, he reaches down and places it beneath the sofa. 'Sure. What about?'

'Just life,' Natalya says. 'We sometimes need to talk about life.'

'OK,' Tim says doubtfully. 'Fine.'

'I'm sorry about speakers, really.'

'Why are you sorry?'

'Because you're sad. So I'm sorry.'

'Oh, OK. I'm not really sad,' Tim says. 'Well, maybe a bit, but . . .'

'I don't understand why you keep this. The man says he can return them, yes?'

'I know. I guess I just felt a bit . . . Not sure . . . Obligated maybe? I mean, he came all the way out here and everything. And a bit daft too.'

'Daft?'

'Stupid,' Tim says. 'I feel a bit stupid for spending that much.'

'Is not stupid,' Natalya says. 'Is a mistake.'

'Well, sometimes mistakes are stupid.'

'No, in Russian, mistake is mistake. Stupid is stupid.'

'All the same . . . Actually, you know what?' Tim says, the decision forming as he speaks. 'Can you do me a favour?'

'Yes?'

'A really big favour?'

'Of course.'

'Can you make them disappear?'

'The speaker?'

'Yes. If I leave you the number for Midland Hi-Fi . . .'

'The man from the shop? This man?'

'Yes. Can you phone him and get him to come and get them? Tell him I'm happy to pay a restocking fee, or delivery costs, or his time or whatever. But can you just make it so that they're gone when I get home? So it's like it never happened? The whole thing is making me feel ill.'

'Yes,' Natalya says, 'I can do this. Is making my ear hurt.'

'And get him to bring the old ones back, before he sells them.'

'The white ones? He has these?'

'Yes, I traded them in. Get him to bring them back. I think this room's gonna sound shitty whatever speakers we have, so we might as well just keep the old ones.'

139

Natalya nods and runs a hand across Tim's hair. 'OK,' she says. 'I think this is good decision.'

'Thanks.'

'And can you maybe do for me something also?'

'Sure,' Tim says. 'Anything.'

'Because I do a stupid thing too.'

'Yeah?'

'Yes, so you don't get angry, OK?'

'Of course not.'

'OK, I'm going to tell you now. So you've promised not to be angry, OK?'

'I promise.'

'You're sure?'

'Yes!' Tim laughs. 'Now what? You haven't boil-washed the kids again, have you?'

'Uh huh,' Natalya confirms. 'They're like babies again. But that's not it.'

'OK.'

'Look at table.'

'The table?'

Natalya nods towards the coffee table.

'OK,' Tim says doubtfully. 'What about it?'

'Look carefully.'

Tim sits up. He leans forward and drags the coffee table towards them. 'Oh, shit,' he says. 'How did that happen?'

'I try to clean window.'

Tim nods. 'I, um, saw that they were clean,' he lies. 'But I don't see the . . . Oh, you stood on the table? In what – stilettos?'

Natalya shakes her head. 'So stupid,' she says. 'I put chair on table. To reach up high.'

'You put a chair on a brand-new table? To clean the windows?'

Natalya nods. She looks as scared as she feels.

140

'No kidding,' Tim says.

'No kidding,' she repeats.

Tim sinks to his knees just as Natalya had done, and again, just like her, he runs his fingertips across the damaged surface.

Natalya has a lump in her throat. She thinks she's probably going to cry. 'You're angry?' she asks.

'No,' Tim says, sounding stern if not actually angry. 'Is this from . . .?'

'Tu Casa,' Natalya confirms. 'Yes. Expensive.'

'What are we talking? Five hundred?'

'More.'

'A grand?'

'Yes. It's bad, huh?'

Tim raises his hands to his mouth and exhales slowly, then regains control of himself and says, 'No, it's fine. I'll take it back tomorrow. They'll fix it. They owe me.'

'You think so? Really?'

'Sure,' Tim says. 'Don't worry about it.' Then, noticing the tremor in his wife's voice, he sits back on the sofa and throws one arm around her shoulders, pulling her in. 'Hey!' he says. 'Babe. It's fine, really.'

'I'm so stupid,' Natalya whispers.

'As we say in Russia,' Tim says, imitating her accent, 'mistake is mistake. Stupid is stupid.'

'And you're sure? That they can fix this?'

'Of course,' he says. 'When you buy stuff at that kind of price, the customer service has to be amazing.' In truth, Tim thinks that he'll probably have to pay for a new table. But, yes, he's sure at least that they'll fix it.

'Oh, Timski!'

'It's done,' Tim says. 'Forget it.'

'And you must forget this speakers,' Natalya says.

141

'Exactly. It's a deal.'

'They were fifteen, right?' Natalya asks. 'Fifteen thousand?' Once she has said it, she doubts that this is possible. 'No, I get this wrong. It's less, yes?'

'Erm, yeah,' Tim says, embarrassed now about the ridiculous extravagance of the purchase. 'Something like that.' He'll have to phone Edwin in the morning and get him to keep the price secret. He can refund the cost to Tim's Amex card and if Natalya asks, he can tell her that . . .

'You know what?' he suddenly says. 'They weren't fifteen. They were fifty.'

'Fifty thousand?'

'Yep.'

'Wow,' Natalya says, wide-eyed and restraining a smile. 'Is big mistake, huh?'

'Yes,' Tim concedes. 'My mistake was even bigger than yours. My mistake was waaay bigger than yours. So you get to feel just fine.'

'No, we're same,' Natalya says.

Natalya is in the kitchen cubing potatoes and a slab of beef while simultaneously frying diced dill pickles. It's Sunday morning, and Tim's parents are due sometime within the next two hours. Natalya hopes that they'll come later rather than sooner. She's running behind schedule and what's more, the later they come, the shorter their visit will be.

She has been putting this off for weeks. It was easy enough at the beginning to claim that the boxes needed to be unpacked first, that they needed a sofa for guests to sit on before inviting the guests themselves, or that as the new stove didn't work, she couldn't cook . . . But as the weeks have gone by, her excuses have been getting flimsier, and finally, yesterday, Tim declared that his parents wouldn't 'give a shit' about the pool having been emptied. They were coming and that was that. And Natalya, who knows Tim's various tones of voice only too well, capitulated. 'It will be nice to have them over,' she lied.

It's not that she particularly dislikes Alice and Ken – she really doesn't. It's simply that it's impossible for Tim to spend a day with his parents without ending up furious about something they have said. And having no family of her own, Natalya can't quite see the point in subjecting oneself to that. Not repeatedly, at any rate.

'Why don't you get Vlad to do that?' Tim asks. 'Get yourself ready.'

Natalya looks up and sees him hanging on the door frame. His hair is wet from the shower. 'I am ready,' she says, then, 'and I like it. And her rassolnik is not so good as mine, you know?'

'That's certainly true,' Tim says, even though, other than the fact that Vladlena's is slightly more peppery (which he rather likes), he's unable to spot the difference.

'Where are the boys?' Natalya asks. They've been quiet for a while now and that always makes her suspicious.

'In the garden with Vlad and some kid from next door. The three of them are running her ragged.'

'It's good,' Natalya says. 'They will be more quiet when Alice is here.'

Alice actually suggested that Boris might have 'that ADHD thing' during her last visit, something Natalya has struggled to forgive her for. They're just rowdy boys, after all.

The doorbell rings and Natalya stops stirring the frying pickles in order to look all the more outraged. 'Surely not so early!' she says. 'It's only ten.'

'Nah,' Tim says. 'It won't be them yet. I'll go. You cook.'

143

Natalya returns to her cookery, but as Alice's voice rings out across the house, she sighs in dismay. '*Vot tak*,' she mutters – here we go.

'. . . so big!' Alice is saying as she approaches. 'We couldn't believe it, could we, Ken?'

'I checked the street name twice before I even dared press the doorbell,' he says.

'But our name's on the doorbell,' Tim points out.

'Yeah,' Ken says vaguely. 'We, um, we didn't really see it at first.'

'Yep, dump the coats there,' Tim says, 'and come on through. Natalya's cooking right now so I'll show you around first – Mum? Mum!'

'I'm only going to say hello,' Alice calls back, and Natalya, who can hear Alice's heels clip-clopping across the floor, braces herself. 'Gosh, this room's going to be difficult to heat in winter, isn't it?' Alice adds, as she approaches the kitchen door.

Natalya tips the diced potatoes from the chopping board and wipes her hands on her apron, then turns to greet Alice. She crosses the kitchen to head her off before she starts meddling, but Alice manages to manoeuvre herself to the stove-side of the embrace even as she kisses Natalya in greeting. 'Gosh, you need roller skates to get around in this place,' she says, already heading for the frying pan. 'Russian soup again, is it?'

'Yes,' Natalya says, frowning and following her back to the stove. 'You said you like it before?'

'Um,' Alice says, picking up the wooden spoon and stirring the potatoes. 'These are sticking. You might want to turn them down a bit. And maybe not so much pepper as last time, huh?'

Eventually, to Natalya's relief, Tim manages to lure both Alice and Ken from the kitchen on a tour of the house and gardens.

Alice's comments are all expressions of surprise about the scale of the place, about the size of the rooms, about the length of the garden. And yet, somehow, she manages to express all of this without ever offering a compliment. The house is so big it's going to be difficult to heat (twice). The floors are going to take a whole day to mop (three times). Who, she wants to know, is going to do the gardening? Because let's face it, neither Tim nor Natalya have exactly got green fingers. Nothing, not one single thing, is lovely, for example. Nothing is perfect or beautiful. And though Tim had prepared himself to expect nothing more from her, by the fifth comment he's already annoyed.

Ken, for his part, offers platitudes. 'Nice,' he says repeatedly. 'Very nice.' Occasionally something's even, 'Very very nice.' But Tim's not sure his father actually sees anything these days. He seems lost inside his own head. Tim thinks he could probably show Ken around a council house and garner much the same reaction.

Once the soup is simmering and the shop-bought beef stroganoff is discreetly defrosting (no one need ever know), Natalya washes her hands, removes her apron, and, taking a deep breath, joins the others in the lounge.

Now Vladlena has gone, the boys are playing with two plastic Slinkys that Ken has brought, chucking them with increasing vigour down the stairs and then running back to the top to do it all again.

'I love these thing,' Natalya tells Ken. 'Proper old-fashion toy.'

Ken smiles. 'Certainly beats all that computer rubbish they have these days.'

'Yes, you're right.'

'I'm not sure the boys would agree with you on that one,' Tim says, his arms crossed.

Natalya walks towards Alice. She is perched on the edge of the leather sofa and is succeeding in making it look like the most uncomfortable piece of furniture that anyone has ever owned. She

145

looks, Natalya thinks, like she's in an airport, waiting for a plane. She looks like she's about to be interrogated, perhaps by Judge Judy.

Natalya wonders if the sofa was a mistake. It's a difficult one, because the room requires something outsized, something huge, something flashy. The problem is that Alice's diminutive frame and her meek posture require something completely different. What Alice needs is a little floral armchair like the one she has at home.

What it boils down to, Natalya realises, is that Tim's parents just don't fit the room. She wonders if any of them do and feels suddenly like an impostor herself.

She sits down next to Alice, then, realising that she's perched on the edge in exactly the same way, forces herself to slide back in her seat, to throw one arm casually across the back of the sofa as if she owns the place. But despite her efforts, she's unable to make herself feel any more at home than Alice looks.

The sensation reminds her of when she was younger, when she had first arrived in London, before she'd escaped from that horrible hostess club. They had made them wear ridiculously high heels, and she used to be fine until she became aware of the men looking at her, until she tried to concentrate on the mechanics of putting one foot in front of another. Once that happened, she was lost. Once that happened, she felt like her body was an alien machine she had to somehow pilot across the room. She had tripped more than once. She had even tipped a whisky and soda over a client.

In Russian you can say that someone feels comfortable in their skin, and she felt the exact opposite of that back then, and she feels almost as uncomfortable right now. She feels no more, no less than a fake. Like the fake she really is.

She looks at Tim for reassurance but his arms are crossed, his features closed. It's his 'talking to Dad' posture. She looks at Ken, his legs splayed in a manly but ultimately unconvincing attempt at taking possession of the room.

146

None of them should be here really – that's the thing. Being self-assured in a space like this requires something that they simply don't have. It requires perhaps what they call breeding. It requires something from a previous generation, something passed on in DNA.

The boys, now bored with the Slinkys, come rioting into the room, and it's a relief, visibly, to everyone. They begin to tear around the new sofa. Alex is chasing Boris, shouting, 'Ooooh! I'm a monster! Ooooooh!'

Alice relaxes a little, even as she tries to catch the boys as they fly repeatedly past her. 'You'll hurt yourselves,' she tells them. 'These concrete floors are going to hurt your knees if you fall over.'

But the boys run on regardless, and as she watches them, Natalya realises that they at least are comfortable here. Perhaps the next generation won't feel like frauds after all. Perhaps Natalya and Tim will have managed at least that.

Alice turns to Natalya. 'They'll hurt themselves,' she says again. 'It'll all end in tears.'

'Boys! Slow down!' Tim shouts, and they do, almost imperceptibly, slow down.

'So how have you been?' Alice asks, having to lean and stretch to pat Natalya on the knee. 'Have you got over the move yet? Have you got used to the place?'

'Yes,' Natalya replies, glancing at Tim again. 'We're fine, aren't we?' She wonders if Alice can tell, wonders if her own inability to be comfortable in her skin, to be comfortable in the room, is as visible as Alice's incapacity to be at ease around Natalya.

When Natalya met Tim, she made up a whole story about her grandparents having come from the Russian aristocracy. She had told him that their wealth had been confiscated by Stalin. Actually, she hadn't really made up that story, she'd stolen it wholesale from

147

an article she'd read in a magazine. It was someone else's story – a Russian violinist's story, in fact.

She had known it was a mistake almost as soon as she'd said it, but there was no going back, so she'd written all the details in Russian in a notebook. She checked them regularly. And she has never once slipped up.

Nowadays, she has told the story so many times that she's not entirely sure it's untrue – it almost feels real. Sometimes it's the years in the orphanage, it's the mafia guys and their offer of 'work' in London, it's the years in that horrific club that feel like a nightmare.

But Alice, she fears, sees through it all. It's a woman thing, and Alice, she senses, has always been able to tell that Natalya is not quite who she says she is.

She wonders now how long you have to be someone new before you're allowed to forget the past. She wonders how long you have to live a different life before it defines you, before it washes away the stains – and the sins – of who you were before.

Alice slides back in her seat, but then shuffles forwards again. Tim and Natalya's made-to-measure sofa certainly wasn't made to measure for her. It's so deep that she can't quite work out how she's meant to sit, especially seeing as she's wearing a skirt. If she moves back far enough to use the backrest, her little legs jut out horizontally. If she sits on the edge, on the other hand, it compresses and tilts, seemingly trying to tip her on to the floor. In the end she links her arms around her knees and manages, just, to find a stable position. But she feels silly somehow, perched on the edge of this bus-length sofa. She feels silly in this room, too. It's all too big, too self-conscious, too demonstratively wealthy.

148

It's impersonal and cold, and, Alice can't help but think, all a bit nouveau-riche-Russian-bride.

Tim has given them a tour of the house and it's all more of the same. Alice has done her best to enthuse, but it's difficult because in truth she simply doesn't get the point. For who could possibly need five bedrooms? Who could need three bathrooms or a stove that heats the pan magically without getting hot itself? Who would even think of buying a kitchen tap with a pull-out shower head (good for washing vegetables, apparently!) or a sofa with an iPad in the armrest, or a hi-fi you can control from your telephone? Who needs any of it?

'Name a song, Mum, any song,' Tim is saying now. He wants to show off his new gadget, a Sonos music box that he claims can play any song ever recorded.

'I don't know,' Alice says. She's aware that the challenge is fraught with danger, though she hasn't yet identified quite why. 'How about "Old Man River"?'

'"Old Man River"?!' Tim spits, and Alice isn't sure why it's a bad choice any more than she understands from whence the song popped into her head.

'Come on, Mum,' Tim says. 'You can do better than that.'

'I'm not sure what you want from me,' Alice tells him.

'Something rare,' Tim tells her. 'Something only you would want to hear.'

Alice licks her lips and looks up at the ceiling and tries, as the boys run repeatedly past her, to rise to the challenge. 'Oh, I know,' she says. 'Something by Pérez Prado.'

'Pérez Prado?'

'Yes,' Alice says. 'The song was, um, "Cherry Pink and Apple Blossom White". That's it.'

'Now we're talking,' Tim says, tapping away at his iPhone screen.

149

Alice blushes at the memory of the song, at the realisation of where this one popped up from. Incredible, the way these things can lodge in the recesses of your mind. Most days, she can't even remember to take her shopping list to the shop, but there it is: Joe's favourite song from fifty years ago.

She glances at Ken, but he looks back at her blankly. Actually, he's not even looking at her. He's looking through her. He doesn't know the song's significance. All is well.

When she looks back at Tim, she sees that his face has a pained expression. 'It hasn't got it,' he says miserably. 'Maybe you got the name wrong?'

'I don't think so,' Alice says. 'But never mind. Play any song by him.'

'Is that P, E, R, E, Z, then P, R, A, D, O?' Tim asks.

'Yes, that's the one!' Alice enthuses, thinking that Tim has found it.

'Sorry, but it's never even heard of him,' Tim says.

'Maybe it's too old,' Alice offers. 'It is very old.'

'How about Madonna?' Ken asks. It's his own clumsy attempt at easing the mounting tension in the room.

'Don't be daft,' Tim says. 'Of course it's got Madonna.'

Ken sniffs and with a circumspect expression, looks down at his shoes, which he taps together. He thought that was what they were trying for: something that the bloody machine does have.

Alice tries desperately to think of a song that might seem rare enough that it reassures Tim while not being so rare that it trips him up again. The atmosphere in the room feels like her life depends on finding that perfect song, but it's precisely that atmosphere which is making her mind go blank.

That's the trouble with Tim these days, she thinks. His ego is so fragile, you have to look at every word you say before you let it out of your mouth just in case you say something wrong. And Alice

150

knows that's one particular game she's never been very good at. She wonders how he got to be so uptight. It must be something to do with his relationship with Natalya, because he certainly wasn't like that when he was little.

'How about that woman who won the TV programme?' Ken asks, suddenly back in the room. 'That mong woman.'

Tim turns to face his father with an expression of such hatred that both Alice and Natalya fear that an actual fight is going to kick off.

'The term "mong", Dad,' Tim says emphatically, 'hasn't been acceptable since about 1922. And anyway, I have no idea who you mean.'

'I don't think it was acceptable even back then,' Alice says, her own expression pained, then, to Ken, 'I can't believe you just said that.'

'Oh, come on,' Ken blusters on, unruffled and seemingly unaware. 'It's what everyone thinks. You know – the one who sang "I Dreamed A—"'

'Dad!' Tim shouts. 'Just shut the fuck up.'

Ken raises his hands in submission. 'Jesus,' he says, 'I was only trying to help.'

'There's no need to swear, Timothy,' Alice mutters.

'Just play something nice,' Natalya suggests. 'Play The Wild Beast.'

'The Wild Beast?' Alice repeats, leaping at this escape route that Natalya has so generously offered from Tim's Music Challenge Nightmare. 'What's The Wild Beast?'

'It's The Wild Beasts,' Tim says, emphasising the s. 'They're a group Matt put me on to. And you'll probably like it. It's very mellow. OK, here goes.'

The music starts to play. It is, indeed, smooth and agreeable if a little echoey in the cavernous lounge.

151

Ken starts to tap his hand against his knee in a visible attempt at expressing his approval, even though they all know that the only music he likes is James-Last-style easy listening.

Alice opens her mouth to ask if Tim has had any news from Matt recently, but then closes it again. She's under the impression that she is supposed to listen carefully to the music for a least a minute before she can reasonably speak. It reminds her a little of when she was at school. Mr Withers used to put a scratched record of Tchaikovsky on the gramophone player and they had to write down what the music inspired in them. The music rarely had much effect on Alice – she's never been a fan of classical music. But she had always enjoyed the exercise. It was a great excuse to write about anything you wanted, to say whatever was on your mind.

Alice's shoulders are aching a little from hugging her knees so she stands and crosses to the big picture window. As she looks out at the empty pool, Boris runs to her side. 'Are we going outside?' he asks.

'No,' Tim says immediately. Which is a shame, because Alice would have quite liked a short walk around the garden with Boris. 'You've been out all morning. We're staying in for a bit now,' he tells the boy.

Alice reaches to smooth Boris's hair, but he flinches from her touch and returns to where Alex is lying on the rug.

She starts to ask why the pool is empty, but thinks better of it. It probably has some kind of problem. Best not to mention it.

'They must be enjoying having all this space to run around in,' she says instead, and the atmosphere in the room seems to lighten under the relief of her compliment. But then, before she has even realised what she's saying, she has added, 'They're so hyperactive, those two. They need a lot of room!' And the atmosphere has noticeably darkened again.

152

Alice pulls a handkerchief from her sleeve and starts to rub at a smear on the window. 'These must be a bugger to clean,' she says.

'Yes, we need a proper window cleaning company to do them,' Tim says. 'Poor old Vladlena can't even reach as high as you.'

'I try too,' Natalya says, 'but is hard. You think you have done it, and then the sun is moving, and it's not so good.'

'Yes, I hate that,' Alice agrees. 'Newspaper and vinegar, that's what you want. Newspaper and vinegar.'

'Newspaper and vinegar,' Natalya repeats. 'This one I must remember.'

'If you've got some, I'll show you,' Alice offers.

'Mum,' Tim whines.

'What?'

'Just sit down. Just relax a bit, won't you?'

'I just wanted to . . .'

'You're not going to start cleaning the windows now, OK?'

Alice shrugs and returns to the uncomfortable sofa just as Boris and Alex start to wrestle on the rug in front of her.

'Boys, calm down,' Tim says.

Boris looks up and his little brother makes the most of the distraction by whacking him across the back of the head. The boys resume their fight.

'Alex!' Natalya shouts. 'Sorry, Alice. They're very exciting since moving houses.' She stands and pulls the two boys apart, then sits them either side of Alice on the sofa.

'Excited,' Alice corrects. 'They are excit-ed.'

'Yes, sorry,' Natalya apologises.

Alice has always been drawn more to little Alex. Boris is something of a bruiser, a future rugby player no doubt, but with his blue eyes and David McCallum mop of hair, Alex looks like a sort of cartoon child, like one of those Japanese manga children. She

153

tries now to put one arm around Alex, but he pushes her away and runs off.

Natalya, who sees this happen, and who notes Alice's pain, knows that it's because Alice always tries to kiss them on the lips – which they hate – and because they both claim that she 'smells funny', which can only be because of that horrible perfume she always insists on wearing. It doesn't suit her at all. In fact, Natalya's not entirely sure that YSL Parisienne suits anyone.

She has tried, on many occasions, to nudge Alice in a different direction perfume-wise. She has boxed and wrapped tens of bottles containing different expensive fragrances. But Alice, who is as stubborn as a mule, always goes back to Parisienne. Natalya suspects that she dumps her perfume gifts directly in the dustbin. She once gave her a jumbo bottle of Chanel No 5. She hopes she didn't bin that one, at least.

Alice, now desperate for a cuddle with one of the children, makes a lurch for Boris but he's too fast for her. He, too, takes flight.

It happens, she thinks, because the boys don't know her well enough. Natalya and Tim virtually never come and visit them these days, and invitations to visit them are even rarer occurrences. 'So how long have you been here now?' Alice asks, that thought leading to this one.

'Six weeks,' Tim says. 'That's right, isn't it, Nat?'

'Yes, nearly six.'

Mentally, Alice rests her case. She bets there aren't many parents out there who don't get to see their children for six weeks in a row.

Boris and Alex now reappear from the kitchen. Boris is making train noises and chasing Alex with a broom.

'Boris, put that down,' Tim says.

'If he falls over with that . . .' Alice warns. She's imagining him running the broom head into some piece of furniture – imagining the broom handle knocking his teeth out.

'Boris! Stop!' Natalya orders, but the boys carry on regardless. Ken raises one eyebrow and catches Alice's eye. And Alice knows what he means, and agrees.

Tim makes to stand up, so to save him the effort and perhaps the shame of having to physically intervene, Alice grabs Boris's arm as he runs by. When he kicks out at her shins in an attempt to break free, she instinctively slaps at his legs.

Everything stops. Even The Wild Beasts stop singing – by coincidence it's the end of the track. Boris, looking furious, turns to check out his parents' reaction. And seeing them surprised, concerned, angry even, he starts to howl. He rolls to the ground and clasps his leg.

'Ha!' Ken laughs. 'He'll make a good footballer, that one. Oh, me leg, me leg!'

'Boris,' Alice says, reaching half-heartedly towards him. 'I didn't hurt you. You know I didn't.'

'I'd sign him up for Man United right away if I was you,' Ken says.

Tim glances at Natalya, then turns to face Alice. 'You didn't hurt him, Mum,' he admits, 'but please don't hit the children. You know we don't do that here.'

'I didn't hit him,' Alice protests. 'It was just a little slap.'

'No, well, please don't. We don't physically abuse our children in this household. We've been through this before.'

Ken snorts. 'Physically abuse?' he repeats derisively.

'It was just a slap,' Alice says, turning to Natalya for support. 'Not even a slap – a tap. That's all it was.'

But Natalya looks as upset as Tim about it.

'Kids need a slap sometimes,' Ken offers.

The temperature in the room seemingly drops ten degrees.

'I'm sorry?' Tim asks, sitting up straight and gripping the arms of the chair like he's on a roller coaster about to loop the loop. 'Would you like to repeat that?'

'Oh, don't start making a fuss,' Ken says. 'I'm just saying what everybody thinks. That sometimes kids need a bit of discipline. Sometimes a slap is the only thing they can understand.'

Tim chews his bottom lip. 'I can't believe you're saying that to me though,' he says.

'Oh, come on, Tim,' Alice pleads. 'You know what he's saying. And, after all, it never did you any harm, did it?'

What Tim wants to say, the phrase that runs through his mind, is, 'So which bit are we talking about? Which bit specifically never did me any harm? Are we talking about the boot in the face? Or the belt across the back? Are we talking the chipped tooth, or the broken wrist? Are we talking about my head being held under the bath water, or my being locked in the cupboard with Matt for a whole night?'

'I'll, um, go set the table,' is what he actually says.

'But it's done, Tim,' Natalya tells him.

'Then maybe I'll do it again,' Tim says, already leaving the room and closing the door behind him.

Boris continues to wail theatrically. The noise, amplified by the resonance of the room and perhaps by her impossible desire to slap the boy again, drives Alice to distraction. Ken, she can see, is getting edgy too.

'Any chance of a drink?' Ken asks.

'Oh yes, sorry,' Natalya says, standing. 'I tell Tim.'

She finds him in the kitchen, already fixing a tray of drinks.

'A Bloody Mary for you, I'm guessing?' he says with a wink.

Natalya smiles weakly. 'A double,' she says. 'And quick.'

'So you're waiting for hotter weather, I assume,' Ken asks once she returns. Natalya frowns, so he points outside towards the swimming pool.

'Oh, a fuse is broke,' she explains.

'Broken,' Alice corrects.

'Actually, in England, we say "blown",' Ken offers gently. He thinks Alice is too hard on Natalya about her English. Natalya is a pretty lass, and in Ken's book, pretty lasses get extra leeway.

'Yes, blown is even better. A fuse has blown,' Alice agrees.

'Is it heated?' Ken asks.

'No, we switch it off.'

'But when it's full, it's heated?' Ken asks, speaking slowly as if Natalya might be stupid rather than foreign.

'Oh yes, it has a heat pump. I think this is right, yes?'

'Yes, love, that's right,' Ken says. 'A heat pump. That'll be nice. The kids will love it.'

'I hope.' Natalya turns and smiles at Tim, who is returning.

He places the tray on the coffee table and starts to hand out the drinks.

'Ooh, Martini,' Alice says, taking her own glass from Tim's hand. 'You know me so well, Timothy.'

'I should hope so after all these years,' Tim says. He hands Ken a can of Stella.

'Are you cold, Mum?' Tim asks, and Alice becomes aware that she's rubbing her arms.

'A bit,' she says. 'I dressed a little optimistically, I think. I thought it was summer when I looked out this morning.'

'It's not that warm in here,' Tim admits. 'Can we turn the heating up a bit, Nat?'

'It's that big window,' Alice says. 'You can feel the cold air coming off it when you sit over here.'

'Is up already,' Natalya says, 'but it will take a while. An hour maybe. The room is so big.'

'It's too big,' Alice says. 'It's going to be a bugger to heat in winter.'

'That's the third time you've said that,' Tim points out.

'Well, it's true,' Alice says.

'I think we can move to dining room,' Natalya suggests, trying to interrupt the flow of that particular conversation. 'It's warmer there.'

'I suppose it's lunchtime anyway,' Alice agrees, glancing at her watch. 'And I'm starting to feel quite peckish.'

Once everyone is seated in the dining room, Tim returns to the lounge for Alice's glass of Martini. He stands and looks back out at the garden. The sun has vanished now. It might even rain.

He forces himself to take a long, deep breath. He's feeling stressed and anxious. He's feeling angry, he realises, and he needs to calm down before he joins the ordeal of the dinner table; otherwise he's likely to lose the plot.

Just two more hours, he tells himself. In two hours' time, they'll be gone.

He had imagined, rather stupidly, that Alice might congratulate him on the house. He had imagined her patting him on the back and saying, 'Well done, son. You've done good.' But instead of that, it's too big, it's too cold, there are smears on the windows, and yes, it's going to be a bugger to heat in winter.

So it's still not enough. It's never enough. Not for Alice, not for Natalya, and not, ultimately, for Tim himself. It's like being at the gym on one of those rolling roads, running to keep still. And just like at the gym, the only real measure of progress is how fast you can run in order to stay still and how long you can keep it up for. And Tim is running. He's running at full tilt right now. And he doesn't think that he can possibly run any faster. But it's still not enough.

His chest feels tight. His left arm is hurting, too, and isn't that meant to be the sign of an impending heart attack?

Alice and Ken, he thinks. Bloody hell. Alice and Ken! He shakes his head in despair and laughs sardonically. And then he laughs again a second time, only this time it's real. Because a revelation has just popped into his head from a source unknown.

The revelation is this: that he needs to abandon the idea of ever gaining his parents' approval. Because he can see that clearly now, so clearly he wants to write it down somewhere in case he forgets it again and the moment is lost. Yes, for some reason, for some reason that is entirely beyond his comprehension, a reason that has nothing to do with Tim himself and everything to do with his parents' personal brand of madness, nothing Tim has ever done has ever been enough, and nothing – he sees this now – will ever be enough. He needs to give up on the idea of pleasing them. Because how much weight would be removed from his shoulders if he just stopped expecting their praise?

He snorts and shakes his head, and at the sound of heels, he turns to see Natalya crossing the room to join him.

'You're OK?' she asks.

Tim nods and lets his wife take his arm.

'Come,' she says. 'We can do this. We're halfway through now.'

Tim rolls his eyes comically. 'Yes,' he agrees, 'we're halfway through.'

Lunch goes off without a hitch. Tim's revelation about his relationship with his parents lasts through three full courses of traditional Russian dishes.

159

Alice, who is making an effort, manages not to mention the temperature of the house. She even remembers, in extremis, to thank Natalya for the food. 'That soup was still very peppery,' she's shocked to hear herself say, 'but lovely. So thank you!' she adds.

'And your stroganoff was bloody marvellous,' Ken tells her. 'The best ever.'

It's after coffee, when they're pulling on their coats, that things go haywire again.

'So when do we get to see you next?' Alice asks as she buttons her coat.

'I don't know, Mum,' Tim says, sounding pre-exasperated by the question. 'Soon.'

'Tim's going to come over one night and help me fix the roof,' Ken says, then to Tim, 'We've got a leak and I need someone to hold the ladder. You'll give me a hand, won't you?'

'He's too old to be going up ladders,' Alice says. 'It's too high up.'

Tim laughs. 'Sorry, Dad, I don't do roofing. But I can send a guy over to fix it for you.'

'Some Pole, I expect,' Ken says. 'All gaffer tape and sawdust and spit. That's the trouble with roofers – the only bit you can see is the bill they hand you at the end.'

'He's not Polish,' Tim says. 'Not that there's anything wrong with the Poles. Bloody good workers actually. But Gary's from Runcorn, if you must know.'

'A Scally?' Ken says. 'A genuine Scally from Liverpool? Well, that's reassuring! Renowned for their honesty, they are!'

'Look,' Tim says, 'I can give Gary a call and it can all be fixed by the weekend, or you can just buy a bigger bucket to catch the drips. It's your choice.'

'I don't want some stranger tramping about on the roof breaking more tiles than he fixes,' Ken says. 'All I need is someone to hold the bloody ladder.'

'Whatever,' Tim says. 'Take it or leave it.'

Because just like anything Tim is able to offer his parents, it's never quite what they need. If he did go to help Ken repair the roof, it would all end in tears anyway. The repair wouldn't work (and that would be his fault) or he wouldn't be holding the ladder properly, or Ken would want him to climb the ladder and fix something he has no idea how to fix and then shout incomprehensible instructions at him while he did it. Yes, there's always something wrong. And it has always been thus.

'I'll leave it then. Thanks a lot!' Ken says sarcastically.

'So how about next weekend?' Alice asks, trying to bring the conversation back to the subject at hand.

Natalya looks at Tim. She looks alarmed, so Tim pulls her to his side and links one arm around her. 'Sorry, but we've got a thing next weekend, haven't we, Nat?'

'Yes,' she lies. 'A . . . birthday. Tim's work friend.'

'That's right,' Tim says. 'I knew there was something. It's Perry's birthday.'

'It can't last all weekend, can it?' Alice asks. 'Because they're doing a special kids-go-free deal over at—'

'There's no way, Mum,' Tim interrupts. He doesn't want her to finish her sentence. He doesn't want her getting the kids onside with whatever it is.

'OK,' Alice says sourly. 'I get the picture. Come on, Ken.'

'What picture?' Tim asks, his anger suddenly frothing like a pan of boiling milk. 'We've just spent the whole day together. And you're already getting in a huff because we can't do it all again next weekend?'

'I'm not in a huff,' Alice says. 'But we never get to see you any more. We never get to see the boys.'

'You're seeing us now,' Tim says, waving one hand in front of her eyes. 'We're here, Mum. Right here, right now.'

161

'But it'll be months before we see you again, I know it will,' Alice says. 'You know what it's like. If I phone Natalya, she doesn't even answer. And she certainly never phones back. And if I phone you, you tell me you need to talk to Natalya first. It's like . . . I don't know . . . getting a hang-glider through that Israeli defence shield.'

Natalya has moved away from Tim and crossed her arms. 'You know what, Alice?' she says, switching into combative Russian mode. 'I am so busy. With no help from anyone. With . . .'

'Well, except for the maid,' Ken says, stepping in to defend his wife. 'And the designer.'

'I am SO BUSY,' Natalya repeats, 'with the moving and the boys and . . .'

'That's not the point,' Alice says. 'The point—'

'YES is point,' Natalya says. Tim tries to reach for Natalya's arm again, but she jerks it away. 'Because I am not . . . how you say . . . social secretary for Tim. If you need to see your son, you should phone him. I can't decide when Tim is free. I don't even know this.'

'That's not exactly fair,' Tim says, feeling torn between his mother and his wife – feeling stressed and anxious again. 'You know that pretty much anything you decide goes, Nat. As far as the weekends are concerned, anyway.'

'Look,' Alice says, her tone placatory. 'I just want to see more of you. You're my son.'

'You have two, actually,' Tim reminds her.

'Yes, and it's not like I get to see much of the other one, is it?'

'Well, he is in France, so . . .' Tim says, feeling a pique of jealousy at Matt's clever escape from all of this.

'I just . . .' Alice says. But she realises that she simply can't say that. There is no reasonable way for her to express to her son that her life with her husband would be a little more bearable if she got to see her children (and her grandchildren) just a little more often. And in front of Ken, she daren't even imply it. 'Oh,' she

162

says, unexpectedly changing tack, 'I didn't tell you, did I? Dot's left Martin!'

Ken looks surprised, Natalya confused. Tim, searching for connections, wrinkles his brow. 'And?' he asks.

Alice can see how that thought led to this one, but again, it would be dangerous to attempt to express that. 'I just thought you ought to know,' she says.

'Why?'

'Because you've known them for years. Because it's shocking. Still, I suppose nothing lasts forever, does it? Not even an apparently solid marriage like that one.'

'Let's go,' Ken says. 'Come on. I want to be back in time for Ireland–England. You know I do.'

Well, thank God for that, Tim thinks.

Once Ken's Mégane has pulled away, Tim sets the kids up with *Bug's Life* in Boris's bedroom, then joins Natalya in the lounge. 'Phew!' he says, chucking himself on to the sofa. 'Thank God that's over.'

Natalya shrugs. 'You invite them here,' she says.

'I know. I think it's like childbirth.'

'Childbirth?'

'Yeah,' Tim says. 'People say that you always forget the pain and end up wanting more. I always forget what hard work they are. It's weird.'

'Yes,' Natalya says, 'only is a myth. A woman never forget what childbirth is like, believe me. Is like shitting a bus.'

'OK,' Tim laughs. 'I'll take your word on that one.'

'So why did she say that thing?' Natalya asks. 'The one about Dot.'

Tim shrugs. 'Mum's mind works in mysterious ways, its wonders to perform.'

163

'I think she says we will split up.'

'Us?'

'Yes, I think it's what she wants to say.'

Tim pouts and shakes his head. 'Nah,' he says, 'it won't be anything as calculated as that. Being Mum, it was probably pretty straightforward. She probably just suddenly remembered that she hadn't told me.'

'She thinks I stop you seeing her,' Natalya says. 'She said this, yes? So she thinks if we split up, it's better for her. This is what I think.'

Tim shakes his head. 'You're slipping into full-blown paranoia now,' he says.

'In Russia we say that just because you feel paranoid . . .'

'. . . it doesn't mean they're not out to get you,' Tim completes. 'Yes, we say that here too.'

'But it's Russian,' Natalya says. 'It's from Soviet times.'

'OK. Sure. But Mum loves you to bits – they both do. You know that.'

Natalya pulls a face. Because, no, she doesn't know that at all. 'I can't believe she hit Boris,' she says – a remark specifically selected to get Tim to close ranks with her.

'Yeah, well, they were very slap-happy parents,' Tim says. 'My childhood was like an episode of Punch and Judy, only without the crocodile.'

Natalya is looking puzzled.

'Never mind. You don't know about Punch and Judy, do you?'

'No. What is . . .'

'It doesn't matter. The important thing is that I told them. We both did.'

'Yes,' Natalya says. 'Thanks to you for that.'

'It will be so difficult to heat in winter,' Tim says, mocking his mother's Brummy accent.

'You see how she cleaned the window?' Natalya says. 'With her handkerchief?'

'Newspaper and vinegar,' Tim says, still mocking Alice's accent. 'That's what you need, love, newspaper and vinegar.'

'And this soup is so pepper,' Natalya says, trying to join in but sounding more like a Russian-speaking Pakistani than she does like Tim's mother.

Tim runs one hand over his face and groans. 'I don't know why we bother,' he says. 'Really, I don't.'

And having got Tim to the conclusion she was hoping for, Natalya steps back from the precipice. Tim would never forgive her if she pushed him over the edge. If he chose, one day, to leap, on the other hand . . .

'Well, they're your parents,' Natalya says. 'This is what we do.'

'Indeed they are,' Tim agrees.

After half a minute of silence, Natalya moves to the kitchen. She starts to stack the dishwasher.

Tim, in the lounge, switches on the television and channel-hops for a minute until he finds a suitably soothing wildlife programme. It's about a female octopus who dies as soon as her thousands of baby octopuses have hatched. *If only*, Tim thinks cruelly.

But he catches himself thinking the thought and berates himself for it. As the onscreen octopus quits this mortal coil he lets himself wonder why it is that they still have Alice and Ken over. Why do they do any of it? Why for that matter does the lady octopus bother to have babies if she knows that doing so will kill her? Why . . . anything?

The answer, evidently, is unknowable. It's the same as when he was a child and he asked Alice questions. Why was she cleaning the oven if she hated it so? Why did he have to go to school in the rain? Why couldn't they eat dessert for every course? Alice's answer was always, 'Because!' Just, because.

165

And ain't that the truth?

Tim has his parents over for the exact same reason the octopus stops eating. Because, like Natalya says, this is what we do.

Tim battles year on year to earn more money to pay for ever bigger houses, because that's what we do.

Natalya returns from the kitchen and pours herself a large glass of vodka. The perfect anaesthetic against the inevitable pain of existence, Tim thinks.

'Pour me one, would you?' he asks. 'I'm gagging for a drink.'

Natalya reaches for the whisky bottle.

'Ooh, whisky!' Tim laughs. 'You know me so well, Natalya.'

As they drive away, Ken says, 'Well, it's a big old place, that's for sure!'

'Yes,' Alice says doubtfully. She's fiddling in her handbag, hunting for mints. The bag has got upended and they're all mixed up with everything else. 'You wouldn't get me living there,' she says, handing Ken a mint.

'I don't think they invited you, love,' Ken jokes.

'You know what I mean.'

'I do. It reminded me a bit of the council offices to be honest,' Ken says. 'It's all that concrete everywhere.'

Alice smiles wryly. 'That's exactly it,' she says. 'It's all very showy. It's all very expensive. But it's not actually very comfortable, is it? It's not very cosy.'

'Nope,' Ken agrees. 'Cosy, it is not.'

'And I may have already said it three times, but it really is going to be a bugger to heat in winter.'

'They look like they can pay the heating bill though.'

166

'Tim looks like he can pay the heating bill,' Alice points out. 'It's Tim not Natalya paying for it all. Natalya just does the spending.'

'Yes,' Ken says a little proudly. 'You're not wrong there. He's done OK, our little Tim has.'

'And all these gadgets everywhere,' Alice says. 'What's that all about? The thingy that heats the frying pan by radio waves or whatever it was. The computer in the armrest . . .'

'That contraption didn't have your song though, did it, eh? You got him there.'

'Is this the way?' Alice asks, turning her head to look back at the junction behind them. 'I thought we went left there.'

'I thought I'd try the 442,' Ken says. 'Avoid all those roadworks.'

'Oh, OK. And I wasn't trying to catch him out,' Alice says. 'It was the first song that came to mind, that's all.'

'The second.'

'I'm sorry?'

'The first was "Old Man River". But that wasn't good enough for him, was it? Nor was bleedin' Madonna.'

'We didn't bring them up to be like that, did we?' Alice asks.

Ken glances in the rearview mirror, then flicks on the indicator before replying. 'Like what?'

'To be so . . . you know . . . materialistic.'

'Dunno,' Ken says. 'I'm certainly not that way inclined.'

Alice snorts indignantly. 'Well, neither am I.'

'You like to shop more than I do, love.'

'If I didn't shop, we'd starve to death,' Alice says. 'But I'm not out buying expensive computer thingies every day, am I?'

'You wouldn't know what to do with an expensive computer thingy.'

'I could buy other things. I could buy clothes and make-up and perfume . . .'

'Only I wouldn't let you.'

'That's not . . . Oh, never mind,' Alice says. She sighs. Ken, as so often, is missing the point. She has spent most of her marriage feeling like she and Ken are having two different conversations about the same thing. It's like their brains live on different floors most of the time.

'I think it's Natalya's influence,' Alice says. 'Did you see those shirts the boys had on?'

Ken frowns and looks at her a little too long for comfort. 'The road, Ken,' Alice prompts.

'The check ones?' Ken says, turning back.

'Yes. By Dolce & Gabbana, they were. God knows how much they cost!'

'They'll grow out of them in a couple of months, too.'

'Exactly! It's like every single thing they have needs to be brand new. Every single thing needs to be the most expensive one. And I'm sure we didn't bring them up to be like that.'

'Nah, it can't be our fault,' Ken says. 'Because the other one sure isn't that way inclined.'

'No . . .' Alice agrees thoughtfully. 'No, I suppose not.'

'I don't think Matt even had a decent pair of socks the last time he came. They all had bloody holes in them.'

'His jeans, too,' Alice says.

'His arse was hanging out when we met him in London,' Ken says. 'Do you remember that?'

'I do. I was so embarrassed, I wanted to buy him a pair of jeans, right there. That lovely restaurant, and there he was with his underpants showing.'

'Wasn't having it though, was he?' Ken says. 'Thought he was the bee's knees with his ripped jeans.'

They drive on in silence for a while, and Alice thinks about Matt and feels that familiar flutter of concern in her chest for her second

168

son's well-being. For all Tim's faults, at least they never have to worry about him. With his pretty wife and his boisterous boys, with his big house and their two cars, he has life pretty much sewn up.

She had tried so hard to instil some kind of thirst for success into Matt, too, but like seeds on stony ground, nothing would ever take root. She remembers telling Matt off for his report cards. Ken had threatened to disown him at one point if they didn't improve; that's how bad they were. She remembers pushing him to do his homework, remembers telling him he could move up to a better stream if he only tried harder. She had tried bribing him and Ken had tried punishing him – they had used both the carrot and the stick liberally – but it was all to no avail. She remembers trying to convince Matt to take a paper round like Tim had. 'Wouldn't you like to be able to buy nice things, like Tim can?' she had asked him. 'Wouldn't you like to have a Walkman too?'

Matt had just shrugged at her as if she was speaking to him, perhaps, in Japanese. 'I use Tim's when he's not around,' he had replied. 'Why would I want one?'

Once they had accepted that Matt wasn't going to shine at school, they had pushed him to do better at sport. He had been a promising swimmer at one point, but again, the more they pushed him, the harder he had pushed back. Eventually, Ken had promised him a music centre if he made the second-grade swimming team, and as if simply to rile them, Matt had dropped out completely. They hadn't realised this until the competitions at the end of the year though, so well had Matt dissimulated. For the entire school year, he had arrived home with wet hair and wet trunks wrapped up in a towel, when in fact he had spent every evening smoking behind the bike shed with that tarty Judy Musselbrooke's lad. Ken had taken his belt off to the boy, but again, it hadn't done any good.

A fresh sensation of unease sweeps through Alice's stomach in this instant, born of the fact that she has spotted an error in her

169

own logic. For how can she blame Matt for being so resistant to their efforts to make him strive harder? How can she blame Matt for failing to work harder, for not wanting success and status and nice things and yet still exonerate herself of any responsibility for Tim's constant, determined, pushy pursuit of those same goals?

The thought makes her so uncomfortable that she closes it down with a simple, *All we ever wanted was for them to be happy.* But she has not quite managed to convince herself – it feels like a lie, or at least a half-lie – so she says it out loud. 'All we ever wanted was for them to be happy, wasn't it?'

'Of course,' Ken says. 'And Tim's certainly done OK for himself, hasn't he?'

Still a little unsettled by the experience of feeling dissatisfied with both her children and her own parenting, she turns her thoughts to Natalya, who seems like a far easier target.

'I must say, I'm getting pretty bored with that Russian soup,' she says. 'Aren't you?'

'Oh, you know me,' Ken says. 'As long as it fills a hole.'

'I swear the principal ingredient is pepper.'

'I thought it was all right,' Ken says. 'And that stroganoff thing was very nice.'

'Yes,' Alice agrees. 'It was good. A little too good, actually. I think Vladlena probably made that one.'

'That's not what Natalya said.'

'No,' Alice says. 'Well. You know what I think about a lot of what Natalya says.'

PART THREE: JOAN OF ARC

8

MAY

Alice wakes up to the sound of drumming rain on the kitchen roof beneath her bedroom window.

Ken, she knows, will be fretting about the roof leak. She's not particularly thrilled about it herself, and is more than a little fed up with mopping the bathroom floor. But left to her own devices, she would have phoned a roofing company from the Yellow Pages months ago. Only Ken's stubbornness prevents that particular problem from being fixed.

She dozes for a while, soothed by the sound of the rain, yet depressed a little at the thought of being trapped indoors all day with Ken. But when she finally does get up, she finds him pulling on his overcoat.

'Where are you off to in this downpour?' she asks.

'To the bookies,' Ken says. 'I fancy a little flutter.'

'Oh, OK then,' Alice says, trying to mask any expression of relief at this unexpected good fortune, at the joy of anticipating a lazy morning listening to Radio Four. 'Will you be back for lunch?'

Ken freezes for a moment. He's staring through Alice as he thinks about his options. He looks like someone has pulled his plug out of the wall socket. 'Maybe not,' he says, when he lurches back to life. 'I think I'll pop into the offices and check how things are going without me. I'll probably go for a pub lunch with Michael.'

Alice nods. Michael is the new managing director of Ken's remould business. He won't be thrilled to have Ken interfering, *but rather him than me*, Alice thinks. 'So I won't make you lunch then?'

'Nope. I guess not. See you later.'

'Yes, see you later.'

Once Ken has pulled the front door closed on the whooshing of cars driving past in the rain, Alice moves to the kitchen. Beyond the window, the back garden looks almost like it does at twilight. Rain is bouncing off the birdbath, but rain or no rain, it's a good day. Today is the kind of day that makes all the other days bearable. Alice can slouch around, drinking tea and eating biscuits. She can listen to *Book of the Week* without Ken turning the sound down every time he walks past. She switches on the kettle, then the radio, and settles to stare out at the rain.

The postman passes just as she's pouring the milk, so she replaces the carton in the refrigerator and scoops the post from the doormat before returning to the kitchen table.

She's shocked to find a letter from the Nationwide Building Society addressed to her. She glances a little nervously back at the front door and then rips the envelope open.

The letter informs her that her new cash card is ready to be picked up from the branch. It contains her new PIN code, a completely unmemorable sequence of numbers hidden under a little flap of waxy paper. She must not write these down, the letter says. But she must not forget them either. As if those two things were compatible.

174

She shakes her head in dismay at the malfunctioning nature of the modern world. For what is the point in specifying that you don't want the card delivered to the house if they then send a letter telling you it's ready? She thanks her lucky stars that Ken was out when it arrived.

She taps the back of the letter as she argues with herself – perhaps she can't spend the morning lazing around after all. Perhaps she needs to go and pick up the card. That way she can make sure they don't send any more letters to her home address. Ever.

Sitting on the toilet some twenty minutes later, she makes a more radical decision. She'll return to the bank and she'll close the damned account. The stupid money can simply go back in the tin. The whole thing was a silly idea anyway – she'd been pushed into it by Dot – and this way at least she can be sure that they'll never send her another letter. This way, at least she can be sure that Ken won't—

She freezes. Her eyes widen. Her heart begins to race. Because downstairs, someone is opening the front door. Someone is stepping inside. Ken is back, and the letter, the damned letter, is sitting on the kitchen table. How stupid could she be?

She wipes herself dry and flushes the toilet. She returns downstairs as fast as she possibly can without looking panicked.

'It's just me,' Ken says. 'I forgot my bloody wallet.'

Alice nods and forces a smile. 'You'll forget your head one of these days,' she says.

But she knows she's too late. Because in Ken's right hand is the letter.

She imagines various scenarios. She could run over and snatch it and run away. She could distract him by lurching at him for a kiss. That would certainly surprise him! She could pretend to see something, someone in the back garden. She could – and this, she

175

decides, is the best idea of all – feign a fainting spell, or a heart attack.

But as good as this final idea may be, it has come to her too late. She's taken too long to think about her options, and she hasn't taken enough care over her facial expression as she does so. She can see that Ken has noticed something's wrong. He's looking suspicious and creasing his brow. He's following her terrified regard, tracing the treacherous line of her own vision to the letter in his hand. And now, he's removing his glasses and raising it to his eyes in order to read it.

'So what's this then?' Ken asks, his features tightening as he scans the page.

'It's nothing,' Alice replies, her voice far more trembly than she'd intended. She crosses the kitchen to take the letter from his hand but Ken moves it away from her and turns towards the window.

'Cash card?' Ken says. 'Nationwide?'

'It's nothing,' Alice says again. She's pleased with her voice. That came out sounding far more casual. 'It's for a surprise, that's all.'

'What is?'

'I wanted to put some money away for a surprise.'

'What money?' Ken asks.

'Nothing,' Alice says. 'Just small change. You know, left over from the shopping and stuff.'

'My money then?'

'Our money.'

'Since when did we have any dealings with the Nationwide?' Ken asks, his face reddening. 'We're with HSBC.'

'I know. But as I say, it was a secret. For a surprise.'

'You've gone and opened your own bank account?'

'Yes, Ken. I've gone and opened my own bank account. Now calm down.'

176

'Without telling me?'

'This isn't Saudi Arabia,' Alice says. Ken frowns at her. He doesn't seem to know what that means. 'Anyway, it would be hard for it to be a surprise otherwise, wouldn't it?' Alice continues, struggling to soften her tone. 'If I'd told you, I mean.'

Moving the letter from one hand to the other, Ken shrugs off his wet coat.

'I thought you were going to the bookies,' Alice comments.

'I was going to the bookies. But that was before I found out my wife's been sneaking around behind my back opening bank accounts,' Ken says. 'Now I'm inclined to stay here and find out what the hell is going on.'

'Ken! There's nothing going on,' Alice says. 'Just go.' She swipes at her mouth with the sleeve of her dressing gown. She can sense beads of sweat sprouting on her top lip. Her heart is racing and she has a strange high-pitched ringing noise in her ears.

'Now just sit down and tell me exactly what's been going on here,' Ken says.

'Nothing's been going on,' Alice says again.

'Sit down!'

'No!' Alice says, her sense of outrage swelling. 'I don't want to sit down.'

'Sit the fuck down,' Ken says, now grabbing her arm and pulling her towards the table.

But Alice shakes him off. 'Who the hell do you think you are, Kenneth Hodgetts?' she asks. 'How dare you!'

'How dare I? How fucking dare I?!' Ken's rage is visibly swelling.

'That's what I said. How dare you.'

'You seem to be forgetting something here, love,' Ken snarls. 'You seem to be forgetting who's the man in this house. And it's me. I'm the man. I'm the husband. I'm the breadwinner around here. And every penny, every single bloody penny—'

177

'You're the man?' Alice interrupts with laughter in her voice. 'Do you have any idea how pathetic that sounds?'

Ken's hand flies at her, catching the edge of her cheekbone in a hard, heavy, open-handed slap, causing Alice to stagger backwards. She raises one hand to her cheek. She's shocked. Despite everything that has gone before, she's stunned. Because she didn't believe that this could still happen. It's been years, after all.

'Now bloody sit back down,' Ken says slowly, spittle spraying from his mouth as he speaks. His face looks swollen, double-sized almost. 'Sit down and tell me why you're sneaking around opening bloody bank accounts.'

'I won't,' Alice says, shaking her head and wiping fiery tears from her eyes. 'I won't sit down. If you want someone who sits to order, get a dog, Ken.'

Ken steps towards her and slaps her again with his left hand, catching her by surprise. This time the blow collides with the back of her head. Alice staggers sideways and gasps.

'SIT. DOWN!' Ken orders.

Alice slowly raises her regard to meet Ken's. She looks him straight in the eye. Time stretches strangely and during a second that seems to last thirty, Alice finds herself thinking calmly. She feels wise and clear and brave – heroic even.

This is enough, she thinks. *I'm bored with all of this. Let him kill me. Let me die, right here, right now. Let him send me away from all of this. And let the bastard spend the rest of his life in a stinking jail for it.*

They continue to stare crazily at each other like two animals facing off. Alice can see the anger, ever-present in Ken's regard. But she can see fear and confusion, too. She wonders if they were always there or if it's a new development.

'Fuck you,' she tells him quietly, her top lip curling. The F word isn't one that she's ever used before, or if she has, she certainly hasn't used it often. But exceptional circumstances call for exceptional words.

'I'm sorry?' Ken says. He sounds almost amused.

'You heard me,' Alice says. 'And you want to know why I opened a bank account? I'll tell you.' Some demon is rising within her. Some devil has taken hold of her tongue. She feels strong and angry and reckless, like some famous martyr in history, like Joan of Arc perhaps, riding into hopeless, suicidal battle. 'Oh yes, I'll tell you,' she snarls. 'Because you're a bastard. Because I don't love you. Because I never loved you. That's why I opened a bank account. I'm leaving you. Just like Dot left that bastard Martin. That's the surprise I was planning, darling. And you know what—'

She sees the fist as it forms. She sees the arm as it starts to swing. But unlike every other time, she doesn't flinch. She doesn't cower. She steps into it. She dives into the wave. *Kill me*, she thinks again ecstatically. *Do it! Kill me now.*

Even by the time the punch is over, Alice hasn't flinched. She raises one hand to her eye. She checks her fingertips – there's no blood. She licks her lips. She smiles slightly. 'You see?' she says. 'You see what you're like?'

'You're crazy,' Ken says. 'You need to get help.' He swipes his coat from the back of the chair and stomps from the room. He slams the front door hard enough to make Alice jump.

I am crazy, she thinks. She feels so unlike any version of Alice she has ever known that craziness is the only logical explanation. She wonders if she is truly possessed.

Ken will go to the pub now. He will go to the pub and get blind drunk. And then he'll return and, if she's contrite, he'll apologise. But she's not feeling contrite. So she needs to not be around when he returns.

The vision in her left eye is blurred. She probes the area with her fingertips in an attempt at measuring the extent of the damage.

179

She moves to the hallway and looks at herself in the mirror. Her cheek is red from the slap and she's going to have a classic boxer's black eye. But surprisingly, she's not dead. Surprisingly, the damage isn't even that bad. She's certainly known worse. Perhaps Ken's getting old. Perhaps Joan threw him off his stride.

She glances at her wristwatch. She has two hours before he returns, maybe three. She'll be fine. She'll do what Dot suggested and write a big cheque to herself from the joint account. She'll pack a bag and she'll leave. Finally, yes, she'll leave. And she'll be fine.

She heads to the freezer for frozen peas to calm the swelling, but then changes her mind and closes it again. Let her eye swell. Let Timothy see what his father has done. She's done sparing everyone's feelings. And she'll be needing his support, after all.

She crosses to the kitchen drawer to look for the chequebook, but it's not there. She checks Ken's office. She checks the bowl of random things in the lounge. Damn! He must have taken it with him.

She finds her purse and verifies that she still has her Visa card. She wonders if Ken can put a stop on it. She wonders how much cash she can take out in one go.

So is she really doing this then? The idea seems absurd. The adrenalin of the moment is already fading, her certainty leaking away like so many times before.

In ten minutes she'll be crying. In twenty, she will have taken to her bed. And by this time next week, she'll have forgiven him. She pushed him to it after all, didn't she? She goaded him, knowing exactly what was going to happen, didn't she? She leant into the punch.

You see? It's already happening.

Alice sinks on to a dining chair and raises one trembling hand to her lip. Joan of Arc has deserted her, taking all of her certainty with her. Her body shudders. She can taste salt. She has started, she realises, to weep.

180

She cries for ten minutes, maybe even a quarter of an hour. The sobs come in unpredictable waves and every time she thinks it's over with, every time she starts to wonder what comes next, another wave rolls in. Because that thought, of what comes next, fills her with a void, with a sense of utter hopelessness.

And then finally, thankfully, it's over. All is calm. She feels cried out. She feels tired, as tired as she has ever felt. And her eye hurts. It hurts a lot.

Her phone rings so she slides it towards her and peers at the screen. It's Dot calling.

Alice had forgotten. She was supposed to call her back last night. 'Hello?' she says. She's not quite sure why she's answering. Perhaps to share some of the blame with Dot. This is partly her fault, after all.

'Hello!' Dot says brightly. 'I'm bored to death with this bloody rain! I wondered if you fancy a film this aft'.'

So surreal is Dot's enthusiasm that Alice struggles to think how to reply.

'Alice?' Dot says. 'Alice? Are you there? Damned phones.'

Alice clears her throat. 'I can't come.'

'You can't?'

'No, I'm . . . I'm busy.'

'What's wrong?'

'Nothing.'

'OK,' Dot says. 'Go tell that to someone who doesn't know you. You're upset about something so tell me what. Is it me? Have I said something?'

Alice swallows with difficulty. It's not that she doesn't want to tell Dot, it's just that she's struggling to find the energy required to even begin to explain any of it.

'Alice!' Dot says. 'Tell me!'

181

'I'm sorry,' Alice says. 'Ken found out. About the account. That's all. They sent a letter.'

'He found out?!'

'Yes.'

'Oh, Jesus. What did he say?'

'I . . .' Alice's voice starts to wobble. 'I'm feeling very confused right now, so perhaps we can talk later?' Her voice doesn't sound like her own.

'Is he there?' Dot asks.

'I'm sorry?'

'Is Ken there?'

'No, he's gone to the pub.'

'You should come here then.'

'I can't.'

'OK, I'm coming there then.'

'No, don't.'

'I'm coming over,' Dot says. 'I'll get a minicab. I'll be half an hour, OK? Don't move.' The line goes dead.

Alice phones Dot back twice. She sends her a text too. She tells her not to come. She warns her that Ken will be back soon. But she knows Dot well enough to know that she's coming, and that nothing can stop her coming. And she's glad. She needs a friend right now. She needs someone to tell her what to do. The only trouble is that she knows what Dot will say and she doesn't think that it will be the right advice. And even if it were, she doesn't have the courage to follow it.

After fifteen minutes, Dot's imminent arrival shakes her from her stupor. Pausing to look in the mirror (Mike Tyson looks back out at her) she climbs the stairs to the bathroom. She showers and painfully applies make-up, then dresses and pulls her old sunglasses from a chest of drawers. Looking at herself in the mirror she thinks, a little obtusely, of Jackie Onassis. When she was younger she used

182

to convince herself that the sunglasses hid everything. She used to tell herself that they made her look like Jackie O. But at sixty-nine on a rainy May day, the only thing they look is silly.

I'll just open the door a crack and send her away, she tells herself. But even as she thinks this, she's imagining Dot saying, 'Oh my God! Did he do this? Has he hit you?' And she knows that she won't send her away. She knows that she'll collapse instead into Dot's arms. She'll fold into a fresh bout of tears.

Alice stares at her mug of tea. She watches the steam rising from it, then raises her head and looks out of Dot's window at the rain, gentler than before, but still falling. She's avoiding Dot's concerned, questioning regard. Her friend is waiting for her to say something profound, something definitive about the situation. She can sense this without looking at her. But her mind is a complete blank so she stares at her tea instead.

At her feet, on Dot's woolly rug, sits her hastily packed bag. So unable was Alice to think about what she might need for whatever comes next that the contents of the bag are, she knows, almost useless. But Dot had insisted, so, through tears, she had thrown random things into the bag. She sips at her tea and clears her throat, and this is apparently a mistake, because Dot takes it as a sign that she's ready to speak. She isn't.

'So what are you going to do?' Dot asks predictably.

Alice shakes her head. The spirit of Joan of Arc is a mere memory. She's just another bashed-up housewife now.

'OK . . .' Dot says slowly. 'Then do you want to know what I think you should do?'

Alice half-shrugs but still doesn't look up. She's feeling ashamed. She should be more like Dot, she thinks. She should have a plan all

183

worked out. She should have a flat and money and the gumption to build a new life for herself, but instead she's just a woman on a sofa with a mug of tea, a badly packed bag and a black eye.

'We need to go to the bank and get you some money out,' Dot says. 'That's the first thing. As much as we can.'

Alice snorts. Dot's advice is based on the assumption that Alice isn't going to go back and she has never been less sure of anything. Fifty years feels like an eternity. After fifty years it's impossible, it seems, to imagine anything different. But she's too ashamed to tell Dot that.

'And then we need to go to the police,' Dot says.

Finally Alice looks up. She pulls a face, and the process of pulling it hurts her swollen eye, causing her to flutter one eyelid behind her sunglasses. 'I'm not going to the police, Dot,' she says, imagining just how tooth-numbingly embarrassed that would make her feel.

'Why the hell not?' Dot asks. 'He punched you in the face, for God's sake.'

Alice shrugs again and pushes her sunglasses a little further up her nose.

'No, come on,' Dot says. 'Tell me why on earth you wouldn't go to the police.'

Alice clears her throat again. 'Because this isn't a sitcom,' she whispers. 'Because this is my life, not some Channel 4 documentary.'

'That makes no sense and you know it,' Dot says. But Alice doesn't know it at all. It makes perfect, albeit inexplicable, sense to her.

Dot gasps with frustration and runs one hand through her hair. She still has lovely hair, Dot has. 'OK. We can think about it later. In the meantime, let's at least deal with the money thing. Whatever happens next, you'll need money. So we need to get you some money from the bank. Ken could lock you out of the joint

184

account at any moment. He could transfer all of the money to a different account. So you need to get there first.'

'Stop,' Alice says. 'Please. Just stop.'

'Look, I understand that you're not thinking all that clearly . . .'

'Stop, Dot,' Alice says again.

But still Dot continues. 'You have to trust me on this one thing, Alice. Money is everything.'

'Money is nothing,' Alice replies.

'You won't be saying that in a week when you're penniless, living under a bridge,' Dot tells her. 'Let me take you to the bank.'

'No.'

'No?'

'Dot! I don't want to think about money. And I don't want to go to the bank.'

Dot looks exasperated. 'Why the hell not? Is it your face?'

'Yes,' Alice says, simply because it's easier than trying to explain to Dot, trying to explain to herself even, why she doesn't want to go to the bank. 'Yes. It's my face.'

'All right,' Dot says hesitantly. 'OK . . . um. Then give me your card then. I'll go.'

And again, because it's easier than fighting, because giving Dot her card and her PIN code means that she gets a break, alone, Alice gives in. 'It's two-two-seven-three,' she says as she hands over the card. 'And don't take too much. I don't want Ken calling the police.'

During Dot's absence, Alice lies on her back on Dot's sofa. She stares at the ceiling and listens to the refrigerator clicking on and off, to the neighbour upstairs walking around. She doesn't think about what's next, and she doesn't think about what happened. She's numb, but that numbness feels comfortable. And didn't Matt once like a song about being comfortably numb? It was by Pink Floyd, she thinks. She can almost remember the tune.

It's almost an hour later by the time Dot returns. 'I only managed to get three hundred,' she announces, handing over Alice's card and a wad of banknotes. 'I asked inside the branch and it's a daily limit, so we can get more tomorrow. And if you go inside, they'll give you as much as you want. You just need to take ID with you.'

'Thanks,' Alice says, stuffing the cash into her handbag. She's glad that Dot could only take out three hundred. It's still enough to make Ken angry, but at least he won't be able to claim that she was trying to clean out the account.

'Now,' Dot says. 'I had a think and—'

'I did too,' Alice interrupts, realising only as she says it that it's true. 'I'm going to Tim's place. I'm going to go back and get my car and then I'm going to Tim's place in Broseley.'

She knows, as soon as she has said it, that it's the right decision. Dot's flat is not a neutral space. Dot is not neutral either. And what Alice needs now is neutrality. She needs to be able to think properly in an unhindered way about what to do next. She needs to be able to decide without Dot pushing her this way and that. Tim and Natalya will have a much more balanced view of things.

'I really don't think that's a good idea,' Dot says.

'It's OK. You don't need to,' Alice replies.

'I think you should stay here.'

'Thanks, but that's not what I've decided,' Alice says. 'But you're a sweetheart for offering.'

'Oh, Alice,' Dot says. 'Please.'

'I'm going to get a taxi back and pick up my car. And then I'm going to Tim's.'

'I don't think you should drive either.'

'I'll be fine.'

'And what if Ken's there? What if he sees you?'

186

'He won't,' Alice says. 'The car's around the corner and I've got the keys. I don't even need to go in.'

'Let me come with you then,' Dot says. 'Just in case. You can drop me home afterwards.'

'No,' Alice says. 'Thanks, Dot, but no. My mind's made up. And that's what I'm doing.'

As the taxi approaches the end of her street, Alice thanks her lucky stars that there were no spaces available in front of the house when she had parked her car. 'Can you do me a favour, dear?' she asks the cab driver, a young muscular Pakistani lad with a pink turban. 'Can you just wait till I'm in my car and my doors are locked before you drive away?' Though she had entertained the idea of entering the house and repacking her bag properly, her heart is racing now that she's here.

'Sure,' the taxi driver says, looking worried. 'You having problems, lady?'

'Hopefully not,' Alice tells him as she hands him a twenty-pound note. 'But I'd just feel safer that way.'

The cab driver nods and frowns, then reaches for the keys and switches off the ignition. He climbs out, rounds the car and yanks open Alice's door. Then standing over her like a bodyguard while constantly scanning the horizon, he walks her to her car. She's so grateful to him that it's as much as she can do to avoid crying again.

She throws her bag on to the passenger seat and starts the engine immediately. The young man, after all, is waiting. With a wave of her trembling fingertips, she drives away.

After about a mile, she turns down the same road to the cemetery from which she had phoned Dot just a few weeks before. Here, she turns the engine off and sits and watches the drips from

187

the recent rain as they fall from the trees on to her windscreen. Once her nerves have settled, she continues on her way.

At Tim's house, she can tell even before she rings the doorbell that only Natalya is home. Neither Tim's nor Vladlena's cars are outside.

'Alice!' Natalya says when she opens the door. She looks more surprised than pleased. 'Tim's not here,' she says, confirming Alice's perception of the situation.

'Can I come in, please?' Alice asks – Natalya is body-blocking the entrance.

'Um . . .' Natalya replies, clearly struggling to invent a circumstance whereby refusing entry to your mother-in-law might be acceptable.

'It's a bit urgent,' Alice tells her.

'Urgent?' Natalya repeats. And then she notices something about Alice's face. Perhaps the sunglasses don't hide everything, or maybe Natalya has simply worked out their significance. 'Of course,' she says, stepping aside. 'Come in. Something is wrong, yes?'

'Yes,' Alice confirms. 'I'm afraid it is.'

Natalya leads Alice through to the lounge. 'Boys are still at school,' she tells her.

'Yes,' Alice says. On the lounge table, playing cards are spread out. 'You're playing Solitaire?' she asks.

'Sorry?'

'Solitaire? The cards?'

'Ah,' Natalya says. 'Nearly. This is Russian game, but almost Solitaire. Yes. You want a drink, Alice? Tea or coffee, or . . .' Her voice peters out. She leans, frowning, towards Alice. 'Your face!' she says, now reaching, rather rudely it seems to Alice, to remove her sunglasses. Alice raises one hand to retain them but then relents and removes them herself instead.

'*Bozhe moy!*' Natalya exclaims breathily – my God! 'Who do this to you?' she continues. 'You are rob or mug or something?'

Alice shakes her head gently. 'I had a fight,' she says. 'With Ken.'

Natalya is frozen in a caricature of shock. Her eyes are wide, her mouth ajar.

'Do you know what time Tim will be home?' Alice asks. 'I tried to phone him but there was no answer.'

'He is meeting all day,' Natalya says, shaking her head. 'Maybe seven, maybe eight. But God, Alice . . .' She reaches out to gently touch Alice's cheek. 'Ken do this to you?'

Alice nods.

'So you need to stay here,' Natalya says. 'Yes! I put Boris in with Alex tonight. There is no bed in the spare rooms yet, but . . .'

'I can sleep on the sofa,' Alice offers.

'No, Boris's room is better. And he likes to share.'

'OK. Then, thank you,' Alice says.

Natalya slides her hand into her pocket. She is, she realises, trembling. She has seen many bruised faces in her time, including a few looking back at herself from a mirror. Horrible memories are surfacing, memories of every bruise she ever tended to.

'You need drink maybe?' she asks, heading for the bar. 'Vodka or whisky? Oh . . . Martini, yes?'

'No,' Alice tells her uncertainly. 'It's a bit early for . . .'

'Huh! I don't think,' Natalya says, slopping some Martini into a glass for Alice and some vodka for herself.

Natalya downs hers in one, and though she's not sure why, Alice emulates her and does likewise. Something about Natalya's certainty has convinced her that this is maybe what she needs after all.

'More?' Natalya says, reaching for the bottle again.

'No, really,' Alice says, 'but perhaps I could sleep for a bit? I'm so tired.'

'Of course. Come.'

Once she has shown Alice to Boris's room and offered to change the sheets (an offer Alice refuses), Natalya says, 'I wake you when Tim is home, yes?'

'Oh, I won't sleep that long. I'm sure I won't,' Alice replies.

Whether it's because of the alcohol or sheer nervous exhaustion, she does sleep that long. She sleeps without dreams, without tossing or turning – she sleeps the sleep of the dead.

She's woken just after seven by Tim. The room is lit red by the setting sun outside the window. 'Mum,' he says. He's crouched beside the bed. He's still in his work clothes: a checked blue shirt and a pink tie, shiny cut-glass cufflinks.

'Um,' Alice murmurs as she tries to convince her mouth to work. She feels like she's taken one of those sleeping pills the doctor used to give her back in the seventies.

'Natalya told me what happened,' Tim says.

'Um,' Alice says again, blinking to clear her vision and managing, just, to sit up.

'Ouch. That looks serious. What did you argue about this time?' Tim asks.

This time, Alice thinks. Because in those two words are a whole encyclopaedia of meanings. 'This time' means that Tim has remembered every other time. Of course he has. 'This time' reveals realms about how Tim is going to react as well. By saying 'this time', he's telling Alice that he's used to this, that he's not shocked – he's telling her that, considering their shared knowledge of every other time, it couldn't be any other way.

'You don't want to know,' Alice says. 'I'll get up.'

And she's right. He doesn't. 'OK,' Tim says. 'I'll see you downstairs.'

Once Alice has washed her face and brushed her teeth (with a finger – her toothbrush is one of many essential things she has failed to bring with her) she descends the cold concrete stairs.

Boris and Alex are watching television. They are wearing dishevelled school uniforms, and Alice wonders how they got home. Perhaps Tim brought them.

'Hi, Gran,' Boris says. 'Mum says you're sleeping in my bed.'

'If you'll let me,' Alice tells him.

Boris nods. 'I'm in with Alex,' he says, 'but that's cool. He doesn't snore. Not like Dad.'

Alex, hearing his name, looks up. 'Where's Grandad?' he asks.

'At home.'

Alex rotates his head, zombie-style, so that it faces the television again.

'What happened to your eye?' Boris asks.

'I walked into a lamppost,' Alice tells him.

Boris laughs. 'Well, that was silly! Did it hurt?'

'A bit.'

'Mum and Dad are in the kitchen shouting,' Boris says as he too turns back to face the television. 'But you can watch *The Simpsons* with us if you want.'

Alice tunes her hearing. And yes, now she too can hear the argument.

Glancing back at the boys to check that they're not watching her, she crosses to the closed kitchen door. From beyond it, she can hear Tim's voice saying, '. . . whole life. It's what they do, Nat.'

'But he did hit her,' Natalya replies. 'Did you see her face?'

'Yes, but . . .'

'This is not OK, Tim. Never.'

'But you can't help them, Nat. It's just what they do.'

'I cannot believe that you say this. This is your mother!'

191

'Yes, she's my mother. And Ken is my father. And this is what they do. She winds him up until he whacks her one, and tomorrow it'll all be forgotten. And there's nothing . . .'

As Alice opens the door, Tim's voice fades. He turns to look over his shoulder at her and blushes deeply.

'It's OK,' Alice tells him. 'Whatever it is, it's OK. Just don't you argue about it as well. Please. Just don't.'

'I'm sorry, Mum,' Tim says, sounding emotional. 'I just . . . I can't deal with this shit any more. I just can't.'

'I know, son,' Alice says. 'I'll get my bag. I'll leave.'

'No!' Natalya says. 'You will stay.'

Tim glances back at his wife, and though Alice can't see his face, she can see Natalya's expression of outrage as it forms. 'Tim!' Natalya says. 'Tell her she must stay.'

'You don't understand,' Tim says. 'It's best not to get involved.'

'Tim!' Natalya growls, in a tone of voice that makes even Alice feel scared.

Tim half-turns to face Alice. 'You should stay tonight,' he tells her. 'It's late. So you should stay the night. Just tonight.'

'Sure, I get the message,' Alice says. 'And it's fine, really it is. I was leaving tomorrow anyway.'

'Tim!' Natalya protests again, her voice even deeper.

'I'm sorry,' he tells his wife, 'but that's my limit. I can't get involved. You don't know . . .'

He walks briskly from the kitchen leaving Natalya and Alice alone. 'I'm sorry,' Natalya says. 'He is stupid sometime. I talk to him. It will be OK. I will talk to him later. I promise you this.'

Alice smiles sadly. She's unsettled to find herself allied with Natalya against her own son. That was unexpected. 'It doesn't matter,' she tells her. 'Really it doesn't. I only wanted to stay one night.'

'I don't understand him,' Natalya says. 'How he can say this things.'

192

'You don't need to understand, really. But Tim's been through a lot too. With Ken. With me. And he's right – it's been going on a long time. It's been going on for too long.'

'But . . .'

'So I understand him. And it's fine! So really, just, you know . . . leave it,' Alice says.

Natalya shakes her head confusedly. 'I will talk to him,' she says. 'Now, you are hungry, I think? There is pizza in the oven if you want.'

'Yes,' Alice says. 'Yes, some pizza would be lovely, Natalya. If you have enough?'

'Of course,' Natalya says.

Alice returns to Boris's bedroom almost as soon as they have eaten. She feigns tiredness, but in truth it's just too hard to make polite conversation with Tim and Natalya. It's like the elephant in the room – namely, Alice's swollen eye – is sucking the oxygen out of every other possible conversation they might have.

She hears Tim put the boys to bed next door. She hears them talking and giggling together once he has left. She hears Natalya read them a short story, her voice rhythmic, the words indistinct. *Family life*, Alice thinks. *It can be so simple.*

She watches the patterns from Boris's stargazer nightlight as they drift across the ceiling and remembers Tim and Matt as children. It's a terrible cliché, but like most clichés, it's true: they grew up so fast. It really does seem like only yesterday.

She thinks of Tim saying 'this time', and she wonders how many of Ken's outbursts Tim had to witness. More than a few. And more than Matt. Ken calmed down a little as he got older, so Matt perhaps suffered less. Should she have left him? Would depriving them of a father have been the right choice? Even now, she doesn't know.

193

She tries to remember the good bits as well, and slowly memories resurface. Tim clamped to her back as she swam at Morecambe Bay. Matt on her shoulders watching the trains. He'd been so excited he'd peed down her back. How everyone had laughed! It had been a good day. Yes, there had been good days.

She wonders if Tim remembers that. She wonders if he remembers any of the good times, or if they've all been wiped away by the ever-present fear of his unpredictable father.

Just before midnight, she hears Natalya and Tim arguing again. This time, they're in their bedroom at the end of the hall, too far away for her to hear the words. But the tone is the same as before. Tim, being manly, sounding sane and reasonable. Natalya, sounding outraged. Yes, family life should be so simple, but it rarely is.

Alice is woken at three by Natalya opening her bedroom door. She crouches down at the bedside exactly as Tim had. 'Alice!' she whispers.

Alice rolls on to her side and then pulls the quilt around her. She sits up. This time she feels wide awake. She feels as if she was barely asleep in the first place. 'Yes?'

Natalya glances back at the door and raises one finger to her lips. Then she straightens and returns to quietly close it. 'I have to tell you something,' she whispers. 'Tim calls Ken on the telephone.'

'He phoned him?'

'Yes, he will come in the morning to take you home.'

'Oh, OK. Was he angry?'

Natalya shrugs. 'He says it's rain in cup or something.'

'A storm in a teacup?'

'Yes, this is the one.'

Alice raises one eyebrow. It still hurts slightly. She sighs.

194

'Anyway, I think you should know,' Natalya says, 'in case you don't want.'

'Yes,' Alice says. 'Thank you.'

'You will stay?' Natalya asks. 'You are not scared?'

'I don't know,' Alice replies blankly, 'but thank you.'

'OK,' Natalya says, reaching out to stroke Alice's arm. 'I go to sleep now.' She stands and turns towards the door, but then hesitates and looks back at Alice. 'You know, Alice, you should not let him do this things.'

'I know,' Alice says sadly.

'You should never let a man do this things. If someone do this thing to me, I am running away.'

Alice's eyes begin to water. She swallows with difficulty. 'Yes. Thank you, Natalya.'

And then Natalya blinks at her slowly and is gone.

'What a strange day,' Alice murmurs, dabbing at the corner of one eye.

Following Natalya's intervention, Alice can't sleep. She tosses and turns.

She watches the stars on the ceiling and tries to remember the names of the constellations. After an hour, she stands and crosses to the window. She opens the curtains and looks out at the garden. Each of the oak trees is illuminated by an uplighter set in the grass. She never noticed it before, but the garden looks magnificent by night, like the garden of a stately home, like the garden of the White House perhaps. Lit by these spotlights, the trees don't look like nature, but like opulent monuments to wealth and power.

She imagines the Mégane coming up the drive. She imagines Ken arriving at the house. He'll be relaxed and jokey. He'll act like

195

nothing has happened. As long as no one challenges him, that is. As long as no one asks him why he punched his wife in the face.

Alice won't ask him. And Tim won't ask him either. But Natalya might. There's an unpredictability about Natalya that sets Alice's nerves on edge. Because if Natalya lays into Ken, the fact of a woman standing up to him could make things turn very nasty very quickly.

Alice thinks of Tim's words. *It's what they do. It's always the same. It never changes.* And he's right. As long as they're talking about the past, he's totally right. But the future? Who knows? Not even Alice knows what the future holds. Yesterday, she had thought she was about to die and she'd been happy at the idea. Who would have thought that could ever happen?

She turns from the window. She looks at her absurd little bag again. Of course she'll go back, she thinks. But not right now. Not just yet.

She crosses to Boris's desk and retrieves her slacks from the back of the chair. She puts them on, then tugs her T-shirt over her head, followed by her old cashmere jumper.

She puts her shoes in the bag and silently opens the bedroom door.

She's able to leave the house without a sound. These concrete floors have one advantage – they do not creak, and the newfangled-looking alarm next to the front door does not, thank God, go off.

Outside, the wet gravel hurts her bare feet, but thinking that it's quieter this way, she continues barefoot until she reaches her car.

The car will make a noise, she thinks, as she pulls on her shoes then slips the key into the ignition. But if Natalya hears her, she'll say nothing. She'll perhaps smile, she'll perhaps feel glad, but she won't tell Tim. And if Tim is woken up by the sound of her car, Alice is betting that he'll pretend he didn't hear a thing.

Such a weak child, Alice thinks. She's surprised at the thought because she has never thought of Tim as the weak one before – not once. But she sees it now. She sees that behind all his bravado, behind his million-pound deals and his glitzy cufflinks, he's still just that scared little boy who cowered in the corner. He's still just the child that she couldn't protect.

We did that to them, she thinks as she starts the engine. *We made them both exactly the way they are.*

Alice drives along the empty 4 a.m. streets. Initially, out of habit, she heads along Ken's route towards Birmingham, but after crossing the River Severn she turns, on impulse, the other way.

She drives, turning randomly towards places that sound nice, but which turn out to be full of housing estates or disused factories. She drives through places she's never heard of, through Coalbrookdale and Horsehay and Lawley and Dawley before, starting to feel anxious, she heads towards a name that is at least familiar to her.

When she reaches Telford, she heads for the park, and more specifically, for the Blue Pool car park. They had come to the Blue Pool with the children many years before. Mike Goodman had given them both radio-controlled boats and Tim had raced his along the edges of the pool while Matt had been, to Ken's disgust, more interested in an ants' nest he had found.

She pulls into the little empty car park and reclines the seat as far as it will go. She's suddenly aware of being a woman, of being alone, of the darkness outside the window. She tries to summon the spirit of Joan once again. *The doors are locked*, she tells herself. *The key is in the ignition.* She pulls a coat over herself and tries to sleep.

At sunrise, she sees a woman walking an Alsatian. It's cold in the car and she's feeling damp and cramped, so deciding that she'll

197

be safer near a woman with a big dog, she gets out and walks at a respectful distance behind them. The woman walks fast, constantly jerking at the choke chain around the dog's neck. He must be a youngster. She must be trying to train him.

The grass is wet and the cloud cover still heavy but the sun is managing to shine through a gap on the horizon. It reflects beautifully on the water of the Blue Pool, not blue this morning but pink.

Eventually, they reach the far side of the park and the woman walks on towards the city centre. The dog, Alice now sees, is old. *Trying to teach an old dog new tricks*, she thinks.

Alice hesitates about the idea of following the woman, of searching perhaps for a coffee shop, but her purse is in the car, so she turns back. It's daylight now so at least she feels unafraid and, attracted by some flower beds, she takes a new path off to the other side of the park. She wonders if she'll ever find her car again. She wonders if she cares.

She checks her watch. It's almost 6 a.m. Ken will be getting up soon. She wonders what time he'll get to Tim's house. She reckons it'll be about nine.

She comes across a bandstand and, searching for some lost memory connected with the place, or perhaps merely with a similar place, she sits on the damp steps. But the memory evades her.

She tries to think clearly about what to do next. She attempts to make a proper adult decision but none of the options (go home, return to Tim's, go to Dot's) appeal.

She starts again to cry. She had thought she was all out of tears, but here they are again. She wonders if all this crying is dehydrating her. She supposes that it must be. She promises herself she'll drink more when she gets to . . . wherever she's going.

She fails, through her tears, to see another dog walker approaching. The man, in his fifties, stops in front of her. His cute black-and-white collie dog looks up at her. It wags its tail.

198

'Are you OK?' the man asks.

Alice wipes her eyes and laughs falsely. 'Yes,' she says, instantly more embarrassed than she is upset. 'I just . . . A friend died,' she says, thinking only as she says it that this is somewhat incompatible with her laughter, and then remembering that she has a black eye to boot.

'But I'm fine,' she says, forcing a smile and already standing, pulling her sunglasses from her pocket and striding away.

It takes her half an hour to find the car park again. She lets herself in and locks the door. She grips the steering wheel. She runs her tongue across her teeth – they feel furry. She could do with a shower; she could do with a change of clothes.

She pulls her mobile from her pocket. She's almost out of battery power. The charger is yet another thing she didn't bring with her. The screen says she has two per cent remaining, but even though it usually shuts down at around four per cent, it lets her check her messages before the screen goes blank. There's a text message from Ken. 'Come home,' it says simply. And there's a voice message from Dot. 'I'm worried about you, Alice,' she says. 'Are you OK? Please call me back. You're my best friend, and I can't sleep for worry, damn you.'

PART FOUR: THE OTHER SON

9

APRIL

'Put your finger there would you, honey?' Connie says, pulling the ribbon tight.

Bruno, momentarily distracted by a woman peering in, turns his attention to the package his mother is in the process of wrapping. 'There?' he asks, placing his finger at the point where the two ribbons cross.

'Uh huh,' Connie confirms.

'So who's this one for, eh?'

'Oh, some walk-in guy,' Connie replies. 'Well, the walk-in's wife, actually. It's her birthday. He's coming back for it at five.'

'Which one is it?' Bruno asks, glancing at the walls and trying to play spot-the-missing-painting.

'One of Hugh's,' Connie tells him. 'He's selling well at the moment.'

'Hugh Fleetwood?'

'Uh huh.'

'Lucky wife, eh?'

'Actually, it's kind of a funny choice for a birthday present. It's very sombre.'

'The Fleetwoods often are,' Bruno says. 'But we love 'em.'

'We do.'

'It's not that one of the dead guy holding the woman in his arms, is it?'

Connie laughs gently. 'You got it,' she says.

'That's a weird gift for a birthday.'

'Beats flowers, I guess.'

'I guess.'

'You can have that back now.' Connie pushes her son's finger away, then adds, 'So have you had any inspiration about what to get for yours?'

Bruno pulls a face. 'Not really,' he says.

'That boy is so difficult to buy for.'

'Yes, he is!'

'Clothes? A shirt? Some pants maybe?'

'He doesn't really care about clothes so much, you know?'

'No . . . I don't know . . . Some gadget?' Connie suggests. 'He lost his iPod thing, didn't he? They make really tiny ones now. I saw it on the TV.'

'No, he just uses his phone nowadays. Everyone does.'

'A trip somewhere then?'

'We're all travelled out, I think,' Bruno says.

'Yes, I guess you must be.'

'The only thing he really wants is a dog.'

'A dog?'

'Yeah. It's kind of weird the way it keeps coming up. When we were travelling together, it became like a tour of the world's dogs, you know? I don't think we ever saw a dog without him letting the darn thing lick him all over.'

Connie wrinkles her nose. 'Eww.'

'I know. Even in India, where they were, like, street dogs?'

Connie appraises the parcel, then flips it over to check the back. Finally, its having met her approval, she slides it to the edge of the counter. 'Well, maybe that's your answer,' she says, looking up at her son. She's just under five feet and her husband is barely taller. She's used to feeling dwarfed, but today, with Bruno in his tattered cowboy boots and Connie in flats, he seems even taller than usual.

'They're such a drag though, Mom,' Bruno says. 'What if we need to move to some tiny apartment over the winter?'

'You could get a tiny dog maybe. A chihuahua or something?'

'The lil ones suck – neither of us like 'em. What he wants is a cocker spaniel. He loves those dogs.'

'Well, it could be worse. They're not so big, eh?'

'Sure, but what if we want to go travelling again? What if I suddenly miss home and want to go back? What'll we do then?'

'Do you think you might?' Connie asks. She looks concerned.

'Not really,' Bruno says, 'but you never know.'

The door to the gallery opens, causing the mechanical bell hung above it to ring. Mother and son look up and then Connie steps out from behind the counter. Murmuring, 'We'll think of something, honey,' she gives her son's arm a squeeze and moves gracefully across the gallery to meet the client. '*Bonjour*,' she says.

'*Bonjour*,' the elderly woman replies. '*J'ai vu les vases en vitrine et . . .*' – I saw the vases in the window and . . .

'Yes, they're lovely, aren't they?' Connie replies in French, gesturing towards the glass display cabinet. 'There are more here. And some beautiful new raku objects we just received from the artist this morning. Do you know about raku? It's a Japanese technique.'

Bruno senses himself blushing. He grabs his jacket from the hook behind the rear wall and heads for the door. Watching his mother trying to sell his work is so excruciating that it actually makes his teeth hurt, plus not a single sale has ever happened while

205

he has been present. It's best if he escapes the scene. It's best if he leaves her to it.

His mother claims to sell his work regularly but Bruno suspects that it's all a set-up designed simply to support him. He thinks that one day he'll probably stumble upon a locked cupboard somewhere containing every pot he ever made. But for now, he, too, plays along. He needs the money. As he passes, the woman replies, 'No, it's the ones in the window I liked.' Connie winks discreetly at her son.

Bruno pauses in the doorway to the gallery and takes in the beauty of the Cours Mirabeau. Aix-en-Provence does this to him, and often. He forgets where he is and suddenly is struck by the sheer aesthetic harmony of the place.

It's a beautiful April morning, one of those mornings when the sky is of pure deepest blue and the light is what they used to call in the detergent ads whiter than white. It seems to make all the colours vibrate.

The temperature is perfect, neither hot nor cold, and yet there's a suggestion of heat in the air, a hint of the summer to come, a sense that picnics and midnight dips are just around the corner. The air, if that's possible, seems filled with optimism.

Around him, the terraces of the cafés are already buzzing with people drinking coffee and eating croissants and, being French, smoking. Waistcoated waiters are flapping white tablecloths and arranging glistening cutlery and perfectly polished wineglasses. At the top of the square, three market sellers are trying to outshout each other with news about today's selection of vegetables.

France always somehow manages to look so much like itself, Bruno reflects. It's a country that has such a strong sense of self, and that's even more the case within the sunlit streets of Provence. But

Aix-en-Provence and the Cours Mirabeau in particular look, Bruno reckons, a bit too French, like perhaps parts of a film set. Aix looks the way Canadians think France should look, the way American films make France look. He sighs and smiles. *No*, he thinks. *Not tempted by home one bit. Not yet, at any rate.*

He starts to walk towards the top of the Cours Mirabeau. The plane trees, he notices, are sprouting green. The French hack them back to ugly stumps in winter, but by August they will have spread wide and bathed the entire square in dappled shade.

As he passes in front of Les Deux Garçons café, another whiff of espresso hits his nostrils. *Hmm, coffee*, he thinks. He continues on to the top of the square, and then into the side streets beyond. Even with his mother pretending to sell every piece of work he makes, he still can't afford the prices at Les Deux Garçons.

He walks through the backstreets of the ancient city and marvels again at the effect the place has on him. For even though he has visited Aix often since his parents moved here from Toronto five years ago, and even more often since he too got 'stuck' here last September, these streets, these sounds, these smells of bread and cheese and coffee still make his senses tingle.

It's a strange thing, but there's something magical about these French streets that makes him feel more alive than he does elsewhere, more alive, in fact, than he does anywhere else in the world.

He turns a corner into Rue Aude and almost bumps into his father and Matt coming the other way. 'Ha!' he laughs. 'Fancy meeting you here.'

'Where are you going?' Matt asks. 'I thought you were at the gallery with Connie.'

'I have a coffee craving,' Bruno says. 'I was heading up to Coffee to Go.'

Matt glances at Bruno's father questioningly, and he shrugs in response. 'Sure,' Joseph says. 'Why not?'

Matt and Joseph turn back and begin to walk alongside Bruno.

'Someone's been shopping,' Bruno says, bumping his hip against Matt's waist as they walk.

'Your dad bought me jeans,' Matt says.

'Thank God,' Bruno laughs, glancing down at Matt's knees, poking as ever from his trousers.

'He made me choose Levis!' Matt says.

'There's no point in buying rubbish,' Joseph explains.

'What's wrong with Levis?' Bruno asks.

'Oh, nothing. They're great,' Matt says. 'But do you have any idea how much a pair of Levis costs these days? It's about what I earn in a week. It's criminal!'

'Never complain about the price of a gift,' Bruno says gently. 'It's not graceful.'

Matt snorts. Bruno has a whole new theory about life, the latest of many. This one comes from some philosophy book he read recently. It says the whole point of life is to negotiate it with grace. The book says, apparently, that the whole process, from birth to the inevitability of death, is like a dance. And the only reason for any of it is to make the whole process as artful, as graceful as possible, for yourself and for those around you. The Creator, the book reckons, likes (and rewards) elegance.

'Anyway, thank you,' Matt tells Joseph. 'They're great. They're beautiful.'

'And you really need them,' Bruno says.

'Yes, I really need them.'

As they cross the Place de l'Hôtel de Ville, Joseph asks his son, 'Any action at the gallery this morning, son?'

'Yeah,' Bruno says. 'Someone bought one of the Fleetwoods. And a woman came in to look at vases just as I left.'

'Your vases?'

208

'Nope,' Bruno laughs, 'but that didn't stop Mom trying to sell her one of mine.'

'Huh,' Joseph says. 'I wonder if she managed it.'

'I'll bet my bottom dollar she did,' Bruno says.

After coffee and then lunch, as Bruno drives them home in the battered Citroën C1, Matt reaches across and places his hand on Bruno's knee. To their left, the Mont Sainte-Victoire rises from the fields, dominating the landscape.

'Your folks are too nice,' Matt comments distractedly, some thought he has already forgotten leading to this one.

Bruno glances at him briefly and smiles. Returning his gaze to the almost empty autoroute in front of them, he says, 'They're nice, but they're just regular nice.'

'They're not,' Matt laughs. 'They're crazy nice.'

'You're bound to think they're nicer than they are,' Bruno says. 'They're not your folks. They're not perfect. Believe me.'

Matt laughs. 'Name one fault,' he says.

'Eh?'

'Name one fault for each parent. I bet you can't.'

Bruno frowns.

'You see,' Matt laughs, squeezing his leg. 'You can't think of anything.'

'Hold on,' Bruno says, feigning irritation. 'Gee!'

Matt rolls his eyes and turns to look out of the side window at a car they're overtaking. It's driven by a grey-haired old man. He's sitting so far forward in his seat that his nose is almost touching the windscreen. Beside him, his wife is asleep, her mouth wide open.

Bruno's parents are so much younger than Matt's, that's half the difference. Being closer in age to Matt than they are to Alice and Ken, they're an entirely different generation. Plus, at fifty-five and fifty-seven, neither of them have ever had to live through the misery of the aftermath of a world war. But even so, they are, Matt reckons, exceptionally relaxed and unusually generous.

'OK,' Bruno says, 'so Mom's really insecure about the whole art world thing, yeah? So if you ever get into any kind of argument to do with art, she'll argue with you endlessly. She'll argue with anyone about art until they surrender.'

'That's not much of a fault,' Matt says.

'It is when you work in the art business,' Bruno says. 'And Dad? He's scared of so much shit, you have no idea.'

'Scared? Of what?'

'Doctors, for one. He won't go and see a doctor, ever.'

'OK . . .'

'And dentists, and banks as well. He won't ever go to the bank. And he won't open his bank statements either. Actually he never opens any post. Mom has to do it all.'

'I never knew that,' Matt says.

'Well, now you do.'

'Anyway, I said they were nice, not fault-free. They're still the nicest parents I ever met.'

'I bet I'd find your parents cool, too,' Bruno says.

'I'll bet you wouldn't.'

'Let's say I'd at least like to have the opportunity.'

Matt blows through pursed lips. 'We've been through this,' he says. 'My parents are not like your parents. You have no idea how much not-like-them they are.'

'And?'

'And you wouldn't get on. I know you wouldn't.'

'You can't know that. You can think that you know that, but . . .'

'I do know that,' Matt says, then, 'Careful along here! Don't forget the speed camera.'

210

'Ah, yeah,' Bruno says, easing his foot off the accelerator. 'Thanks for that.'

When they get back, Matt lights a fire while Bruno heads off to a house down the road to feed the absent owner's cats.

Their three-room cabin, crafted from massive pine trunks, is set in the foothills of the French Alps. It was originally meant to be Bruno's parents' summerhouse (plus a base for occasional ski-trips in winter) but when their son returned from his travels with a surprise – namely, Matt – they had generously handed him the keys.

Being regularly snowed in during December and January, and needing a roaring fire every night up until June, it's not most people's idea of an ideal home, but once the fire is lit, the place feels to Matt like a made-to-measure love nest. He can barely believe his luck.

Bruno returns muddy-handed and brandishing four tatty leeks.

'How were Virginie's cats?' Matt asks.

'Fine. They still had loads of crunchies left,' Bruno says. 'But these are the last of the crop,' he declares, wiggling the leeks in Matt's face.

'Almost the last or really the last?' Matt asks.

'Totally the last,' Bruno says. 'Not one leek remains.'

'They don't look good,' Matt says, pulling a face.

'They don't,' Bruno agrees. 'It's snow damage. But they'll taste fine in the soup. You'll see.'

As Bruno, behind him, prepares the soup, Matt sits and stares at the flames behind the window of the stove. He lets his mind drift and physically jumps when ten minutes later, Bruno places one hand on his shoulder.

'You OK, hon?' Bruno asks.

211

Matt looks up at him and smiles. 'I think so,' he says. 'I was just thinking about that boy.'

'The kid in the store?' Bruno says.

'Yes.'

On their way into Aix they had stopped in a small supermarket to buy cans of Coke. At the checkout in front of them, a drama had been unfolding.

A father, his young boy by his side, had been trying to buy two plastic bottles of cheapest cooking wine. He had looked (and smelt) like a fully fledged alcoholic.

The cashier, a young pretty girl in her twenties, was refusing to let the man leave the shop with the wine. His Visa card, it appeared, had been refused.

But as Bruno and Matt reached the checkout, the father had started to rant, and then to shout, and then finally to bang his fist against the counter. And his child, a beautiful brown-eyed boy of six or seven, began to plead, his voice quivering, for him to stop. '*S'il te plaît, Papa*,' he kept saying, pulling at his father's sleeve. '*S'il te plaît, on y va!*'

'That kid was scared,' Bruno says.

'He thought he was going to hit her,' Matt says. 'That's why. It was heartbreaking.'

'I wondered about that. I wondered if he might hit her. Or the boy.'

'He needed his booze,' Matt says. 'That's all.'

'Huh. Still not sure that buying it for him was the right answer though,' Bruno says.

Matt nods. 'I know. But I needed it to stop. It was unbearable.'

'You were shaking.'

Matt nods again. 'He reminded me of Dad,' he says. 'That's why.'

'Really?'

212

'Yep. He used to get out of hand like that. I hated it.'

'Out of hand?'

'Yes,' Matt says. 'Nothing that bad. But it was hard as a kid to see your father out of control. And you saw how grateful that boy was when I made it all stop, right?'

'Yes,' Bruno says. 'He had tears in his eyes.'

'Isn't that what your graceful thing's all about?' Matt asks. 'Isn't it about making some six-year-old's nightmare stop?'

'Maybe,' Bruno says. 'But it only stopped till he went home and drank those two bottles.'

'And once he'd drunk them, he'd fall asleep,' Matt says. 'We bought that kid four hours of peace. Maybe five. That's less than one euro an hour.'

'If you say so,' Bruno says.

'I do say so,' Matt tells him earnestly.

As Bruno returns to the kitchen area and begins noisily to liquidise the soup, Matt remembers pleading with Ken, remembers tugging at Ken's sleeve in exactly the same way.

He had been seven or eight at the time, and Ken too had been drunk. Tim had, it seemed, broken something. Matt struggles to remember what it was but the memory escapes him. It could have been something important, something expensive like a clock or a vase, or it might have been just a cheap mug from Woolworth's. That was the thing about Ken's moods – they were utterly unpredictable.

Anyway, Ken had been drunk and furious about whatever it was, furious enough to meet Matt from school, furious enough to demand, 'Who broke it?' and to shake Matt's arm so hard he feared he would rip it from him. 'Tell me, you little sod. Who broke it?' he had shouted.

213

But Matt hadn't known, that was the thing. He was like Dustin Hoffman in *Marathon Man* being asked, 'Is it safe?' And like Dustin, though he didn't know, he had eventually caved in and replied, 'Yes, it was Tim.' After all, that was probably true. And so they had waited for Tim at the school gates.

Matt had tugged at Ken's sleeve. 'Let's go home, Dad,' he had pleaded.

'Shut it!' Ken had replied.

So they had continued to wait, Ken's foot tapping angrily, the sole of his shiny shoes sounding hollow against the playground and Matt constantly scanning the horizon, praying that Tim would for once be held in detention, or that he would see them and run away until Ken had calmed down or at least sobered up. But there he was, as bright as a button, walking towards them, wondering what was wrong, wondering why the welcome committee had turned out to greet him.

Ken had slapped Tim's face so hard that he'd crashed into the railings and cut his ear. It had bled profusely. But also like Dustin, Tim had no idea who'd broken the bowl, either. Yes, Matt remembers now: it had been a wide, low-edged fruit bowl and Ken had stuck it back together. They had continued to use it for years, lest anyone dare try to forget.

Once Tim had been reduced to a snotty, snivelling mess, grovelling on the floor, Ken had hit Matt hard across the back of the head too. 'Just in case,' he had said, 'because it must have been one of you little bastards.'

Back at the house, while the boys hid in their rooms, Ken had laid into Alice. Matt, his heart racing, had hidden under the covers and put his fingers in his ears until it was all over.

The next morning, Alice, with a hefty bruise on her arm and a strange matted patch of hair at the back of her head, had told them in apparent amusement that 'silly Dad' had broken the 'stupid

214

bowl' himself. And Matt had vowed, for the first time of many, to kill him. It was the only way, he had decided, to liberate them all from his tyranny.

'So if your father gets crazy,' Bruno asks unexpectedly, 'don't you worry about your mom?'

Matt clears his throat. Has Bruno somehow been listening to his thoughts? 'Not really,' he replies. 'She knows pretty much how to deal with him by now.'

'She does?'

Matt shrugs. 'If she doesn't, then she's had long enough to leave him. It's just not something I can help her with. She knows the score. That's their deal – it's like some kind of S&M thing almost. If she didn't like it, she would leave. You have to step away from other people's craziness at some point. I learnt that in therapy. You have to stop owning it on their behalf. Even when they're your parents.'

'That sounds . . . I don't know . . .' Bruno says.

'Harsh? Uncaring?'

'Maybe.'

'It's like that AA thing. You know, help me to accept the things that can't be changed or whatever.'

'But she's still your mom.'

'And like I said, he's still my dad.'

'OK . . . but do you miss them?'

Matt laughs. 'Define "miss",' he says.

Bruno, leaning on the counter behind him, frowns.

'There's kind of a hole where they're not,' Matt explains with a sigh. 'If that makes any sense.'

'Not much.'

'There's an absence, OK? But it's an absence of something very complicated. So it's an absence of love and fear and hatred and . . . I don't know . . . exhaustion maybe?'

Bruno nods. 'And Tim?'

215

'You'd have to ask him.'

'No, I mean, do you miss your brother?'

'Of course I miss him. But you know, we're so different. We—'

'How so?'

'Oh, Tim's very into his stuff. His CDs and his—'

'But you like music too.'

Matt rolls his eyes. Bruno is always trying to find empathy, even where there isn't any. It's sweet, but it's tiring sometimes, too. 'Sure, I like music. And Tim likes CDs. He likes hi-fi. He likes things. We didn't see that much of each other even when we lived in the same town. But sure, I miss him. And I'm kind of hyper-aware that the boys are growing up and I'm not around.'

'How old are they again?' Bruno asks, giving the soup a final stir and then joining Matt on the sofa.

'Seven and eight maybe. No, seven and nine, I think.'

Bruno is staring at Matt strangely.

'What?' Matt asks.

'I don't know,' Bruno says. 'I mean, suppose your folks died tomorrow . . .'

'They're not that old.'

'No, sure. But if they did. How would you feel? Wouldn't you have any regrets?'

'Obviously! I'd be sad not to have seen Mum, but I will see her. I'll go back soon and see everyone.'

'And your pa?'

'Ah,' Matt says.

'Ah?'

'Perhaps I'd be sad too. But not really for him. For a version of him that never existed, maybe. For the relationship we could have had if he'd been someone different. That doesn't make sense, I know.'

'It makes perfect sense,' Bruno says.

216

'Yeah, well . . . Is that soup ready?'

'It needs to simmer for half an hour.'

'Then we have time for a walk around the lake?' Matt asks, nodding towards the door.

Bruno stands. 'Sure,' he says.

Matt pulls on Bruno's thick Aran jumper. He loves to wear his boyfriend's clothes (even though they're all too big). Wearing Bruno's jumper feels like being wrapped in Bruno's arms.

The two men leave the doors to the cabin unlocked (there's no one for miles around) and head across the garden and then on into the pine forest that surrounds them. This walk is a daily ritual and their footsteps have worn a track in the feeble undergrowth.

But today, a trunk has fallen across their usual path. Bruno is able to step over it but Matt, being short, has to take Bruno's hand and climb.

'What days did you say you're working at the restaurant this week?' Bruno asks as the first glimpse of the lake comes into view through the trees.

'Just Wednesday,' Matt says. 'Plus the weekend.'

'The whole weekend?'

'Yep. That's when the plates get dirty.'

'Damn. I wanted to go over the border to San Remo or Bordighera,' Bruno says. 'Just for a day trip. Get some real Italian pizza and some cheap booze, you know?'

'We can go during the week,' Matt offers.

'You know I work weekdays.'

'I know. But you could make an exception. You could work through the weekend instead.'

Bruno nods. 'OK,' he says, 'I'll do that. Do you think it'll last all summer? At the restaurant, I mean.'

217

'I should think so. The season lasts till September. And they like me. I'm a very good washer-upper apparently.'

'And after September?'

Matt shrugs. 'Maybe the ski resorts again, if we need the money?'

'I think I need to get a proper job,' Bruno says.

High above them, a large bird, perhaps a vulture, perhaps even an eagle, screeches and flies away. 'I'm twenty-nine,' Bruno continues, 'and I've never had a job.'

'It's overrated,' Matt tells him. 'Anyway, you do have a job. You earn almost as much as I do.'

'Only because Mom pretends to sell all my work.'

'She doesn't pretend,' Matt says. 'You're just being paranoid.'

'Huh. You know, she tried to give me two hundred euros today?'

'Yeah?' Matt replies, feeling suddenly guilty, because Bruno's father made him take two hundred euros too. 'Bruno won't take it,' he had said, 'so I want you to. That way his pride doesn't get hurt and he gets to eat.'

Bruno's parents' generosity always feels so alien to Matt that he's at a loss to know how to respond. So he alternates between awkwardly refusing and awkwardly accepting their help. Today it seems that he was accepting even as Bruno was refusing. He wonders if he should tell him. 'I think it's sweet,' Matt says, testing the subject. 'The way they look after you is really touching. They really care about you.'

They reach the lake and begin to walk towards the dam along the scrubby beach.

'Water's low,' Matt comments.

'We need rain,' Bruno says. 'And I know it's sweet, but I'm twenty-nine.'

'You keep saying that like it's old,' Matt says. 'Are you trying to make me feel bad?'

'I just mean that I need to stand on my own two feet. It's important at a certain age to say, "Yes, I'm your child, but I'm an adult now." You know what I mean?'

Matt wrinkles his nose. Because though in a way he understands exactly what Bruno means, in another, having stood on his own two feet since he was sixteen, he also doesn't. And Bruno's life is so tied up with his parents' lives, Matt can't see how you could even begin to separate them out. They do, after all, sell his work. And the boys are living in Bruno's parents' summerhouse rent-free. They're driving Connie's car, too. Matt struggles to imagine what standing on his own two feet might imply for Bruno, or indeed for both of them.

'Do you miss Canada?' Matt asks.

'Why do you ask?'

'I'm not sure,' Matt says. 'I suppose I'm wondering if standing on your own two feet implies you're going back there?'

'No,' Bruno says. 'It doesn't.'

'But do you miss it at all?'

'I miss poutine,' Bruno says, laughing.

'What's poutine?'

'It's like cheese and French fries and gravy all mixed up. It's dee-lish.'

'Sounds good.'

'And Coffee Crisps.'

'Which are sweets presumably?'

'Candy bars. Yes.'

'But that's it?'

'Uh huh. I miss the people too, sometimes. Canadians are very relaxed.'

'That's what everyone says. Your folks certainly are.'

219

'It's true,' Bruno tells him. 'You Europeans are all so intense.'

'People,' Matt says, pointing along a footpath to their right where a couple are coming towards them. 'Oh my God!' he exclaims, starting to stride towards them, or, more specifically, towards their brown cocker spaniel.

Once the dog has licked every inch of Matt's face (unhygienic, but, Bruno knows, inevitable) and the couple have dragged their reluctant dog away, the men continue towards the dam.

'That's the kind of dog I wanted when I was a kid,' Matt explains, glancing regretfully back. 'There was a pet shop below the Bullring and I used to cycle there after school to muck around with the puppies. I used to go almost every night.'

'You have bullrings in England?' Bruno asks in dismay. 'I thought that was, like, a Spanish thing.'

Matt laughs and links his arm through that of his boyfriend. 'It's just a shopping centre,' he explains. 'Or a mall, as you'd say.'

'So you don't have them?'

'No,' Matt confirms. 'No bullrings in England, thank God. Though the Bullring's not much better. It's just a different kind of carnage.'

'Is that your favourite kind of dog?' Bruno asks, mentally trying out the idea of dog-as-birthday-gift and mentally rejecting it even before Matt can reply.

'You know it is,' Matt says.

'But I meant out of all the other brands of dogs that exist out there.'

'I think they're referred to as breeds,' Matt says, laughing.

'OK, breeds then,' Bruno repeats in a silly voice.

'And yeah, I think so. I really love those Tibetan mastiffs too. But they're crazy big. Like, seventy kilos or something. So . . .'

'Seventy?!'

'Yeah, but they look like big teddy bears. They're amazing.'

'But other than that, you like those spaniels, eh?' Bruno asks, nodding vaguely in the direction of the couple with the dog.

'Yeah, especially the roans – they're really mellow. They're the black and white ones like we saw the other day. Anyway, why all the questions? Are you going to buy me one?'

'Sure,' Bruno says. 'I'm gonna buy you a dog so we can never go anywhere ever again.'

'Oh well,' Matt says, feigning disappointment, 'I guess I'll just have to make do with my existing pet. I call him Bruno.'

Bruno laughs and jabs Matt in the ribs.

They reach the steps up to the top of the dam and Bruno pauses, one hand on the railings. 'Across or back?' he asks.

'Back, I think. I'm starving.'

Bruno pulls his phone from his pocket to check the time. 'It's not even seven.'

'My stomach doesn't seem to know that. I'm still starving.'

'So your folks wouldn't let you have a dog?' Bruno asks, as they start to walk back.

Matt snorts. 'It was worse than that,' he says. 'They promised me one and then changed their minds.'

'That's shitty.'

'Oh yes,' Matt agrees. 'Shitty, it was.'

The dog was to have been Matt's reward if he passed his eleven-plus exam. Matt had never wanted anything more and he had never worked for anything harder.

When he wasn't at school or at home – revising his vocabulary lists or his hated times tables – he was at Heavy Petting beneath the Bullring, leaning against the window, and, when invited in by Janine the owner, caressing the constant stream of puppies that passed through her shop.

Matt had isolated himself from his few friends in order to study for the exam. The eleven-plus had been phased out in the

Midlands by then, but Matt (or rather Ken) had 'elected' to take it anyway. The hope was that by so doing he would be able to go to the local King Edward Grammar School rather than Bournville Comprehensive where Tim went. Matt would, for the first time ever, be one up on his brother. Or so the theory went.

When the day came, he passed the exam with flying colours. His grade had been 152, which everyone said was 'exceptional'. It was certainly beyond Ken's expectations. And it definitely put competitive Tim's nose out of joint.

But on the evening before Matt's interview at King Edward's, Ken had come home drunk, and in yet another drama-filled evening, he had wiped out any hope of a dog. He had changed his mind, he said, matter-of-factly.

Matt failed to turn up at King Edward's for the interview the next morning. He was peering into the window of Heavy Petting with tears in his eyes instead. And a week later, when the interview was rescheduled, he had hidden in the park. If he wasn't getting his dog, then he wasn't going to King Edward's, that was for sure. Cutting off his nose to spite his face, Alice had called it. And perhaps it had been.

For a while he had kept returning to look at the dogs. Sometimes it made him cry, and sometimes Janine invited him in to help her clean out the cages and he got to cuddle the puppies too. But ultimately, that only made him feel worse. He wasn't a child who had a lot of friends at school, and Tim, who was older, was less and less interested in playing with him, or even being seen with him. The dog was to have been his new best friend, his confidant. Without it, he felt lost.

He had bought a dog lead, too, he remembers now – a pathetic gesture of defiance, a child's declaration that one day he would have his dog. He had even put the collar on Tim's old teddy bear, Barney, and dragged it around the room. He had made Barney's fur wet

222

with tears. Yes, the dog incident had been a huge childhood trauma for him. Perhaps unreasonably huge.

Many years later he discovered in therapy that it had also been a turning point in his life, a crucial event in the construction of his 'self', as the shrink had put it.

Because from that moment on, Matt made sure that he never met Alice or Ken's expectations of him again. Those expectations were, he had learnt, movable goalposts. Nothing would ever be enough.

Even Tim – who, with his suits and his cars must be a member of the One Per Cent that everyone loves to hate these days – never quite seems to have succeeded enough for Alice and Ken. And that really proves the hopelessness of the endeavour.

'You're so lucky to have your parents,' Matt says, linking arms with Bruno.

'Hey, Mom never let me have a dog either,' Bruno says. 'The closest I ever got was a guinea pig.'

'OK. But they never promised you a dog either, did they?'

'No,' Bruno admits. 'No, I guess they didn't. Like I say, that was a shitty thing to do.'

'So what about if your parents go back?' Matt asks. His mind has jumped back to a previous conversation.

'I'm sorry?'

'If your folks moved home. Would you still stay here then?'

Bruno shakes his head. 'They aren't going home. This was always the plan. As long as I can remember they've been saying they'd retire to France and open a little gallery.'

'Running a gallery isn't really retirement,' Matt comments, pausing to hunt for flat stones he can skim on the surface of the lake.

'Well, Mom was a counsellor,' Bruno says. 'She spent her life counselling grieving kids. Kids who'd lost their parents. Kids who'd lost brothers and sisters. Kids, sometimes, who'd lost everyone. That was her specialty. So I guess that compared to that, running a gallery probably does feel like retirement.'

'Yes, I suppose that must have been pretty full-on,' Matt says, spinning a stone and watching it hop magnificently across the surface of the water.

'Some days we couldn't talk to her when she got home,' Bruno says. 'She was never mean or anything, but some days she didn't have the energy left to talk back.'

'I can imagine.'

'She's much happier nowadays. Much more relaxed.'

'So that's it? They're where they want to be.'

'I guess,' Bruno says. 'And you? Are you where you want to be?'

Matt launches another stone, this one less successful than the last, and then straightens to look at his boyfriend. He smiles. 'You know I am,' he says.

'So I won't have to follow you back to rainy England?'

'Nope,' Matt says. 'Nope, I don't think that's going to be necessary.'

Bruno's features relax, so Matt is glad that he has said it, even if he's unsure if it's true.

It's not that he 'misses' rainy England, that much is certain.

His boyfriend is perfect. He's beautiful and calm and sexy and clever; he's young yet mature, he's tall and bearded. He's everything that Matt ever hoped for.

His adopted family are amazing too. It's no exaggeration to say that Matt feels more relaxed, more welcome, more loved, in fact, than he ever felt back home.

His life here is lovely. The house is cute – like living in some children's picture book – and even his job, washing up in a hotel restaurant, he enjoys. Katya, who he works with, is cheeky and

224

funny. Stephane, his boss, is polite and understanding. So, yes, everything here is as perfect as it can be.

And yet, and yet . . . it feels like something is missing. It feels like something is still gnawing away at his subconscious, and this most of the days and most of the time.

Sometimes he thinks it's his country calling to him. Sometimes he puts it down to a simple lack of Marmite, or *Doctor Who*, or stumbling upon Graham Norton on the telly being hilariously sarky about the Eurovision contest. At other times he suspects it's his family, who, for all their failures, are just too far away for comfort. Certainly he still thinks about them a lot. Despite the years of psychoanalysis, he still dreams about his childhood, still wakes up scared and sweating.

Then again, it could be his lack of material success that's tripping him up. He fights this one on a daily basis, seeing it as a great capitalist myth. *Buy this and look better*, the adverts say. *Buy this and feel like you've succeeded.*

Most of the time, Matt feels he's moved beyond the advertisers' reach, believes he really has risen above the poor manipulated masses. But then something on the car will break and Bruno will have to ask Joseph to pay for it to be fixed and he'll feel inadequate all the same. Something in the house will get broken and he won't mention it because he's not able to afford to replace it, and he finds himself feeling like a scared child all over again. He thinks sometimes of Tim, swimming in wealth, drowning in wealth, and he imagines how Alice would see his own life in comparison. Yes, he wishes still that he could make his parents proud.

Perhaps that's the one, perhaps that's what's still causing the gnawing feeling. Maybe even now, even at forty-two, that's what's eating away at him: the lack of parental recognition, the destabilising knowledge that his mother, his father, his brother, and along with them much of modern society, would look at his life and see nothing but failure.

How amazing to still be waiting for a pat on the back at forty-two. Maybe that's something you just never lose, because recognition is the one thing you never get. Or at least, not in a form you can recognise, not in the way you need.

When they open the door to the cabin a cloud of smoke bellows out.

'Looks like it's gonna be packet soup tonight,' Bruno comments as he calmly crosses to remove the burning pan from the stove.

Matt grabs an LP from the rack to use as a fan – it's Kurt Vile's *Smoke Ring for My Halo*, which strikes Matt as amusingly appropriate. He stands in the doorway and fans the smoke from the kitchen and watches as it mixes with the rapidly chilling evening air.

Secretly he's glad that Bruno has burnt the soup. Though Bruno is incredibly proud of his home-grown, home-cooked leek soup, it's not really that good, and Matt prefers by far the packet kind. Whatever chemicals they put in, it simply tastes better than Bruno's snow-damaged, muddy leeks.

10

MAY

Matt carries the tray downstairs to the kitchen. It's his birthday today and Bruno, who has already brought him a cooked breakfast in bed (eggs, tomatoes, mushrooms and some sumptuously delicious spinach), is preparing dishes for lunch.

'Thanks,' Matt says, sliding the tray on to the drainer. 'That was gorgeous.' He pecks Bruno on the cheek and then reaches out to dip his finger into one of the bowls. 'Home-made hummus!' he says. 'Yum.'

Bruno slaps his hand away in exactly the same way Connie always used to slap his own little fingers away from the cake mix. 'Not until lunchtime!' he says. 'Now go and make yourself look handsome while I get this all ready.'

'You're a bit full-on, aren't you?' Matt says mockingly, glancing at the kitchen clock. 'What time are they coming?'

'Not till twelve-thirty or one. But there's lots to do, so bzzzz!' He makes a shooing gesture at Matt, who laughs bemusedly and wanders off to the bathroom.

Once he's dressed in his new birthday shirt and the Levis Joseph gave him, he steps out into the garden. The table is yellow with pine pollen, so he returns for a sponge and begins wiping down the table and chairs.

It's a stunning May morning and the air is still and fragrant. A bird, unseen, is tweeting crazily from one of the taller pine trees. It sounds uncannily like a 1980s Trimphone.

'Perfect day for it, eh?' Bruno says from the doorway. Matt turns to see him proffering a red checkered tablecloth.

'Tablecloth? Really?' Matt says. 'My, we're feeling fancy this morning.'

'It's not every day your partner hits forty-three,' Bruno says.

'This is true,' Matt replies, pushing out his bottom lip.

'What?'

'I can't help but think about the big one,' Matt says. 'Fifty. Imagine that.'

'And after that comes sixty and seventy and eighty and ninety and then we get buried,' Bruno says.

'Don't be like that. I was only thinking about—'

'Yeah, but there's no point, is there?' Bruno interrupts. He waves the folded tablecloth at Matt again, and once he has taken it, returns inside the house.

Bruno has a particular aversion to any discussion about age. Perhaps, Matt thinks, it's because his age difference with Matt is a sorer subject than he likes to admit.

But he's right. The philosophers are right too. Neither the future nor the past exist. There is only now. But forty-three . . . All the same!

At five past twelve, Joseph's car appears at the bottom of the sloping, twisting, dusty driveway. Though his car is a four-wheel drive and though even the C1 manages the track with ease, Joseph always parks at the bottom of the slope next to Bruno's little

228

motorbike. 'I just prefer it that way,' he says whenever anyone challenges him about it.

'Do you want me to come down?' Matt calls out.

'No, we've got it, honey,' Connie calls back. She's carrying a large cake box and Joseph a woven picnic basket.

Once the contents of the basket – pots of tapenade and olives and pats of smelly goat's cheese – have been added to Bruno's mezze-type spread, and once the cake box (a secret – no peeping!) has been placed in the refrigerator along with the Champagne, Bruno asks, 'So what about the other thing?'

'What other thing?' Connie asks. 'Oh, that!'

Matt glances at the faces around him, one by one. Everyone is looking strangely amused.

'I might need Matt to help me with that,' Connie says. 'It's a bit unmanageable for one person.'

Matt frowns in puzzlement. Everyone still looks amused, but somehow also expectant. They look like the thing in the car might not be any old thing.

Despite years of training to keep his expectations low, Matt starts to feel excited as he accompanies Connie back down the track. She is making small talk about their drive out from Aix this morning, but there's something in her tone, some artificiality, something mocking almost, that reveals it for what it is: a carefully designed distraction from whatever's in the car.

The fact that Bruno and Joseph also follow on, either to help carry the thing or to witness Matt's reaction to it, makes him even more excited, and by the time they reach the car his heart is racing a little. He feels like a child at Christmas.

'Here,' Connie says, reaching for the handle to the Dacia's hatchback. 'I threw a blanket over it to keep the sun off.'

As the hatchback opens, Matt glances back at Bruno. He's chewing his top lip nervously. And are those tears in his eyes?

229

And then there's a sound: a whimper, a scuffle. Matt's head snaps back towards the open rear of the car. A lump forms in his throat. He stops breathing.

'We didn't have time to wrap it,' Connie is saying, still in her false, disinterested voice. 'But you can remove the blanket yourself. That's almost the same thing really, isn't it?'

Matt reaches out, and there it is again. That noise. A strangled little squeak. He tremblingly grasps the blanket. He tugs it away.

Through vision instantly blurred by tears, he peers in at the contents. He opens his mouth to speak, but only manages to gasp.

The puppy – a tiny roan cocker spaniel – rolls on to his back and writhes around and continues to whimper. He looks the same, exactly the same, as the one Matt chose all those years ago in the window of Heavy Petting. Matt pushes his fingers through the bars of the cage and as the puppy starts to lick them, he begins unexpectedly to weep.

Bruno places one hand on Matt's shoulder, but this only makes things worse. His sobs intensify to the point where he is forced to crouch down on to the dusty earth.

'Don't you like him, honey?' Connie asks, her voice, too, trembling with emotion.

Matt links his arms around his knees and begins to rock a little. 'I'm sorry,' he mumbles, still peering through his tears into the rear of the car. 'It's not that . . . I'm not, you know . . . He's beautiful. I just . . . I can't . . . breathe.'

Connie crouches down and wraps her arms around Matt. 'Honey,' she says simply. Bruno joins her, and then Joseph too, until all three of them are crouched down on the dusty earth, their arms surrounding shuddering, gasping Matt.

Eventually, Matt's tears subside, only to start up again when Bruno removes the puppy from the cage and places it in his arms.

'This is for you too,' Joseph says, reaching into the car for a carrier bag full of dog food and dog bowls and toys.

'I think he wants to walk,' Bruno says as they start back up the track towards the house. The puppy is writhing madly in Matt's arms.

'I wouldn't put him down just yet,' Connie says. 'I'd wait till you have a lead on him.'

'He needs to learn to be cuddled,' Matt says. 'He's going to have lots of cuddles, aren't you?'

'He is the kind you wanted, isn't he?' Joseph asks. 'Because they did say that if he's the wrong kind . . .'

'He's perfect,' Matt interrupts. He can't even bear for Joseph to finish that phrase. His voice breaking again, he continues, 'I can't even begin to tell you how perfect he is. And I can't think how to thank you both either.'

'It's Bruno's gift really,' Connie explains. 'Bruno chose him for you.'

'When did you do that?' Matt asks.

'Last Friday.'

'When you had the car trouble?'

'When I had the car trouble.'

'So there was no car trouble?'

'None,' Bruno laughs.

'Our gift to you,' Connie says, 'is more practical.'

'Practical?'

'Yes. It's not the dog, it's our commitment to the dog.'

'I'm not sure I understand,' Matt says. In truth he doesn't much care about anything now. He just wants to bury his face in the puppy's fur and forget everything else.

'If you ever want to go away, we'll look after him,' Connie explains.

'I always wanted a dog,' Joseph says.

231

Bruno seems shocked. 'Really? I never knew that.'

'He did,' Connie admits. 'But you were bad enough on your own. Imagine if you'd had an ally.'

'But then why couldn't we have one?' Bruno whines.

'We used to travel a lot,' Connie says, choosing to explain to Matt rather than her son. 'We went to India and Asia and all over Europe. We couldn't have done any of that if we'd had a dog.'

'And then we wanted to move here,' Joseph adds. 'To France. And that would have been complicated too.'

'Anyway, now we're settled,' Connie says. 'We're not going anywhere. And we love this little chap.' She reaches over and tickles the puppy's head. 'So any time you two want to go anywhere, you just leave him with us. That's our gift. A puppy. And no ties.'

When they reach the house, everyone sits down except for Matt. The puppy, after a two-hour drive, is frantic, so Matt puts the lead on him and gives him a tour of the garden. He pees against every tree and every bush.

'Why did Matt get so upset?' Connie asks while Matt is out.

Bruno shrugs. 'I think he wanted him a lot. I think he just wanted him a real crazy lot.'

'I hope he'll be OK. I hope we haven't opened some old wound.'

Bruno shakes his head. 'Look at his face,' he says, nodding at Matt who is walking back up the garden with a face-splitting smile.

'Have you thought of a name?' Connie asks, when Matt reaches them.

'Raspberry,' Matt says instantly. 'Or maybe . . . What's Raspberry in French?'

'Framboise,' Connie says. 'But it sounds like a girl's name.'

'Framboise. I like it,' Bruno comments. 'But why?'

'Because . . .' Matt starts. But he can sense fresh tears rising up, so he changes his mind. 'You know, I'll tell you another time if that's OK? It's a long story.'

'His official name has to begin with an L,' Joseph says. 'It's a weird French thing because he's a pure breed. The letter this year is L.'

'But they said if you're not putting him in for competitions, you can call him anything you want,' Bruno explains.

Matt pulls a face. 'No,' he says. 'No competitions. And it's Framboise. Definitely Framboise.'

'OK,' Bruno agrees with a shrug. 'It's your dog. Framboise it is then.'

Once the birthday cake has been eaten (a triple chocolate extravaganza) and Champagne has been drunk, once Connie and Joseph have moved to hammocks at the bottom of the garden to 'sleep it all off', Matt tells Bruno a little more of the story of the puppy he never had. Framboise is sleeping beside him on a deckchair and Matt gently caresses one ear as he speaks.

When he finishes the story, Bruno shakes his head dolefully. 'That's a terrible story, babe,' he says. 'That's horrific.'

'I know. When I was in therapy, it came up again and again,' Matt says.

'I'm not surprised. I mean, parents are like gods at that age. And if even they don't keep their promises . . .'

'I know.'

'And your mom didn't stand up for you?' Bruno asks.

Matt shrugs. 'She tried. But no one could ever stand up to Ken.'

'I'm not sure I want to meet him after all.'

'Well, no,' Matt agrees. 'I don't think you do.'

233

It's a strange experience for Matt, telling these stories. Because for Matt, growing up in the midst of Ken's madness, it had all seemed normal. It wasn't until he saw a therapist in his twenties (for an 'inexplicable' bout of depression) that he started to understand that most childhoods were not like this.

But even now that he has assimilated this fact, he's still always taken by surprise when he sees the shocked reactions on other people's faces.

Bruno, right now, is staring at him wide-eyed. And yet Matt hasn't even told him the full story. He still hasn't told Bruno (or anyone except his shrink, in fact) what happened following Ken's change of heart about the dog.

For though he sometimes needs to explain just enough of his past for people to understand his own sometimes bizarre reactions, he draws a line at making people hate his father unconditionally. Whatever understanding he might require to get by, he still doesn't want anyone seeing his mother as the helpless, hopeless victim that she was. And so, with the exception of when he was seated opposite the therapist, he has always edited certain details out.

Like the fact that Alice had tried to stand up to Ken that night. Like the fact that she was furious at Ken for breaking his promise to their child. Like the fact that she had insisted, over and over, that Matt must have his dog.

The more Alice had gone on about it, the angrier Ken had become, and the angrier he became the more bottles of beer he consumed and eventually, once Matt and Tim were in bed, he had started hitting her. He had wanted her to 'shut up', that was 'all'. And she wouldn't shut up. She would not stop.

Matt had, as ever, hidden under the covers. He had plugged his ears with his fingers, but tonight they couldn't block out Alice's shrieks, and they couldn't block out the resonance of the body blows which seemed to carry through the walls and floor.

Crying in his bed, Matt had tried to beam a message to Alice, *Star Trek* style. THE DOG DOESN'T MATTER, he told her, over and over. GIVE IT UP.

But Alice wasn't receiving him. On and on she went about 'that poor boy', and 'all the work he's put in', and what a bastard Ken was. Matt had never heard her rage so violently against what was, after all, Ken's almost constant injustice.

About 11 p.m., Tim had prodded Matt through the covers, and he had winced at first, then dared to peep out. Through tears, he had seen Tim in the moonlight, fully dressed and holding a cricket bat. 'We have to stop him,' he had said, above the background noise of screams and thumps. 'He's gonna kill her this time.'

Matt had doubted the ability of an eleven-year-old and a thirteen-year-old, or indeed, the ability of anyone, anywhere, of any age, to stop the monster that was Ken on a bender. But he had nodded and wiped his face on the blanket and summoned all of his bravery and got up.

The boys had crept down the staircase as far as the final landing from whence they could see the scene through the open lounge door: Alice, bloody-nosed, still swearing, still fighting, and Ken shouting, then slapping, then shouting some more.

Tim had stroked the cricket bat. 'Come on,' he had said. He had seemed to Matt as cold and fearless as a secret agent in a film. Matt had felt proud of his elder brother.

But despite his pride, he had found himself unable to follow him. He had found himself, to his shame, literally paralysed by fear. And so, when Tim reached the doorway and looked behind him for backup, he had seen his little brother still stuck on the landing, still peering through the banisters.

'Matt!' he had said. 'Come on!'

By then, though, it was already too late. Ken had spotted him and before Tim even turned back to face the room, Ken had ripped

235

the cricket bat from his grasp and hurled it across the room. As it fell, it smashed Ken's side table cleanly into two.

'You fancy a go as well, do you?' Ken had spat, kicking Tim's legs from beneath him even as Alice launched herself at his back.

But Ken, drunk, had the power of ten men, and swatting at his wife – about as annoying to him as an insect – while kicking his son in the face proved no challenge at all.

As for Matt, once he had seen how quickly his valiant older brother had fallen, he had understood that he had nothing to contribute here. And so he had run, shaking, back to his bedroom. He had hidden yet again beneath the covers. He had put his fingers in his ears and had prayed as ever for the violence to remain downstairs. And when momentarily he had found the headspace for something other than his own safety, he had prayed that his brother and mother might, too, survive this night.

And they had survived. Sure, Tim had lost a tooth (he had an implant inserted when he hit thirty to hide the fact). And Alice had broken a finger (it healed a little crooked but still worked, she insisted, just fine). There had been psychological wounds too. Neither Alice nor Tim would ever attempt to stand up to Ken again. And Tim never quite seemed to look at Matt the same way either. That was fair enough, Matt reckoned. He was clearly a wimp to the core. He knew that now. He couldn't be relied upon in a crisis. But, yes, somehow all of them had survived. And wasn't that the main thing?

'So why Raspberry?' Bruno asks, dragging Matt from his memories. 'Where did that come from?'

'Ah!' Matt says. 'Well, I told you I used to go to this pet shop, yeah?'

'In the Bullring?'

236

'Exactly. Well, more below it, but . . . Anyway, I used to look at the dogs and help clean the cages. So, the day we got my exam results, the day I knew I was going to get a dog – or thought I knew – I went down there.

'She had three eight-week-old puppies, just like this little guy here.' He nods at Framboise. 'Two of them were fighting – just play-fighting the way puppies do. But the third one was on his own, and when I opened the cage, he came over to me.' Matt clears his throat before continuing. 'He was lame. He had a dodgy back leg. Nothing serious, he could walk and everything, but he limped. And when I picked him up, he farted. And the woman – Janine, her name was – said, "Oh, he's blown a raspberry!"'

'Huh,' Bruno says. 'So you called him Raspberry.'

'I would have. But of course, I never got him.'

'Did you find out what happened to him?'

'Not really. I . . .' Matt's voice fails him. He looks away, takes a deep breath, and then manages to continue, his voice wobbling. 'I went back for a while to see him. His brothers vanished first, but Raspberry was still there. I guess people weren't so keen on a limping dog . . .'

He starts to cry again, so Bruno stands, then moves to his side. 'Babe,' he says.

'It's fine,' Matt replies, now laughing at his own silliness for crying. 'I'm just being stupid.'

'You're not,' Bruno says. 'You're being so cute, you have no idea.'

'Anyway, Janine said I could have him for half price so I held on to the dream for a while. But in the end, to be honest, I just stopped going.'

'It upset you too much?'

'Exactly. It used to make me cry. But I'm sure someone took him. He was so cute.'

237

'And your father never relented.'

Matt laughs sourly. 'No,' he breathes. 'Ken never relented about anything.'

Bruno glances towards the bottom of the garden where Connie is sitting on the edge of her hammock, rubbing her eyes. 'Mom's awake,' he says. 'I'll put some coffee on. D'you want some?'

Matt nods. He clears his throat again. 'Sure,' he croaks. 'That'd be nice.'

Matt does not sleep well that night. Framboise, at the foot of the bed, fidgets, waking him almost constantly. And even when he does get to sleep, Bruno prods him awake. 'You were having a nightmare,' he tells him. 'Are you OK?'

By the time he gets up in the morning, he has forgotten the content of his dreams. Only the tiredness and the bleary vision, only the sour taste of a tormented night remains.

When Matt looks out of the kitchen window, he sees Bruno in the garden playing with Framboise. The dog is trying to pull a stick from Bruno's grasp. He smiles at the scene and then turns towards the kitchen. He needs coffee this morning. Lots of coffee.

When eventually he steps outside, Bruno and Framboise come to meet him. 'You're up,' Bruno says, reaching out to stroke Matt's cheek. 'You had a rough night, eh?'

'It was the dog, I think,' Matt says, crouching down to cup the puppy's face in his hands. Addressing the dog, he adds, 'You kept kicking me, didn't you?'

'I think he was having dreams too,' Bruno says. 'Those little legs were running like crazy. Do you remember you had a nightmare?'

Matt pushes out his lips. 'Not really,' he says.

'I had to wake you up. You were shouting.'

238

'What was I saying?'

'Nothing comprehensible,' Bruno says. 'Just noises.'

'It was about Mum, I think,' Matt says. 'It's maybe because she didn't call. She always calls on birthdays. Birthdays and Christmas.'

'Maybe she lost your number.'

'Yeah, I expect that's it. Can I use your mobile? It's free to the UK, right?'

'Yep,' Bruno says. 'Free and unlimited. It's charging in the kitchen.'

After breakfast, Matt calls his parents' landline but there's no answer; just Alice's familiar voice and the beep of the answerphone. He doesn't call Alice's mobile, partly because he doesn't know the number by heart and he can't be bothered to get it from his own mobile, and partly because Alice so rarely answers the damned thing anyway.

'They're out, so I'll try again later,' he tells Bruno when he returns to the garden. 'So what do you say we introduce Framboise to the lake?'

'Sorry, I'm working today,' Bruno says.

'God, it's Monday! I forgot.'

'We can go tonight,' Bruno offers, 'but I really want to work. I've got an idea.'

'No worries,' Matt says. 'Framboise and I will be fine, won't we?'

Once he has showered and dressed, Matt crosses the garden to the shed where Bruno works. He leans in the window and sees Bruno pounding a lump of clay. 'We're off,' he says. 'See you in a bit.'

Bruno raises one grey slimy hand and gives him a wave.

As Matt leads Framboise into the shadowy pine forest, he wonders what Alice will say when he tells her he has a dog, then instantly

239

decides not to tell her after all. *Better not to open old wounds*, he thinks, and then, with a smile, *better to let sleeping dogs lie*.

The puppy goes crazy at the smells of the forest floor, and runs left and right, his nose to the ground, as he snuffles through the massed pine needles. Because the lead snags constantly on fallen branches, Matt quickly unclips it to let the dog run free. But Framboise never strays far from Matt, not at least until he catches a glimpse of the lake, whereupon he starts to bound ahead. Resigning himself to the idea of a chilly, life-saving swim, Matt runs after him, shouting, '*Framboise, Framboise! Ici!!*' He discovers that he hates shouting this name out loud. It makes him feel self-conscious. Perhaps it'll have to change.

When, out of breath, he reaches the lakeside beach, Matt finds the dog simply barking at the tiny waves as they break upon the shore. He starts instead to try to convince the dog to swim. He throws sticks into the lake, but the puppy just continues to bark from the water's edge.

'So you're no swimmer then!' he says.

'Woof,' the dog replies.

When they get back to the house, Matt detours to avoid Bruno's cabin. He doesn't like anyone to see his work-in-progress.

Luckily, Bruno's phone is still sitting on the kitchen counter, and this time Ken answers immediately. 'Hello?'

'Hello. It's Matt.'

'Matt!' Ken exclaims. 'How the hell are you? Where the hell are you?' Ken's voice sounds unlike himself, like a TV drama version of himself, like an actor perhaps, playing Ken.

'I'm in France still,' Matt says, frowning. 'In the Alps.'

'That sounds good. That sounds great,' Ken says, and again, those just aren't quite the right words for Ken to use.

'It was my birthday yesterday,' Matt tells him. 'Mum usually calls, so I thought I'd phone and check everything's OK?'

240

'I remembered it was your birthday. I remembered yesterday morning, as soon as I got up,' Ken says. It's almost certainly a lie. 'I just couldn't find your number.'

'Did you not get my postcards?' Matt asks.

'Of course we got them.'

'They all have the number on.'

'Yes, well, I couldn't find them. I expect your mother tidied them away. Did you get anything nice?'

Matt rubs his tongue across his teeth before replying. 'Yes, a dog,' he says. His tone, he realises, was more challenging – more aggressive – than he had intended. He's met with silence.

'I got a dog,' Matt says again, more softly. 'A puppy.'

'A dog, eh?' Ken replies. 'Well, there's a thing.'

Matt sighs and shakes his head. He's not sure what he expected. He's not sure what he ever expects. Some meaningful comment perhaps? An apology maybe? An apology for everything that ever happened? 'Is Mum there?' he asks.

'Um, no,' Ken says.

'Is she at the shops? Should I call back later?'

An overly long silence ensues until eventually, Matt prompts, 'Dad? Are you still there?'

'Yes, son, I'm here.'

Matt pulls a face at the sound of the word 'son'. He can't remember Ken ever having used it before. 'Is something wrong?'

'She's, um, gone off, Matt. That's the thing.'

Matt drops his left hand to the ground where Framboise immediately starts to lick it. 'What do you mean, she's gone off?'

Ken clears his throat. Matt can imagine him shuffling from side to side in his favourite chair. 'She's gone away for a bit, Matt.'

'Gone away?'

'And there's no point asking me where, and there's no point asking me why. You know what your mother's like.'

241

Yes, I know what she's like, Matt thinks. *And she never goes any-where.* 'You had a fight?'

'Not really. She just went off. It's that Dot's fault.'

'Dot? What's Dot got to do with it?'

'She left Martin,' Ken says. 'And I think it gave your mother ideas.'

'Mum's left you?!' Matt says.

'No! I didn't say that. I said she's gone off for a bit. Look, I have to go now, son. I've a meeting with the accountant. But do call again soon.'

The line clicks dead. Matt lowers Bruno's phone from his ear and frowns at it. 'Do call again soon?' he repeats in a silly voice. 'Do call again soon?!'

'You stay there,' he tells the dog. 'I need to find Mum's number.'

With an increasing sense of anxiety, Matt calls Alice's number repeatedly. But it goes straight to voicemail every time.

Hunting through the contact list on his old mobile for num-bers, he calls Dot's house (no reply), then Tim's landline (discon-nected), then his mobile (voicemail), and finally Natalya. He's never felt particularly close to Tim's Russian wife – she has always struck him as something of a cold fish – but at least she tends to answer her phone.

'Hello?' she says. 'Who is?'

Matt exhales a sigh of relief. 'Nat,' he says, 'it's Matt. Tim's brother.'

'Oh, Matt! I see some foreign number and I worry who it is. You OK?'

'Yes, I'm OK. But I phoned Dad. What's going on, Nat?'

'Ah yes,' Natalya replies. 'Big dramas. Tim says she has lose the plot, but between you and me, I think she has made good decision.'

242

'Has she left him? Is that what's happened?'

'Yes, he hits her. You know about this?'

'Oh, um – well, he used to. Not for years, but yes. Where is she?'

'She is with . . . Oh, I forget. It's a secret. If I tell you, you don't tell Ken, OK? And you don't tell Tim neither.'

'Of course not.'

'She is with her friend Dot. This is Dorothy, yes?'

'Yes.'

'For two weeks now, I think . . . Yes . . . Monday. So it's two weeks.'

'So this is serious,' Matt says. 'Jesus.'

'I think it is. Her face . . . You know . . . It was not so good.'

'He hit her?'

'Yes! I tell you this.'

'I thought you meant . . . never mind.'

'He hits her, and I say, you must leave him, Alice. But don't tell Tim. He wants to stay neutral, he says. He thinks he is Switzerland.'

'No,' Matt says. 'No, I won't tell anyone. Is she OK though?'

'I'm sorry. This is all I know. She is with Dot. But you can call her. She has her mobile.'

'It's not answering,' Matt explains. 'I've been trying all morning.'

'Is probably just empty,' Natalya says. 'She never charges. But keep to try. And don't worry. I'm sure she is OK with Dot.'

Matt tries Alice's number twice more but gets only the same result: voicemail. He finally leaves a message giving his own French mobile number, then plugs his own phone in to charge.

He paces back and forth across the kitchen floor a few times. He kneels down and buries his face in the warmth of the now sleeping puppy's fur. But nothing can calm his nerves. He's surprised at his own distress. He had lied to himself. He had told himself that he'd distanced himself from Alice's and Ken's dramas. He had convinced himself that he was beyond their reach. But suddenly he wants to hide beneath the covers and put his fingers in his ears. Suddenly he wants Tim to hit Ken with a cricket bat all over again.

Unable to settle, he breaks his own rule and walks down the garden to Bruno's shed. 'Hey,' he says, leaning in through the window.

Bruno, in the middle of some delicate operation involving gluing sheets of clay together, looks up. 'Hey,' he says.

'I know you're busy, but can we talk?'

'Sure,' Bruno replies, albeit distractedly. 'These tubes are bastards to stick together.'

'My mum's left my dad.'

'Uh?' Bruno says, glancing up again. He looks at Matt blankly for a moment until the meaning of the words sinks in. 'Really?' he says, finally letting go of the rolled sheet of clay which sinks, in slow motion, until it's flat again.

For an hour, Bruno accompanies Matt in his worrying. He holds him in his arms, he paces the garden beside him. He tries to think of intelligent things to say.

But in truth, he can't help. In truth, no one can help Matt, and until they have more information, there are no intelligent things to say. And eventually, seeing that far from soothing Matt, his attempts at conversation are in fact irritating him, he gives up and returns to his pottery.

At two, Matt finally hears a ring tone. 'Mum!' he almost shouts into the phone. 'I've been trying to call you.'

'Matt?' Alice says.

'Yes.'

244

'Oh, I'm sorry. I forgot to type that code thingy in. So the damned thing was off, even though it was on.' Her voice sounds strangely relaxed considering the circumstances.

'Right,' Matt says. 'Are you OK? Are you at Dot's? Natalya said you're at Dot's.'

'Calm down, dear,' Alice laughs. 'I'm fine.'

'But you are at Dot's?'

'Yes, that's right. I needed a few days on my own, that's all.'

'You had a fight? With Dad?'

'Yes, something like that.'

'Natalya said he hit you again.'

Alice sighs at the end of the line. Discussing this with anyone makes her incredibly uncomfortable, but to discuss it with her son seems almost impossible. 'We had a bit of a fight, that's all. You know how he gets.'

'Yes, I know how he gets, but I thought that was all over.'

'I'm just at Dot's for a few days while I think things through. It's nothing to worry about.'

'While you think things through?'

'Yes.'

'Are we talking . . . I mean . . .' Matt coughs. 'Are you leaving him? Permanently, I mean.'

'I don't know, dear,' Alice says. 'I'm having trouble . . .' Her voice has begun to wobble a little, so she pauses and takes a calming breath. 'I'm having a little trouble seeing things clearly at the moment,' she says in a monotone voice.

'Don't go back,' Matt says. He's as shocked at his own words as Alice is. 'Don't go back, Mum,' he says again.

Alice, welling up on the other end of the line, struggles to reply.

'You deserve better,' Matt says softly. 'You always did. Don't go back.'

Alice coughs. 'It's complicated though, isn't it?'

245

'Do you want me to come home?' Matt asks. 'I should come home and help you sort things out, shouldn't I?'

'No,' Alice says. 'No, that wouldn't solve anything. There wouldn't even be anywhere for you to stay. You'd have to stay at the house, and . . . No, really. Don't. Please don't do that.'

'But if you're at Dot's . . .'

'Yes. It's only tiny.'

'Tiny? Did they move?'

'Oh no, dear. They split up. Dot's in a flat now. I'm staying on her couch.'

'Oh yeah,' Matt says. 'Dad mentioned that. Christ. It's like *Drowning by Numbers*.'

'I'm sorry?'

'Oh, nothing. It's just a film. They all kill their husbands. Tell me how you are, Mum. I'm worried.'

'I'm absolutely fine.'

'You can't be fine.'

Alice laughs. 'No. OK then, all things considered, I'm OK though. Really I am. Dot's been wonderful.'

'So what are you going to do?'

'I . . .'

'Mum?'

'You know what?' Alice says after a pause. 'Can you do me a favour?'

'Anything.'

'Can you tell me a bit about you?'

'Me?'

'Yes, I'm exhausted with thinking about me. So tell me about you. I'd love to know what you're up to.'

'Um, OK . . .' Matt says doubtfully. 'What do you want to know?'

'I don't know,' Alice replies. 'Where are you living? What job are you doing? Are you happy?' *I so want someone to be happy*, Alice thinks, *just to prove that it's possible.*

So Matt describes the cabin. He tells her about the lake. He tells her about the hotel he works in. 'And yes,' he says. 'I'm pretty happy right now. Well, I was. Now I'm worried about you.'

Bruno resurfaces from his shed just after four to find Matt in a deckchair chewing his fingernails.

'You done?' Matt asks. 'Or just having a break?'

'Done,' Bruno says. 'It's not working anyway. What's up with you?'

'Nothing.'

'You look stressed.'

Matt snorts. 'I got through to Mum,' he says. 'She has left him. She's staying with a friend who also left her husband. Mum's sleeping on her couch. Can you believe that? She's almost seventy, and she's sleeping on someone's couch.'

'Wow,' Bruno says, then, 'Where's Framboise?'

'Sleeping,' Matt says. 'He sleeps all the time. Do you think that's normal?'

Bruno nods. 'The guy in the store said that he would. It's because he's still just a baby.'

'I'm not sure about the whole Framboise thing,' Matt says.

Bruno looks horrified. 'Really?! What's wrong with him?'

Matt laughs. 'Not the dog. The name! I felt really stupid calling him when he ran off. It's a bit . . . I don't know . . . cutesy, I suppose. He doesn't really look like a Framboise to me after all.'

'I know what you're saying,' Bruno agrees. 'I thought the same thing. But he's your dog, so . . .'

'I might try to find a better name,' Matt says.

247

'Can I tell you what I wanted to call him?'

'Sure. Fire away.'

'Jarvis!' Bruno says. 'Like Jarvis Cocker. Jarvis Cocker spaniel. Get it?'

Matt snorts. 'Jarvis,' he repeats. 'I like that.' He starts to chew his fingernails again.

A shadow crosses Bruno's features. He pulls a chair up next to Matt and takes Matt's hand between his own. Bruno's skin has been dried out by the clay and his hands are rough and papery. 'You're really worried about her, eh?'

Matt shrugs. 'She's never left him before. This is all new territory.'

'And you're scared she won't cope on her own?'

'No! I'm scared she'll go back,' Matt says. 'I mean, she can't stay on a friend's couch forever. I'm thinking I should go over and give her some support or something. I need to look at flights.'

'Can't Tim give her support?' Bruno asks. 'He lives nearby, doesn't he?'

'Huh!' Matt says. 'Tim sounds like he's being an arsehole. Natalya says he thinks he's Switzerland.'

'Switzerland?'

'You know . . . neutral.'

'But if your father's hitting her . . .'

'Well, quite. But he's always been like that. He's never been one to take sides, no matter how obvious the wrongdoing is. Exactly like Switzerland, I suppose.' The image of Tim holding the cricket bat flashes up in Matt's mind's eye. 'Well, not for years anyway,' he adds. 'He wasn't always like that, I suppose.'

'If you need to go, then you should,' Bruno says. 'We can afford the flight, and Dad will help out if we need him to. But what would you be able to do if you did go?'

248

Matt sighs deeply. He pulls his hand from Bruno's and reaches for a long blade of grass. He starts to chew the end. 'I don't know,' he says, causing the blade of grass to bob up and down. 'I just think she needs someone on her side. I think she might need someone to tell her she's right not to go back to him, that's all.'

'If it was my mother, I'd go back,' Bruno says. 'But I'd call my brother first.'

'Yeah . . .' Matt says doubtfully. Bruno, being an only child, tends to think that family are far more powerful, far more magical even, than they really are. 'I will. I'll call him this evening. He doesn't get in until late anyway. And I'll have a look at flights, too. Just in case.'

'So how about we walk the dog?' Bruno suggests. 'That'll calm your nerves.'

'If you can wake him,' Matt says. 'But he looked all out of batteries the last time I looked.'

The conversation with Tim that evening starts out well enough, with the brothers exchanging news about Matt's travels, the boys' progress at school, Tim's job, the new house, the newly filled pool . . . But when Matt attempts to discuss Alice, things quickly degenerate.

'I'm sorry, Matt,' Tim says crisply. 'I don't want to get involved.'

'But you are involved,' Matt says. 'We both are. They're our parents.'

'Oh, you finally found that out, did you?' Tim asks.

'I'm sorry?'

'Never mind.'

'No, go on . . . What was that supposed to mean?'

'Nothing. Look, what do you want me to do, Matt?' Tim asks, the tempo of his voice increasing. 'Go round and punch him for her?'

249

'No, I—'

'Call the police maybe? That could be dramatic. And fun!'

'Yeah, OK. Why not call the police?'

'Because Mum can do that perfectly well herself,' Tim says. 'She could have called them years ago if she'd wanted to.'

'Look, I know that,' Matt says. 'I understand. But—'

'No, you don't. You don't understand anything. You fuck off around the world and you leave us here to deal with it all, and then you phone up to tell me what I should be doing. It's the bloody nerve of it, that's what gets me.'

'I wasn't under the impression that you were dealing with anything,' Matt says, his own hackles rising. 'I was under the impression that you weren't getting involved.'

'We go and see them, OK?' Tim says. 'We sit in their shitty little lounge and listen to them moaning about the leak in the bloody roof. We have them over here, too, so they can moan about how cold it is. Nat cooks for them, not that they ever appreciate anything. We're here for them, Matt. But you? What do you do for them? What did you ever do for them other than be a worry? What did you ever do except quit your job and move to a squat, eh? When did you ever even phone them other than to ask them for money so you could fuck off around the world with your backpack?'

'Fuck you, Tim,' Matt says.

'No,' Tim replies. 'Fuck you.'

The line goes dead.

Bruno, peering around the door frame from the kitchen, comments, 'That didn't go well, I take it?'

Matt, though red-faced and sweating, still manages to laugh. He rubs one hand across his face. 'Oh, babe!' he says. 'You have no idea.'

The next morning, Matt wakes up to the sound of heavy rain. He glances at the alarm clock – it's not even six – then rolls towards Bruno beside him. But the puppy has inserted himself between them. 'Move, Framboise,' Matt says, giving the dog a push.

'I thought it was "Jarvis",' Bruno groans sleepily.

'Jarvis! Move!' Matt tries again, nudging the dog with one knee. And this time the puppy stands, stretches, and moves to the foot of the bed.

'You see,' Bruno murmurs. 'He just needed the right name.'

When Matt wakes up again, it's almost eight-thirty and the smell of freshly brewed coffee fills the cabin. He gets up, pulls on jogging trousers and a T-shirt, then heads through to the kitchen where Bruno is seated, feeding bits of toast and jam to the dog.

'Are you sure he can eat that?' Matt asks, sleepily scratching first his balls, then his head, then raising his hand to caress one of the roughly hewn logs that make up the walls of the cabin.

'They can eat anything except chocolate,' Bruno says.

'I'd still rather you didn't. He's barely weaned off milk.'

'Sure, OK,' Bruno says, withdrawing the toast from the dog, who immediately starts to whimper.

'Plus, if you feed him at the table, he'll do that every time we ever eat anything,' Matt points out.

'OK, OK!' Bruno says. 'Message received. Oh, are we going with "Jarvis", by the way? Because I'm worried he'll have some personality disorder if we don't choose a name soon.'

Matt leans to the right and looks at the dog. 'Yep,' he says. 'Jarvis is good. It fits him.'

Matt walks to the counter and pours himself a mug of coffee, then pulls out a chair and sits opposite Bruno. The dog, more interested in Bruno's toast than in Matt, ignores his presence. 'Shit weather,' Matt comments, glancing past his boyfriend at the wet garden beyond.

251

'I wanted to go to Italy again, too,' Bruno replies. 'You're working tomorrow, right?'

Matt sips his coffee. 'I am. But we could go on Thursday.'

'Unless you go to England.'

'Unless I have to go to England,' Matt confirms, pulling his laptop towards him across the kitchen table and opening the lid. 'I suppose I'd better look at those flights.'

Even though he's looking at the screen, he sees Bruno slip Jarvis another square of toast. But he doesn't say anything. He has bigger things to worry about today. 'Wow,' he says, after a few clicks on the mouse pad. 'These flights are crazy expensive.'

'The last-minute ones always are. You have to book months in advance for the prices they advertise. Have a look at that Irish one from Marseille.'

'Ryanair,' Matt says. 'That's what I'm looking at. Three hundred euros, round trip.'

'Gee. And what about easyJet? Mom flew with them when she went to that arts expo thing.'

'Yep,' Matt says, clicking away on the keyboard. 'I'm just checking that now. Shit. It's even more. Well, only eight euros more, but all the same . . .'

'How long would you go for?' Bruno asks through a mouthful of toast.

'A few days, tops,' Matt replies. 'I can probably get the Wednesday off, but I'd have to be back for the weekend shift.'

'Maybe I could fill in for you,' Bruno offers. He finds the prospect of stacking the hotel dishwasher surprisingly appealing. As long as it's only for one weekend.

'I doubt it,' Matt says. 'But I could ask.'

At that moment, Bruno's mobile starts to vibrate. He leans back in his chair and swipes it from the kitchen counter behind

252

him, glances at the screen, and then slides it across the table towards Matt. 'UK number,' he says. 'I think it's for you.'

Puzzled, Matt answers the phone. 'Hello? Hello?' he says. Then, addressing Bruno, he adds, 'Too late, I think.'

But then a voice comes from the handset. 'Is anybody there?'

'Mum?' Matt says. 'Is that you?'

'Is that Matthew?'

'Yes.'

'Oh, hello. This is Dot. Do you remember me?'

Matt glances across at Bruno who is watching him questioningly, his second slice of toast suspended in mid-air.

'Yes, Dot,' Matt says, more for Bruno's benefit than for Dot's. 'Of course I remember you. Mum's friend. She's staying with you, right?'

'Yes. I can't talk for long,' Dot says. Her Midlands accent is even thicker than Alice's. 'She's only nipped out for a minute. I got your number from her phone, sneaky loyke.'

'OK . . .'

'I need your help, love,' Dot says. 'I'm in a bit of a pickle with your mother.'

'Really?'

'Yes. I love Alice to bits, Matthew – you know I do. But she's been here two weeks now, and it just can't carry on like this much longer.'

'Oh,' Matt says.

'The thing is – and I shouldn't really tell you this, so not a word, eh? – but the thing is, I've got this gentleman friend. Your mother doesn't know about that, and he doesn't want me to tell anyone just yet. But with Alice here, I can't even get to see him. So it's all getting a bit sticky. Do you see what I mean, love?'

253

'Yes,' Matt says, struggling not to laugh. Who would have ever imagined Dot with a secret lover? 'But what are you thinking? How can I help?'

'I thought you could have a word with Timothy,' Dot says. 'I thought maybe you could convince him. He seems to be being ever so difficult.'

'You want him to take Mum in?'

'Yes,' Dot says. 'Yes, it's time her family took up some of the slack.'

'Tim won't want to get involved,' Matt says. 'I can almost guarantee that much.'

'But he has to get involved,' Dot says. 'Alice needs his help.'

'I spoke to him already, Dot. He told me to . . . well, to bugger off, basically.'

'Oh,' Dot says. 'Can you think of anyone else? Because if someone doesn't step up to the mark soon, she'll end up going back to that . . . Sorry, Matthew. I know he's your father and everything, but . . .'

'Sure,' Matt says. 'I understand.'

Bruno, opposite, is waving one hand around, trying to get Matt's attention. He's mouthing something at him, too. Matt waves back that he should 'cut it'. He's trying to think, and it's hard enough without Bruno jumping around. But Bruno continues ever more frantically until finally Matt gives in.

'Hold on one second, Dot. I just need to . . . hang on. What?!' Matt asks, holding his hand over the base of his mobile so that Dot can't hear him addressing Bruno.

'Tell her to come here,' Bruno says. He says this as if it's the most obvious thing in the world.

'Here?'

'Yes. Your mother. Tell her to come visit.'

'You're crazy,' Matt replies. 'And anyway, there's no room here. We don't even have a sofa.'

'We could call Virginie,' Bruno says. 'I'm sure she wouldn't mind. It's not like she's using her place. Your mom could feed her cats.'

Matt shakes his head sharply. 'Sorry, Dot,' he says, resuming the conversation. 'That was just . . . someone distracted me.'

'Why not though?' Dot asks. She apparently heard every word. 'I can't think of anything that would do her more good than getting away right now. Unless you don't want to get involved either, that is.'

Tim's words suddenly ring in Matt's ears. *What did you ever do for them except be a worry?*

'It's not that,' he says, wondering as he says it if it's a lie. 'It's just that . . . I don't know. I'm really not sure that would work. And Mum never travels anywhere on her own.'

'She does,' Dot says. 'She flew back from Spain on her own.'

'Did she?' Matt says, pulling a pained expression. 'Look . . .'

'I've got to go,' Dot says. 'She's on her way up. Just have a think, all right, love? I'll . . . I'll call you back.'

'So why not?' Bruno asks, once Matt has hung up.

'Just . . . don't . . .' Matt says, batting the question away with one hand. 'You don't know her. You don't know my family. So just . . . Please. Let me deal with it, OK?'

11

JUNE

Matt raises a finger to his lips only to remember that he has no fingernails left to bite. *I need to buy some of that horrible-tasting nail polish*, he thinks, not for the first time.

The arrivals board has been showing Alice's flight as having landed for over half an hour, but still there is no sign of her. Matt wonders if she could have changed her mind at the last minute. He wonders if that mightn't be a good thing after all.

He chews the skin along the side of his thumbnail instead. He chews the inside of his mouth. Yes, he's nervous. He's even, he admits now, a little scared. Not of Alice, but of his own inability to remain calm in her presence. She has a tendency to get on his nerves.

Their relationship has never been an easy one, but above all, it has never comprised the kind of intimacy that her coming to stay implies. But after weeks of poking and prodding, by Dot over in England, and by Bruno here in France, here she is, pushing through the turnstile, struggling with her suitcase.

She looks older than when he last saw her. That's the first thing that Matt notices. She has aged ten years in less than three.

He raises one arm and waves, then strides across the hall to greet her. 'Mum!' he says. 'You made it!'

'Ah, Matthew,' Alice says, her features relaxing slightly. 'You're here!'

'Of course I'm here!'

'I was scared you'd change your mind,' Alice jokes.

Matt and Alice embrace awkwardly, and then Matt takes control of her crazed, veering suitcase. 'Do you want a drink or the loo or anything?' he asks. 'We've got a long drive ahead.'

'No, thanks,' Alice says. 'I had a horrible sandwich and a cup of tea on the plane. Seven pounds twenty, it came to. Can you imagine that? Seven pounds twenty for a cuppa and a cheese sandwich.'

'It's how they keep the prices of the flights so cheap, I suppose.'

'Only it wasn't cheap,' Alice says. 'It wasn't cheap at all.'

Matt starts to walk a little faster towards the exit. Alice follows on. He leads the way out across the car park.

'Gosh, it's hot!' Alice says, looking at the tarmac shimmering in the sunshine.

'It's the south of France. Anyway, you love the heat,' Matt reminds her.

'What a strange little airport,' Alice replies, glancing around.

'It's just the low-cost terminal,' Matt says. 'The main airport's back that way.'

'Like I said,' Alice says, tripping along beside him, 'it wasn't low cost at all. You know, most of the other people on that flight had picnics with them? Which, once you know what the food is like and how much it costs, makes sense, I suppose. I just wish I'd known in advance. The woman beside me – she had her daughter with her, a fat little girl – she had sandwiches and drinks and chocolate bars and crisps . . . She just kept pulling stuff from her

258

bag. It was like a magician's bag, you know? Bottomless. In the end there was so much stuff on her little table that she had to use mine. It looked like – do you remember when you used to play shops? – well, it looked like that. The mum was a bit overweight too. I felt like saying, maybe you should cut out the crisps and the chocolate, love. She kept elbowing me as she ate. I almost said something. But in the end, there's just no point with people like that, is there?'

Matt weaves his way between two cars and glances sideways at Alice. He thinks, *Oh! This isn't going to work after all. How could I forget?* 'This is it,' he says, pausing behind the C1 and fumbling in his pocket for the keys.

'This one?' Alice says. 'My, it's tiny! Is it safe?'

'It's no smaller than your Micra. And yes, Mum, it's safe. It had its *contrôle technique* thingy – its MOT, that's it – just two weeks ago.'

'I hope it's got air conditioning,' Alice says as Matt opens the hatchback and a rush of superheated air hits them. 'I'm melting here.'

'It hasn't, Mum. But it's much cooler up there. You'll see.'

'Gosh, what a tiny boot,' Alice says as Matt heaves her case into the car. 'It's a good job I packed lightly.'

'You could have filled the entire back seat, Mum. There's room for two more cases like this one.'

Alice has moved to the driver's side, so Matt has to remind her that they're in France, that the passenger's side is on the right.

'Oh, of course it is,' Alice says. 'Silly me! You'd think I'd never been abroad before.'

'I still forget sometimes, too,' Matt says. 'Occasionally, I even drive off on the wrong side of the road.'

'Not today, please,' Alice says. 'So is it far?'

'It's, um, just over two hours,' Matt replies once they have negotiated the ticket barrier.

259

'And Marseille is the nearest airport?'

'Yes, Mum!' Matt says, his tone of voice already starting to express irritation despite his best efforts. 'This is the nearest airport.'

'I was only checking,' Alice whines. 'I was only worrying that I'd made you drive out of your way.'

'I told you to fly here, Mum,' Matt reminds her, 'so it's fine.'

'What a lot of traffic,' she says, as Matt moves into the start-stop queue of cars on the slip road.

'It's only till we get to the autoroute, Mum. After that, it'll be fine.'

'You have to pay for those here, don't you?'

'The autoroutes? Yes.'

'They cost a fortune in Spain. They cost us more than the petrol.'

'Yes,' Matt says. 'Well, they're pretty expensive here too.'

Mainly because Alice keeps asking him to slow down, it takes them three hours, not two, to get home. And by the time they reach the cabin, Matt's nerves are already frayed.

'Really?' Alice says, as they bump up the drive. 'You live here?'

Matt pulls up outside the front door and turns the ignition off.

Bruno quickly appears to greet them and Matt catches his eye and pulls a face before opening the car door and helping Alice out. 'Home sweet home,' Matt says. 'And this is Bruno. Bruno, my mother.'

Alice looks confused as she shakes Bruno's hand. She hadn't been expecting anyone at Matt's house. '*Bonjour*, Bruno,' she says, wondering if he's a neighbour or the gardener, all the while noting how good-looking he is.

'Bruno's Canadian, Mum,' Matt tells her. 'You can speak English.'

260

'Thank God for that,' Alice says. 'I speak a few words of Spanish, but my French is non-existent. I know "baguette" and "*bière*" and "*bonjour*" and I think that's about it. I don't think I got past the letter B.'

'Those are very useful words,' Bruno says. 'With those three you need never go hungry. Or thirsty.'

'Do you need anything from your bag, Mum?' Matt asks. 'Or can we just leave it in the car?'

Alice is looking confused, so Matt reminds her, 'You're in a house down the road, remember? There's only one bedroom here. And no sofa bed either. I explained it to you on the phone.'

'Yes, that's right,' Alice says. In fact, she has no recollection of this conversation, but her mind has, admittedly, been rather occupied recently.

'You get to share the house with Virginie's five cats,' Bruno says enthusiastically. 'They're awesome.'

'I'm not that keen on cats,' Alice replies in a tone that implies she's sharing a confidence with him.

Bruno laughs. 'You might have to work on that one,' he says.

Once Alice is seated at the garden table, Matt joins Bruno in the kitchen.

'This is never going to work,' Matt says distraughtly as he closes the door behind him.

Bruno, standing over the kettle, looks up. 'Already?' he says.

'Yes, already. I don't know about saving her from Dad. I'm starting to want to kill her myself.'

Bruno pulls a face.

'Joke, babe,' Matt says.

Bruno pours the water into the mugs and adds teabags. 'Yeah, well don't. Not about that. It's not . . .'

'Graceful?'

'Exactly. It's not graceful at all. How does she take her tea?'

'White,' Matt says. 'No sugar.'

Bruno crosses to the refrigerator. 'I should have said to get more milk,' he says. 'We're almost out.'

'I'll steal some long-life stuff from Virginie's place. If we get that far.'

'You need to calm down,' Bruno tells him gently. 'You're getting yourself all worked up where there's no need.'

'No need?' Matt says a little too loudly. He glances guiltily at the door. 'No need?' he repeats softly. 'I've just spent three hours in the car with her. And believe me, you've no idea. Ooh, Matthew,' he says in a comedy Birmingham accent, 'do slow down a bit – it's not a racetrack.'

'You do drive fast,' Bruno says.

'Where on earth do you get your shopping? It's so remote!'

'She has a point,' Bruno says. 'Like I said, we're almost out of milk.'

'What happens if you need a doctor?'

Bruno shrugs. 'Old folks worry about stuff like that.'

Matt snorts. 'I hope there's no more bends,' he continues. 'This road's making me feel quite carsick, Matthew.'

Bruno smiles tightly and shrugs.

'Oh, and best of all,' Matt says, waving one finger at him, 'who on earth would choose to live out here? I mean, can you believe that? I'm in the process of driving her to our house, and she asks who the hell would want to live here?'

'Maybe she's nervous,' Bruno says generously. 'People can be difficult when they're nervous.'

'Maybe she's a nightmare,' Matt says, comically wiggling his fingers either side of his face, monster-style.

Bruno laughs, then sighs deeply and returns his attention to the drinks.

'Yep,' Matt says, 'I know. Not graceful.'

Alice fidgets in her plastic garden chair and looks around at the garden. Up the hill, to the right, is the beginning of a dense pine forest. In front of her, a large sweep of scrubby lawn leads to five fruit trees; she's not sure which kind. And to the left, a series of terraced levels lead down to the distant main road. Most of these have been cultivated as vegetable plots, it would appear, though Alice can't imagine by whom. Certainly Matt never showed the slightest interest in gardening.

She turns her head and glances back at the cabin, but the door is shut, the shutters still closed. There's nothing to be seen.

She's having trouble feeling present right now – she's struggling to convince herself that this is reality rather than a dream or the edgy lead-in to a nightmare, the phase when everything feels wrong, just before the spooks appear. Though her surroundings are what people traditionally describe as 'beautiful', she has never been a great one for isolation – remote locations have always made her feel edgy. And beyond this, something really does feel wrong. In fact, everything feels wrong. The feeling is hard to put words to, but none of this looks like a logical version of reality to her.

She's been feeling peculiar for weeks, has been floating around in an almost dreamlike state ever since she walked out of number twenty-three. Because how, her brain keeps asking, can she really be doing what she's doing? And she finds herself unable to reply.

Every morning she has opened her eyes and had to blink twice before accepting the reality of Dot's luminous lounge, of her suitcase in the corner, of Dot herself, bustling around behind her brewing coffee. But this, being here today, is even stranger.

Firstly, of course, she's in France. Everything is foreign. Everything is strange.

And she's staying with Matt! She can't remember having had a proper conversation with Matt since he was about ten. Should she feel guilty about that? Probably. Then again, so perhaps should he.

Add then to the fact that she's staying with Matt in France, the fact that Matt is living, of all places, in a remote wooden cabin in the Alps, for God's sake, and you have all the ingredients of a dream sequence. It feels a little like one of the strange scenes from that *Twin Peaks* TV series Matt and Tim were so addicted to.

She scans the edges of the garden, but instead of one-armed men or midgets in red suits, she sees Bruno walking towards her with a puppy on a lead. 'So, Alice,' Bruno says, 'it's time for you to meet Jarvis.'

'Oh, hello!' Alice says, leaning down to caress the excitable puppy. 'My, you're just a baby, aren't you?'

'He's ten weeks old,' Bruno says. 'He was Matt's birthday gift.'

'Oh, that was nice of him,' Alice says.

'Oh no,' Bruno explains. 'We got the dog for Matt.'

A dog! Alice's mind is suddenly swamped with memories – terrible memories. She pales. 'And his birthday,' she says. 'I forgot it!'

'I guess you had a lot on,' Bruno says. 'Don't worry. Matt's OK with that.'

'But all the same.'

'You're here now. That's the main thing.'

Alice looks up at Bruno and he smiles at her and she feels a little better. She manages to push the ghosts from her mind. She notes again how tall he is, how attractive. With his dark brown eyes and his neatly trimmed beard, his long upper body and his muscular arms, and that constant friendly smile above all, he really is quite extraordinary. But who is he? That's what Alice can't work out.

'So how do you know Matt?' she asks.

264

'We met travelling,' Bruno says. 'In a backpackers' in Thailand. It was horrific really. Matt and I fought the roaches together. The roaches won.'

Alice nods and frowns. Because though this reply answers everything, it also explains nothing. An idea is forming on the edges of her consciousness, like a child jumping up and down trying to be noticed in the crowd. But Alice rejects it out of hand. Yes, Matt has always been a little 'other' to her. And yes, he has always been intensely private, secretive even. But surely he wouldn't invite her out here without telling her *that*, would he?

'Do you live nearby?' Alice asks, smiling neutrally to disguise her confusion.

Bruno, now crouched down to play with the puppy, looks up. He smiles and frowns simultaneously. 'I live here,' he says. 'This place belongs to my folks. It's their summerhouse.'

Alice nods. She runs her tongue across her front teeth. Hadn't Matt said there was only one bedroom here? 'How lovely,' she says after a pause. 'So how about you show me around the house? I don't think I've ever been in a log cabin before.'

Bruno shows Alice around the house and it doesn't take long for her to garner the only pieces of information that really interest her. Yes, there is only one bedroom. No, the couch does not convert into a bed. Yes, there are two toothbrushes in the bathroom. The day feels suddenly even stranger.

'It's lovely,' she says, once the short tour is over and they're back out in the sunshine.

'There's an outbuilding too,' Bruno says, 'behind the plum trees. Come.'

For a moment, as they cross the lawn together, the dog yapping at their heels, Alice breathes more easily. But the outbuilding is really just a shed – a tatty ramshackle shed at that. It's filled with pottery equipment and bags of clay. In the corner is an electric kiln.

265

'This is where I work,' Bruno explains.

Alice peers in and smiles weakly.

'You can go in,' Bruno tells her.

'Um, thanks,' Alice says, stepping tentatively inside. Once her eyes adjust to the gloom, she sees that the rear wall is covered in roughly cut shelving containing roughly glazed, roughly shaped pots. It's all very rough.

'Those are mine,' Bruno says.

'How nice,' Alice says unconvincingly. Her mind is far more occupied with the sleeping arrangements than with finding the right thing to say about Bruno's ugly vases. 'Are you, um, having trouble with the varnish thing?'

'I'm sorry?'

'The, er, glaze? Is that what it's called?'

Bruno laughs. 'Ah, yeah,' he says, 'and no. Not really . . . It's called raku. That's what it looks like.'

'It's meant to look like that then? It's meant to look all cracked and burnt?' Alice asks, only vaguely aware that she's being tactless, and still too distracted to compensate.

'Yep,' Bruno says. 'You pull it from the kiln and plunge it into sawdust to get it that way. Otherwise it would look like every other pot.'

'I see,' Alice says blandly. 'How interesting.'

'Here you are!' Matt exclaims from the doorway. 'I thought you'd both run away together.'

'Nope,' Bruno says in an unusually sarcastic tone of voice. Matt glances at him questioningly, but his face remains expressionless.

'Bruno's been showing me his pots,' Alice says.

'They're gorgeous, aren't they?'

'They're certainly very novel,' Alice replies – it's the best she can offer. 'I . . . I'm just going to nip to the loo if that's all right?'

266

Feeling a little trembly, she squeezes past Matt and scurries off in the direction of the house.

'Did I miss something?' Matt asks. The atmosphere in the shed feels strained.

Bruno shrugs. 'Not a big fan of raku, apparently,' he says drily.

'Mum's not a fan of anything. I did warn you.'

'You did tell her about us, didn't you?' Bruno asks.

'I'm sorry?'

'You did tell your mother who I am?'

Matt looks at him blankly.

'Matt?'

'I just introduced you,' Matt says. 'I said, "Mum, this is Bruno. Bruno, this is Mum." What do you want?'

'You know perfectly well what I mean.'

Matt continues to look blank, but it's an unconvincing, bad-faith kind of blank that makes Bruno start to feel angry. 'God, you didn't, did you?' he says.

'Didn't what?'

'Matt!' Bruno says. 'You cannot be telling me this. You cannot be telling me that you invited your mom to come and stay in our house without telling her that I'm your boyfriend, surely?'

Matt shrugs. 'She's old, Bruno,' he says. 'And anyway, I don't see a problem. Is there a problem?'

'You don't see a problem?'

'No! If she wants to come and stay, then she has to accept me for who I am. I don't have to justify myself to my mother. Not at forty-two . . . Not at forty-three, I mean.'

'Unbelievable,' Bruno says, shaking his head slowly.

'What's so unbelievable?' Matt asks, repeating the word in a mocking voice. 'That I didn't say, "Hi, Mum, this is Bruno. We fuck?" Is that what you wanted?'

'Jesus,' Bruno mutters. 'You asshole.'

267

'Bruno,' Matt whines. He steps towards him and opens his arms, but Bruno sidesteps him. 'No,' he says. 'Just no, Matt.'

'Babe,' Matt pleads. 'Look, your folks are all young and trendy, OK? And you can sit up till 3 a.m. discussing your sexuality with them, and that's grand. But Mum's not like that. She's from a whole different generation, and that's not the kind of relationship we have.'

'So . . . what?' Bruno asks. 'She has to work it out for herself? Because you're too damn scared to tell her you're a fag?'

'A fag?' Matt repeats disgustedly.

'It's a term people who don't like gays use to describe gays,' Bruno says. 'People like you.'

'Now you're being ridiculous.'

'I'm being ridiculous?' Bruno splutters. 'Jesus. No wonder she's freaked.'

'Plus, you know what?' Matt says. 'I haven't been thinking that much about telling her I'm a fag recently, if that makes any sense to you. I've been worrying about getting her away from my violent father before he kills her.'

Bruno nods. 'Well, aren't you just the greatest guy around, eh?'

'Bruno,' Matt pleads. 'Don't be like this, babe.'

'Babe?' Bruno says. 'I thought I was just the guy you fuck.'

'I didn't say that.'

'You did, actually.'

'Then I didn't mean that.'

'OK. Then apologise. Because that is what you said.'

'Then I'm sorry,' Matt says. 'I, I . . . wasn't thinking clearly.'

'Fine,' Bruno says, though he doesn't look to Matt like he's fine at all. 'Now go tell your Mom.'

Matt pulls a face. 'Go tell her?' he repeats.

'Yes, go tell her.'

'It's like I said,' Matt says. 'She'll work it out for herself.'

268

'Why?'

'Why?'

'Yes, why can't you tell her?'

'Because . . . Because . . .'

'Yeah?'

'I don't know,' Matt says. 'Because, like I said, that's not the kind of relationship we have. We don't talk about things. We just . . .' He shrugs. 'I don't know – we observe how things are. We . . . watch what's happening, and we work it all out from there.'

'Hey, you know what? If your mother is staying in my parents' house, then the least you can do is tell her I'm your partner. Unless you're too ashamed of me. In which case, that's a different conversation we need to have.'

'But she's not really staying here,' Matt offers in a tiny voice that implies he knows just how pitiful he's being by saying it.

Bruno raises his hands. 'I give up,' he says, stepping out of the shed. 'You're pathetic. Just . . . just stay away from me. Stay away from me until you've found the balls to tell your mom who I am. No, you know what? Stay away from me until you've found the balls to tell your mom who you are.'

In the bathroom, Alice stands, flushes the toilet, but then puts down the lid and sits back down again. She has often favoured the cold, clean surfaces of bathrooms at times of crisis. She couldn't explain why, but it has always seemed easier to think in a bathroom or a kitchen than in the cosy clutter of a lounge or a bedroom.

She looks around the room. She's stalling, taking time out before she forces herself to confront that thing she needs to think about.

Here in the bathroom, the external walls are also made out of massive tree trunks. They form a series of rounded horizontal

269

bumps. Dust has collected on the more difficult-to-reach ones. *Men*, Alice thinks. *Why can't men dust?*

Only the wall around the bath has been boarded and tiled, and this many years ago, judging from the old-fashioned tiles. But despite the age of the place, the entire house still smells of pine sap. It's rather lovely, like having a built-in air freshener.

Alice looks out of the small window at a branch tapping in the breeze. She can hear a bird tweeting maniacally too. She coughs. She swallows. She lets the thought surface. Matt. Her son. Homosexual?

She feels a little tearful, but isn't sure why. She thinks unexpectedly of Jeremy Thorpe. She tries to remember what his lover's name was. Norman Bates perhaps? No, that was the son in *Psycho*. Norman something, anyway.

The surprise is that it makes sense. She remembers a science fiction film they had watched one Christmas at Tim's. It had been terribly confusing and she hadn't really been concentrating properly, but in essence everyone had been lost in some kind of virtual reality contraption. But when they ate the red pill (there were other colours, as far as she can remember), everything was revealed and everything that had never quite made sense suddenly did make sense. She feels a little as if she's just eaten the red pill herself. Because though she feels shocked (and she really does) she also feels instantly as if she understands everything she ever struggled to understand about Matt, from his strange childhood taste in toys (the My Little Pony flashes through her mind's eye) through his random grasping of fashion changes from Goth to punk to whatever it was that came next, to his eyeliner, his piercings, his desperate need to get as far away as possible from home. *He wanted to transform without witnesses*, she thinks. She remembers her conversation with Dot. Dot was right, then: he's been finding himself.

She wonders if Ken's violence made Matt that way. She wonders if she did. But she's read enough, she's seen enough TV about homosexuality to know that no one is really to blame. That's what they say, anyway. But even so, Ken can't have helped things, can he?

And Bruno. He's so young. Can he really be Matt's boyfriend? Despite herself, she shudders at the word, not because she has any great problem with homosexuals – gays, that's the preferred term, isn't it? – it's just that an image of Matt and Bruno, you know . . . doing it . . . flashed through her mind, and it wasn't pleasant. That, she supposes, is like trying to imagine one's own parents having sex. Best never to go there.

But wouldn't Matt have told her? Perhaps she has it all wrong. With everything she knows thus far, could she have got completely the wrong end of the stick? She asks herself the question. She wrinkles her nose in reply.

So Matt, she supposes, will now tell her at some point. Or he'll ask her if she's worked it out. Or he won't. Maybe he'll tell her about some girlfriend in Marseille. And perhaps it will be true, and perhaps it will be a lie.

A spider on the ceiling catches her eye. Tim had been terrified of them when he was little, and to avoid feeding his phobia, Alice had trained herself to catch them barehanded, to throw them out of the bathroom window. You can get used to anything if you try.

When he tells her, she'll be calm then. She'll be calm and accepting. She won't ask any difficult questions either. She doesn't want to know who plays the man and who plays the woman anyway. But seeing as Bruno is much younger, Matt must play the boy, mustn't he? She thinks that in some strange way she would prefer that to . . . She shudders again. Yes, definitely best not to go there.

And AIDS. God, she hopes neither of them have AIDS. They say they live normal lives these days, don't they? They say the

271

treatments have got better. But all the same. She would find that far harder to deal with, she thinks.

Outside, she hears Matt shouting Bruno's name. 'Bruno, please!' he is calling, pleadingly.

If they look like a couple and they sound like a couple, Alice thinks. She takes a deep breath and stands.

When Alice steps back into the garden, she finds Matt leaning against a tree, chewing a finger.

'Everything OK?' she asks.

Matt nods. 'Uh huh,' he confirms.

'It's really time you stopped chewing your fingernails,' Alice tells him. She can't help herself. It's a parent thing.

'Um?' Matt says distractedly. Then pulling the finger from his mouth, he adds, 'Oh yeah, I know.'

'Where's Bruno?' She wonders for a moment whether Matt will reply that he's 'gone home'. She wonders if that would make the day seem more or less peculiar.

'He's taken the dog for a walk around the lake,' Matt says.

'Ah, the lake, yes. I haven't seen that yet.'

'Yeah, I'm, err, sorry, Mum,' Matt says, 'but I'm working tonight – I told you that, right? And I'm going to have to get moving pretty soon. But Bruno will be back. He said he'll take you down to Virginie's place and get you set up and everything. I'll drop your case off as I go past so you don't have to lug it down the road.'

'Oh, OK,' Alice says, a little distraught at the idea of being left with this stranger, Bruno, before she even fully understands who he is. 'And you? What time are you back?'

'Midnight,' Matt replies. 'Maybe one.'

'Right,' Alice says. 'That's OK. I understand. And there's no need to worry Bruno. I'll just sort myself out.' After a month at

272

Dot's place, the idea of an evening alone with her thoughts is surprisingly appealing.

'Only you can't really,' Matt tells her. 'There's no food in Virginie's place. We have to sort that out tomorrow. But Bruno said he'll cook for you tonight.'

'I could perhaps take something from here to heat up?' Alice offers. 'Or just some bread and cheese perhaps?'

'No, Bruno's looking forward to it,' Matt says. 'He's not a particularly good cook, but what he lacks in skill he makes up for in enthusiasm.'

'Right. But . . .'

'Sorry, but I really do have to . . .' Matt says, pointing back towards the house.

'Of course,' Alice says. 'Feel free.'

Once Matt has vanished indoors in order to change for work, Alice walks down to the car and retrieves her e-reader from her suitcase. She sets herself up beneath the widest of the plum trees and switches the device on. But though her eyes keep scanning the onscreen page, her mind refuses to take in the meaning of the words today, so she gives up and stares out at the garden. She watches three butterflies flirting or perhaps fighting among some wildflowers. She sees a bird soar overhead. She listens to the cicadas. *What a strange day*, she thinks again.

Almost as soon as Matt has driven off, Bruno reappears with the dog. 'Hi, Alice,' he says as if they haven't seen each other for a while. 'Did Matt get off all right?'

'I think so,' Alice says. 'Everything OK?'

Bruno nods nonchalantly. 'Just a tiff,' he says. 'You know how it is.'

'I think I do,' Alice says hesitantly.

273

'I . . .' Bruno begins. He hesitates, then ties the dog to a branch in the shade before pulling a chair over beside Alice. 'An e-reader, huh?' he comments, nodding at Alice's Kindle. 'That's modern.'

'Tim bought it for me a couple of Christmases ago. It's easier on my old eyes,' Alice replies. 'I can make the characters as big as I like. I have to hold paperbacks so far away these days . . . I'll be needing longer arms soon.'

'Right,' Bruno says.

He looks a little sad, so Alice asks again, 'Are you sure everything's OK?'

Bruno nods vaguely. 'I just regret letting Matt go,' he says. 'Without making up, I mean.'

'You argued then?'

'Uh huh.'

'I hope it wasn't about me.'

'Not really.'

'Oh,' Alice laughs. 'That sounds ominous.'

'I was just angry that Matt hadn't told you,' Bruno explains. 'About me, I mean.'

So I was right, Alice thinks. And even though she has prepared herself for this, her heart flutters a little. 'You're . . . together, then?' she asks.

'You worked it out. Matt said you would.'

Alice smiles knowingly. 'I counted the bedrooms.'

'Huh. Well, he should have told you.'

'Maybe.'

'Definitely.'

'You know, it's not all his fault. We're not a very chatty family.'

'No, that's what Matt said.'

'Your parents know, presumably?' Alice says, thinking that it's a rather good, relaxed thing to say. 'I mean, if this is their place and everything.'

274

'Oh yeah. They've always known.'

'Always?'

'Pretty much. Mom's best friend was a gay guy, so I never even imagined there might be a problem, you know?'

'It's a generational thing, I think. I mean, I'm not sure I've ever known a . . . a gay person . . . not in real life.'

'In real life?' Bruno asks, grinning. He seems to think this a rather ridiculous thing to say.

'On the telly,' Alice explains. 'And in books. Actually, maybe my hairdresser . . .' Bruno laughs again, so Alice says, 'That's a horrible cliché, I suppose.'

'Most clichés are horrible. And most of them are based on reality, too.'

'Yes,' Alice says. 'I suppose they are. How old are you, Bruno? Do you mind me asking that?' She's thinking that he seems exceptionally mature compared with his youthful looks.

'Twenty-nine,' Bruno says. 'Why?'

'No reason.'

'And you?'

Alice smiles. 'Me? I'm sixty-nine,' she says. 'But people don't generally ask women of my age that kind of question.'

'OK,' Bruno says thoughtfully. 'And how do you feel about it? I mean, are you OK about Matt and me?'

Alice tries to locate her feelings about Matt being gay, about Matt living with Bruno, but she finds them absent, or at the very least too confused to be quickly identified. She fears that her 'feeling' circuits have been overused recently, leaving her a little slow on the uptake, a little numb, a little dumb even. 'I think so,' she finally replies. 'Why wouldn't I be?'

'Thanks,' Bruno says brightly. 'I knew you'd be cool.'

Alice laughs. She's not sure anyone has ever called her cool. 'Matt said you'd show me wherever it is that I'm staying?' she says.

275

She feels the need for something concrete to do, something practical rather than all this searching for missing feelings.

'Yep,' Bruno says. 'We'll have to walk it though. Unless you want to go on the bike?'

'The bike?'

'The old Suzuki down by the road. That's mine,' Bruno says. 'I could take you on that. If it'll start. The battery might be flat though. I haven't moved it for weeks.'

Alice shakes her head. 'Um, I don't think so,' she says. 'Not today, anyway,' she adds. She doesn't want to completely cancel out her cool-ness. 'Is it far?'

'Half a mile maybe. So no, not really.'

'I think a walk might be nice,' Alice says.

'A glass of water before we go?'

'No, thanks,' Alice says. 'I've never much liked water.'

Bruno laughs again.

'Is that funny?'

Bruno grins at her. 'Well, yes,' he says. 'You'd be dead without water. We'd all be dead without water.'

Once Bruno has drunk two full glasses of the life-saving stuff, he locks the cabin doors and he and Alice start to make their way down the track towards the main road.

'This must get muddy when it rains, doesn't it?' Alice asks.

'Yes,' Bruno says, 'it does.'

'So why did you decide to live here of all places?' Alice asks. 'Oh, it's your parents' place. That's what you said, wasn't it?'

'Yeah, it's their summerhouse,' Bruno says. 'But that's not why we live here. We live here because we like it.'

Alice nods. 'It's pretty, I suppose,' she says. 'As long as you don't mind being so far away.'

'Far away from?'

'I'm sorry?'

276

'As long as we don't mind being so far away from what?' Bruno asks.

'I don't know,' Alice says. 'From everything really.'

'I love it here,' Bruno tells her. 'Matt does too.'

'Yes, that surprises me really,' Alice says. 'He always seemed such a city boy.'

As they round the second corner, the intense noise of the cicadas suddenly stops. Once they continue along the track it stutteringly starts up again behind them.

'Noisy buggers, aren't they?' Alice says lightly.

'The sound of summer,' Bruno replies.

By the time they've reached the main road, the silence has begun to feel uncomfortable, so Alice takes a deep breath and asks, 'Did you say you met Matt in Thailand?'

'Yeah,' Bruno says. 'I was trying to block the bottom of the door with toilet paper to stop the roaches coming in.'

'It sounds horrible.'

'It was, but kind of fun, too,' Bruno says. 'Anyway, Matt had insecticide. He gave me a squirt of it and stole my heart.'

'Very romantic.'

'Well, quite. And I kind of just liked him there and then, you know? He's very likeable.'

Alice nods and thinks about this for a moment as they continue to walk side by side. 'But how did you know?' she asks. 'I mean . . . how could you tell?'

'That he was gay?'

'Yes,' Alice says. 'I couldn't.'

'Really?'

She shrugs. 'No, I don't think so. I wasn't as surprised as I might have been. But . . .'

'It's called gaydar,' Bruno says. 'If you're gay, you can just tell.'

'Always?'

277

'Nah,' Bruno says. 'No, I get it wrong all the time. But often.'

'Maybe I did know,' Alice says. 'Deep down.'

'Anyway, we got together against the roaches and decided to travel on to Indonesia together. And we've been together ever since.'

'Well, I'm glad you . . . you know . . . get on.' She winces. Her choice of words sounded wrong there, but then again, even she's not sure quite what she meant to say.

'We do get on. Matt's very cool. You should be proud.'

'Huh! I don't think I had much to do with that.'

'Well, someone did,' Bruno says. 'And by the sounds of it, it wasn't his dad.'

'I really don't think it was me either,' Alice says. But she feels a flush of pride all the same. Because, yes, for all her failings as a parent, here is Matt, alive, apparently healthy, and apparently happy. And partnered with rather lovely, relaxed, honest Bruno.

She's proud of herself also, she realises, for her ability to conduct this conversation. Chatting to her son's partner does feel, after all, rather modern. She can think of plenty of parents her age who would struggle with that.

Perhaps it's because Bruno is, essentially, a stranger to her. She has often noticed how much easier it is for her to talk about things – particularly *intimate* things – with someone she has never met before. Which is strange, really, when you think about it.

'So is it true that Matt's dad hit you?' Bruno asks unexpectedly.

Alice is so blindsided by the question that she momentarily stops breathing as she glances sideways at him. But from his expression – neutral, open, interested – it really would appear that he thinks this is just a reasonable thing to ask.

'I'm not sure I want to talk about that right now,' Alice says. 'Sorry.'

'Wow,' Bruno says. 'He did then.'

'Yes,' Alice replies coldly. 'Yes, he did.'

As they cross a small road bridge, Bruno pauses and points down at the brook below. 'Look,' he says.

'What?' Alice asks, leaning over the railings beside him.

'The river.'

'Yes?' Alice asks, looking up and down the length of the river as she attempts to spot whatever Bruno has seen.

'It's pretty,' Bruno says in a funny pedantic voice. 'So look at it.'

'Oh!' Alice laughs. 'OK. Yes. Lovely. God, it's hot though, isn't it?'

'Yes, it is.'

They start to walk again. 'I hope it doesn't get much hotter than this, does it?' Alice asks.

'It most definitely does.'

'I love the sunshine,' she confides. 'But I've never been that good with the heat.'

'That must be a challenging combination,' Bruno says. Alice frowns, so he expounds, 'What with the sun being the source of all the heat on the planet and everything.'

'It's not that challenging in England,' Alice says sarcastically.

'No, I guess not,' Bruno laughs. He points to a hamlet of houses in the distance. 'That's where you are. That's the village.'

'Thank God for that,' Alice says. 'I think I need that drink of water after all. But my, it's tiny. Is that it?'

'Yep,' Bruno says. 'That's it.'

The hamlet comprises fewer than a dozen narrow stone houses, squashed one against the other on the roadside. 'Virginie's is that one,' Bruno says, pointing at the second house. 'The one with the cats.'

A small staircase leads up from the narrow road to a tiny garden with a tatty vine-covered pergola leading to the front door. On every other step sits a flowering pot plant, and five of the steps are occupied by mangy country cats.

279

'Are they friendly?' Alice asks, as Bruno leads her past them. 'I've never been that fond of cats.'

'No,' Bruno says, 'you said. And yes, they're lovely.'

'And where is Virginie?' Alice asks once they've reached the trellis. 'I never thought to ask.'

'Her mother's ill,' Bruno says. 'She's in Marseille looking after her.'

'Nothing too serious, I hope?'

'Very serious, I'm afraid,' Bruno says. 'She's dying.'

'Oh, how sad.'

'Yes,' Bruno says. 'She's lovely too. Ah, there's your case.'

Alice looks over to see it partly hidden behind a small marble garden table. She tuts. 'That Matt!' she says plaintively. 'I can't believe he just left it outside.'

'Um, not too much crime around here,' Bruno replies.

'All the same,' Alice says, grabbing the handle of the case and yanking it towards the front door.

Bruno fiddles with the lock, then leads Alice into a small kitchen-cum-dining room. The furniture is old but has been repainted in Provençal yellows and greens. With the vine-covered entrance, it's like a postcard of Provence.

Alice looks around at all of Virginie's things, and the reality of staying in someone else's home suddenly hits her. Surprisingly, she hadn't thought much about it. 'Gosh, all her stuff's still here,' she says, looking at a bottle of deodorant on the sideboard.

'Well, yes. This wasn't exactly planned.'

'Are you sure she doesn't mind?' Alice asks. 'I'd feel very funny about someone living in my place.'

'She said not,' Bruno says. 'I didn't even have to ask. I just told her you were coming and she offered.'

Two of the cats have followed them into the kitchen, and the brown, shabby tabby has leapt on to the kitchen counter. Alice

280

raises her hands to scare him away. 'Go on, you,' she says. 'Outside. Shoo!' The cat looks at her nonchalantly and then rubs his chin against the fruit bowl and meows.

'Shoo?' Bruno laughs. 'This is where they live.'

'Yes, but not on the kitchen counter,' Alice says. 'I bet even Virginie doesn't allow that.'

Bruno doesn't reply. He just grins at Alice disarmingly. 'Come upstairs,' he says. 'Come see the other rooms.'

Alice follows him up a narrow, whitewashed stone staircase. It reminds her of those photos you see of Greek villages and amusingly, on the landing, is a photo of a Greek church. Virginie must have had the same thought.

The lounge, exactly the same size as the kitchen, contains a sofa and an armchair. These have been covered with red and orange throws that look like they might have come from India. The red hexagonal tiles of the floor are covered with small rugs, and the walls with heavily laden bookcases.

'Cosy, huh?' Bruno says.

'Yes,' Alice replies. 'But look at all that cat hair! I hope she's got a vacuum. And I'll give those bookcases a dust for her too. It looks like they could do with it.'

'She has great taste, huh?' Bruno says. 'Come on. Only one more floor to go.'

On the third floor is a very feminine bedroom. An iron four-poster takes up most of the space. It has been draped, prettily, with mosquito netting.

'Do you have mosquitos here?' Alice asks.

'Yep. We use those plug-in things, but Virginie prefers nets.'

'Ooh, I think I'll need a plug too,' Alice says. 'I hate mosquitos. So how old is Virginie?' To Alice, it looks like quite a young girl's bedroom for some reason.

281

'Not sure,' Bruno says. 'Her mother's ninety-one, and I think she had her quite young.'

'So . . . seventies?'

'Something like that.'

'And the bathroom?' Alice asks. 'I didn't see a bathroom.'

'Ah!' Bruno laughs. 'That's the catch.'

'The catch?'

'Yeah. I hope you're not like Matt. I hope you don't pee in the middle of the night.'

Bruno leads her back down. 'Gosh, all these stairs!' Alice says.

They step back out on to the courtyard. On the opposite side, a small blue door is set into the stone wall. 'Tada!' Bruno says, opening it.

The bathroom, though tiny, contains everything one might need: a toilet, sink, mirror and a small tiled shower area. The ceiling has been painted the same deep blue as the door, and the walls again have been whitewashed.

'Is Virginie Greek?' Alice asks, pointing at another photo, this time of two women posing in front of a higgledy-piggledy Greek village.

'Nope. But she loves Greece. Especially Santorini.'

'Is one of these two her?' Alice asks, pointing at the photo.

Bruno leans in and studies the picture. 'Yes. That's Virginie on the left,' he says. 'But a long, long time ago.'

Alice looks around the bathroom again. 'It reminds me of when I was a girl,' she says. 'We had an outside loo as well.'

'So you'll be OK then.'

'Yes, fine. As long as it doesn't rain,' Alice says, stepping back out into the courtyard.

'Hah,' Bruno says. 'We'll get you an umbrella. This over here is mint.' He walks to a rockery in the corner and picks a leaf and

282

puts it into his mouth. 'You might want to water this for her. It's a bit dry.'

'And you might want to wash that before you eat it,' Alice says. 'It's probably got cat pee all over it.' A clattering noise behind her makes Alice jump. She turns to see the white longhair bursting back out through a cat flap. 'Oh,' she says. 'They have their own door.'

'Like I said, this is their home.'

'But I can lock it, presumably?'

'Why would you want to lock it?'

'Well, to keep them outside,' Alice says.

'But why would you want to lock Virginie's cats outside? I don't get it.'

'Not all the time,' Alice explains. 'But perhaps at night. I mean, there are no doors, are there? I don't want them running all over me all night. I don't want them bringing me dead mice and things.'

Bruno strokes his beard. He pushes his tongue into the side of his cheek. He stares at Alice. He looks bemused.

'What?' she asks.

Bruno scratches his neck. 'I'm just surprised,' he says. 'Matt was right, I guess. He said you were like this, only I thought he was exaggerating.'

Alice frowns. 'Like what?' she asks. She's really not sure what she's said.

'Is it because you're stressed?' Bruno asks. 'Because I know you've had a hard time. And some people get weird when they're stressed. My dad does, actually.'

Alice pales. 'Stressed?' she says. 'I'm sorry . . . I . . .'

Bruno raises his hands in a gesture of peace. He smiles gently. 'Hey, I'm not, you know, having a go, Alice,' he says. 'I'm just trying to understand.' And indeed, his tone is gentle, friendly, entirely devoid of anger or aggressiveness.

283

'I'm not sure what I've done,' Alice replies honestly. She's running conversations through her mind, trying to spot the error. 'I didn't realise that I was being weird, to be honest.'

'Really?' Bruno asks.

'Really.'

'OK, here's the thing,' Bruno says, chewing his lip. 'I guess . . . Well . . . You might wanna work on your positives, is all.'

'My positives?'

'Yeah!'

'I'm sorry, Bruno,' Alice says, 'but I'm really not following you.'

'OK,' Bruno says softly. 'You seem nice, Alice. Really you do. And I know you've had a hard time. But since you arrived, I've heard nothing but negatives from you. The house is remote. You don't like cats. You don't like water. It's too hot. There are so many stairs . . . Matt said that in the car you actually asked him who would want to live in a place like this? Is that true?'

'I . . . I was only thinking about how remote it is,' Alice says. 'For youngsters like yourselves.'

'That *is* your point of view,' Bruno says, 'but you're here for a month, eh?'

Alice nods and swallows with difficulty. She's being gently berated by a seven-foot, twenty-nine-year-old Canadian boy – her son's boyfriend. And she has absolutely no past data on how to react to that.

'So you might wanna try to find some positives here,' Bruno continues. 'You might wanna try to execute this whole thing with a bit of elegance, for us, but for you too. For you mainly, in fact. That's all I'm saying here.'

Alice nods and wipes a bead of perspiration from her top lip.

'Your son's driven for five hours today to pick you up before going off to work a seven-hour shift. We've found you this great place to stay.' He gestures around him. 'Most people say . . . In fact,

284

you know what? I think you're the first person ever to come to our cabin and not say how awesome it is. And this place? Look around you, Alice – it's fucking incredible.'

Alice nods. 'I hear you,' she says.

'You're going through some really difficult shit, Alice. I know that, OK? We all know that. But we don't need to make this whole thing as difficult as possible, do we? We can actually find some pleasure here if we try, don't you think?'

Alice swallows and nods silently. She can't think of a single word to say. She feels about five again.

'It's like Mom always says. You have to take the time to smell the roses.'

Alice sighs deeply. She has an inexplicable desire to say, 'I've just left my husband. He beat me.' Instead, she licks her lips.

'I'm sorry,' Bruno says with concern. 'I think I've upset you, huh?'

'No, not really,' Alice says vaguely. 'I'm not sure how I feel.'

'OK. Well, I'm going to go home and give you some space. I'm gonna make some dinner, too. And then I'll see you about eight, OK? You remember the way?'

Alice nods robotically.

'Great,' Bruno says. 'Oh, the keys are on the side there. And don't forget to feed the cats – the crunchy things are under the sink. And they need water too, otherwise they die.'

Alice watches Bruno as he skips down the stone steps and strides off into the distance. She sinks on to a hard cast-iron garden chair behind her and remembers seeing a round cushion for it some-where indoors. She can't find the energy to go and get it right now though.

285

One of the cats, an old skinny grey one, jumps up on to her lap, but she pushes it off and crosses her knees to discourage it from returning. The cat rolls on to its back at her feet instead. It looks like it wants its tummy tickled, but Alice knows how quickly cats go from tickle-me to bite-you. She's not falling for that one.

She tries to think about her conversation with Bruno, but she's feeling stunned. Her brain seems devoid of sensible thoughts about it, or even any kind of emotion, yet his words – many of which are her words – are running as if on a loop through her head. *Nothing but negatives . . . driven for five hours . . . who would choose to live in a place like this?*

And yes, she had said that to Matt in the car. She had asked him exactly that question. And yes, perhaps she had been tactless. But then who would choose to live up the top of a mountain? Who would look at a map of the world and choose somewhere without a shop, or a restaurant, or a bar? It was hardly unreasonable to point out that most single young men did not actively search out this kind of isolation. But then Matt, she remembers, isn't single. And he's not really young any more either. As a parent, one tends to forget that. As a parent, one often tries to forget that.

And this Bruno – the way he spoke to her! No wonder she's in shock. Because, frankly, how dare he? *He's nothing to me*, Alice thinks. *He's not my son. He's not my friend. So how come he dares give me lessons in etiquette?*

Some emotions finally are surfacing. Alice is starting to feel angry. The heat of it is rising up from deep within like the uncomfortable rush of a blush. It sweeps through her body like that scorching wind they have in Spain. The scirocco, isn't that the one?

'How dare he?' she whispers, as her skin prickles with the heat.

Bruno's young enough to be her grandchild, for God's sake. 'You might want to work on your positives' indeed! The impertinence of it, that's what gets her, an impertinence so typical of

286

all these new world cultures, these people from places where no one ever learnt how to speak to an elder, where deference and tact are unknown values, where only brashness and newness have any worth, where so-called honesty trumps politesse every day of the week.

The form of it, that's part of why she's feeling so shocked, she realises. No one has ever spoken to her like that before. Yes, she's seen people have these heartfelt 'for your own benefit' conversations in American films, but it's not the English way. It's not the English way at all.

We prefer to say nothing, Alice thinks. *We bottle it up until we're so upset that we cry. Or we bottle it up until we're so angry, we punch our partners in the face.* That's one thing she has always understood about Ken's anger, for example. That the punch was never the result of whatever had just happened, but the culmination of a thousand unmanaged slights. Or perceived slights, anyway. Ken's punches were always expressions of an entire lifetime of bottled-up disappointments – that's why there was no sensible way to deal with them. Alice meets the revelation that she is crying again with a sense of exhaustion. Will the tears ever end?

She wonders if Bruno talks to Matt in the same patronising tone he used with her. She wonders how he copes with it. Perhaps he has learnt to talk like an American too. But no, because when Alice in the car had asked why anyone would live here, Matt hadn't asked her why she'd said it, had he? He hadn't pointed out that it wasn't a very nice thing to say, either. He had smiled at her blandly and then bitched to Bruno about it behind her back. Like Alice herself, English to the core.

Alice pulls a handkerchief from her pocket and wipes her eyes. So why had she said that? She runs the rest of the conversation through her mind and decides that, no, it was not an unreasonable question to ask. But all the same, why would a mother complain about the heat, complain about the bends, about the distance, about the isolation? Why would a mother choose these things to say to her son, rather than thanking him for driving for five hours? Simple habit perhaps? Simple bad habit?

She thinks about being (supposedly) the first ever person not to comment on how pretty the log cabin is. It's not something to be proud of. And yes, now she thinks about it, it is pretty. So why hadn't she said so?

At the time, she simply hadn't noticed, she decides. But then that begs the question, why hadn't she noticed?

She thinks about the river that Bruno had tried to get her to look at. Because she hadn't been able to 'see' that either. Yes, she had looked at it. And yes, like the house, once she had looked at it, she had perceived that it was pretty, that, in a logical, rational way, it was something worth looking at. But she'd had no emotional response to the river or the cabin. She's had no positive emotional response to anything for a long time. *Perhaps I'm clinically depressed*, she thinks. *Perhaps this is what it feels like.*

Alice struggles to look afresh at her immediate surroundings, and again, rationally, she can see that the vines are pretty, that the dappled shadow beneath them is picturesque. She looks at the mint in the corner of the rockery – vibrant, almost fluorescent in the sunshine – and her words come back to her. Cat pee, she thinks, shamefully. That was the only thing she had found to say. Cat pee!

Perhaps I can't see beauty any more, she thinks. *Perhaps I'm dead inside. Perhaps fifty years with Ken killed me.*

The tears are flowing freely now and Alice lowers her head into her hands and lets herself sob. She's been busy, that's the thing. She's been very, very busy for a very long time – busy avoiding conflict. She's spent her life not mentioning things, not noticing things. She's had to become an expert at not thinking about things, at not having emotional responses, just to survive. Yes, she understands

288

that now. It's not really her fault. She's just been too busy surviving to even think about smelling the bloody roses.

When Alice's tears run dry, she feels exhausted and a little hopeless. So coming here was a bad idea after all! The problem is that wherever you go, people expect things from you. No matter what's happening in your life, people have expectations of how you're supposed to behave. And Alice has nothing left to give. Not tonight at any rate. Perhaps not ever again.

A car drives past, the first one she has seen since she got here, and suddenly aware of the fact that other people must live here, and fearing a challenging conversation with one of the French locals (a conversation that she really doesn't have the energy for) she returns to the interior of the house. She locks the front door behind her.

She looks around at the hard chairs of the kitchen, two of which are occupied by cats, then climbs the stairs to the lounge. Here, she opens the windows and shutters. A strip of sunshine falls across the sofa. *Huh!* she thinks. *So I finally get my sofa in the sun.*

An image of Dot's place comes to mind, and then Dot herself, and Alice remembers that she is supposed to phone her. But she doesn't have the energy right now to fulfil Dot's expectations of her either, so she fishes her mobile from her bag and sends a text message instead. She's not sure if the message sends or not. Do they work from France? She'll have to check with Matt later.

She pushes Virginie's cat-hair-covered cushions on to the floor, then retrieves the cleanest one as a pillow. She stretches out on the sofa so that the sunlight falls across her face (it feels heavenly) and then, listening to the sound of the crickets outside the window, she falls into a deep sleep.

By the time she wakes up again, the sunlight has moved from her face to her feet. She's groggy from sleep and initially unsure as to what woke her. One of the cats has installed itself between her ankles but when she moves her legs, it instantly jumps down.

289

The noise, a noise she now realises she had integrated into her dream, sounds again. *Tock, tock, tock*: knuckles on a window. She lies still for a moment. She holds her breath. But then she hears Bruno's voice. 'Alice? Alice? Helloooo?'

Alice doesn't want to see Bruno right now. Alice isn't sure if she wants to see Bruno ever. And if not seeing Bruno means that she doesn't get to eat this evening, then she'd really rather not eat. She's easily tired enough to sleep right through anyway.

But the rapping gets louder. Bruno's cries become more strident. And Alice realises that she's not going to get away with just hiding here, so, deciding she'll simply send him away (she can do it tactlessly; she can do it with fully fledged Canadian honesty after all), she drags herself from the sofa and on down the stairs.

When she reaches the sombre kitchen, Alice realises that she must have slept for longer than she thought. She crosses to the door where Bruno's face, framed by his cupped hands, is peering in.

'Ah, thank God,' he says through the glass.

Alice unlocks the door and opens it.

'I thought I'd done all of this for nothing,' Bruno says. 'I thought you'd phoned a taxi and gone home or something.'

'Wishful thinking maybe?' Alice offers.

Bruno gestures behind him, so Alice glances at the tiled garden table upon which Bruno, bless him, has laid out a dinner party for two. 'Oh!' Alice exclaims, her mood instantly shifting. 'Gosh.'

'Dinner is served, Madam,' Bruno says through a grin.

'Yes . . . yes . . . I can see that! I . . . I was asleep, that's all.'

'And I can see that,' Bruno says, with meaning.

'Do I look awful?' Alice asks, one hand fluttering to her hair.

'No, but you do look like someone who just woke up from a siesta,' Bruno says. 'Take your time. I need to cuddle Paloma here anyway.'

290

'Paloma?'

Bruno steps towards the windowsill on which the old grey cat is sitting. 'This is Paloma,' Bruno explains. 'She's not going to be with us much longer, I don't think. She's very ancient, aren't you, Paloma?'

Alice returns inside the house and washes at the kitchen sink. She checks her face in the mirror. Her hair is squashed to one side and she has the seam of the cushion embossed across her cheek, so she squashes her hair back into shape and then massages her cheek a little before returning to the courtyard. 'You really didn't have to do all of this,' Alice says, taking in the three Tupperware containers of salad and the quiche Bruno is busy slicing. 'And you carried it all here, too!'

'Well, I waited for a while,' Bruno says, 'but then I got hungry!' He crosses to the doorway. 'Now, I just need plates and shit,' he says, 'and we're ready to go. Sit down. I'll bring them.'

Alice rubs her eyes and attempts to wake up, attempts to feel present right here, right now, but it's hard. This tiled table, this unexpected meal, is all so far away from Dot's apartment where she was this morning, after all. It's all a bit surreal, this air-travel lark.

'Here,' Bruno says, handing her a plate and dumping a handful of cutlery in the middle of the table.

'Thanks,' Alice says, constraining a yawn.

'That's beetroot and quinoa and mackerel,' Bruno says, pointing. 'That's Matt's favourite.'

'Really?' Alice asks. 'I could never get either of them to touch beetroot.'

Bruno shrugs. 'Sure,' he says. 'But when?'

'When?'

'Yeah, I mean, how long ago?'

'Ah,' Alice says. 'Yes, I see your point. It was a very long time ago.'

291

'And that one's tomato, mozza, basil, and that one's tabbouleh and mint. Oh, and before you ask, yes, I washed the mint. And the basil!'

'I wasn't going to say anything about the mint,' Alice protests.

'Well, good,' Bruno laughs. 'We're making progress here.'

'I wasn't aware that I needed to make progress,' Alice replies drily. She's a little surprised at herself for the spunky reply, but then again, why not? She's spent enough years sparring with Ken, after all. Even if he never once noticed.

'Touché,' Bruno says.

'Touché yourself,' Alice retorts.

Bruno picks up the beetroot salad and points it at Alice. 'Some salad number one, Mrs Hodgetts?' he asks. 'I take it you still go by Hodgetts?'

'I suppose so,' Alice says. 'And yes, thank you, Mr . . .' She frowns. 'And your surname is?'

'Campbell,' Bruno says. 'Like the soup, unfortunately.'

'Then yes, Mister Campbell. Some soup would be lovely.'

'Some salad?'

'Sorry, yes, of course. Some salad would be lovely.'

'Gosh,' Bruno says. 'More positivity.'

'You're a very rude young man,' Alice says. Her tone of voice implies that she's vaguely amused by his rudeness. 'Has anyone ever told you that?'

Bruno shakes his head. 'Not till now,' he says, slopping wine into their glasses. He raises his. 'To honesty then,' he toasts.

'To tact,' Alice offers, raising her own.

'Tact's overrated,' Bruno says.

'But nowhere near as overrated as honesty.' Alice sips her rosé – it's cool and fruity and delicious. She forks some beetroot salad into her mouth. 'This is nice,' she says. 'I can see why Matt likes it.'

'Tact or honesty?' Bruno asks.

Alice shrugs. 'A bit of both maybe? If that's possible.'

'I reckon,' Bruno says.

'So tell me something else I don't know about Matt.'

'Something else?'

'Well, I didn't know about him being . . . you know . . .'

'Gay?' Bruno asks.

'Yes.'

'It's OK,' Bruno says. 'You're allowed to say it these days. They changed the rules.'

'I know that, it's just . . . Anyway. So I didn't know he liked beetroot either. What other surprises have you got for me?'

Bruno shrugs. 'I don't know,' he says. 'I'm not sure what stuff you know already.'

'Not much, to be honest,' Alice says. 'He was always very secretive.'

'He likes dance music,' Bruno says. 'Techno and trance, and really boppy electronica.'

'He used to like The Smiths and The Cure.'

'He still does. But he DJs now, so he listens to dance music too.'

'He DJs?'

'Yeah, at parties and stuff.'

'Then that's a thing I didn't know.'

'He loves dogs,' Bruno says. 'All dogs. Any dog. Every dog.'

'Oh, your puppy,' Alice says. 'Where is he?'

'He's at home. He's fine. He sleeps a lot.'

Alice teases a chunk of mackerel from the salad. 'I knew about the dogs, of course,' Alice says. 'He drove us mad for one when he was little.'

'Yes,' Bruno says. 'He told me about that.'

'Oh, did he?'

'Yes . . . Um, moving quickly on,' Bruno laughs, 'he hates rosé. And capers. And anchovies.'

293

'Not keen myself,' Alice says.

'Careful now,' Bruno laughs, tapping the neck of the bottle.

'The anchovies, I meant. The wine's lovely.'

'So it's genetic then? The anchovy thing?'

'Possibly,' Alice says.

'He's scared of motorbikes.'

'Fearless Matt?' Alice asks. 'Scared of something?'

'Not-so-fearless Matt,' Bruno laughs. 'But then that might just be my driving. I don't think I'm very good.'

'Well, that's lots of things I didn't know. And you? Tell me some things about Bruno Campbell.'

'Er . . . I'm Canadian. I make pots,' Bruno says.

'And you like beetroot.'

Bruno wrinkles his nose. 'It's OK,' he says. 'I like cooking. And gardening – especially growing vegetables. I get really excited when they start to form. Things you can eat, sprouting from nowhere. It's like magic.'

'I could never get anything much to grow,' Alice admits. 'I've never had green fingers, me.'

'Matt's not much cop either,' Bruno tells her. 'He lacks patience. But he's good at other stuff.'

'Such as?'

'DIY.'

'Really?!'

Bruno nods. 'Really,' he says. 'He can build pretty much anything. And he's very good at his job, apparently.'

'Washing up?'

'Yes – well, clearing tables and stacking the dishwasher.'

Alice sighs. 'OK, there's a thing where you can maybe enlighten me, Bruno. Why does Matt always do such silly jobs?'

'Silly?' Bruno repeats.

'He's got an art degree, for God's sake!'

294

'He has?'

'Well, almost,' Alice says. 'He did four years. I mean, he dropped out before the end. But it really was just before the end.'

'I didn't know that.'

'Ah!' Alice says. 'You see – we can trade secrets.'

'But to answer your question, I guess he doesn't think that they're silly.'

Alice looks doubtful.

'Don't you eat in restaurants?' Bruno asks. 'Don't you stay in hotels?'

'Well, yes,' Alice says, 'not as much as I'd like to, but . . .'

'So someone has to deal with the dishes.'

'But Matt's so clever,' Alice says. 'He could be so much more.'

'He is so much more.'

Alice squints at Bruno as she thinks about this. And just for an instant, she thinks she knows what he means. But like some complex mathematical problem, her comprehension has vanished almost before she has finished grasping it. 'It still seems such a waste to me,' she says. 'That's all.'

'I thought we were watching our negatives.'

'You said that, not me,' Alice replies. 'Why don't you watch your own?'

'I do,' Bruno says. 'All the time. But anyway, getting back to Matt, I'm just saying that he's happy. So maybe you could try to concentrate on that instead.'

Alice nods. 'OK,' she says, 'I'll try. But you really are a very strange young man.'

'Strange is good,' Bruno says. 'Strange is what we strive for.'

'Well, I'd say you're doing pretty well then,' Alice laughs.

'And you?' Bruno asks. 'Tell me about you.'

'Oh, I don't know,' Alice says. 'There's really not much to tell.'

295

'OK then,' Bruno says mockingly, 'let's talk about me again. I've got masses to tell. Salad number two?' He points the second Tupperware container at Alice.

'Yes,' Alice says. 'Thank you.' As Bruno serves her with tomato and mozzarella, she smiles. It's strange, but in fact this bad-natured sparring is shifting to good-natured sparring, and she's starting, despite herself, to enjoy it. It's been so long since she has found herself opposite someone quick enough to fight back. 'So I like to read,' Alice says, 'if that counts.'

'Sure. What kind of thing?'

'Anything. Fiction, non-fiction, biographies, everything. I just devour books.'

'Like Matt then?'

'If you say so. And black pudding. And fish and chips. I know it's not haute cuisine or anything, but I do like fish and chips. And asparagus. God, I love asparagus.'

'It's nice, but it makes your . . .' Bruno's voice fades out.

'Yes?'

'Never mind,' Bruno says. 'It's not, you know . . . tactful dinner conversation.'

'It makes your pee smell?' Alice laughs. 'Was that it?'

'Yeah,' Bruno says. 'You know about that then?'

'It would be hard to like the stuff as much as I do and not know that really.'

'Eww,' Bruno says.

'Hey,' Alice says. 'You started it.'

Alice and Bruno spar on into the night. Around them, the light fades, the temperature falls, and the mosquitos appear, prompting Bruno to fetch and light a huge yellow citronella candle from Virginie's larder.

The cats, ever-present, take it in turns to attempt an invasion of Alice's lap, but she's not having it.

'You'll give in eventually,' Bruno tells her. 'Cats are incredibly tenacious.'

'So am I,' Alice tells him. 'They've met their match.'

By the time they've polished off the bottle of rosé, Alice is feeling tipsy and cocooned, as if wrapped in cotton wool. She's also surprised to find herself feeling something approaching happiness. At some point, the sparring has ceased and the conversation has become pleasant, intimate even.

Right now, Bruno is telling Alice about his parents, about their move to France, about the gallery in Aix and his suspicions that his mother merely pretends to sell his work. He's explaining about the Japanese technique called raku – he's describing the pots that he's trying to make, groups of smooth, perfectly formed cylinders, mounted on a base, each designed to hold a single flower. His eyes are sparkling in the candlelight. His pottery, Alice can see, really is a passion.

At some point, Alice checks her watch. She's surprised to see that it's almost half past eleven. 'At least it's cooler now,' she says.

'That's what's so great about living up here,' Bruno replies. 'Even in the hottest part of summer, you can still sleep properly. It's horrific down on the coast. In Aix, I used to get up to take cold showers every couple of hours, otherwise I couldn't sleep at all.'

'That must be horrible,' Alice agrees.

'So how are you feeling about everything?' Bruno asks. 'We've talked about just about everything except you, really.'

'That's true,' Alice admits. 'But I think it's done me good, to be honest. I almost forgot for a moment what a mess I'm in. It's been quite restful.'

'Are you in a mess?' Bruno asks.

'Yes,' Alice says. 'Yes, I think so.'

'Matt's incredibly proud of you, you know. For not going back.'

'Ha,' Alice laughs. 'For not going back yet.'

'Do you really think you might?'

She shrugs. 'I struggle to see what other options I have, to be honest, Bruno. But we'll see.'

Bruno nods thoughtfully. 'You could stay here,' he says. 'You could rent a little place like this one. Rents are dirt cheap around here.'

Alice laughs. 'Matt would love that,' she says.

'I guess that depends how easy you make it for him. Or how difficult.'

'You know, I did go back,' Alice says, fulfilling a sudden desire to tell Bruno something real about herself. He has shared so much with her this evening, after all.

Bruno frowns. 'I don't understand.'

'After it happened, I stayed with my friend for a few days. And then I got up one morning and decided I was being silly. So I packed my bag and went home.'

'Wow. And what happened?'

'Ken wasn't in,' Alice says. 'I don't know where he was, but he wasn't in, thank God. But he'd left me a note. On the kitchen table. Do you know what it said?'

Bruno almost indiscernibly shakes his head.

'It said, "Alice. If you come back while I'm out, can you iron me some shirts?"' Alice starts to laugh, but her moist eyes bely the complex mix of emotions that she's feeling.

Bruno, opposite, stares at her wide-eyed. 'And that was it?' he asks, grinning in disbelief. 'He was worried about his shirts?'

'Exactly.'

'Oh my God, Alice,' Bruno says. His hand, on the table, reaches forward and momentarily cups Alice's own. She can't remember the last time someone touched her hand across a table and it feels lovely

298

but also surprisingly, shockingly intimate. Reaching for her glass of water as an alibi, she quickly pulls it away.

'Can you believe that?' she says, swiping at a tear in the corner of her eye with her free hand.

'So you turned around and walked out, eh?'

'Yes. I packed some clothes in a bit of a panic. I was scared he'd come back.'

'I bet. And then you just left – good for you.'

'I wrote a note first. And then I left.'

Bruno raises one eyebrow. 'What did you write?' he asks.

'You really want to know?' Alice asks, restraining a smirk.

'Uh huh.'

'It's a bit rude. You might be shocked.'

'Go ahead,' Bruno says. 'Knock me out.'

'I wrote . . . You're really sure you want to hear this?'

Bruno blinks slowly. 'Yes,' he says.

'OK. I wrote, "Iron your own fucking shirts",' Alice says. She raises one hand to cover her mouth and glances left and right as if checking for eavesdroppers.

Bruno starts to laugh. 'Iron your own fucking shirts?' he repeats.

Alice nods and laughs (and cries a little) all over again. 'Iron your own fucking shirts,' she whispers again. 'That's the only thing I wrote.'

Once the dirty dishes have been moved to the kitchen and Bruno has once again walked jauntily off down the road, Alice returns to the courtyard.

The temperature now is just on the cool side of comfortable, so she goes inside for a pullover and the round cushion she spotted, before returning to the cast-iron chair.

The sky here is as deep and dark as she has ever seen, and as she sits and stares at it, hundreds and then thousands of stars come into view. She's never seen so many stars. It's stunning, simply stunning.

A flashing light in the corner of the garden catches her eye. It looks like one of those green LED lights and for a moment she thinks that Bruno must have left his phone on the wall. But when she crosses to retrieve it, it surprisingly takes off and drifts away.

Alice gasps. She's never seen a firefly before and it really is the most shockingly beautiful thing, if somehow a little silly. She sniffs at the air, then realises that she's picking up a hint of mint. Still watching the fading flashing light of the firefly, like some distant erratic aeroplane now, she brushes her hand through the leaves which release a pungent burst of minty air. She pulls a leaf from the plant and hesitantly places it in her mouth, then returns to the garden chair and looks back up at the night sky.

She thinks about Bruno talking about his pots, how animated he'd been, how excited. She asks herself if she isn't a little in love with him and wonders if that's wrong. He is her son's boyfriend, after all. What a strange concept that is. Her son's boyfriend! It's amazing how times can change, how suddenly you can decide to date a man or a woman and everyone thinks that's just fine. Still, that's better, she supposes. Compared with all the suffering of the past, that's got to be progress, hasn't it?

What a lovely evening, Alice thinks, and she's surprised at herself for the thought. But, yes, despite the circumstances and against all expectation, she has spent a lovely evening. And who would have thought that could still happen?

A tiny gust of breeze makes her shiver, so she blows out the candle and turns towards the house. There, in the doorway, is the ancient grey cat. Paloma, Bruno had called her, hadn't he? He had said that she wouldn't be around much longer.

300

'What do you want, old cat?' Alice asks it. Because the cat is clearly waiting for something.

'Food? Water?' Alice asks. But when Alice reaches the doorway, the cat trots ahead. It waits for her on the fourth step, tracking her movements as she moves around the kitchen. And when finally Alice switches the light out and crosses the room, it runs upstairs and waits for her, purring, on the bed. 'You just want company then?' Alice asks, and the cat rolls on her back and squirms a little in reply.

'Then you'd better not fidget,' Alice tells it. 'You'd better not keep me awake or I will kick you out, Paloma.'

The next morning, Alice steps out of the tiny bathroom to find Matt in the process of tying Jarvis to the railings. 'Morning, Mum,' he says. 'I thought we should bring you some breakfast.'

'We?' Alice queries, looking around for Bruno.

'Me and Jarvis,' Matt explains. 'Bruno's pottering today.'

'Isn't it potting?'

'Not sure,' Matt says. 'Potting sounds like gardening, doesn't it? Like potting compost? And potting shed.'

'Maybe,' Alice admits, pulling her wet hair back into a ponytail and tying it with a band. 'It's not like you to be up this early.'

'The dog wakes me up,' Matt says, 'which is tough, because I didn't get back till two.'

'A hard night?'

'A birthday party for thirty,' Matt says. 'I thought they'd never go to bed. And the worst music ever – "La Bamba" and the bloody Gipsy Kings and stuff like that. It was horrific. Did you sleep OK?'

'Like a log, actually,' Alice admits. 'I woke up covered in cats though.'

301

'Ah!' Matt laughs, heading into the kitchen and filling the kettle. 'And how are you getting on with the mogs?'

'They're very undisciplined,' Alice says, following him inside. 'I think Virginie must let them run riot.'

'They're cats,' Matt laughs.

'I just mean that they go everywhere,' Alice says. 'On the counters, on the furniture, on the bed. I don't think there's a single place they consider out of bounds. One of them tried to follow me into the bathroom.'

'Yes,' Matt says. 'That's what cats do.'

'Well, I intend to train them,' Alice tells him.

Matt laughs. 'Good luck with that,' he says.

Alice crosses to the kitchen table and peers into the paper bag Matt has placed there. 'Ooh, hot croissants!' she exclaims. 'Where did you get those from? I didn't think there was even a shop up here.'

'There isn't,' Matt says. 'They're from the hotel. I warmed them in the oven, that's all. They're leftovers from yesterday, but they're fine warmed up.'

'Can I?' Alice asks, reaching tentatively towards the bag. 'I'm a bit hungry.'

'Sure,' Matt says. 'It's what they're for.'

'So how did you get on with Bruno?' Matt asks, once the coffee's made and they're seated at the garden table.

'He's quite strange, isn't he?' Alice says. She watches Matt frown and hears her own words and wonders why she said it. Perhaps she does need to watch her negatives. 'I meant that in a good way. He's very surprising,' she adds. 'And shockingly direct.'

'I think it's a Canadian thing,' Matt says.

302

'But I liked him,' Alice admits. She wonders why it costs her to admit this. Because it does. She can feel the cost as she says it. 'I liked him a lot, actually.'

'He liked you too,' Matt says. He sounds almost as surprised at this as Alice feels at learning it. 'He said you talked till midnight or something?'

'We did.'

'About?'

'Pretty much everything, really. I blame the wine.'

Matt grins. 'He got you drunk then? Figures.'

'Not quite drunk. But, you know . . .'

Matt clears his throat. 'I suppose we need to talk too.'

'Do we?' Alice asks, sipping at her coffee, then feeding another chunk of buttery croissant to her lips.

'I think so, Mum,' Matt says. 'I mean, what happened? And what are you going to do?'

Alice stops chewing for a moment. Matt, opposite, looks at her expectantly.

'Can we leave it for a few days?' Alice says finally. 'Would that be possible? Only it's all a bit fresh. And I only got here yesterday, after all.'

'Sure,' Matt says, relieved. 'But just so you know, I think you should leave him. I mean . . . you have left him, but I think you should stay away. Definitively. Make a new start.'

'Yes,' Alice says, sounding distant. 'Like I say, can we leave it for a few days? I need some time to get my thoughts together.'

Jarvis, still tied to the railings, starts to whimper now, so Matt crosses the courtyard and unties him, then returns to the table with the writhing dog in his arms. 'He tends to chase the cats,' Matt says as he reties him to the chair. 'I think he only wants to be friends, but they don't seem to know that.'

303

Alice looks around, but the three cats present in the courtyard have already vanished. 'That's one way to get rid of the cats,' she says. 'Maybe you can lend me the dog tonight.'

'Only you're not much keener on dogs, are you?'

'I've never had anything against dogs,' Alice says indignantly. 'Well, except the big dangerous ones. The ones that bite your face off.'

Matt shrugs. 'Oh,' he says. 'OK.' He nuzzles the dog's head with his nose.

'I . . .' Alice starts. She clears her throat. 'I'm glad you got your dog,' she says. 'Finally, I mean.'

Matt swallows and looks soulfully up at her. 'Thanks. It was a huge surprise. I burst into tears actually.'

Alice nods thoughtfully. 'I can imagine,' she says. 'I am sorry about . . . you know . . . when you were little.'

'It's OK, Mum. It's all in the past now.'

'But I am sorry,' Alice says again. 'I want you to know that. And we've never spoken about it. I . . . I was sad for you. I was so sad for you. I felt I had really let you down.'

Matt sighs and looks back up at Alice, his expression pained. 'It's OK, Mum,' he says again. 'It wasn't your fault.'

'I tried,' Alice says, her voice starting to break. 'I don't think you ever knew that, but I really did try. But your father . . . he was always so stubborn.'

'I know. I always knew that,' Matt says softly.

'Really?' Alice asks. 'Because I always felt you blamed me.'

Matt shakes his head. 'I never blamed you. I heard everything, after all.'

'You did?'

'He nearly killed you, Mum. What more could you do?'

Alice tips her head sideways. 'I don't think it was quite that bad, but . . .'

Matt pulls a face and clears his throat. 'OK . . .' he says.

For a minute, they sit in silence, the mother and the son. They're both wondering the same thing. They're both asking themselves why Alice has always done this, why she has always understated Ken's violence. It's just a reflex, Alice is thinking. It's just another bad habit, one designed to make the whole situation just a tiny bit less unbearable. But what if making the unbearable bearable turns out to be counterproductive? What if it only makes the unbearable last longer?

Matt plays with the dog's floppy ears, folding them across the top of his head like a hat, while he debates attempting to get Alice to admit the truth of what took place that night. He's wondering if she needs to be forced to face up to things if she's to avoid doing them all over again.

But Alice gets there first. 'You're right,' she admits, her voice squeaky and strange to her. 'He did nearly kill me that night. I thought he'd broken my nose. I had to go to the hospital.' Tears start to roll down her cheeks.

'Shit, Mum,' Matt says. 'I'm sorry. You said you didn't want to talk about it. I should have listened.'

'It's fine,' Alice says, looking bravely up at her son, seemingly accepting the past, accepting all of it simply by not hiding her tears from him. 'This is fine. This is good. I think it's what your Bruno would call a "healthy process".'

The days come and go without form or reason, their progression marked only by Alice's progressive surrender to the law of the cats and an ever-increasing number of fireflies at night.

Some days Matt appears with breakfast and some evenings Bruno prepares supper, but as often as not Alice finds herself

305

alone with some bread and cheese, reading – her Kindle propped up against a misty bottle of wine. The cats, untrainable, are ever-present.

Occasionally Alice tries to think about the future and on such occasions she inevitably cries a little. And sometimes, lying on the sofa in the sunshine with Paloma between her ankles, she finds herself feeling unexpectedly happy; surprisingly, shockingly contented.

She goes for daytime walks with Matt and Jarvis around the magnificent lake behind their house, and at nights, when Matt's working, on 'firefly' expeditions with Bruno. They're called *lucioles* in French, he tells her. It's such a beautiful word that she writes it down when she gets back. Near the lake, the countryside flashes and glitters with them so madly that it looks as if someone has strewn disco lights across the land.

In Virginie's courtyard, Alice tries to photograph these stunning insects, but not one of them shows up in the picture. When she complains to Bruno about this, he asks, 'Why do you want to photograph them anyway?'

'So I can remember them,' Alice replies.

'Can't you just remember them with, you know, your memory?' Bruno asks.

And for once, Alice finds herself lost for a reply.

Twice, Matt drives her over the mountain for supplies, and Alice nervously presents her Visa card. But it continues, against all expectations, to function. All is well.

On the second Saturday of her visit she heads to the cabin for lunch, only to find Bruno's parents have arrived, too.

Observing Connie and Joseph with Bruno, Alice finds that she perhaps understands Bruno a little better. They're so relaxed together, so completely natural, so informal, so caring – it's such a shocking contrast with any family gathering that Alice has ever attended that she can't help but wonder where she and Ken went wrong. Of course, she figures, Connie and Joseph seem to actually like each other. That must, after all, help a bit. Plus Joseph doesn't seem to be a psychopath, either. And they're both young and clever and educated, and, she guesses, reasonably wealthy. That must make life easier. She starts unconsciously to hate them.

For a moment, sprawling on blankets beneath the apple tree, Alice forces herself to smile through one of the most acute pangs of jealousy she has ever experienced. For a few seconds, she detests all three of them for being such shiny, happy people. But then Connie throws back her head and laughs uncontrollably at one of Alice's strange metaphors, and Joseph rolls his eyes and winks at Matt, and Alice caves in to the inevitability of loving Connie and Joseph also. It's simply impossible, she realises, to do anything else.

In the midst of this summer lovefest, Alice carries some plates into the cabin, where she finds herself alone with Matt at the sink.

'Let me do that,' Alice offers. 'You must be sick of doing dishes.'

'Dad just phoned me,' Matt replies, his voice stony.

Alice gulps. She feels as if she has been cut loose from her balloon. She feels as if she has hit the ground with a nasty bump. 'Oh,' she says, her smile on entering the kitchen a mere memory.

'He wanted to know . . .' Matt coughs. 'You know . . .'

'If I'm going back?' Alice says quietly.

Matt's hand, engaged in slow, circular motions as he scrubs the plate, freezes. 'He wanted to know when you're going back,' he says, without looking up. 'Not if.'

Alice reaches out to grip the draining board. She feels suddenly dizzy. 'What did you say?'

'That I had no idea,' Matt says. 'I didn't think it was my place to . . . you know . . . pre-empt . . . or whatever.'

'No,' Alice says. 'Of course not.'

307

'You're not going back though, are you?' Matt asks, nervously looking up from his dishes at Alice beside him.

Alice licks her lips. Her eyes dart around her son's face as if perhaps the answer lies there. And then before she even knows that she has found the said answer, she hears herself speak. 'No,' she says. 'No, I'm never going back.'

Matt screws his features up. His eyes are glistening. 'Good,' he croaks. 'That's good.'

'You think?'

Matt nods. 'You've been so different, Mum. These last few days . . .'

'I . . .' Alice starts.

But then Bruno bursts into the kitchen and the moment is lost. 'Come on!' he says, wrenching the sponge from Matt's grasp. 'You can do that later. Or I can. Come outside. We need you for charades!'

Once Connie and Joseph have driven away, arms hanging out of windows, and once Matt has 'suddenly' realised that he's late for work and rushed off in a flurry of excuses, Alice finds herself alone with Bruno again.

'I should be getting home, too,' she tells him once they've cleared away the remaining lunch things from the table.

'Really?' Bruno says. He sounds surprised. 'Why?'

'Oh, I'm sure you've had enough of me by now!'

'Nope,' Bruno says. 'So sit down. It's aperitif time.'

Alice smiles indulgently. 'Oh, OK,' she says. 'But just for the aperitif. And then I'm going to leave you be.'

Bruno fetches a fresh bottle of rosé and some delicious, salty pistachio nuts. 'Here,' he says, handing Alice the corkscrew. 'You do the honours. I'm just gonna put some music on and feed the dog.'

Once he has connected a small portable speaker to his telephone and settled Jarvis in his basket, he takes a seat and raises his glass. 'To family,' he says. 'And rosé.'

'To family,' Alice agrees. 'I must say you seem to get on very well with yours.'

Bruno nods. 'They're pretty cool.'

'I feel a bit jealous really,' Alice admits.

'Jealous?'

'Oh, I don't know. Of the way you all get on, I suppose. There doesn't seem to be any tension at all. And Connie and Joseph seem to have led quite a charmed life really.'

Bruno looks thoughtful. 'They've had their share of heartache,' he says.

'Really?' Alice asks. 'If they have, they hide it well.'

'Dad wanted to be a pilot,' Bruno says, 'but he's colour-blind. It meant it was impossible back then, apparently. Not sure about now. But he's scared of heights, so I'm not sure how that one would've panned out anyway!'

'But he had a whole career in electrical goods, didn't he? It sounded like he built a whole empire.'

'I'm not sure about an empire, but they had ten stores. It's not what he wanted to do though. Not at all. And Mom wanted babies. She wanted lots of babies. But she could never have kids. Something wrong with her womb, I think. She lost a few before they gave up trying. Dad said it was really tough on her.'

'Yes,' Alice says. 'That will have been tough.'

'I think that's why she became a grief counsellor,' Bruno says. 'So she could, you know, help herself.'

Alice frowns confusedly. 'So does that mean . . . are you . . .?' she stammers.

'Adopted,' Bruno says, matter-of-factly answering Alice's unfinished question. 'Yeah. My mother was a junkie apparently.

309

Heroin. She died of an overdose when I was two. I never knew her or anything.'

'Gosh!' Alice says. 'I didn't know that. I'm so sorry.'

'It's fine,' Bruno says. 'Mom and Dad are awesome. It was a lucky escape, I guess.'

'That's amazing,' Alice says. 'You couldn't possibly tell. I mean, you all get on so perfectly.'

Bruno flashes the whites of his eyes at Alice. 'Maybe that's why,' he says. 'I mean, they chose me from all the other abandoned babies out there. And I've always kind of known how lucky I am. People always say you don't choose your family, but I guess we kind of did.'

'Yes,' Alice says, 'I suppose you might be right.'

'More wine?' Bruno asks, waving the bottle at Alice.

She glances at her glass and sees that she has emptied it during Bruno's brief and surprising story. 'More wine!' she affirms, pushing it forward.

'So what do you think of this?' Bruno asks, nodding at the speaker.

'The music? It's strange,' Alice says.

'Just strange?'

She shrugs. 'No, it's OK actually. I hadn't really thought about it. It is strange. But in a good way.'

'They're called Boards of Canada.'

'So they're Canadian?'

'Not even,' Bruno laughs. 'I thought they were – it's why I got into them in the first place. But no, they're Scottish.'

Alice concentrates on the wafting waves of sound coming from the speaker, then says, 'It sounds like something from a film really. Or a dream.'

'A dream sequence in a film maybe?' Bruno offers.

'Yes, perhaps. So tell me about Virginie,' Alice says. 'I found some photos. I mean, I know I shouldn't have, but . . .'

'Who could ever resist forbidden photos?'

'Not me, sadly. That's for sure.'

'She's lovely,' Bruno says. 'She's coming up soon to meet you. Well, to see the cats mainly, but she wants to meet you too. You'll like her. She's fun. She speaks a bit of English, too.'

'And she's my age, you say?'

'Uh huh. Maybe a bit older. She was a nurse, I think. But she's retired now.'

'A nurse? That explains the uniform in the closet,' Alice says. 'I thought it might be for fancy dress or something. It's a very old-fashioned nurse's uniform.'

Bruno laughs. 'Matt tried to get into that for a party once. But it was waaay too small.'

'Was she ever married?'

'Not that we know of.'

'And no children either?'

'Just the cats. The cats are her children, I think.'

'So do you think she was just unlucky in love?'

'Ha!' Bruno laughs. 'The million-dollar question. We're not sure. There are some pictures of her with a woman. On holiday and stuff. Did you see those?'

Alice nods.

'Probably just a friend though.'

'It's not like you not to ask.'

'I guess,' Bruno says. 'But I always got a bad vibe about that one. Like there was some heartache in that story, you know? It's always seemed best not to go there. Matt agrees.'

'So you can be tactful when you want to?' Alice says with a wink.

'Apparently so,' Bruno says. 'I just try, you know, to negotiate things with some grace. It's not always easy.'

311

'With grace?' It strikes Alice as a strange word for a young man to use.

'Yeah. To do the right thing. To say the right thing. But sometimes you need to be tactless, I reckon. Sometimes you need to push people so that they open up a bit. Otherwise there's no contact. Otherwise it's all shouting over walls, you know?'

'Like with me, for instance?'

'Maybe.'

'That sounds very wise,' Alice says. 'Actually, you are very wise for – how old did you say you are? Twenty-nine?'

'Yeah. I'm not so sure about wise though,' Bruno says.

'I am. Honestly. You seem very . . . I don't know . . . centred? And you seem to have a lovely simple life here. You both seem very settled.'

'Most of that is Matt's doing,' Bruno says. 'I would never have dreamed of living up here without him. But Matt fell in love with the place. He convinced me that we could be happy here. And he was right.'

'Really? That surprises me. I thought that was your influence.'

'Nope. Matt worked out that if we lived here, I could carry on doing my ceramics. And he could work part-time so we can do more stuff together. And Mom and Dad don't mind. Not for the moment anyway. Yes, Matt's the great anti-consumer around here. The rest of us are just playing catch-up.'

'He's an anti-consumer, is he?' Alice says doubtfully. 'I don't think I'm even sure what that means.'

Bruno smiles. 'You should talk to him about it. He reads loads, you know: religions, Buddhism and stuff, ecology, new age philosophies, psychology . . . He's made having no money into this whole lifestyle thing.'

'Isn't that just an excuse though?' Alice asks. 'Isn't it just an excuse for being broke all the time?'

312

'Maybe,' Bruno says, 'but I don't think so. You should talk to him about it, Alice. Talk to him about life, about happiness. He has heaps of things to say.'

Alice forces a smile and takes a moment to look around her, a moment to think about this. She sees the log cabin and the tatty plastic table. She sees Bruno's vegetable patch and thinks of their battered car and his rusty motorbike. She sees the tumbledown garden shed at the bottom of the lawn and pictures Bruno in his potter's shed. And in her mind's eye, she compares it with Tim and Natalya's place, with the sleek sheer expanses of concrete and glass and shiny, shiny success. She compares Matt's kind of happiness with Tim's, too, Bruno's frugality with Natalya's constant spending, her constant grasping for status. And suddenly she sees that Matt's lifestyle isn't born of constraint, as she had imagined. It's not born of failure, as she had feared; it's a choice – of course it is! She's still not convinced that it's the right choice, but it's perhaps no more crazy than its exact opposite. It's no more unreasonable than continuous, unsustainable consumption, after all. And that thought feels like something of a revelation to her.

'So what about you?' Bruno asks, interrupting her thoughts. 'Did you ever date anyone else? Or was there only ever . . . Ken? Is that his name?'

Alice stares at Bruno. His question, as often, strikes her as impertinent. But as she looks questioningly into his eyes, she realises that it's nothing of the sort. He's treating her as an equal, that's all. He's treating her like someone who might want to get tipsy with him on a bottle of rosé, like someone who might enjoy listening to this strange electronic music. It makes such a change from the usual compartments we put each other in. It makes such a change, as Bruno would say, from all of that shouting over walls.

313

Yes, Bruno is treating her like a real human being who might have something interesting to share with him. She wracks her mind for a story to prove him right.

'OK,' she says finally, 'but if you want that story, I'll be needing to eat. Because all this wine on an empty stomach is making me too tipsy to think straight.'

'Food!' Bruno says, standing. 'You got it!'

By the time Bruno has returned with two doorstep sandwiches, Alice is hesitating about telling her story after all. Fuelled by rosé and the intimacy of the moment, it had seemed like a good idea, only now she's not so sure.

'So,' Bruno says, sliding a plate towards her, 'you were going to tell me your story.'

'Yes,' Alice says, 'but I think I've changed my mind.'

'Oh, go on, Alice,' Bruno pleads. 'I made you a sandwich and everything.'

'OK, I'm not sure how much of this . . .' Alice starts hesitantly. 'But, OK, here goes. There was someone before Ken. I was . . . in love . . . perhaps. In a way.'

'You were, huh?'

'We used to go for long walks together. We liked the park. Joe wanted to become a gardener. I'm not sure if that ever came to pass or not.'

'You didn't stay in contact?'

'No,' Alice laughs. 'No, not at all.'

'But you think you were in love with this Joe?'

'As I say, in a way . . . It's complicated. But we used to laugh a lot. Just silly stuff. We were still kids really. But we used to have lots of silly in-jokes. Things only we understood. We used, for instance – and I

314

still do this actually – but we used to make up these silly metaphors together. We would say that someone was as fat as a ferret. That was a favourite one. Or that someone was a thick as a fiddle. Or as difficult as a difficult Tuesday. I'm not sure that will make any sense to you. As I say, it was an in-joke.'

Bruno nods enthusiastically. 'Matt still does that,' he splutters, his mouth full of sandwich. 'Sorry,' he mumbles, belatedly covering his mouth with one hand.

'Does he?' Alice asks. 'Really?'

Bruno chews and swallows before continuing. 'Yeah, Matt's always saying things are as flat as a ferret. Or as pernickety as a pumpkin. Weird, funny stuff like that.'

Alice laughs. 'Well, that all came from Joe. And it used to make us giggle so much . . .'

'Complicity,' Bruno says.

'I'm sorry?'

'You had complicity.'

'Yes, I suppose we did. We made each other laugh a lot, anyway.'

'But Matt doesn't know about Joe, eh?'

'No, nobody does.'

'I won't tell him if you don't want me to, don't worry.'

Alice shrugs. 'It's all so long ago anyway,' she says. 'It's ancient history now.'

'So what happened? How did you end up with Ken?'

'Ah,' Alice says. 'I'm not sure I can explain that. Not satisfactorily, I mean. Joe wasn't right for me. It was just a silly crush really. It was one of those blips that happen. Like a freak whirlwind that sweeps through. It was obvious to everyone that it wasn't any kind of normal relationship. My parents were against us seeing each other, so . . .'

'Because?'

315

Alice sighs. 'Joe wasn't right,' she says. 'Anyone could see that. And my father knew Ken's father. He had his own business. He was successful. We were quite poor back then, so . . .'

'So it was like an arranged marriage?'

'Almost,' Alice says, then, 'Yes, pretty much.'

'And Joe didn't fight for you?'

'No,' Alice says. 'No, um, Joe knew as well as I did that it couldn't work out.'

'But I don't get why,' Bruno says. 'If you loved each other.'

'Like I say,' Alice says, 'it was a funny kind of relationship. Childish, perhaps. And it's so long ago. It was a whole different time. The rules about what you could and couldn't do were very different. I know this isn't making much sense to you now, but . . .' Alice shrugs. 'And Joe didn't have a penny. And nor did we. And with our parents against us even being friends . . . Well, it was nigh-on impossible. It was impossible.'

Bruno is staring at Alice intently. It's making her feel nervous.

'Anyway, I wasn't against marrying Ken. Not at first, at any rate. I mean, I got to stop work – I was doing shifts in a horrible soap factory. And Ken gave me Tim and Matt, after all.'

'Were you scared of the thing with Joe?' Bruno asks. 'It sounds a bit like you were. When you say it was like a freak whirlwind and stuff.'

'In a way, yes,' Alice says. 'In a way I hid from it all by marrying Ken, I suppose. I hid in my marriage to a certain degree. Plus it's all very well thinking you're in love, but if you're hungry and homeless . . . We were scared of poverty. People tend to forget that nowadays, but it is possible to be too hungry to be happy.'

Bruno sighs. 'I don't know,' he says. 'I just can't believe that Joe never came back for you. That you never heard from him again.'

316

Alice shuffles in her seat. 'Joe lived right over the other side of town. They were slums, really. I never had any reason to go there. And once I was married, well . . . It was best to stay away.'

'Don't you regret it though?' Bruno asks, dipping his finger into the yellow wax of the candle. 'I mean, you could have had a whole different life. Matt could have had a whole different family.'

'Matt wouldn't have existed,' Alice says. 'You can thank Ken for your boyfriend.'

'You don't know that,' Bruno says. 'Maybe he inherited everything from you. Maybe he would have been just the same. Who knows how that shit works.'

Alice sighs and shrugs.

'Have you ever tried to find him?' Bruno asks. 'You can find most people on the Internet these days if you try. I could help you look. What was his surname?'

Bruno reaches for his phone and unlocks the screen, but abruptly, Alice puts down her sandwich and stands.

'You know what?' she says. 'I suddenly want to be on my own. Is that OK? Can I say that without upsetting you?'

Bruno looks concerned. 'Have I hurt your feelings, Alice?'

'No, really,' Alice says. 'You've been perfect. But I just suddenly want to be on my own. Is that OK? Can I do that?'

Bruno puts down his phone and raises his hands. 'Sure, Alice,' he says. 'Whatever.'

Alice does not go home. When she reaches the point where the track meets the tarmac, she turns right, and not left. She glances nervously up at the cabin in case Bruno is watching her. She feels as if what she's doing, heading to the lake rather than the house, is somehow irresponsible, illicit perhaps. She suspects that he would tell her off.

The official footpath, as opposed to the boys' shortcut, zigzags up the side of a small green hill before weaving through the pine forest as it descends the other side.

It's another beautiful moonlit evening, but Alice feels a little scared all the same. She has never thought to ask which animals roam among these trees. She hopes there's nothing dangerous.

The air is still warm from the heat of the day, and the pine needles beneath her feet crunch and exude a gorgeous scent, a mixture of pine freshness and earthy decay. Here and there, fireflies drift erratically among the trees like floating, flashing garlands of light.

When she reaches the lake, she crosses the beach and sits on a rock. She stares out at the deep grey of the water and thinks about the fact that this lake is supposedly man-made. *At least we made something pretty for once*, she thinks.

As she starts to walk again, she thinks of Joe and remembers the impossibility of the times. Because, yes, Joe had fought for her. Joe had begged her not to marry Ken. She had even appeared on the night before the wedding. 'Please don't, Alice,' she had wept, over and over. 'It'll be the end of everything.'

'The end of what?' Alice had asked her. And Joe had been unable to reply. Because neither of them could name that thing which would be broken. Neither of them had any vocabulary to describe what they were feeling, or to envisage what might continue if only Alice did not marry Ken. There were no words for these things, back then.

You could have had a different life, she hears Bruno saying, and it's so easy to say, yet so difficult to live. For how can you live something when you don't even have a word for it?

'A crush,' her parents had called it. A silly childhood crush. That was the best anyone had managed back then, vocabulary-wise. And how could Alice possibly choose a fragile, insubstantial 'crush' on a girlfriend over the weight and heft of a marriage, of a family?

318

But it was no crush. It's taken her a lifetime to admit it, but she knows this now. And perhaps she owes it to herself, owes it to Joe even, to build a different life for herself now. It's all here, all apparently laid out for her.

Her son and Bruno, lovely Bruno, have shown her that something else is possible. A life without anger? A life without constantly striving for something else? A life of accepting, of coming to terms with the nature of one's own desires perhaps? A life with a smidgen of grace? Could it really be that simple?

Matt seems happy. Not smiley, laughing, sitcom-happy, but content, deep down, with his lot. And with Bruno waiting for him and the cabin to live in . . . with Jarvis at the foot of the bed and the warmest, most understanding, generous in-laws ever, who could blame him? Bruno, too, seems happy. For the child of a dead addict, he's done well. He's doing what he wants. He's living where he wants. He's with the person he loves.

And Alice, too, has felt unexpected moments of happiness these last days, moments of acute happiness occasionally. There's been no walking on eggs, no tiptoeing around other people's delicate egos. There has been no worrying about dinner or traffic, no watching the horizon in case of sudden explosions of anger. Or violence.

Could she really just stay here?

A bird swoops across the lake – an owl perhaps. The bird. The lake. The mountains. The stars. It's stunningly beautiful here. It's heartbreakingly beautiful here.

So yes, could she live here? Could she really just stay here? Can she perhaps simply carry on like this? Or is this one of those crazy childhood crushes? Is the reality a return to rainy, grey King's Heath? To frozen meals and economy lightbulbs? Can life, can change, really be this simple? It feels possible. It feels like a fog that kept everything in place is lifting, revealing other roads winding off into the distance, roads she never even knew existed.

319

She's not sure of the details yet. She's not sure how or where she could live. Virginie will reclaim her house at some point, no doubt. But perhaps she could rent somewhere similar. Bruno has said, after all, that rents are cheap here. So perhaps she could. Perhaps she doesn't need as much as she thought she did.

She could try to learn French perhaps. She could get her own annoying cat. She could spend her evenings eating French cheese and baguettes with her e-reader propped up against a bottle of cheap rosé, couldn't she? Perhaps she could get her pension sent here. Dot's adviser guy would know. And if she could, then what more would she need? Her son and his partner don't seem to need much, after all.

And Joe. Is it just madness to think that Bruno might really be able to find her after all these years, lurking somewhere in the depths of the Internet? The idea both terrifies and thrills her. Because what if Joe is dead? And what if she's alive?

It takes Alice almost an hour to walk to the far end of the dam. She leans over the edge and watches water gushing from a vent into the distant river below. The air here is cool and moist.

She swipes at a mosquito, then thinks she sees a fawn running through the trees and doubts her own eyesight. And finally, she turns and starts to head back.

As she passes in front of the cabin, she pauses to look up at the cosy orange glow from the windows. The light inside is flickering and she imagines Bruno on the sofa, watching TV with Jarvis beside him. He'll be waiting for Matt to get home from his evening of washing dishes. Tonight, even that thought of her son washing dishes fails to provide its familiar pang of angst. Someone has to wash the dishes, she hears Bruno saying. And he's right, of course. Someone does have to.

She pictures Matt coming home to Bruno and Jarvis and the flickering television screen. Happiness. It can be so simple. All you have to do is stay away from those who would ruin it for you. She's happy that Matt's with Bruno, she realises. And she's shocked at herself for the realisation.

But it's true. For the first time ever, Alice no longer needs to worry about her other son. Because her other son is no longer 'other' to her. And because Matt, her lovely Matt, has Bruno to look after him now. Bruno who is so big and strong and calm and kind. Her eyes are starting to mist, so she smiles through the tears and forces herself to walk on. Yes, Matt's safe now. Matt's happy now.

As she reaches the edge of the hamlet, a car comes into view. It squeals to a halt beside her and Matt looks up at her from the side window. 'Mum!' he says.

Alice smiles gently at her son. He looks incredibly handsome tonight, smiling in the yellow of the streetlight. He looks suddenly like a man. When did that happen? Yes, it seems like only yesterday that he was pleading with them for a dog.

She wonders if her tears are showing in the lamplight, but resists the temptation to wipe them away. That would be a dead giveaway. 'You're early, aren't you?' she says. 'Or is it later than I thought?'

'It's ten,' Matt says, glancing at the car clock. 'There's some fête thing happening in the next village. There were only three people in the restaurant so they sent me home. Any chance of a cuppa?'

'Wouldn't you rather go home?' Alice asks.

'I will, but let's have a cuppa first,' Matt says, putting the car back into gear and pulling over to the side of the road.

Back at Virginie's house, Alice makes them both mugs of tea, then carries them out to the table in the courtyard. Paloma jumps on to Alice's lap and she lets her remain there.

'You're not getting over your cat aversion, are you?' Matt asks.

'I never really had an aversion,' Alice says. 'I just don't like them all over my worktops.'

'If you say so.'

'And I quite like this one, actually. The others all want food – you know, when you come in, they just want food and then they bugger off – but this one, all she wants is company, don't you?' Alice says, stroking the cat's head. 'Which is rather special for an animal really. Plus she's old, like me. We have that in common.'

'You're not that old, Mum,' Matt says. 'So did you have a good day with the in-laws?'

'I did,' Alice says. 'They're rather lovely really, aren't they?'

'Yeah,' Matt says. 'They're OK!'

'And that Bruno,' Alice says. 'You'll be wanting to hang on to that one.'

'You like him, huh?'

Alice nods. 'A lot.'

'Well, I intend to,' Matt says. 'Hang on to him, that is. I even thought we might, you know, get married.'

'Yes, that's possible now, isn't it?' Alice says. 'I forgot about that.'

'The Catholics here kicked up a stink about it, but it went through in the end.'

'They'd do better to deal with their paedophile priests,' Alice says.

'You're right,' Matt agrees. 'They would. Um, Dad phoned again, by the way.'

Alice sighs. 'He's been calling my mobile over and over. I just switched it off in the end. I don't want to talk to anyone anyway.'

'I told him you were staying for a while. For a few months,' Matt says, chewing at the edge of a fingernail.

'You did?'

Matt nods. 'That's a good idea, don't you think?'

'If it's possible,' Alice says, 'I think that would be a very good idea. I bet Ken didn't like it though.'

322

'He surprised me actually,' Matt says.

'He did? How?'

'He said not to worry about money. He said to keep on using the card. That there's plenty more where that came from.'

'Oh,' Alice says, pulling a face. 'Gosh.'

'I know,' Matt says. 'Maybe he had a bump on the head.'

'Maybe. But I bet it won't last.'

'No,' Matt agrees, 'probably not. But are you having a good time here?' he asks. 'I mean, despite everything?'

'I think so. I feel . . . I feel . . . more free, I suppose you'd call it. I feel a bit more free with every day that passes. Like a mist is lifting.'

'That's good,' Matt says. 'And you don't mind being stuck up here? Because we could maybe look for somewhere down on the coast. Or in Aix-en-Provence.'

'No,' Alice says. 'It's a surprise to me, but I do like it here. I think this life you've built for yourself is wonderful.'

Matt laughs. 'Careful, Mum,' he says. 'You almost sound like you approve of me.'

Alice reaches across the table for her son's hand. She places her own on top of his, exactly as Bruno had done when she first arrived. 'Matt,' she says. 'I don't approve of you . . .'

Matt frowns. 'I thought that was too good to be true,' he says. He tries to pull his hand away, but Alice grabs it and forcefully yanks it back towards the centre of the table.

'It's more than that, son,' she says. 'It's as if . . . I don't know how to explain it. But when you were little, I always thought you'd grow up to be a painter or a writer or something creative like that. I thought you'd do something like Bruno does, really.'

'The Other Son disappoints again,' Matt says drily.

'Listen to me, Matt,' Alice says. 'That's what I used to think. I did. I was disappointed. But now I see that it's this . . .' She gestures

323

around her. 'It's all of this. It's this life you've built. It's France and the cabin and the pots and it's Bruno and the dog. And it doesn't look like any other life, does it? Because that's it – that's your creation, and it's beautiful. And I'm so proud of you, really I am.'

Matt finally pulls his hand from Alice's grasp. He looks up at her wet-eyed. 'I've been waiting so long for that, Mum,' he says, his voice wobbling with emotion. 'I've waited so long just for one of you to say that. I gave up really. I thought it would never happen.'

'I'm sorry,' Alice says through her own tears. 'I should have said it a long time ago.'

She pushes back from the table and crosses to Matt's side. 'This is where we hug,' she says, when Matt remains seated.

Matt looks up at her sheepishly. 'I'm not a very huggy person, I'm afraid,' he says.

'I'm not surprised,' Alice replies, crouching down to throw her arms around his rigid frame. 'You didn't come from a very huggy family. But we can try. We can change. We can get better at things. There's still time.'

They embrace, albeit awkwardly, for a few seconds, and then Alice releases him and straightens. 'I am sorry,' she says again, 'that this has taken so long.'

Matt stares at his feet. 'It's OK,' he mutters. 'We got there in the end. That's the main thing.'

'It's late,' Alice says. 'Shouldn't you be getting back to that . . . to that . . . fiancé of yours?'

Matt looks up at her through a fresh bout of tears. 'Fiancé?' he laughs.

Alice shrugs cutely.

'But, yeah, I suppose I should,' Matt says, then, 'Would you come? To a wedding, I mean? If we did do it, would you come, Mum?'

'Of course I would,' Alice replies. 'I'd be proud to.'

324

Matt stands. 'Thanks,' he says.

'Drive carefully.'

'I will. And I'll see you tomorrow, right?'

'Yes, I'll see you tomorrow,' Alice says. 'Bruno said he'd help me look for something on the Internet.'

'Fair enough,' Matt says. 'You'll be OK, won't you?' he asks, hesitating with one hand on the railing.

Alice nods. 'I'll be fine,' she says. She glances at the house and sees that Paloma is sitting in the open doorway, waiting expectantly for her to go to bed. 'Yes,' she says again. 'I'll be absolutely fine.'

ACKNOWLEDGMENTS

Thanks to Fay Weldon for encouraging me when it most counted. Thanks to Allan for his proofing and to Rosemary and Lolo for being there. Thanks to Karen, Jenny, Diana, Annie, Sergei and everyone else who gave me feedback on this novel. It wouldn't have happened without you. Thanks to Amazon for turning the writing of novels back into something one can actually earn a living from.